D0614403

BLIC LIBR

WINNIPEG
3

FIVE WIVES

FIVE

HARPER AVENUE

WIVES

A NOVEL

JOAN THOMAS

Five Wives

Copyright © 2019 by Joan Thomas.

All rights reserved.

Published by Harper Avenue, an imprint of HarperCollins Publishers Ltd

First Canadian edition

No part of this book may be used or reproduced in any manner
whatsoever without the prior written permission of the publisher,
except in the case of brief quotations embodied in reviews.

This novel is a work of fiction based, in part, on real-life events and individuals
but including imagined elements and characters. See the Author's Note
on page 383 for further details.

Excerpt from *Lines: A Brief History* by Tim Ingold reproduced with the permission of
Routledge, via Copyright Clearance Center.

The cartoon caption on page 358 is from the cartoon titled "God" by Liana Finck/The New
Yorker Collection/The Cartoon Bank; © Condé Nast. Used with permission.

Map by Mary Rostad

HarperCollins books may be purchased for educational, business,
or sales promotional use through our Special Markets Department.

HarperCollins Publishers Ltd
Bay Adelaide Centre, East Tower
22 Adelaide Street West, 41st Floor
Toronto, Ontario, Canada
M5H 4E3

www.harpercollins.ca

Library and Archives Canada Cataloguing in Publication information
is available upon request.

ISBN 978-1-4434-5854-2

Printed and bound in the United States of America
LSC/H   3 4 5 6 7 8 9 10

For my loving father, Ralph Thomas

ALSO BY JOAN THOMAS

Reading by Lightning
Curiosity
The Opening Sky

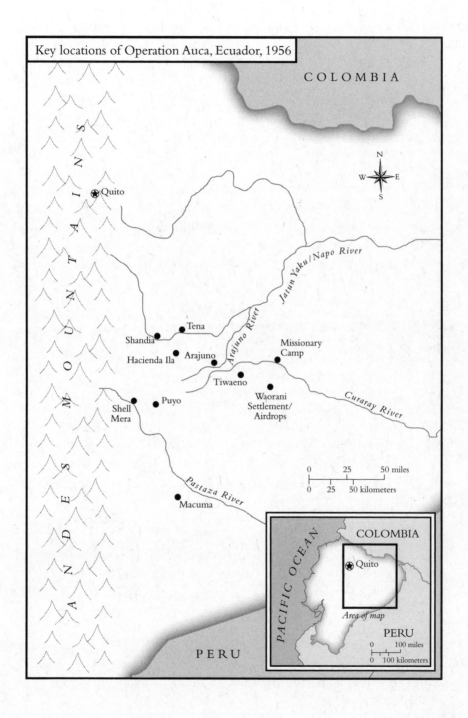

Key locations of Operation Auca, Ecuador, 1956

COLOMBIA

N
W   E
S

Quito

Jatun Yaku / Napo River

Arajuno River

Tena

Shandia

Hacienda Ila   Arajuno

Missionary
Camp

Tiwaeno

Curaray River

Waorani
Settlement/
Airdrops

Shell
Mera   Puyo

A N D E S   M O U N T A I N S

Pastaza River

Macuma

0   25   50 miles
0   25   50 kilometers

PERU

COLOMBIA

PACIFIC OCEAN

Quito

Area of map

PERU

0   100 miles
0   100 kilometers

There is no point at which the story ends and life begins.

—Tim Ingold, *Lines: A Brief History*

READY YOURSELVES

1

THE WIVES SPENT THE EVENING putting the story together. Kids finally asleep, so the women could talk uninterrupted in the lounge, mugs of cocoa cooling on the floor beside their chairs. They were hoping for photographs soon, but in the meantime they had the letters the pilot had carried out on his supply runs, and the journals the doctor brought them at the end. Everything scrawled in pencil, but the women were good at deciphering their husbands' handwriting and also at reading between the lines; it was amazing what they were able to piece together.

The site where the men set up camp was a white sand beach, a sandbar really, because the river was so low just then. An open and airy vestibule to the rainforest, dotted with palms; imagine the grounds of a swanky tropical hotel. At its edge grew a giant ironwood tree, perfect for a tree house, and the men built on one of the massive limbs. They'd prefabbed the scrap-lumber floors and walls and flown them in, strapped to the undercarriage of the small yellow plane. The beach was just long enough to serve as an airstrip. Eventually the pilot was confident in his landings, but the sand was very soft and for takeoffs he counted on a little extra lift from the Lord.

The men were excited, almost giddy at being there at last. They had no idea how long this adventure would last, and they cherished discipline, they thrived on it. They all had designated tasks. Every morning one of them surveyed the beach for strange footprints. Every hour on the hour somebody got out the binoculars

3

and systematically scanned the forest wall. Somebody carried clear water from a spring. Somebody dug a latrine and covered it with a board. They worked together to cook proper meals in a stove improvised from a hacked-open iron drum.

An iron drum?

Roger carried it in, one of the women said. He thought it would be useful as body armour.

Oh.

Mornings were spent in the shade of the ironwood tree, reading and writing, and afternoons relaxing at the river. It was hot, hot, hot, and the bugs were bad—tiny gnats and those red-brown sweat bees with furry bodies. The men built a second fire by the water and threw termite nests on it, the way the Quichua do, draping themselves in acrid smoke. They waded into a deep pool and killed the hours fooling around in water up to their necks; you put that gang together and the jokes and teasing never stopped. When it was cooler, they waded out and got their fishing rods, and they ate their catch for supper. *This is the day that the Lord has made, let us rejoice and be glad in it.*

But the nights—they were scarier. The sudden darkness, and the way it transformed the clearing into a place you'd never seen before, and the unfamiliar sounds. Once the sun dropped below the canopy, they'd clean up the campsite and use the latrine and climb the wooden ladder to the shelter in the ironwood tree. A *rope* ladder! one of the wives said, still planning. Why didn't we think of that? Something you could pull up after you. But the men had a hand-crank two-way radio and they had the guns, all loaded. The idea had been to keep watch in two-hour shifts, using the gaps intentionally left in each wall, but once they were cozily ensconced high up off the ground—well, it seemed a little silly. Stretched out on the floor, they arranged their mosquito nets and talked and prayed and eventually turned off the lantern. Think of what the stars must have been like, that far back in the forest. No, the moon was full those nights—but think of how big and how bright, pouring silver light onto the palm fronds and the white sand. Think of the noises all around, the howler monkeys, the puma. Think of their husbands, together and alone, lying on their backs on their sleeping bags and listening until sleep overcame them.

Mornings they woke to the realization that God had delivered them safely to a new day. Their surprise at this was less as time went by. You could say the glamour was wearing off just a little. It was cloudy and the bugs were worse and the things the men enjoyed about each other began to grate. What exactly was the point of a designated latrine-hole in the vast, ravenous compost pit of the Amazon basin? How many hours a day could one man whistle the same tune? Each wife frowned over the pages in front of her and pictured her husband on a bad day—restless, testy, needy, petulant, silent, et cetera.

By the fourth day, the men's fears had begun to prey on them and they got the distinct impression they were being watched. The pilot's mate said it first and the others agreed. Silence fell over the camp. But silence was counterproductive; they wanted to be found! They were bait in a trap, you might say. The battery-powered megaphone came to mind and one of the men climbed the tree house to fetch it. He knew a handful of phrases, and all afternoon he stood by the river and shouted them into the forest. After he went to bed that night, the phrases knit themselves together into a sermon in his mind, and the morning of the fifth day he stood in the river preaching it. Friday, it was the Friday when his congregation revealed itself. A voice rang across the water, a strong male voice, and a figure stepped out of the forest—a naked brown-skinned man. A girl joined him. Farther up the bank, the men spied a second female. Right out in the open, they stood in the open, their arms at their sides.

The preacher was the first to react. He tossed his megaphone onto the sand and waded across. On the other side, he reached out a hand, and said words he had taken great pains to acquire: Welcome, I want to be your friend. The naked man stepped forward and took his hand. They strode into the water and the women followed, and all of them waded calmly across the river to the camp.

Three, it was astonishing! And no spears, no weapons at all. The fellow they judged to be in his early twenties, one of the females a girl in her late teens, the other a woman of maybe forty. They looked just as the men had been led to expect: long hair with bangs cut short over their ears, big balsa plugs in stretched-out earlobes. All naked except for a band of fibre around their bellies and lianas tied around their wrists and ankles. No body paint. They looked healthy and well-fed, although the older woman's breasts were long and flat, like inner tubes empty of air. The young man— his gear was pinned by the foreskin into his bellyband, one of the wives read out in a soft voice.

Having meticulously planned against failure, the husbands found they had no immediate plan for success. Eagerly they set about being hospitable hosts. They had been frying hamburgers for lunch, and they saw there would be enough if they held back a little. And so the forest people were served grape Kool-Aid and hamburgers on buns with mustard. They squatted easily beside the stove and the men demonstrated prayer to them, bowing their heads and thanking God for the meal and for their new friendship, gesturing to the heavens to make it clear who they were talking to. The three forest people ignored the prayer, but they scarfed down the hamburgers, and the young fellow, especially, seemed to love his.

The husbands relaxed and began to joke around. The pilot dug out his camera and they shot off a roll of film. George, they took to calling the young fellow. The girl they named Delilah. If this delegation had a spokesman, it was Delilah. She was desperate to tell the men something. She said the same thing over and over, getting more and more frustrated, speaking in sounds the men had never heard and could not begin to approximate. I wonder why they called her Delilah? one of the wives said. I guess she was pretty, someone suggested. No, it's because they thought George had seen white men on the beach and had brought her along as a gift. Or in trade. *For them.* This theory was recorded in two of the diaries. A very good thing their husbands were decent men.

As for George, well, they saw him eyeballing the plane, reacting when occasionally the two-way radio in the instrument panel came to life and blasted out static and human voices. So the pilot buckled him in and took him up for a ride. Apparently he loved it, he hollered the whole way. The pilot knew where their long-houses were, and he flew over and buzzed them. When he banked to fly back, people on the ground caught sight of their fellow tribesman in the cockpit, and oh, their expressions were a thing to behold!

After they landed back on the beach, George was unresponsive to anything they offered. The husband who had done the preaching got out his bag of tricks, his yoyo, his harmonica. They blew up balloons and batted them around. They showed photographs. They had a yellow model plane with them, and they tried to demonstrate how the forest people should clear an airstrip close to their longhouses so the men could visit. They stuck sticks into the sand to represent trees, and showed how the plane would crash into the trees and flip. They acted out their distress at this catastrophe. The three seemed baffled by these theatrics. There was a moment of mutual resentment, there must have been. The men, after all this effort—had they ever pictured the forest people as so incurious, so uncommunicative, so indifferent to all they were offered? So *small?*

Towards evening, the young pair slipped back into the forest, and the pilot took off on a supply run. The older woman stayed. She sat on a log, feeding the fire they had built close to the water, and when darkness fell, she began to chant. It was like nothing they had ever heard, and at first they were curious. But it went on and on and on, and soon the bugs drove the men to the tree house. Except for the husband who had hauled in the body armour; he sat and listened to her. Finally he too had had enough and he went to bed. In the morning, embers still glowed on the beach, but the forest woman was gone.

That was the end of the story. If you could call it a story, given its unsatisfying plot and lack of obvious meaning. Nevertheless, the women found they could not stop talking about it—those gleaming, heart-stopping days when their husbands were separated from them but still inhabited this earth. A child started wailing down the hall and the mothers avoided each other's eyes, disavowing ownership.

"He says the tree house was thirty-five feet up," one of them said, indicating the page she was reading. "Can that be right?"

"It was a *catfish* they caught the first day."

"They put a shirt on George for the plane ride. Oh, that was thoughtful. It's always so cold in the plane."

This was just a chapter, of course, not the whole story. The question was how this chapter led to the next. And then, of course, to the next—to their unthinkable lives.

The children, oh, the children.

One of the wives was eight months pregnant and her ankles were terribly swollen. "Put your feet up here, Marilou," Olive said, slipping down to the linoleum floor to make room.

ABBY IS CALLED

2

He spies Abby as soon as he steps into the foyer of the chapel, and feels a rush of pleasure and pride. Her hair is partly up and partly down, and she's wearing her best dress, a colour he thinks of as Pontiac blue.

He edges over to her. She's staying with friends in the college dorm and he hasn't had a private word since they landed in Chicago. "All good, honey?"

"All good, Dad."

She's got her speech rolled up in her hand. As Betty's only grandchild, she's been asked to share a personal memory. David's been suggesting Scripture passages that might be suitable, just as a way of driving her reflections home. *Now we see through a glass darkly, but then, face to face.* "Dad, I'm good," she keeps saying. She is in fact a terrific public speaker.

Abby is going to be seated on the stage, and an usher leads David to the side room reserved for family. It was David who suggested earlier in the day that they define *family* loosely and include all the Operation Auca offspring and their kids, the McCullys, the Saints, and the Youderians. So it's quite a gang. Sean Youderian's parents slide over to make room for him. He hasn't seen them since Abby and Sean broke up. "I'm so sorry," Martha says, squeezing his fingers briefly, and he says, "Well, you never know with kids," before he gets that she's offering condolences on the death of his mother-in-law. But her face is so vacant that he decides to let it ride.

"Did Sean come?"

Mike Youderian shakes his head.

David's asked to accompany Betty's husband, Stan, at the front of the line. They walk into the chapel to "Jesu." He's calling up Sharon in his mind, trying to feel her hand on his arm. This chapel was built after he and Sharon were students together at Wheaton College. It's a fine space, panelled with blond wood in different grains, all fitted cunningly together to create a subtle pattern. The chandeliers are rings with lit candles fixed to them. An image rises of long-haired girls balancing affairs like that on their heads; can that be an actual thing? Probably not, the hot wax. He's ushered to the front row, between Stan and the Youderians, and sitting down, he steals a peek at the audience. The "formerly young" (as he's started to call them) have turned out in droves, but they're by no means the majority. It's a pretty impressive assembly. It's not for Betty alone; this crowd is here because of Operation Auca. Betty died at the home she and Stan shared in Massachusetts, but Wheaton College is the de facto headquarters of the mission. Decades after it all happened, when David and Sharon arrived on the Wheaton campus, they discovered that they were already known and loved. Even now, when David visits, people murmur to each other as he walks by, or come up and introduce themselves. You're the spitting image, they say—and it strikes him sometimes that his father, Nate, is more vivid in other people's imaginations than he is in David's.

They stand and sing with full hearts, "We rest on Thee, our Shield and our Defender!" The melody is beautiful and old. *Finlandia*. Five wonderful young men stood beside his dad's plane and sang this hymn that fateful day in early 1956 when they flew into the camp on the Curaray River. Five who knew the terms of their mission. They knew, and still they went. "When passing through the gates of pearly splendour, Victors, we rest with Thee through endless days."

A formal eulogy from the dean of Wheaton College, way too long—but in point of fact, Elisabeth Elliot accomplished enough in her lifetime for any three lives. Martha shifts on the pew and her elbow touches David's and again Sharon is beside him, leaning on him slightly as she always did. At least she was spared the ordeal of her mother's terrible decline. The last time David and Abby went to Massachusetts, they were horrified at how Betty had changed. Could that silent goblin hunched in a wheelchair be his brisk, articulate, clever mother-in-law? Aphasia, it was called, but how could a woman so gifted in words lose them entirely?

A Scripture reading (*In my father's house are many mansions*), a rendition of "Make Me a Channel of Your Peace," a song Abby happens to hate, and as the soprano struggles with that monotone melody line, his daughter's eyes begin to glitter and search out his from the stage. She's nineteen, but what is nineteen? They're either twenty-four or they're fourteen, a mom at the church said to him. You get whiplash trying to keep up. He and the mom had a long conversation about why it's such a challenge for Christian parents to raise a faithful child: there's no drama connected to their conversion. He remembers Abby saying to him once, her face wistful, "I wish I remembered what it was like before I was saved." She was maybe ten, and they had been on a hike and were sitting at the picnic table in the backyard scraping mud off their shoes with (if he remembers correctly) the barbecue spatula. "Abby," he was inspired to answer, "you don't have to remember the sunrise to know that the sun is up."

Then it's Abby's turn, and she stands poised and graceful at the podium, a tall basket of white flowers on either side, her hair a bright cascade over one shoulder.

"Thank you for coming to honour and celebrate Elisabeth Elliot's life. It's a joy to speak to you about my wonderful grandmother. I have to start by telling you something amazing that happened yesterday while my dad and I were flying here from Portland. I was trapped in a middle seat beside a very large gentleman reading a massive newspaper. For a while I tried to peer around his paper, and under it, and over it, and then I just gave in and started reading along with him. And do you know what he was reading? An article about my grandmother! In the Sunday *New York Times*. I can't tell you how proud I felt. I was pretty inspired just now, too, hearing Dean Morrow's account of all Betty accomplished in her life. But I've been asked to share something different, something you might not know. The private side of Elisabeth Elliot—and here's the thing. I'm not sure I can give you much insight, because my grandmother lived her ministry every minute of every day, whether she was on a public stage or behind closed doors."

Nicely done, Abigail, David thinks, smiling up at her. Because it's a fact that Betty didn't place a lot of value in the grandmother role. A kid wasn't going to get gingerbread and hand-knit mittens from Elisabeth Elliot.

Abby tells the story of a family trip to the shore near Portland. She gets a laugh describing Betty walking across the sand in a tweed jacket and leather pumps. "I was an eight-year-old in a polka-dot swimsuit, and I wanted her to help me build a sand castle. Instead, she taught me to write 'Jesus Loves You' in Chinese. It's not that easy to make Chinese characters legible when you're squatting on a beach, drawing in coarse sand with a piece of driftwood. 'You have to make them big,' my grandma said. 'That's the trick.' I think for Betty it was the trick to everything. For a woman born in 1926, my grandmother had a really big life."

Abby's voice is calm and natural, and she never glances down at her script. This is a speech that comes from the heart. She's always been such a fantastic role model for the other girls in the church. That blue dress—raised by a single dad, how did she develop this lovely and modest style? Dress as if Jesus is your boyfriend, she jokes.

"It's been a few years since my grandmother and I have been able to talk, but I guess I'm luckier than most grandkids, because Betty left a shelf full of her books for me to read. I hope with time

I'll understand some of the contradictions of her life. She sat on platforms with world-famous leaders of the church, and she was a better speaker—in my opinion—than pretty much all of them, and yet she believed in women being subservient to men. She wrote books that questioned the way Christian missions operate and yet she accepted the tragedy of Operation Auca and the senseless killings that turned her into a writer."

David's misheard, it seems—but beside him, Martha draws in a sharp breath.

"When her young husband died, Betty said, 'I prayed that God would keep Jim safe, but the Lord had something better in mind.' Imagine being as intelligent as Elisabeth Elliot was, and as willing to think deeply about everything, and then in the end to still have faith that terrible and even bizarre tragedies are planned and carried out by God."

David leans forward. This speech could be saved—*Now we see through a glass, darkly!* Fervently, he telegraphs the words up to the stage. But Abby never looks in his direction. She veers into a secular children's book, that nonsensical *Alice* thing.

"It was my favourite book—I actually know most of it by heart. My grandma liked it too, and when she visited, we would take parts. Grandma would be the Red Queen and I would be Alice. I would say, 'You can't believe impossible things. There's no use trying.' And Grandma would say, 'You just haven't had enough practice. When I was young, I worked at it for half an hour a day. Why, sometimes I've believed as many as six impossible things before breakfast.'"

Not a Scripture passage, no. Asked to speak at Elisabeth Elliot's funeral, his daughter is quoting *Alice in Bloody Wonderland*.

IT SEEMS A sea change has taken place, but he was clueless until the water started lapping at his ankles. It's almost a year since Abby graduated from high school. Most of her friends from the church left town last fall, went to Bible college or nursing school, or to build clinics in Nigeria out of sun-dried bricks, and Abby (their undisputed queen) stayed home, sleeping till noon, tanning on the trampoline in the backyard if there was sun in the afternoon, avoiding David. It had always been his dream to send her to Wheaton College, but she was pushing for the University of Oregon, and he couldn't bring himself to cough up money to watch her morph into one of those vegan hipsters hanging out in Portland's coffee shops, trying to pass their godlessness off as social justice, harassing staff about the purity and provenance of the chocolate sprinkled on their soy lattes. So he and Abby were at a stalemate with regards to her education. He tried hard to get her involved at the church (they could have cobbled together a job in the education programs), but she wouldn't bite. She worked as a waitress for a while, not remotely what he'd imagined of his brilliant daughter, but the café shut down. It was all complicated by Sean Youderian, one of her Operation Auca "cousins." He worked mostly in LA, in the Christian film industry. Abby talked about moving to California if and when they got engaged. She was awfully young to be thinking of marriage, but David saw the rightness of her and Sean together, given the tragic past they shared, given their many talents; you had to think God would use them powerfully. And then suddenly Sean was out of the picture, and Abby was restless and full of attitude. One of her lifelong friends stopped coming to the Portland Church of God. He joined a worship community that met above a nail salon. He wanted Abby to go with him, and David could actually have lived with that for a while, anything to keep her in the fold, but she mocked her friend, she said, "Dude thinks gluten-free communion wafers are going to be enough to lure me in." One night when she wasn't home by the agreed-upon time, David went to the door and changed the security code so she couldn't slip in unobserved, and when the alarm started to shriek around two o'clock, he got up to find her in the entrance, flushed and confused, punching numbers randomly into the keypad. Leaning in to help her, he could smell alcohol. She was laughing inappropriately, and after he got the siren turned off, he wouldn't let her go to her room. He steered her to the living room, recalling stories he'd heard of inebriated people who threw up and aspirated their vomit and died. "Oh, for crying out loud," she protested, but she kicked off her sandals and sank onto the couch. He sat in the armchair and asked her how she'd got home. "Will," she said. Eventually she volunteered that Will was a guy she'd worked with at Fernando's, the café.

"You're seeing somebody new?"

"I'm not seeing him. He's gay, Dad. He's my best friend at the moment." She made a rueful face. "Hopefully he never finds out about *My Two Dads*."

"What?"

"Remember? That protest we held outside the library. About that children's book? What was the sign I carried?" She sighed and closed her eyes and tipped back her head. After a minute she said, "'Gay Sex Is Sin, Christ Can Set You Free.'"

At that hour, in those circumstances, he was not about to take her on. He sat until she'd stretched out and seemed to be falling asleep. She's going to get cold, he thought, and he got up and pulled the light blanket his mother had crocheted off the back of the couch and stooped to drape it over her. Again he smelled the booze on her breath—a pollution, it sickened him. Oh, his lovely daughter, his motherless girl. He sat back on the chair, thinking, God has his ways of humbling us. All over the nation, parents endure scenes like this, their children coming home drunk, or worse. Oh, darling, tell me what to do.

Possibly he uttered this aloud, because Abby opened her eyes and looked at him neutrally.

"I was just thinking about your mother," he said. "Sweetheart, it would break her heart to see you like this."

She muttered something he couldn't make out.

"Abby, is this about Sean?"

"What?"

"Are you missing Sean?"

"No, Dad. *No.* Cripes."

"I'm hoping you two will patch things up."

"I don't think so. Sean's a total hypocrite."

"What do you mean?"

"You don't want to know."

"Yes, I do."

"Well, he was so hung up on me being his virgin bride, but I know what he was up to in LA."

Oh, on every side lay perils.

Her voice came through the dark again. "Dad, tonight. I had a great time. Just a little too great. It was . . . it's *nothing.*"

"It's not nothing, Abby. Maybe other kids can afford to experiment a bit, but God has called you out in a particular way. You carry a glorious legacy. Everybody knows you—not just here, but all across the nation. Even as a child, you inspired a lot of people. You need to think about what that means. Satan is not going to let God's Kingdom be advanced without a fight. The powers of darkness are going to go after you in a vicious way."

"The powers of darkness!" She put a hand over her face, genuinely overcome with laughter. "You can't be serious! Oh, the powers of darkness! Maybe you should hire an exorcist!"

He got up and said good night and went to his room. He'd lobbed his two most potent hand grenades in her direction (her mother, the devil), he had nothing left.

3

Abby wakes to the buzz of her dad's alarm, glad to be in her own bed after three nights in the Wheaton College dorm, and lies listening to the small sounds of his morning routine. The toilet flushes, the shower starts up. He mutters to the dog. Silence while he has devotions in his room. Then he's in the kitchen, his spoon hitting the sides of his cereal bowl. The electronic chirp of the TV (he's carried his coffee to the living room) and the hectic voices of news anchors. Every morning he watches half an hour of news. Conscientiously. As a pastor in contemporary America, he likes to say, you can focus on the everyday concerns of the faithful ("What would Jesus buy?" Abby suggests) or you can try to provoke your congregation to take on the world and its sorrows. Her dad has always aspired to be the latter sort of pastor.

The TV goes off. His briefcase slides across the tile floor in the side entrance. The door slams. Abby holds her breath for a minute and then she turns her face into her pillow and lets out the sobs she's been holding in her throat. Betty is so alive in her mind this morning. A young Betty—there she is, straight out of a photograph in one of her books, striding barefoot along a mud path in the rainforest, a flock of children running to keep up. Looking *hungry*, eager for life and for experience. Abby loved her because she recognized that look. At the funeral, she so wanted to speak the truth, even if it meant upsetting some of the people there. She felt close to Betty as she wrote her speech, Betty who never backed off from challenging others. It was as if she was channelling Betty's courage. But afterwards! No one admitted to being upset by what she'd said—they just wanted to point out how upset *Betty* would have been. And they were right, of course. It was the wrong occasion for a speech like that. She has no judgment, it's obvious.

Her sobs subside and she hears Gizmo whining at her door.

She wipes her face on the quilt and gets up to let him in. "Hey, Dogma," she says, dropping a hand down to him. He jumps onto the bed and she scratches his tummy and goes down the hall to the bathroom. When she returns, he's still writhing on his back. "You little tramp," she says, indulging him with another scratch.

Her weekend bag's on the floor, still not unpacked. She sits on the bed and picks up her phone. Last night, chilled by her dad's silence, she decided she'd drive up to Seattle this afternoon and stay with Olive for a bit. But instead of calling Olive, she presses Will's number. They haven't known each other very long, but he's the only Portland friend she missed during the trip to Wheaton. The day she met him, maybe three months ago, she felt a lurch of longing to know him better. The easy, humorous way he had of holding your eye, and the solemnity with which he served out hamburger platters, as if he was a professional waiter at a bistro in Paris. He's the first gay friend she's ever had (well, that she knows of), and he is so honest and smart and clear about who he is. He has a force of character that fills her with admiration.

To her delight, he picks up. "So you're back."

"Yep."

"How was it?"

"Well, it was, you know, a funeral."

"Did your ex show up?"

"No, he did not."

"And how did your speech go?"

"Oh, it was doomed from the beginning. I couldn't quite say what I wanted to say, but I pissed people off anyway. My dad won't speak to me. The flight home was brutal." This would be the point to plunge into the whole story, but Will lacks the context to understand it. She's been cautious about how much she tells him. Back when her church staged its homophobic protest in front of the library, Abby was interviewed on the radio, and she has this horror that one day Will is going to be listening to her talk and he's going to think, I know that voice from somewhere. Where have I heard that voice before? "Anyway, tell me what you're up to."

"I'm pretending to work on my thesis. You know, reading cool shit online and telling myself it's relevant."

"Like?"

"Well, I just read an article about a group of Buddhist monks on the east coast of Canada. They've been saving money for a long time, and they went to a seafood wholesaler and bought six hundred pounds of lobsters heading to restaurants and rented a truck to carry them back to the ocean."

"That's *so* cool. I hope they cut the rubber bands off their claws."

"I'm sure they did. And then they lowered them one by one into a little bay where lobster fishing isn't allowed."

"Will they stay there? Maybe they'll head right back to their old breeding grounds."

"It's always possible. But that's outside the purview of an act of charity. The monks did their thing and the lobsters . . ." His voice trails off.

Abby calls up his hazel eyes and his thoughtful face. She pictures him in the yellow robe of a Buddhist monk, crouching on a rock, granting a lobster its perilous freedom on the vast dark floor of the Atlantic Ocean.

He asks her whether she's coming to the library today. He's a grad student in philosophy and he can't figure out why she's not in university.

"Nah, I'm grounded."

He laughs.

"You think I'm kidding."

"You're grounded."

"Well, I'm confined to my room by my father's righteous anguish. We have an appointment at two this afternoon. For a formal reaming-out. It's an old tactic of his, to maximize the guilt and stress." Will does not live at home. He got a grant for grad school and has a basement apartment in the Lloyd area. "You have no idea how lucky you are."

"Oh, I kind of do. And even when I was living at home, my parents didn't pull shit like that."

"Like, can I ask—how did they take it when you came out? I mean, if it's not too private."

"It's not private. It was no big deal. My mom suggested it to *me*, actually. I had a huge crush on a guy in junior high, somebody named Joel who, you might be fascinated to know, had a ferret as a pet, and she raised the possibility that guys might be my thing, and we talked about what that would mean. And she was right. About all of it."

We're from different planets, Abby thinks with a fresh surge of emotion. She sits with Will's voice in her ear, widening her eyes to keep her tears from dropping, and feels how alone she is, how deeply bereft. I have nothing, she thinks. No past, no character, no truth to guide me. There's no way forward. It comes to her that what she needs is a ceremony. Like her baptism, when sunlight streamed through narrow windows onto the immersion font and she stepped down four cement steps into cold water, her green choir gown blackening, and Pastor Dave put one hand on her forehead and one hand on her back, and she surrendered and sank backwards, dying to her old life, rising to a new.

They hang up, and Abby lies back on the bed. I'll get on my bike, she thinks. I'll ride and ride. By the time I see Dad, my head will be totally empty and I'll be too tired to fight. I'll go to Forest Park. Or is there time to do the Willamette Loop? She turns her eyes toward her clock.

On the bedside table stands a photo in a silver frame, an old black-and-white taken by a famous photographer. An iconic photo, at least in her world. A brown-skinned man walks up a path in the jungle with a little girl on his shoulders. The girl's blond curls are a splash of silver in the dim forest. The two of them are naked;

the photo's taken from the back. The little girl is Abby's mom, and the man is an Auca named Nincambo, an Amazonian Indian from a tribe that eluded contact for centuries. He was involved in the massacre of the missionaries, this has been established. He may even have led it, he may have been the one who slaughtered the little girl's father. And Sharon told Abby that in those days she called him Baepo, the Auca word for Daddy.

Abby lies and rests her eyes on this photo. All the meanings they impose upon it don't begin to drain it of its power.

THE AUCA. IT's a habit to use that word, but the people her family served are actually the Waorani (or the Huaorani, if you are writing in Spanish). Abby has only one memory of meeting Waorani people. Just before her mom died, when Abby was twelve, her great-aunt Rachel Saint brought two converts from Ecuador to America on a fundraising tour, and their nearest stop was a church in Seattle. Abby's mother really wanted to see them, so they drove to Seattle for the day.

The Ecuadorean contingent was late arriving at the church; their flight had been delayed. Abby and her parents were led to a front pew and then they waited. Sharon was terribly nauseated that night, and the thinness of her face under her peachy-blond wig gave her the look of an aged Barbie. The pew felt very hard. Abby sat close so her mother could lean on her, feeling wretched that they hadn't thought to bring a cushion for Sharon to sit on. She was nursing a childlike fantasy of what lay ahead, something momentous for her mother, a scene in which the Auca warriors would come up to them, tall and fierce and feathered, and bow their heads and beg Sharon's forgiveness on behalf of their people. And Sharon would say something like, Our Lord Jesus Christ forgives you, it doesn't matter about me.

But they were so late that finally the organizers asked Pastor Dave if he would fill in, and he willingly took the podium. No doubt everybody in that audience already knew the story of Operation Auca, but Abby could feel how moved they were, hearing Nate Saint's very own son tell it. Her father was unusually emotional himself. "I have a family now, and I love them more than life itself. And so I think about those five men who gave up their safe and comfortable homes in America, and went into the jungle in obedience to God's call, and I'm in awe at their courage, at their willingness to pay the supreme price, so that these lost souls might hear the gospel. 'Who will go?' God called, and bravely they replied, 'Take me, Lord.'"

He let the words hang over the audience and then he announced that his daughter, Abigail, was going to come forward and favour them with a musical number. So Abby had no choice but to get up from her seat and climb the little stairs to the platform. "I'll Go Where You Want Me to Go," her father murmured when she got to the podium. He took his pitch pipe out of his pocket and blew her a G, and she sang a cappella, not faltering, but also not letting her eyes go to her mother's white face below. In the last refrain he put his arm around her shoulders and joined her, harmonizing in his fine tenor, "I'll go where you want me to go, dear Lord, over mountains or plains or sea. I'll say what you want me to say, dear Lord, I'll be what you want me to be."

Just as they got to the last line, voices were heard in the foyer of the church, and everyone craned their heads around. A very large old woman walked up the aisle, a tall, stout, white-haired woman in a white dress. Rachel Saint. Her hair was pulled back from her round face into a bun. Following her were two short guys in grey suits—her Latino drivers, Abby thought. It took her a minute to realize. Had she really expected the Waorani to arrive in Seattle naked, and painted, wearing just a bellyband made of vine? But it was their shortness that amazed her most as they stepped up onto the stage—they came up to Rachel's shoulder. Their hair was also short, not as in the pictures taken on the Curaray River. They looked very much alike, though Abby guessed that one would be in his mid-twenties, the other maybe sixty. The older man had stretched-out earlobes, empty now of balsa plugs and dangling limply. Apparently Jesus didn't approve of earlobe plugs. The younger man was missing teeth and had visible black cavities. They had grown up in two different eras: one before the missionaries, one after.

It was nothing like her fantasies. Rachel made a presentation and did a Q & A, and when it was all over, they met at the front of the church and stood in a circle of nervous laughter and confusing talk in three languages. Sharon didn't have the strength to stand, she perched on the front pew and chatted with the older man, Enkidi—a few words in the Auca language, and then they moved to Spanish. She was wearing a synthetic wig because the thought of other people's hair freaked her out, and he stared at her in open surprise and disbelief. *La niña rubia*, he kept saying. But Sharon's eyes were shining. Abby knew she was seeing the fearless boy she had known as a tiny girl in the settlement, who scaled branchless trees to collect palm fruit for her, who trapped a gecko and wove a little harness for it so she could keep it as a pet. Over and over, her thin hand reached out to touch his arm.

On the way home in the car, Sharon slipped into a different zone. She had trouble responding to them, and at times they thought she was asleep, but her eyes were half-open. They went straight to the hospital when they got back to Portland. In the weeks that followed, she lay in a high white bed, hooked up to machines and dreaming of Ecuador. A garden that has everything, food for people and different food just for birds and monkeys. A fungus you peel into strips and press like a Band-Aid onto any cut or blister you have and are soon healed. Fruit that opens into waxy white pods you can light with a match and burn like candles. The termite nest you rub on your arms and legs to repel flies. It smelled like Oregon, her mother said. Because termites eat cedar. It seemed to Abby (shrivelled by the fluorescent lights, sick on the smell of antiseptic) that Ecuador was a place her mother could finally die from, that the very gates of heaven were visible from that lush and throbbing forest. Once, Sharon lifted her head from the pillow and saw Abby and said, "When *you* go, sweetheart . . ."

Youderian and two of the other "cousins" did go a few years later. They were all in their teens, the right age to be baptized, and this beautiful idea emerged: they would go back to that playa on the Curaray River, and wade into the water, and there they would be baptized by the Auca warriors. It struck everyone as a breathtaking expression of respect to these new Christians: their murderous past was forgiven, they were elders in the church now, they could minister to the Americans. It made Abby's heart ache—one of those expressions of faith so rich you couldn't take it in, or take it apart, or argue against it, and yet night after night she lay in bed in the dark and resisted it. Her dad desperately wanted her to go. But she kept putting off the decision until her procrastination had to be read as a no, and that spring, after the Ecuador trip was over, after Youderian and the others were back, full of exciting stories, she was baptized by Pastor Dave himself in the cement tank of the Portland Church of God.

4

IN HIS OFFICE, THE DESK phone is blinking. Voice mail from, of all people, Sean Youderian. David calls back and Sean's voice says, "You have the right to remain silent. If you choose to speak, everything you say will be recorded." Cute. David's doubts about the guy have sharpened into distaste, thanks to Abby's revelation. David chooses to remain silent.

He settles at his desk. It's his habit to make a start on his new sermon on Monday morning, and he's coming at it blank this week, having been occupied with other things for four days. But the news this morning—it was a long bit about the Islamic caliphate. They showed a clip from a few years back, Americans in robes kneeling in the desert with swords to their throats. It struck David as Biblical, straight out of the Old Testament, the cavelike dwellings with their low doors, the occasional camel, the single-mindedness, the rage and vengeance and spilled blood. Experience tells him he's being given the seed of a sermon. Isn't the formation of an Islamic state one of the signs of the Second Coming?

It's hard to know where to start in the Scriptures with that, and he's forced to resort to Google. Turns out a lot of people think ISIS forces are descendants of the Amalekites from Exodus 17. He follows the branching tunnels of that rabbit warren for an hour. Around eleven, Karen, the church secretary, pops her head in the door. "Just a reminder," she says. "You were going to change the sign this morning."

She hands him the bucket full of letters. The big sign—it's what you notice first when you drive past the church, it looms over the parking lot. His congregation thinks it makes them look amusing and accessible, and they live in faith that the mottoes Pastor Dave puts up are going to smite the hearts of drivers passing by on Wilmore Street and bring them to their knees, or at least into the church. So in spite of his own misgivings, he works up a list of mottoes and every Monday Karen picks out the letters. The caretaker usually installs the sign, but he's on vacation for three weeks, and he has proven to need close supervision. It's harder than you might think, balancing on a ladder in the rain, plucking the letters from the bucket and sliding them along their little tracks, working from either end and still getting it right. A case in point, the motto David picked last year for the anniversary of 9/11: REMEMBER THAT SATAN HAS HIS MIRACLES TOO. The misspelling of SATAN didn't catch his eye for days. Not until someone said, "Don't you think you're rushing the season a little?"

SANTA, the caretaker had posted! SANTA HAS HIS MIRA-
CLES TOO.

He drags the ladder out from the crawl space and trudges across
the parking lot. After the motto's up, he stands back to check it.

DON'T CONFUSE
GOD'S PATIENCE
WITH HIS FINAL RESPONSE

It's mean-spirited and threatening when you see it up in
all caps. When he picked it out, he was not thinking about his
daughter. He was thinking about, well, the whole USA, which
seems to have surrendered its role as beacon of light in a dark
world. He never actually saw the America his mother conjured
for him when he was a boy in Quito. By the time he moved
here, America had inoculated itself against the gospel in ways that
still baffle him.

He takes the ladder and bucket back to the crawl space. "I have
a pastoral visit scheduled this afternoon," he says to Karen. "I'll be
back at six for the men's fellowship."

"Okey-dokey," she says, looking up with a smile.

Abby's bike is gone when he gets to the house. Gizmo skitters
across the kitchen floor in delight to see him. "So what's to eat?"
David asks, scratching his ears. On the kitchen counter, flats of
applesauce cups, cases of V8 juice, a humongous box of Cheerios,
a carton of green-wrapped granola bars. It's crazy to buy bulk
when it's just the two of them, but he's not very adventurous. He'll
have the usual for lunch: a bowl of Heinz pork and beans heated
in the microwave, with a fried egg on top. Today he cracks an egg
for Gizmo too. LORD, HELP US BE THE PEOPLE OUR DOGS
THINK WE ARE, he thinks as he bastes the yolks with margarine.
Betty used to interrogate him about the big sign when she came
to visit. She thought it was a mistake to pander to secular culture,

she thought it trivialized the gospel. Even homey slogans like the dog one perplexed and displeased her. Where do you get them? she asked, and he was forced to admit, the Internet.

He slides Gizmo's egg into his rubber bowl. "Say grace," he says, and Gizmo crouches with his muzzle on his paws and his little tail whipping. *Amen*, you lucky little beggar.

He sinks onto a stool at the island and pulls a fork out of the drawer. He's not really hungry. His deficiencies are obvious in this lunch. People expect so much of him because of his physical resemblance to his father. You can have an athletic build and be lousy at sports. Betty saw him for who he was, she never thought he was a fitting mate for Sharon. Oh, she never said anything of the kind. But her constant pushing and interrogation wore him down.

He finishes his beans and moves to the recliner in the living room for his lunchtime lie-down. Their last visit to Massachusetts, Betty hadn't spoken a word in several years. But from the minute they arrived, she was entirely focused on her granddaughter. When Abby walked into the room, she would swim back up to life and fix her milky-blue eyes on her. The day they said goodbye, she clutched Abby's hand and lifted a desperate face, shaping her mouth into an urgent thought that refused to come. They mused for months about what she might have wanted to say.

He reaches for a cushion and shoves it under the bend of his neck. And now *he* needs to find the words to help his daughter, who is so confused. He tries to empty his mind so the Lord can fill it. The window in the hall is open and he hears his neighbour's Vespa start, the sewing-machine whine of its engine sharpening as it moves up the street and then narrowing to nothing. He feels the firm, sustaining leather of the chair. He begins to drift, he's sinking fast, and then he hears the door, and the click of Gizmo's nails, and he opens his eyes to see Abby step into the living room. She's wearing her cycling shorts and she looks warmed from her ride. "Hey," he says, surprised into breaking his silence. He sits up, pushing down the footrest of the recliner. Sticks his middle fingers under his glasses and massages his eyeballs awake.

"I brought you an iced coffee."

He's not a fan of iced coffee, but he says, "That's my girl," and sets it on the end table at his elbow. "Have you had lunch?"

"I had a late breakfast."

She wanders over to the couch and sits down. He was counting on an hour to pray and think before they met, but you have to trust God's leading in the moment.

"So what have you got planned for the week, honey?"

"I thought I'd go up to Seattle and see Olive."

"That's a great idea. She'll want to hear all about the funeral."

"Yeah. She's going to find this hard. Being the last one left."

Her hair is damp and flattened from her bike helmet, and she sits running her fingers through it. He's struck by her face: it's deliberately emptied of expression. She's trying to place herself outside his reach. She's waiting for this to be over, so she can go back to feeling what she feels. "It's hard to think of this world without your grandma Betty in it," he says gently.

"*Yes*," she says.

"Betty's been in my thoughts a lot too. It's not that we saw her that often, but she had such a huge presence in our lives." An idea has been flitting through his mind since yesterday and at this moment it takes up residence, a fully formed revelation. Excitement starts to percolate, but he keeps his tone casual and picks his words carefully. "As we were flying home, I was thinking about the incredible care God took when He set the stage for Operation Auca. Not just raising up the five men with their special gifts, but also preparing a brilliantly talented young woman because He wanted to make sure the story went out to all the nations. When you think about it, He had to start thirty years before the event. He created Betty, He gave her the intelligence and the skill with words that made her a linguist and a writer. He guided her education, He kept her close to Himself."

He reaches for his iced coffee. "It strikes me that we're moving into a new phase of the ministry. Every stage has its own mandate and its own challenges, and at every stage, God has provided." He lifts the coffee in a little toast. "You know, Abby, I suspect God is preparing another gifted young woman to carry our story to a new generation. Someone to take up Betty's online ministry, her blog. Stan was talking about it when we were in Wheaton. He's upset about all that's been neglected since she got sick. The books—he's serving as executor for now, but he'd love to pass that job on."

He doesn't take it further, just watches her. She raises her eyes and gives a startled laugh. "Me?"

"Well, what do you think? You might not be ready just yet, but it's something to shoot for."

"I don't think so, Dad."

"No? Why not?"

"I don't know. Maybe we should just let things go."

"What do you mean?"

"Just—maybe it's time to move on."

Then he's the one who's stunned into silence. Finally he says, "I thought you might be excited at the idea. You've always been so proud of your family and how God has used us."

"No," she cries. "No, I'm not proud."

He looks at her perplexed.

"What should I be proud of? That we went to someone else's country and said to people, your ways are wicked, our ways are good? It's horrible! It's racist!"

"It's not *us* saying that, Abby."

"No?"

"No. It's God. It's God's word."

She sits motionless, not taking her eyes off his face.

"What, darling?"

Still she doesn't speak.

"Tell me where all this is coming from."

She makes a helpless gesture. "Are you sure you want me to talk about it?"

"Of course," he says with all the warmth he feels. "You can talk to me about anything."

They sit on their separate sides of the living room for a long minute without moving. In that pause he sees that she's terrified, and he understands heavily the enormity of having put this question out. He has given her her moment, and they'll be on different terms when it's over.

"Okay," she says. "It's just that I don't have God to blame my attitudes on anymore." Her voice is flat, but she doesn't falter. "About a year ago I tried an experiment. I stopped talking to God, or thinking about Him, because I had to figure out if it was just me. And turns out it was. God was my imaginary friend, like people say. As soon as I stopped making Him up, He was gone."

Fury hits him hard. "Oh, Abigail, such a wilful boast. It's blasphemy. You don't toy with God. You don't do *experiments*." He manages to lower his voice. "Abby, when you hit a dry spell, it's not God who's checked out, it's *you*. Remember when Peter went walking out across the water to meet Jesus? He was okay if he kept his eyes on the Lord. But the minute he took his eyes off Jesus, he started to sink."

"Dad . . ." She looks at him with anguish. "Dad, I don't know if walking on water is what I aspire to."

What do you aspire to, Abby? That would have been the thing to ask.

STILL SELF-INCARCERATED, ABBY moves around her bedroom, sorting out her laundry from Illinois and trying not to start crying again. Her dad's in his room too, no doubt kneeling by his bed. It was as if they had a pact, that at least she wouldn't say it. He loves her, she knows it. She's spent her whole life standing straight, so as not to spill the overflowing bowl of her parents' love.

She moves to the closet to pick out a few things to pack for Seattle. "Your room," Olive calls the upstairs bedroom in her condo. It has a bed with a railing along three sides (a daybed, Olive calls it), a quilt with red-breasted birds, a chiming clock, and house plants that are versions of wild plants Olive remembers from Ecuador. And curled up on that daybed is Shadow, the grey cat named after the cat Olive had as a girl.

Olive has always been Abby's favourite of the Operation Auca grandmas. After Sharon died, Abby spent a lot of weekends in Seattle, cutting her last class on Friday to catch the early bus. Olive isn't the force of nature that Betty was, but she is thoughtful and surprisingly honest. Although she rarely talks about herself. Mostly they talk about Abby. Well, Abby was a motherless teenager, wasn't she. It was sort of a project for her, to gradually confide everything important in Olive.

She'll take her library backpack. She's been working through a list she found online: "Reading for Aliens: The Twentieth Century on Planet Earth." Will doesn't know about the list, and he's intrigued by the books he sees on her carrel; he thinks she's some kind of savant, or at least an autodidact. She shakes the backpack open. *1984* by George Orwell and *Things Fall Apart* by Chinua Achebe, both unread. And below them, the red spine of a book she found in the social sciences section. She searched "Amazon Indigenous peoples" just for the heck of it, and felt a pulse of recognition when she went to the shelves and slid out this book with its cover photo of two children scaling a smooth palm trunk. It's a study of the Waorani by an anthropologist who lived in a rainforest longhouse with them for many years. Maybe she'll show it to Olive and maybe they'll talk and she'll learn something.

After she hears David leave for the men's fellowship, she goes to the basement and digs a pizza out of the freezer. Gizmo is alert to her every move. "In your dreams, Dogma," she says as she slides it into the oven. While it bakes, she goes to the living room and picks up the channel changer, but before she can switch on the TV, the land line rings. A male voice asks if this is the Saint residence and whether he can speak to Abigail. He says his name is Walter Varga and that he's a film director. A prank call, obviously—but he goes on to say, "We're working on a film about American missionaries in Ecuador, and there's something I'd like to talk over with you. Do you have a few minutes?"

Well, she does.

He says the movie in question is based specifically on Operation Auca. It's a dramatic feature being made by a company called Veritas, and it's destined for wide international release.

He says that in his view the meaning of those 1956 events has never been fully probed, and it's a story the world is ready for. Their goal is to do it right, to give due attention to the cultural context. They have a prominent anthropologist on board, a guy who's been working with the Waorani to produce a book of oral histories. He's going to be consulting on the film.

"How did you get my name?" Abby asks.

"Somebody saw you at a conference in Sacramento a while back—you were on a panel about Operation Auca, right? I've got the program right here, and, well, we managed to track you down. I understand you're in a unique position. Both your families were part of this story?"

"Nate Saint and Jim Elliot were my grandfathers."

"Wow. Let me ask—do you have any professional experience?"

"What?"

"Have you ever acted?"

"Like, outside daily life?"

He laughs as though he's starting to like Abby. "It's not a

deal-breaker," he says. "We'll be casting a lot of non-professionals, certainly in the minor roles. The Waorani will all be played by individuals from the tribal community. I'm, well, personally, I've been hooked on the Italian Neorealists since college, and I think we're better off with people who bring their life experience to a role." He pauses dramatically. "So. What does your week look like? Could you drop everything and come to LA?"

"You're asking me to audition?"

"Yes."

"For a minor role?"

"Actually, we'd like you to read for one of the missionary wives."

"Seriously."

"Seriously. I've got your photo here and I think you'd be a good fit."

"For which wife?"

"We'll have to see how you read." Another pause. "I understand you're twenty-four?"

"I will be soon enough."

He laughs again. He gives her his phone number and the address of an agency called Breakwater Talent in Beverly Hills. He asks her to grab her smartphone and look it up while he waits. "Click on satellite. Zoom in, zoom in. You see that rooftop with the lime-green patio umbrellas? That's us, right under there, third floor. Put a pin in it."

He pauses then, thinking. "Obviously you don't have an agent."

"Uh, no."

"I'm just thinking, you know, if you were my daughter, I wouldn't want you running down to LA on your own to meet a strange man." Clearly he knows she is nowhere near twenty-four. "I wonder if I should have a word with—"

"No. No, no, no, no."

"Well, why don't you bring a friend along, just so you're more comfortable? And you should know that three of our team will be present for the audition, including a woman named June Shapiro." He says they're moving at warp speed and he wants Abby—well, tonight if he could get her! They settle on Thursday morning. They say goodbye.

What do you do after a call like that? "What?" she shrieks at Gizmo, and he yips his excitement back and they do a dance around the coffee table. The oven timer is pinging. Abby goes to the kitchen and slides the pizza onto the big cutting board and, too agitated to sit at the table, carries it into the living room, where she sinks onto the carpet, her back against the couch. She'll call Ashley. She'll call Bethany. Will. No. Sean, she thinks.

Oh, poor Sean. Sean is *desperate* to get ahead in film. He was involved in one of the sequels of *Left Behind* and he claims to be best buds with Nicolas Cage. He dreamed constantly about making a movie about Operation Auca—he wanted to cash in on his heritage. But cash was exactly the problem, and she thinks how pissed off he's going to be at being scooped. Whereas Abby—nothing like this ever once crossed her mind. And if she ends up landing a role, she'll make a pile of money. Enough to pay for university.

She digs into the pizza, peeling off pieces of pepperoni for Gizmo. Are you going to film in Ecuador? she had asked, and Walter Varga said yes, absolutely. He described the source material as galvanizing. To which Abby replied, "Well, it's a really dark story. Although I guess that depends on when you think it starts and when you think it ends." This observation was not original to her, but it seemed to impress Walter Varga, who used it to wrap things up. "That's why we need you, Abigail. You carry this history in your bones."

A terrifying thing to say, when you think about it. She drops a pizza crust onto the board and gets to her feet, and then happiness wallops her like a tsunami. *Perfection*—it fills the house with its dazzling light. How absolutely brilliant: fun, and glamour, and hard, thrilling work. All the people who are so disappointed in her—she'll totally fulfill their hopes and expectations, she'll spectacularly transcend them, everyone weeping to see her in one of those roles, her friends and critics alike. Her own personal trailer, with her name on the door. The friendly, flattering makeup artist (*Your skin is perfect, my God, do you even have pores?*). The costume trailer, the racks of clothes. It will be a period piece, the *Mad Men* era. She may have to cut her hair, she may have to get a perm. Wear one of those pointy bras. But still, she thinks.

They'll cast the women as younger than they actually were, and as prettier. They always do.

In the kitchen, she catches her reflection on the microwave and lifts her chin. Fine. She can make that cut.

OLIVE OPENS THE DOOR

5

"Just have your lesson before Nate gets here," Peter said as he poured her a mug of coffee. "You don't want to let Panka down." Panka was their language informant and they paid her ten sucre per session.

So that's what Olive did after breakfast, she went to see Panka, and spent the morning sitting on a stump in front of a palm-plank house, rubbing at invisible flies biting her ankles and expanding her Quichua list of household items, because she hadn't mastered the techniques for extracting any words but nouns. Panka's baby tottered over to her, and Olive picked her up, and Panka tilted her lovely face and said a long phrase with the word *baby* (*llullucu*) in the middle of it. She repeated it several times, but Olive didn't write it down because some of its sounds eluded her and because she had no idea what it meant. *You're bouncing my sweet brown-eyed baby on your knee. My baby usually makes strange, but she seems to love you. My baby's chigger bites are infected again.* It could even have been a question: *Where is your baby?*

Then she went back and climbed the steps to their tiny bamboo house and cobbled some lunch together and she and Peter walked through the settlement to the airstrip. They went plenty early so they could scour the surface, looking for protruding roots that would snag the landing gear of the plane, or a rut a wheel might fall into. The airstrip ran from one river to the next, from the Jatun Yaku to the Talac, and the Talac end was new, they had built it after the flood. That part was especially dangerous because roots the men had failed to dig out would rot and the surface might cave in at those points. Peter took the new part, stomping on any stretch that troubled him, and Olive walked the old. It all looked fine. So, standing in the sun with their duffle bag at her feet, she had time to tackle the passion fruit she was carrying in her pocket. She notched it all around with her thumbnail until it came apart in halves to reveal a mess of luscious frogs' eggs in grey sacs, waiting to be slurped. But just as she lifted one of these cups to her mouth, a gang of children raced across the playing field and danced out onto the airstrip, dogs barking, and a minute later Nate Saint's little yellow Piper dropped over the trees like a raptor. Helplessly, Olive bent for the duffle bag, passing the open cups of passion fruit to a small girl named Urpi, who took them with a quiver of delight. Nate taxied towards them, and then his arm darted out and he tossed a handful of hard candies as far as he could hurl them, his method for clearing the runway, and in a flash Urpi had dropped the passion fruit in the dirt and dashed into the fray with the boys.

"Jim already there?" Pete called, running down the airstrip.

"Yup," Nate shouted. "He came straight from the men's retreat." He pushed his cap back and grinned at Olive. "Got your toothbrush?"

"But Betty?" Olive said, glancing over her shoulder in the direction of Jim and Betty's house on the ridge. "Isn't Betty coming?"

"Nope. She's looking after Rachel."

So Olive crawled alone into the back of the plane. She untangled the leather straps of the shoulder harness and took her time fastening them over her breasts; this was her furtive sign of the cross. Peter buckled himself into the front passenger side and put the extra headphones on. Nate turned the plane around and then they were jouncing back along the airstrip. And then the roar, and the lift, and gravity pressed her hard into the seat and the settlement dropped below, the thatched roofs vanishing first and then the tin, a tiny Quichua settlement hemmed in by two rivers. What a thrill to be scooped up and carried out of it, like a man in a fable being shown another world. Up into the sky, a lovely china blue tending towards violet at its edges. She pressed her face against the plastic window and watched the forest shrink and flatten and transform into a rough green sea, a sea that tilted suddenly, showing its misty edges, because Nate had banked to the northeast.

Nate. Even the back of his head transmitted efficiency. He did this all day every day except Sunday, flying his plane out of the mission headquarters at Shell Mera as nonchalantly as a delivery man drove a truck. He read the ridges between the jungle stations like road signs; he knew all the rivers that coiled through the forest, some wide, some narrow, although they were all the same colour, a pale milky brown. This was the Jatun Yaku he was following, a.k.a. the Napo. At one of its bends Olive could make out a clearing, the yucca fields of another Quichua settlement. The Quichua lived along the rivers because they hoped to trade—rubber and tapir skins, mostly. They aspired to T-shirts, outboard motors, liquor, rice, guns, kerosene, machetes, Spanish words, and Pepsi. Farther back in the trackless jungle, the savage Auca were rumoured to live, not along the rivers because, unlike the Quichua, they had no desire to trade and did not want to be found. They made every- thing out of the forest or they got along without it. When Olive was a girl in Seattle, a picture hung above the doorway in the school library: Christopher Columbus arriving on the shores of America and receiving gifts from the Indians. He was holding a wooden cross like a giant staff, and Indians in feather headdresses knelt before him. Now, all these centuries later, she and Pete and the others were at a similar portal of history. *Pacha*—the Quichua word floated into her mind. *Pacha*. It meant space, and world, and earth; it was one word that meant all those things. It meant this vast dreamscape, the sky and the whole curving expanse of earth, as featureless and as outside time as the ocean. It meant, *Are you even here?*

Peter swivelled his head in the massive headphones. "Machu Picchu," he shouted, the joke he made every time they flew into Arajuno. Olive angled her neck to see. She tracked the Napo with its brown coils, as stately as a water boa, and then she spied the writhing worm of the Arajuno River, and there, at their intersection, she saw the Arajuno airstrip catching the sun, the only straight line in the whole scene.

Arajuno, more remote than the Shandia station, and also more civilized. When it was built in 1940, it was going to be Shell Oil's permanent headquarters. For almost ten years it functioned as a tiny model tropical city, a grid of five or six streets lined with neat American-style bungalows, and a narrow-gauge railway to bring in supplies from Shell Mera, and a hotel and swimming pool and tennis courts. But the oil executives had overlooked one crucial fact when they built it: their prized townsite was on the Auca side of the river. They couldn't get Ecuadorean crews to go into Auca territory to build roads and lay pipe. And then they lost a bunch of Americans (six, Olive heard, and someone else said *fourteen*), men who were speared when they ventured into the forest. Suddenly Shell Oil was gone, leaving everything behind—Caterpillar tractors, children's swings, furniture, drill heads. A windfall for the Quichua in the area, and for the jungle, which gobbled up Arajuno at a speed you could almost track with your eyes. That's what people said: the first year it was a topiary park, three years later, pretty much invisible.

Maybe it was Jim who thought of it first, maybe it was Ed, or Nate: how wonderfully situated that ghost town was for reaching the Auca. At Shandia, the Auca felt so far away—forty miles or so of dangerous jungle trekking. But at Arajuno you were right on the edge of Auca territory; it was almost as if God had used Shell Oil to set that town up. Ed made Shell a ridiculously small offer, he bought a whole town for a few thousand dollars, and Nate flew a work party in. They ripped and hacked their way through the swinging curtains of vines, and Ed and Marilou picked out the house they wanted, a big bungalow on the bank of the Napo, and the men rebuilt it entirely with materials scavenged from the site. Marilou's kitchen counter was a beautiful slab of redwood that had formerly been the bar in the hotel. She and Ed had a brass headboard for their bed. They had a huge enamel bathtub, although of course they had to fill it by bucket. They lived in a real house, in contrast to the shack on stilts that Olive and Peter called home in Shandia.

A real house with a screened porch on both the front and the back. The back porch faced the forest, and that's where they were all sitting when Olive and Peter and Nate walked over from the airstrip. Not all—Nate's wife, Marj, wasn't there, she had stayed in Shell Mera with the kids. And Betty was back in Shandia with the thankless job of looking after Nate's sister Rachel, who had malaria. So just Jim and Ed and Marilou, drinking limeade and eating peanuts. Marilou was in the bamboo rocker, her hair tousled and her face flushed. Pregnant or not, she was still running a school in Arajuno. Every morning she rang a bell, and the Quichua kids splashed across from the other side of the river, and she taught them in Quichua and Spanish while her house girl watched her own little boys.

"I kept the kids in school until noon," she was saying in her soft, laughing voice. "They knew what had happened, and they were so wound up they could hardly sit. But I kept them in and I made them practise for the Christmas concert. We'd finish a verse of 'Noche de Paz' and they'd burst out, Señora, we will kill him with our blowgun if he comes around again! I had to keep saying, We want the Auca to be our friends. Remember? We want to tell them about Jesus."

"I don't get it," Peter said. "What happened?"

"Nate didn't tell you? Marilou had a visit from the Auca!"

They finally heard the whole story. Ed had stayed in Punapunga the night before, helping Jim with a men's retreat, and at dawn, while the kids were still sleeping, Marilou got up to use the toilet, and she happened to glance out the kitchen window and saw a naked man standing motionless at the edge of the forest. She threw her robe on and ran out the back door. The man was just standing there staring at the house. His hair was long, with bangs cut in the front. He had balsa plugs in his earlobes and he was carrying a spear, twice as long as he was tall.

"Holy cow," said Pete. "What did you do?"

"Well, my first thought was to take him a gift. Just to let him know we're friendly. I looked back at the house and saw a machete leaning against the porch, so I grabbed it and went towards him. I was calling out, ¡Hola! Quiero ser tu amiga. He looked at me for a minute, and then he spun around and took off into the forest."

"So Marilou radioed me," said Nate. "Cool as a cucumber, she says, One of our neighbours just showed up in Centreville."

Neighbours. Centreville. That was code. It was designed to keep others in the dark, especially a certain someone who did not have a two-way radio but might get word nonetheless.

They sat in a circle, gazing at each other with shining eyes.

"Why was I calling out to him in Spanish?" Marilou whispered. "A pregnant gringa in a yellow bathrobe waving a machete! What could he have thought? I suddenly realized, and I switched to that Auca phrase Jim gave us." She demonstrated for them: "Biti miti punimupa." Trying to say the words made her laugh so hard that tears rose in her eyes.

Everyone jumped in with a different pronunciation, and soon they were all helpless with laughter.

"I blew it," Marilou moaned, wiping her eyes. "I had a chance and I blew it."

"Oh, baby, you didn't blow it," Ed said. He swung his feet in size-thirteen sneakers up onto the railing. "He felt your love."

After the man disappeared, Marilou went back into the house to get the pistol, because she had promised Ed she would if something like this ever happened, and she and Fermin (their yardman) and Tica (their house girl) walked cautiously down the path, Marilou with a canvas bag over the hand holding the cocked gun so if the Auca or possibly his friends were still watching, they wouldn't see it and be frightened. Halfway down the yard, a plank lay over a little ditch and Fermin spied a wet mark on it. They thought it might have been a footprint.

They studied the wet mark carefully before it dried. Marilou was only sorry she hadn't thought to take a picture. "So you'd know I didn't dream the whole thing up," she said.

"Nobody thinks you dreamed it up."

"If it was a footprint, what size feet did he have, would you say?"

"Ten, maybe. And it was wide. At least a double D."

"How old did the guy look?"

"About as old as The Kid here." She meant Peter.

"And he was in his birthday suit?"

"He had a . . . a sort of string. He might have had something tied around his wrists too—I'm not sure."

"Well, we won't ask you about his gear, Marilou, because we're sure you didn't look."

Marilou batted at Jim's arm.

Olive took a sip of her lemonade, loving how cold it was, loving the tinkle of ice. These miraculous ice cubes were from Marilou's kerosene freezer, which had been flown in on a cargo plane; of all the outstations, only Arajuno had a landing strip big enough for a cargo plane. And the veranda was actually decorated for Christmas, with a playful tree Marilou had made of bamboo and hung with the tinsel she'd had the foresight to bring with her from Deerfield, Illinois. Oh, Marilou, so resourceful, so brave, so funny and modest, the star of the party—she was always the star. Not just the prettiest of the wives, but the sexiest, that's what Olive, perched on an upturned Pepsi case beside Peter, was beginning to understand, that it was something beyond her beauty that drew your eyes to

Marilou. Even pregnant! Olive pressed her cold glass to her cheek, and felt her double, troubled heart merge into a single, warmly beating one. The beauty of one was the beauty of all, they were all fools for Christ.

Fermin walked past the porch, calling good night. Three or four other Quichua joined him on the path down to the river. Their houses were all on the other side.

"They don't swim over, do they?"

"It's not that deep right now. You could wade. But they keep a canoe tied to a tree. In case we get a big rain and the water comes up. They really don't want to be stuck on the Auca side after dark."

Swifts sprang from the direction of the river as if they sensed danger, swirling up into a sky so small and glowing, it looked like an open parachute. They sat and ate their peanuts and talked, and the forest vanished into darkness, and soon they were just voices along the porch. And then the tree frogs started their enormous song and gradually they all fell silent.

Olive drained her lemonade. She'd tasted alcohol just once in her life, on a clandestine night out with her friend Carol in college. Gin and tonics, that's what they drank. Sometimes lemonade alone would bring it back, the delicate piney fumes, the blurry joy of that evening. She set her glass carefully on the floor.

"Some nights we hear jaguar," Marilou said dreamily.

"You're kidding. We never hear jaguar at Shandia. What do they sound like?"

"They groan. They sound like an old man groaning."

"It may not be jaguar you're hearing," Nate said. "The Auca are expert at imitating animal sounds. That's what Daniel Boone says."

"Daniel Boone?"

"Carlos Sevilla. You know, the Spanish guy with the hacienda near Shandia."

Silence on the veranda. And then, from somewhere close, a long, graceful fluting.

"What was that?"

"Haven't a clue."

Ed got up to turn the generator on.

"Leave it for a bit, honey," Marilou said. "Just a few more minutes. We're having hamburgers, it's a quick supper."

He sat back down, a big genial shadow slouching in the dark. Not taut and burning the way Peter was, from the constant athletic struggle of holding his sins at bay. Olive reached for Peter, she laid her hand lightly on his thigh and slid it down to his bony knee. He put his hand over hers and wove their fingers together. The man came into Olive's mind, the Auca man, as vivid as if she had seen him herself, sturdy and naked and unselfconscious, standing still against the forest wall like the angel God sent out to guard Paradise with a flaming sword.

"One of their warriors showing up like that and not attacking, it has to mean something." This was Ed.

"Praise God," Jim said. "The Auca know we're not oilmen. They can feel the prayers and the love, we're drawing them in."

That night this seemed to make sense to everyone, although a week later they'd thought better of it, and when they all flew back in to Arajuno for Christmas, the men got to work and strung an electric fence around Ed and Marilou's yard.

6

TOLSTOY SAID THERE ARE ONLY two plots: a man goes on a journey and a stranger comes to town. Olive, sitting at the back of the lecture hall and scribbling down every word that came out of her professor's mouth, thought, Isn't that the same plot? If you just switch the point of view? Not that she put up her hand to argue with him. She was silent, as befitted the invisible. I'll ask Peter, she thought. Peter, who *could* see her. Meeting Peter might be considered the start of Olive's story, but they had known each other their whole lives. If you wanted an inciting incident, you'd have to think of the rainy Sunday in late June 1951 when Jim Elliot arrived in Seattle. You'd start with the hour before Olive heard the knock on the door, before the whole thing started up, because afterwards she could never see as clearly. She got enmeshed, as tightly bound up in it as if a boa had seized her and was gradually tightening its coils around her, squeezing until her eyes paled to white.

They lived a mile or so apart in Seattle, she and Peter. That rainy Sunday, Peter Fleming drove Olive and her parents back from the Gospel Hall in his father's green Packard. The Flemings owned a car and the Ainsleys didn't. Both families were exceptional in the Gospel Hall—Peter's family because they were rich and somewhat worldly, Olive's because they had only one child, her, their cherished daughter. Peter was invited for Sunday dinner, he was with them when they stepped into a cool and silent house that had filled with the smell of roasting chicken while they prayed in the Gospel Hall on Rainier Avenue. A spotless house, the dust motes all settled, and a lemon pie tucked into the dark safe of the tiny refrigerator, oozing amber beads onto the white drifts of its meringue. Sundays: you walked in after church feeling hungry and righteous but also strangely chilled and flattened out, and Olive loved it when Peter came home with them and helped bring her back to life. She loved seeing him take off his jacket and undo his top shirt button, as though he belonged in this modest house where they ate in the kitchen at a white-painted table. At Peter's place they ate in a dining room crammed with heavy oak furniture and draped in lace, and the air was frigid with his stepmother's moods.

That Sunday, Olive's mother held out a blue-dotted apron and Olive took it and tied the strings in a bow and set about putting the vegetables to boil. She made gravy, pressing the lumps out with a wooden spoon, and her mother stood beside her and stirred up a white sauce for the peas. They were still a little shy around Peter, Olive's parents. Olive could tell it moved them, their only child having a private life, choosing a boyfriend all on her own. But that it was Peter Fleming—if they had looked up the components in God's catalogue and had him custom-made, they would hardly have dared ask for so much. A slender, dark-haired boy from a big stone house on Queen Anne Hill, a boy who was going to be a university professor one day, and whose parents drove an expensive new car and had books on their shelves. The Gospel Hall did not believe in putting one man above another; everyone dressed the same, and the men took turns preaching. But the Flemings—you'd have to call them the first among equals.

And now they were talking easily the way families do, about her father's renovations in the kitchen and about the wallpaper, which had a pattern of gnarled trees clutching the earth with gnarled roots. Olive trees, the family's little joke—they could never change the wallpaper.

"You are the only Olives I know," Peter said.

"It's a good name," Olive's dad said. "It's in the Bible. When the flood ended, a dove brought Noah an olive branch as a sign of peace."

"I wanted to call her Faith," Olive's mother said, deftly pouring the gravy from the roasting pan into its little white pitcher. "Alex was the one who wanted Olive. I said it would be too confusing. So then he started calling me Livie. I was never Livie until our Olive came along."

"It's usually the child you give the pet name to," Peter said. His eyes met Olive's as if he'd said something private and outrageous, and, warmed, she turned back to the stove, where the potatoes were tender to the fork. Hollow with hunger, glazed with happiness, she got out the masher and put her weight into it. The potatoes surrendered their shape, and she slopped soft butter into them, and then they set the food on the white table with its red cotton cloth and took their places.

"Peter, would you ask the Lord's blessing on the food?" Olive's father said, and Peter glanced across at her and bowed his head.

"You are mighty, Lord. You furnish all our needs," he prayed in his calm and precise voice, and Olive, watching through her lashes, registered something yellow in the corner of her eye. It was her mother's housedress. For the first time ever with a guest in the house, her mother had gone upstairs and taken off her navy Sunday suit and put on her yellow housedress. Mom knows, Olive marvelled, bowing her head. She knows, and she is happy.

It was a fork-in-the-road day. It would have been anyway, even if nothing else had happened, even if, just as they were settling into their meal, a thump had not sounded loudly on the door. Olive put her fork down, pushed her chair back, and went up the hall. She opened the door. A young man stood on the front stoop with the brim of his hat turned down against the rain.

She had never actually met Jim Elliot, but she knew him as a friend of Peter's. He was from Portland and was scheduled to speak at their assembly that evening. He wore a suit but no tie, like all the Brethren. Not much older than Pete, but while Pete was reading Nietzsche and Sartre at the university, Jim had been going around the country preaching in soup kitchens and jails or buttonholing people on the street. And here he was, springing through the door with his hand out, carrying his celebrity into their little house.

She took Jim's hat and led him into the kitchen and they all got to their feet. "How did you track me down?" Peter asked, looking pleased and embarrassed.

"I have my spies out," Jim said. Olive's dad went to the living room for a chair and Olive went for another plate. She could see her mother at the cupboard, no doubt regretting the yellow housedress, casting around for something to make this meal special. She came back with dill pickles in a cut-glass dish.

"I'm sure you folks have already said a blessing over this

wonderful dinner," Jim said as he sat down, "but I'd like to tell God how grateful I am to be sharing it."

He was not a tall man, but he was powerful and lithe. He looked like a wrestler, which he was. Olive had seen wrestling, she had stood in the entry to the gym at the university and watched muscular, bare-chested men lumbering around each other, stooped and glaring, grabbing as if they were trying to kill each other with their bare hands. "Civilize the mind, but make savage the body," said Peter, who was with Olive at the time. This wasn't from the Bible, it was an ancient Chinese saying. Peter said Jim's wrestling was a wonderful tool for God. He walked into saloons and challenged drunkards to arm wrestling, and when a crowd gathered, he preached to them.

Now he sat holding a big hand out in either direction. It was not something they did, they didn't link hands for grace, but Livie put her hand in his with a smile, and Jim grasped Pete's hand where it lay on the table, and while the chicken grew cold on the platter, they had a second and lengthier grace. Olive's parents valued modesty, her father could hardly bring himself to use the pronoun *I*, and Olive thought it possible that Jim Elliot was over-reaching himself.

"Did you serve, Jim?" Alex asked as he passed the chicken up the table. In the war, he meant. It was a dark preoccupation that he tried to keep hidden.

"No sir, I did not," Jim said, spearing himself a drumstick. He had a disarming dimple, just one. "I count it a blessing that I'm called to go out into the world with the good news of the gospel of Christ, instead of bearing death and destruction. And you folks probably share my belief that as followers of Jesus we are citizens of a heavenly kingdom, not citizens of this world. So I cannot in conscience participate in either politics or war."

This was a question Peter loved to debate, and Olive tried to catch his eye. But he was caught up with his dinner. It struck her how unlikely his friendship with Jim Elliot was. And yet last summer, on a whim, they had spent six weeks travelling together, living on cans of beans heated on the engine block of Jim's 1942 Ford while they drove.

"What do we have here?" Jim asked, lifting a bowl.

"Creamed peas," Olive's mother said. "This is the way we serve peas in Canada." It was the most exotic thing about the Ainsleys, that Livie was a Canadian.

"You're a Canuck?" Jim said, slopping a huge spoonful onto his plate. "Canada's a complete mystery to me. Tell me about it."

That was Jim Elliot, interested in everything. He professed to love creamed peas and he identified Livie's secret ingredient in the tomato aspic (Worcestershire sauce). He learned that Alex was a milkman and he portrayed him as a hero, on the front lines of Washington State's successful battle against childhood rickets. He discovered that Alex and Livie had met when Alex took a vacation trip to Canada to see the goats grazing on the roof of a store on Vancouver Island, that Alex got lost and wandered into the diner where Livie worked, where he ordered liver and onions and handed his waitress a gospel tract. Which opened the door for him to lead Livie to the Lord, and, of course, to court and marry her. "Wasn't that an amazing coincidence?" Livie exclaimed, as she always did at this point in the story. But Jim would have none of it. "You followed God's call, Mr. Ainsley, though you had no idea of all the wonderful things He had in store for you. Praise God for that. Well, the Lord is calling me to a foreign field as well, and I intend to listen."

"To Canada?" Livie laughed, not ready to give it up.

"I pray that some man of God gets to the Canucks before the Commies take the whole place over," Jim said. "But it won't be me, I'm afraid. God wants me in South America." He pressed a shallow dent into his mashed potatoes for the gravy and, while he ate, told them the whole story. He'd thought his calling was to preach in America, but one day, out of the blue, he received a letter from an Englishman named Dr. Tidmarsh, who was serving God in Ecuador, in the eastern region known as El Oriente. Dr. Tidmarsh worked with the Quichua, miserable, impoverished Indians who were indentured to plantations where they dug yams from morning to night, drunk on palm spirits, many of them children with no idea who their fathers were. Dr. Tidmarsh had recently suffered a terrible accident: the little aircraft carrying him and his wife into his jungle station crashed. By God's grace everybody on board survived, but the pilot's back was broken and Mrs. Tidmarsh was badly injured and would have to go home for good. Dr. Tidmarsh had heard of Jim and he wrote to ask him to seek the Lord's will about coming to replace them. While Jim was praying about it, he was led to attend a summer course in Oklahoma to learn how to translate the Scriptures into Indigenous languages. And there, the man assigned to mentor him was a different missionary on leave from El Oriente, that very region of Ecuador.

"What a coincidence," said Olive's mother.

Jim smiled at her and his dimple flashed. "Mrs. Ainsley, if you give your will entirely over to the Lord, you will never again use the word *coincidence*," he said. And then he told them how, after the linguistics course, he shut himself into his room at his parents' house in Portland and waited and prayed. God can't lead you if your heart is clouded by sin, and Satan went after him like crazy. "I was tormented by terrible lusts," he said frankly. "I had murderous thoughts about people who I believed had wronged me." On the tenth morning, weak from these battles and from living on the tea and bread his mother delivered to his room, he woke up and his heart and mind had been washed clean. And then he heard God's voice, which was indeed a still, small voice. God was not leading him to the Quichua Indians after all. His mission was to the Auca, a tribe farther afield, people who had never once had a peaceful contact with civilization. He'd heard about them at the Summer

Institute, and his heart had burned within him, but at the time he hadn't recognized that as a sign.

The Auca were Stone Age Indians who inhabited a vast territory in Ecuador, rich in rubber and oil and possibly gold. All those resources were inaccessible to the civilized world because the Auca speared everyone who tried to enter. "These people live in utmost darkness. They have no culture, no laws, no morality whatsoever. They go about naked. They bury their elders alive. They bury children alive."

"But—" Olive said (how could he possibly know this?), and he cast a quick look of scorn and dismissal her way and kept on talking.

"They act entirely on impulse. If a man wants a woman, he takes her. If a mother is irritated by her baby's crying, she strangles it."

It was her mother who successfully cut him off. "My stars! Why would anyone want to live like that?"

"They don't know any other way. They have never heard the name of Christ."

"Yes, there are many unsaved folks living on this street, and they don't go around strangling their children."

Yes, America was on a dark path, but it was not the Amazon, where Satan had had a free stomping ground for centuries.

By the time the pie was served, Jim had shifted gears and was talking in a low voice, paying her parents the huge compliment of confiding in them. He told them how grieved he had been that God had not blessed his ministry in America; eighteen months in, he had almost no fruit for his labours. But now he understood what God was up to. This is not your place, Jim, God was saying. I want to lead you farther. It was no small sacrifice. Jim knew he could never expose a wife and children to the dangers of this mission. He had had to surrender his most cherished dream of home and family. "But the Lord calls and I obey," he said simply.

They'd pushed back from the table by then. Jim lifted one shoe to his knee, a worn brown brogue, and gripped his ankle in a casual caress. *How beautiful upon the mountains are the feet of him who brings the gospel of peace.* Olive knew this verse and she suspected Jim did too. She sat still, feeling a new calling take possession of her heart: a calling to strangle a minister of God with her own bare hands.

PETER WOULD SPEND the afternoon with her, that's how their Sundays went. If the rain kept up, they'd play Scrabble and then have supper together, and he'd drive them to the evening meeting. But while she was rinsing gravy off the plates, Olive heard Jim Elliot say, "What have you got planned for the afternoon, brother?" and Pete reply, "Nothing," and first thing she knew, they were out the door together.

So Olive spent the afternoon alone in her room, stretched out on her bedspread. She was chilly, but if she crawled under the covers now, she'd sleep until morning. It was that crazy hike they did yesterday, the Chirico Trail. By unspoken agreement, she and Peter did it more or less at a run. They met in a picnic area at the trailhead—Olive had ridden out with the two chaperones and a girl named Marlene—and somebody pumped water. The pump screeched like a donkey and the water was very cold and tasted of iron. When she'd had enough, Olive passed the dipper to Peter. As he drank, he looked at her over the edge of the dipper with eyes that said, *Now.* The group set off and Pete and Olive snatched the lead, dashing up the rocky ways as fast as they could to get ahead. At a bend, the trail separated and they took the narrower way and scrambled up it. It was a path to a lookout high above, an almost vertical path. Peter swung over the lip at the top and reached back for her. He was on his knees and they toppled breathless onto the moss. He undid a button and nuzzled his face into her blouse. His mouth was looking for the secret place between her breasts. Then it searched lower, it found her nipple. He was lying right on her for the first time. She felt the bulge in his jeans against her abdomen and a wave of astonishment went through her. It was true after all, it was the truest thing she had ever felt. And then there were voices on the trail below, Harry Bancroft shouting, and then a girl, it sounded like Marlene: "Hey, look, they went up this way."

She rolled over and pressed her face into her pillow. *I will praise thee O Lord, for I am fearfully and wonderfully made.* There's a verse for everything. And the truly amazing part of it all was this—that what made her parents happy had this wildness in it.

Suppertime came and he hadn't called. Her mother came downstairs in her navy suit, doing up the little safety pin she used to keep her neckline modest, hurrying so they could catch the six-thirty streetcar, and Olive announced that she was staying home.

"Don't sulk, Olive," Livie said.

"I'm not sulking. But I'm not going." So her parents put their hats on and went without her. She hardly ever crossed them.

After they were gone, she stood for a minute in the kitchen and the cat rubbed itself against her leg. "You're shameless," she said, stooping to pick him up. Jim Elliot would be at the door of the Gospel Hall by now, warmly shaking hands, charming all the women. How mercilessly he had turned his blue-eyed charm on her poor mother. *Mrs. Ainsley, God loves an inquiring mind.* He was not so in love with Olive's inquiring mind.

She lifted Shadow, pressing her cheek against his soft side, and went slowly back up the stairs. "You little rodent," she whispered, capping the cat's bony head, squashing his ears flat, staring into his alien face. He stared back with glassy eyes and she watched the foil sleeve of his irises retract. In her room she set him on the quilt and reached up to pull the elastic off the end of her braid, fingering her hair out into its stiff waves. Then she lay down and picked up her book. *Moby Dick.* Peter had written his master's thesis on Herman Melville. Is there a bigger book in the whole world?

When Olive started first grade, her mother walked her up to

her classroom and they stopped to admire a display in a glass case in the corridor. It was a collection of dead bugs on pins with little labels in English and Latin. "Beetles of the North-West. Collected by Pete Fleming, 3A," her mother read out. From the time she could remember, he was her hero and her friend. There were very few Plymouth Brethren children in their school, and the girls with their long braids and shapeless dresses stood out more than the boys did, and were teased for it. But kind and brave, Peter often walked her home, wheeling his bike along the sidewalk. A quiet boy who devoured the newspaper, who puzzled out books in Spanish and French, who copied down Bible verses and taped them to the handlebars of his bike so he could memorize them while he rode. Who talked to her about books, and began to lend them to her. Olive's family did not have books; her father had grown up in a house where only the Bible was allowed. But Peter got Olive reading. When she was eleven, he lent her *The Swiss Family Robinson*, and her parents read it as well. Then he began bringing over adult books for them, Christian stories by Amy Carmichael for Livie, but also *Gone with the Wind* and *The Good Earth. All Quiet on the Western Front* for Alex.

She had never dreamed of going to university, but Peter came over and talked her parents into it. He was the first from their Gospel Hall ever to go to university, where he did a double honours in literature and philosophy. What was philosophy, when you thought about it, but questions? More than once, Olive had seen him striding down a corridor with a professor, elbow to elbow, locked in argument. And still he was the fair-haired boy at the Gospel Hall, where questions did not exist, where the whole point was to clutch on to truth that had come down to you two thousand years ago, while all around you the world careened in crazy, runaway change. Think how intense and disciplined he had to be to navigate all that. For her it was easier; no one expected her to speak up about anything.

She was still pretending to read when her parents came home. She was in the middle of Chapter 46 and they still hadn't clapped eyes on a whale. She got up drowsily and went partway down the stairs. "Did you see Peter?" she asked.

"Saw him up at the front," Alex said. "Didn't have a chance to speak to him, though." He and Livie both seemed agitated. "Just want to look up the verse that Elliot fellow preached from. What was it again?"

"Matthew 19:12," Livie said, pulling out the pins that held her hat in place and setting both the hat and the pins on the sideboard.

Alex sat down with his bible and began to leaf through it. He found the passage he was looking for and lifted the bible and read it aloud. "Matthew 19:12. *There are eunuchs who have made themselves eunuchs for the sake of the kingdom of heaven. He who is able to receive this, let him receive it.*"

He looked over at Livie, troubled. She frowned and reached a hand towards him. It was his reading glasses she wanted, and he gave them to her. She stuck them on, and dug the dictionary out of the drawer in the sideboard and paged through it, muttering, "U-N-E . . . U-N-E . . ."

"No, Mother," Alex said. "It's E-U-N."

"*Eunuch*," Livie finally read out. "'A castrated man, especially one formerly employed by Oriental rulers as a harem guard or palace official.'" She looked up at Olive aghast. "He did talk about the Orient."

"He talked about El Oriente," Olive said. "You heard him—it's a region of Ecuador. And that other—it's just a figure of speech. It means he's taking a vow to be single for the rest of his life." She was still standing on the stairs looking down at them and she could not stand the gormless expression on their faces. "It's a fancy way of saying that he hates women. Like, in his own mind, he's been *fixed*."

═══

OLIVE HERSELF WAS to blame, she always thought (in a certain way): a stranger came to town, and she got up from the table and answered the knock at the door.

She and Peter had been dating for two and a half years. Since a wintry night when the young people's group came over for hot chocolate after a skating party and Peter stayed behind to help Olive wash the cups. As they finished up, she stepped away from him and he pulled his tea towel taut and flicked it in her direction, snapping it against her thigh. She felt it bite through the wool of her skirt, saw it in slow motion, like a big long tongue, like a frog's tongue catching a fly—Peter choosing her—and she turned her eyes to him, and saw in his face that in that moment it was done. For him. As for her, she'd known it forever, and she beamed her love back at him. In those days, she had no experience with lying. Her lips did not lie, and neither did her heart. There had never been the need.

All that summer after Jim Elliot's visit, Olive heard nothing from Peter. He was not at the Gospel Hall on Sundays and he never called and explained. It was thoughtless, it was cruel, and it was nothing like Peter. At first she told herself he was busy, and imagined all the things he was doing, and woke up each morning knowing he'd call that night. She sustained this for longer than you'd imagine any sane person could. And then, well, it was like being in the sort of nightmare where you suddenly discover that you're desperately lost, you've wandered without realizing it into a landscape where nothing is familiar.

One day when her mother was out, she stood in the hall with heart thudding and telephoned the Fleming house herself. Peter's sister answered and called him. He sounded subdued. He said he'd been away, he'd just gotten back, and he was planning to call her. He was going back to his job and he asked her to meet him in Denny Park on his lunch hour. The next day she took the bus downtown and he was in the park when she arrived. They sat side by side on a bench shaded by huge trees. She was wearing a new dress she and her mother had sewed, pale aqua cotton with a narrow yellow belt, and her white sandals. It was the end of August and patches of red already hung in the maple trees.

Under the circumstances, the joy she felt at seeing him was absurd. She spoke warmly because she didn't know any other way. "So, Sillence," she said. This was his strange and beautiful middle name, pronounced (he'd taught her) like the French word for silence, and she used it only when they were alone. "What have you been up to all these weeks?"

That was when she learned he was going to Ecuador, hoping to leave by the end of the year. Jim had been looking for a partner for months, he said. Jesus sent his disciples out two by two. Two men, that is. It was dangerous work and there was no place for girls in it. He opened the neat wax paper packet his ham sandwich was folded into and waited for her to respond, not meeting her eyes.

She sat very still. In that moment what she felt most strongly was her own necessity: she knew he was lost without her. She could see him in his new jungle home, Jim Elliot jawing away in a hammock on the other side of a thatched hut and Peter with the inconsolable face he'd had when he was sixteen and his mother died so suddenly. He came to school the day after her death. Olive never expected to see him, but there he was, walking alone down the corridor. She caught up with him and put her hand on his arm, and said, "Oh, Sillence," and her own tears spilled over. And then he started crying too, and she pushed open a door and led him out onto the playing field, and they leaned against the bleachers and wept. He told Olive that he was the one who found his mother. She was outside under the laundry lines, an artery had burst in her brain. Her eyes were open and at first he had the crazy idea she was just lying there enjoying the sky, which was very blue that afternoon. Olive put both arms tenderly around him. "You shouldn't be at school," she said.

"Why not?" He stooped and pressed his face into her shoulder, sobbing in the dry, rackety way of someone who seldom cries. He was trying to talk, but she could barely make out the words. "Why not? I know she's in heaven with Jesus, there's no reason to mourn."

He sat now clutching his sandwich, misery in every line of his body. He was blind to what he needed Olive for, that was the biggest part of his need. "A wife could make a home for you," she said, feeling her heart begin to beat as though it had been lying dormant in her chest until that moment. "You'll need a home."

"Well," he said stiffly, "when the Lord calls, He provides. I guess we'll muddle along."

Olive stared at him, trying to see him clearly, thinking, This began long ago. It began last summer, when he went on the road with Jim. He was finishing up a master's in English and he spent the summer passing the offering plate at gospel rallies. It was a boot camp in dialectics, he had said at the time, to explain why he did it. *Dialectics.* She'd smiled, and he leaned against her, his weight trapping her against the brick wall of the Humanities Building, and they kissed.

"This call from God," she said. "How do you know? Did He send you some sort of sign?"

"I guess He did." A single steamer fare to the coastal town of Guayaquil is $315, he had said, and when he and Jim tallied up the offerings they collected after speaking to the five Plymouth Brethren assemblies in Portland, the total was exactly $630.

"That's it?" she cried, incredulous. "You're going to give up your whole life because of a coincidence in numbers?"

"No, of course not! You asked me for a sign, so I told you. But of course that's not how the call came. In the last few weeks, Jim and I have immersed ourselves in Scripture. And I can't tell you how much it's changed me. It's changed everything. I was on the wrong path, Olive. How did I think I was going to spend my whole life reading and teaching modern literature? When it's so base and degraded, so devoted to filth?"

She saw that her instincts about Jim Elliot had been right. "What about Jim? Don't you think he's attracted to filth? Think about the horrible things he said about the Indians in Ecuador. He enjoyed telling us that stuff. I think he made it up to shock us."

He was furious with her, for the first time ever. "He didn't make it up. He didn't make it up, Olive."

"Well, how could he know such a thing? If these people have murdered every outsider who ever entered their territory?"

"I don't know how he knows it. But I can tell you he's not lying. And how can you dare say it makes him happy? I've seen how it grieves him. It breaks his heart. He's prepared to give his life to take the gospel to the Auca people. Literally, his life! Can you imagine how much love that takes? How much courage?" He set his sandwich on the bench, mangled from his furious grip, and reached up to his shirt pocket. "Look. God gave me this verse. I wrote it down for you so you'd understand."

He wanted only one thing from her, she saw it in his face: that she would take the note he was holding out to her and vanish from his life without a fuss. So she took it and got up without a goodbye and walked swiftly across the grass and onto the street. She couldn't bear to wait for a bus where he could see her, so she walked up Denny Way, climbing the steep hill all the way to Broadway, where criss-cross wires hung between her and the sky, and there she caught a streetcar. As soon as she got a seat, she opened the paper and read, in Peter's neat hand, *I would like you to be free from concern*, and she heard Peter's voice, her boyfriend's loving voice, and the tears broke through. Leaning her head on the dusty window, she sat and sobbed, indifferent to the curious looks coming her way from across the aisle.

But when the first storm had passed and she was able to read the rest of it, she saw that the "you" in this text was not her at all, that this Bible passage Peter chose to leave her with was all about him. *I would like you to be free from concern. An unmarried man is concerned about the Lord's affairs—how he can please the Lord. But a married man is concerned about the affairs of this world—how he can please his wife—and his interests are divided. I am saying this for your own good, not to restrict you, but that you may live in a right way in undivided devotion to the Lord. 1 Corinthians 7:32–35.*

The words were mild and reasonable, but Jim Elliot came vividly to mind—his thick neck, and the single horizontal line that creased his forehead, and the furious way he hitched his chair around to shut her out of his line of vision. Against Peter's careful, thoughtful ways, the wrestler had prevailed.

She managed to get upstairs without attracting her mother's attention. Her bathrobe hung from a hook on the door, and she leaned against it and pressed her face into the dark terry. The smell of soap and her old life made her cry harder. Finally she wiped her face and turned to the bedside table and picked up her bible. It was a slim, leather-bound bible, a gift from her parents, and on the flyleaf her mother had printed, THIS BOOK WILL KEEP YOU FROM SIN OR SIN WILL KEEP YOU FROM THIS BOOK.

She wanted to get the whole story. She turned the flimsy pages until she found 1 Corinthians, Chapter 7. She began to read from the top, as Pete must have done. She came to this: *If anyone is worried that he might not be acting honourably toward the virgin he is engaged to, and if his passions are too strong and he feels he ought to marry, he should do as he wants. He is not sinning. They should get married. But the man who has settled the matter in his own mind, who is under no compulsion but has control over his own will, and who has made up his mind not to marry the virgin—this man also does the right thing. So then, he who marries the virgin does right, but he who does not marry her does better.*

This was in the Bible! *He who marries the virgin does right, but he who does not marry her does better.*

This was what tore them apart. It was that mossy ridge above the Chirico Trail, it was the afternoons her parents thought she was in the library when Peter picked her up and they drove down an alley off the Pike/Pine corridor and parked, and turned helplessly towards each other. It was the Sundays when Pete came over for dinner and she sat across from him at the table, demure in her long, shapeless skirt and white blouse, her hair pulled into a single braid and the braid pinned modestly up on the back of her head, her heart and her mind carefully fortified with Bible verses (*Put on the whole armour of God, that ye may be able to stand against the wiles of the devil*)—it was the way they sat in full view of her parents, and he slid his ankle against hers and the heat shot all the way up her inner thigh. That was it. All these months, she'd felt not a bit of shame. Peter had been praying for a sign from God, and Olive understood that they'd long ago received it. Would they get engaged before he left for grad school in California? They talked like that was the big question, but it was a different deadline they were racing towards, and they both knew it.

She looked back at the page—*the man who has control over his will*—and rage filled her. How could Peter be expected to resist an enticement like that?

HER PARENTS WERE grieving too. Her father, more silent than ever, spent Saturdays chipping alone at the stump of the sycamore in the backyard, a job Pete had promised to help with. On Sunday afternoons, her mother insisted they play board games, thinking it might console Olive. But not Scrabble, which she admitted was no fun without Peter. So they played Chinese checkers and Snakes and Ladders. The squares on the Snakes and Ladders board were tiny pictures showing children doing good deeds and bad. Olive studied them as she waited for her turn. These sins were easy enough to resist. Who wanted to be a glutton? Who wanted to smash a window with a stick? But when her turn came and she landed on the pointy tip of a snake's tail, she felt her shame flare in her cheeks.

One day when Olive was crying in her room, her mother tapped on the door and Olive ended up handing her the dog-eared slip of paper Peter had given her.

"*A married man*," Livie said after she read the verse from Corinthians. She looked closely at Olive. "Did he ask you to marry him? Before all this started up?"

"He asked me to wait because he was praying God would give him a definite sign. And I said yes, I would wait. But Mama, he wanted to. He really wanted to! I think he was going to propose that very weekend—and then Jim came."

"Why do you think that, darling?"

The thing about Livie was, she had not been a Christian when she was young. She'd seen the inside of a dance hall, she'd tasted whiskey and beer. She had that dark glamour, that she'd known the world, and she sussed out things any other mother would be too innocent to suspect. She looked searchingly at Olive with her warm brown eyes, and Olive felt the blood rise in her face, she felt the memory of Peter's touch on her breasts and thighs. It would never fade, it was like the shadows on the Shroud of Turin.

"Were you ever alone with him, Olive?"

"We dated for over two years. Of course we were alone."

"Did you let him go too far?"

"No!" Her rage and grief burst out in a terrible wail. "No, Mama, I didn't! I didn't let him go far enough."

"Oh, Olive, Olive, hush, hush. It breaks my heart to hear you say such a wicked thing." She tried to take Olive in her arms, but Olive pushed her away and lay face down on her bed, and eventually her mother went out and closed the door behind her.

7

IT WAS LATE JUNE WHEN Jim Elliot dropped into the Ainsleys' little shingled house in Seattle like a cougar dropping from a Douglas fir. All through that fall, Peter and Jim toured the western states, raising funds for their new mission, and she heard updates at the Gospel Hall. In December, she endured Peter's farewell address to the congregation and lined up with everyone else to shake his hand. Then he and Jim were gone, and one Sunday in late winter Kenneth Fleming got up and asked the congregation to pray for them as they moved back and forth between language study in Quito and fieldwork with the Quichua in the jungle.

"Peter is being sorely tested," he said. "He's asked to do a great deal of work in areas he is not well suited for—building construction, engine repair, that kind of thing. Even dentistry. And he's been very ill with malaria. So I know he would appreciate your prayers."

Another man stood up. "Just to point out to Brother Fleming that God often chooses a weak instrument, so that His own glory might be evident in the work."

Olive felt her cheeks warm, hearing the man she loved described that way.

He was everything. She'd been like a tightrope walker, moving between the Gospel Hall and the university, keeping her balance by fixing her eyes on a single spot. And now her spot was gone. When university started that fall, she went back—what else was she going to do? She still had two years for her general degree, and it was a goal she kept moving woodenly towards. He'd dragged her into a godless world and ditched her there. Left her to deal alone with the filthy words girls scratched into the walls of the toilet stalls and the professors who ridiculed God and claimed we came from monkeys.

But at least she was invisible there—until, in one of her classes, she realized with astonishment that someone was watching her.

A tall girl with huge eyes, as heavy-lidded and pale-lashed as a camel's. When the professor asked them to choose partners for a project, the girl blinked those eyes at Olive and then shot her hand up. "Dr. Cortez, Olive Ainsley and I would like to work together."

The girl's name was Carol Howard. They walked to the cafeteria after class and she twirled her fork into her spaghetti and explained: "My cousin Betty wrote me that you were at Washington U. She said I should watch for you. And here we've got a class together."

"Betty?" Olive said.

"Elisabeth Howard."

"I don't know anybody with that name."

"You used to go out with Peter Fleming, right?"

"Yes."

"Well, she knows him. Jim Elliot? He's Betty's fiancé. She sailed to Ecuador last month. Or flew, or took a train, or something. How the hell do people get to Ecuador?" She made a crazy face, as if Ecuador was the moon.

Olive stared at this girl with the long, knobby fingers and the large, off-white teeth. "Jim Elliot is engaged? Wasn't he—?"

"Always preaching about being single! You're right, he was. Betty broke up with him and suddenly he's never going to get married, he's going to be some sort of monk. But that didn't last long, they're back together now. You met him, right?"

"Yes."

"Isn't he a riot? God's Quarterback, I like to call him, just to bug Betty." She gave up the fork twirling and just slurped up a clump of spaghetti, wiping sauce off her chin with the back of her hand, laughing at her own clumsiness. "I don't know how well you know him, but he can't do anything like ordinary guys. He's always striking these Man of Destiny poses. When he reads the Bible, he has to read it in Greek. When he was wrestling, he always had to be matched with the champion. When he decides to get married—"

("He's *engaged*?" Olive repeated stupidly.)

"—he has to marry the most terrifying girl in the entire USA. Because she is, you know, Betty."

"How long has she been his girlfriend?"

"Oh, for years. I think he first got the idea of being a missionary from her. She was going to China. She gets a call from God, so she gives Jim the boot, and that's when Jim decides to go to South America and starts talking about being a *eunuch*. But then, guess what? Last fall, the Communists throw all the missionaries out of China, and God leans down and taps Betty on the shoulder or whatever the hell He does and says, Doll, I've changed my mind. Turns out I want you in Ecuador." The girl rolled her large, pale eyes. "Surprise, surprise."

She had been right about Jim. He had played with Peter like a toy. For a moment her hatred coloured everything. She hated God, the vicious traps He sets. She hated Carol, the over-jocular bearer of ugly news. But along with the fury that threatened to burst her rib cage, a little incandescent flame of joy began to burn: down in Ecuador with his new friends, Peter had been talking about her.

After that, she spent every spare hour with Carol. A born-again Christian friend at university! Olive was like an immigrant over-hearing a voice on a streetcar and knowing it was a cousin from her own village halfway around the world. But how reckless and irreverent Carol was—that was new.

The course they took together was the Pre-modern World and this was their assignment: *Select an artifact and discuss what it reveals about the mores and beliefs of the pre-modern society that produced it.* They arranged to meet in the main library. Olive suggested an artifact from Ecuador and Carol jumped on the idea. But the periodicals catalogue in the library had very few listings about the Indigenous people of the Amazon basin, and the term *Auca* never appeared.

"Well, they have no culture," Olive said. "No mores or beliefs. According to Jim."

"I know," Carol said, "let's write to Betty! It would be brilliant to have a direct source. Maybe she could send us an actual artifact."

"Do we have time?"

"No, course not."

They claimed a table behind the crumbling pillars in the anthropology stacks and pressed each other for confidences, heads down to avoid the dark looks of the library clerks. Carol was from a farm east of Walla Walla. She had three oafish brothers, her mother was desperately downtrodden, and she had been thrilled to leave home. She boarded with an elderly woman named Mrs. Fanistel, where she did housework in exchange for her room. Her grandmother sent her money and she'd bought two dresses, the first store-bought clothes she'd ever owned. She wore them on alternate days. One was a striped, button-fronted sailor, the other raspberry rayon with a flared overskirt—a peplum, she said it was. She looked like a species of dog in those dresses, a thin hound dressed up to play poker in a calendar picture.

She had no more news of Peter, but lots to say about Betty. Betty had grown up in the East, in New Jersey, and Carol had stayed there for a summer. Like herself, Betty was tall and flat-chested, that was a Howard thing. "And she has a gap between her two front teeth. It's the first thing you notice. So she's not exactly beautiful—well, she's not even pretty, no one has ever described her as pretty, and everybody was really shocked when Jim fell for her, because let's face it, that guy could have any woman he wanted. Girls throw themselves at him, left, right, and centre. It's embarrassing to watch. But from the day he met Betty, there's been nobody else for him."

Olive felt a bit of respect for Jim stir, hearing this. "But what's Betty *like*?"

"She is the smartest girl you will ever meet. She's going to be famous someday. And she always speaks her mind. No one shoves Betty around. She's full of sand. That's what my dad always says: 'Your cousin Betty is full of sand.'"

Carol was coy about her own beaux, but she was dying to hear about Peter. In recent months Peter had transformed in Olive's mind from an icon of perfection to a very flawed man—but when pressed, she found this made no difference to her. It was like he had been silver before, and now he was streaked with lead, but heavier because of it, more solid and real.

"He's a fine person," she said. "He's not always trying to impress people, the way Jim is."

"He is not weighed down with the burden of his own charisma," Carol said.

"Exactly."

"But the love just wasn't there?"

How could Olive make her understand? Finally she told her how Peter had given up skiing. "I couldn't understand it. I just love skiing and I know he did too. We had some great times with our youth group at Crystal Mountain." She was remembering the afternoon she'd got stuck on the chairlift, and Peter did a jump turn below and sent her up a doughnut on the end of his pole. His bright, loving face peering up at her. "But suddenly he quit skiing altogether. Because he was starting to get obsessed. He realized it was dangerous to love anything too much." This was a new and profound insight to her, and her voice shook a little as she put it into words.

"Hmm," Carol said, watching Olive skeptically. "I wonder—can you love too much?"

Turned out that Carol had been raised in a garden-variety evangelical church, not as strict as the Gospel Hall. She was aghast that women were not allowed to join in the hymns in Olive and Pete's assembly.

"Well, we can sing," Olive explained. "But only in our hearts. We contribute through our silence."

Carol laughed until she almost choked, but Olive found herself defending it. "Honestly," she said, "sometimes it feels like a better way."

As for Carol, she hadn't been to church since a Sunday morning when she was fourteen and walked out in the middle of the sermon. Her parents tried every tactic, including locking her in her room for a week, including sending her to her fanatical aunt and uncle (Betty's parents) in New Jersey, but she never went back.

"Was the minister preaching about hell?" Olive asked.

Carol grinned. "No, actually, he was preaching about heaven. How we'll stand around waving palm branches and praising God for all eternity. I've had it with buttering up the men in my life. What kind of egoist needs that much praise?" She went to movies now, and drank and went dancing and wore crimson lipstick. This might have fooled others, but it did not fool Olive for a second. Even when Carol smoked, she looked *conscientious*, as if she was in training to be a smoker. Her efforts to be modern and daring were as futile as her efforts at beauty.

They still hadn't settled on a topic. "What about the Plymouth Brethren?" Carol joked. "They're prehistoric."

"We need an artifact."

"We could write about your hairdo."

Somehow Olive never got offended. Even when Carol took the Lord's name in vain. *Gawd*, she said all the time—but it was a breath away from a prayer.

SHE COULD HAVE written to Peter, there were ways to get his address. It was a shameful coward who extracted Elisabeth Howard's address in Ecuador from Carol, and wrote to Elisabeth, and sealed the letter up without reading it over, and carried it to the corner and dropped it in the letter box. And then she had weeks to wait for an answer, and she could hardly recall what she'd said.

Meanwhile, their assignment was almost due. They started pulling journals from the shelves at random. "Look at this," Carol said. Photographic plates showed small clay figures, human figurines, with doors on their chests that swung open to reveal a chamber. In that little chamber sat another human figure. "Are they pregnant?" Carol asked. "Is that their womb?"

"I don't think so," Olive said. "Look." Some of the figures were men, you could see the little clay bud between the legs.

Host figurines, they were called. They'd recently been found in pyramids in the ancient city of Teotihuacán, close to Mexico City. Apparently the Aztecs revered and collected these little figures, but they were not made by the Aztecs. They were from an earlier civilization, one that ended abruptly a thousand years ago.

"How does a civilization end?" Carol asked. "Does it mean they all died, or they just got conquered?" She went to the file drawers to look up Teotihuacán and Olive stayed at the table, examining the plates, which were black-and-white but seemed to her to glow with hidden meaning. Little clay people sitting naturally, cross-legged or with their clay legs scissored to the side, and some of them lifting their heads as though they were taking in the sun. They were beautifully crafted, their faces detailed and expressive, their mouths lined with even clay teeth, their hair raked by a comb. The figures inside their chests were elaborate, with headpieces and feather cloaks.

Real people had fashioned those figurines, Olive thought with a wrench of surprise. If you studied the clay under a magnifying glass, you might find *fingerprints*. Real people from centuries ago used this clay to describe their deepest experiences, and she longed to understand.

Carol came back and they took a break. The cafeteria was full, so they carried their Cokes out to the corridor and sat on the stairs. Olive's mind was still on the last photograph she'd studied, a figurine that had a chest chamber with no little figure in it. But on the door, on the inside of the open door, a human face had been carved in bas-relief. So when you closed the door, that secret face would gaze through the dark into an empty heart. Olive took a drink of her Coke and felt her eyes sting. But Carol didn't see her tears.

"Where were you when you asked Jesus into your heart?" she asked, leaning back against Olive's knees.

"In the kitchen with my mother, apparently. I don't remember."

"Hey, me too. But it was a special moment for my mother."

Olive's free-floating love landed on Carol, sparking off her shoulders and her rough caramel-coloured hair. Both of us are cut loose, Olive thought. And she wondered which of them was on a more dangerous path.

ELISABETH HOWARD. WHEN an airmail letter arrived for Olive, she ran up the stairs and locked herself in the bathroom before she slit the blue form open with her nail file. The ink was black and the handwriting spiky and forceful, like a man's. Olive slid to the floor and read:

Elisabeth was glad that Olive had approached her with her grievance, though it pained her to read of Olive's distress. She wanted to assure Olive that Carol was entirely mistaken regarding her relationship with Jim Elliot. They were not engaged and never had been. True, God had knit their hearts together with a love such as she had never experienced and did not previously know existed. But there is a higher love than the love between a man and a woman—the love of God and service in His Name.

Elisabeth had been called to minister to the Colorado Indians, a tribe situated in the western lowlands. She would be stationed across the Andes from El Oriente, where Jim would soon be serving the savage Auca tribe. The extreme danger of his mission finally confirmed their conviction that they could not marry. They were currently in Quito together, in an intensive language program. "I know you were fond of Pete," she wrote, "and terribly hurt when your friendship ended, so perhaps you can imagine how excruciating it is for Jim and me to see each other daily, to work side by side, but be unable to touch or to speak of our love."

And then Elisabeth was moved to share a precious confidence with Olive:

> *Not long ago, Jim and I allowed ourselves a quiet hour together after a difficult day of language study. We slipped away from the group to walk through one of Quito's beautiful old cemeteries. Soon overcome with emotion, we sat and prayed, dedicating our lives anew to the Lord's service, and I confess there were tears on both sides. When I whispered Amen and opened my eyes, I saw that while we prayed, a full moon had risen and cast the shadow of one of the gravestones onto the smooth bench between us—it was the shadow of a cross. Could God have provided a more powerful symbol of the sacrifice He requires of us? I will carry that image in my heart in the years ahead, and I pray that you might embrace it too. Submission to God's will is never easy in the moment, but the eternal rewards are incalculable.*
>
>

Your sister in Christ,
Betty Howard

Olive read this letter through twice, and then tore it into narrow ribbons and dropped them into the toilet. Stubbornly the pieces floated on the surface, black ink swirling off them, until she banged on the flush handle and they were sucked down the foul, stinking pipes to the freezing waters of Puget Sound.

On a Sunday morning when the smell of spring rose from the damp lawns, Peter's father approached Olive after the assembly and handed her an envelope. "Peter has started to make a carbon copy every time he writes a letter to us. He asked me to pass it on to you, so that you can pray for his work in Ecuador."

There it was in smeary carbon—the small, quick handwriting she knew so well. *Dear Dad and Mother.* He never called his step-mother Mom.

He began by saying that he'd contracted malaria again and had to be airlifted to Quito. He couldn't help but be grateful for this respite from the jungle, where daily his deficits were on display. He didn't know how to use a gun. He couldn't play the piano accordion or fix the generator. He got airsick when they went out in the single-engine plane searching for Auca houses, and spent the whole mission with his head between his knees. He had terrible occipital headaches. "I overhear the Quichua kids refer to me as a *wawa*," he wrote to his parents. "I don't believe the word needs any translation." His honesty was heartbreaking, especially considering how much he disliked his stepmother.

After that, the letters came every two weeks. Olive had to believe that Betty had spoken to Pete, that that's what had prompted this. There was never a line to her or about her, but Olive treated these carbon copies as deeply personal. She never showed them to her parents. She kept them in a special stationery box in her dresser drawer and read them over and over. He did not describe his new home or the people he was working with, but no doubt his earlier letters had done that. It seemed he and Jim were ministering to the Quichua Indians, which was not what they had intended. But they had no idea how to reach the Auca, and God was bafflingly silent and remote on the subject. Pete and Jim spent a lot of time negotiating with Him, pleading for auguries. If God wanted them to go into Auca territory, would He please communicate this by keeping Peter free of malaria for six months? The next letter, Peter was back in hospital in Quito and had dialed this test down to three months. But even when you made things easy for God, He never met you halfway. They had just finished building a school in Shandia when the river rose and washed it away. They moved to higher ground, and then the river rose again and washed away all the outbuildings plus five hundred hand-planed logs, each one the work of a day for a Quichua man. All gone in a matter of hours. Plus a third of the airstrip, which they had just cleared so it was usable again.

God's ways were infinitely mysterious.

One Sunday, Olive found herself walking out of the Gospel Hall beside Peter's stepmother, and she said, "I wonder if I might read Pete's letters from the beginning, just to get a better sense of the mission?" Mrs. Fleming's lips puckered at the corners. "Oh, I'm afraid Peter hasn't authorized that." She wouldn't even look directly at Olive. Olive wished then that she had kept her mouth shut until she'd had a chance to ask Pete's father. But Pete's sister Mary had overheard this exchange, and the Sunday after, she slipped Olive a little packet of letters. And then gradually a vivid picture of Peter's home in the rainforest took shape in her mind.

After leaving Quito, they had moved into the Tidmarshes' house at a Quichua settlement called Shandia, on the Napo River. The house was split bamboo, set up on posts, with a thatched roof. They used kerosene lamps and they threw their waste water into a ditch that ran like a shallow moat around the house. They had a servant, an Indian man named Yapanqui, whose first job every morning was to sweep up the cockroaches that had succumbed to the DDT during the night. He lived with his family nearby. The Quichua subsisted by farming, by hunting, and by selling rubber and tapir skins. They ate yucca, maize, and bananas in every form including soup. Some were indentured to a nearby plantation— they had taken trade goods at massively inflated prices—and would never get out from under that burden. They suffered from intestinal parasites, snakebites, tuberculosis, malnutrition, and malaria. Jim and Pete had learned how to give injections but could not keep enough penicillin on hand. Often the witch doctor would get to people first, and they would die. Shandia also had a resident Catholic priest, an American. Pete and Jim had entered Ecuador as linguists and teachers, and under the terms of their visas they were not allowed to try to convert the people or to set up churches. The priest was watching them like a hawk. But Jim paid off the plantation debt for two young men and hired them to teach him and Pete the language. They were hoping to translate the Gospel of Mark. They trusted the Holy Spirit to rise up off the pages and speak to their informants, who could then share the good news with others.

"I often think of the *echolalia* in the New Testament," Peter wrote, "the speaking in tongues. We Brethren have viewed this gift as overly emotional, a sort of ecstatic babbling, and have not sought it. But I wonder now if we were mistaken in this. Did God give the Apostles the gift of an actual but unknown language so that they might share the gospel more swiftly? This is the subject of much discussion at our supper table. But so far we are acquiring the Quichua language the hard way."

SUNDAY MORNINGS, THE light at the window would pull her from the land of dreams, and she'd be lying on her side, Pete nestled behind her, his hand cupping her breast. She'd float there until her mother called, and then she'd get up and dress and go with her parents to the Gospel Hall, where she sat listening to the silent prayers of the women and their silent songs (almost deafening, the silence of the women). Weekdays, it was her alarm clock that woke her. Then she'd get up in the dark and wait sleepily on Stanley Street until the streetcar came to carry her to the university. She was assigned *Anna Karenina*, and in the library she discovered whole shelves devoted to the nineteenth-century novel. She'd often read for hours between classes, enjoying the thick old paper and the vague lines of type, which occasionally wavered or even lifted from the horizontal like birds taking off. She read hungrily, her heart beating fast for the heroine; whether she was a servant girl or the wife of a high-level government official, she was full of longing, she didn't quite fit. Then terrible things happened, and she'd be desperate, and do something reckless, steal money or take a train to meet the wrong man. But by the end of the book, it would be done. She'd be walking a path along a cliff at dawn, or cradling a child in her arms while rain fell outside the window, and she'd be changed, the meaning of everything fully revealed and throbbing within her.

Olive sat holding the small leather-bound book between her two hands, as it seemed she herself was held and sustained in the mind of the author, a benign god: only things that had meaning were allowed in this world.

It was dark again when she caught the streetcar and walked home from the stop. Walked through drizzle that made gauzy circles in the street lights, and into the room where her parents sat companionably in the heat from the little coal burner, her mother knitting and her father reading, the two of them oblivious to how stale the house smelled, a smell Olive traced to her father, to his exhaustion. All her life he'd gotten up in the dark to do his milk route. Afternoons he lay down for a nap, but he seldom slept. Saturdays he went to the library to feed his recently uncovered passion for warfare. *Battle Stories of German Tank Commanders. The Siege of Leningrad. Blood of Our Heroes.* This was what Peter had given him by bringing books into the house, fuel to stoke a bellicose fire. He read every evening now, just getting up occasionally to open the door of the stove and tip in a shovelful of coal. He was preoccupied with the state of the world, and troubled at the way the rules of decent conduct had been forgotten since the servicemen came home from the war. It was his most cherished grievance, the new wave of permissiveness sweeping America, and he had a new culprit to blame for it, Christian men like Peter and Jim who had gone overseas and abandoned their country to its folly. Abandoned it to the Communists, who were everywhere and invisible, eating their way like termites into the foundations of government, planting messages in newspapers and films, corrupting people's ideas and values, so that some ordinary morning Americans would get out of bed and find that their way of life had been entirely stolen away.

One day Olive asked her father if she could do his milk route with him. At three he was in her bedroom doorway, dressed in his white uniform and bow tie. They were picked up by a van that ferried all the milkmen to the dairy at Licton Springs, where their trucks were parked. The milkmen walked across a big parking lot to the office while Olive stood shivering alone in the dark. Above her, individual stars stood out white from a milky field. She tried to make out shapes, but she could never see the constellations other people saw. When her father had joined her again with the keys to his truck, she said, "I wonder sometimes if the constellations are just made up. Wouldn't you see entirely different pictures if you just picked different stars?"

He shoved his cap up so he could look at the sky. "The Big Dipper is real," he said. The dipper! He was making a milkman joke.

She had never seen her father drive, and this hidden competence moved her. They drove all the way to Holmann Road, through a city that had nothing to do with them, the ships in the harbour below, the warehouses and the sinister locked-up taverns with their neon signs dark. Her father turned off into a modest neighbourhood and parked. He swung his iron rack out of the truck with ease and set off up the street, leaving two or three bottles on each stoop, picking up the empties. Sometimes a housewife had forgotten to put out her empties and Olive thought he might show mercy and leave milk anyway, but his rules were clear, grace did not figure into it. She trailed after him and marked his sales in a little notebook. They worked in the dark for a couple of hours, and then lights came on one by one in the houses and Seattle woke up around them. Boys slipped out of back doors and gathered in a little park and began to pitch a ball around, a happy pre-breakfast game of catch in the ringing air. As Olive and her dad walked by, she glanced at his face. It was as closed as ever. He took no joy in the scene. They were all perishing, those kids, going to hell.

He did not preach at the Gospel Hall like most of the men, he did not have that gift. He did not build cabinets, or write books, or plant trees. He had no work that would last. Olive was his only enduring project. Three or four times a week for her entire life, he'd taken her into a hall to sit in silence and learn about God's intention to condemn most of humanity (and possibly her) to the lake of fire, where they would be tortured forever with hot pokers. She did not really hold this against her parents; they did what they thought they had to do, but they also clothed her in love, so that she was immune to it. The sermon would thunder to an end and she would step out into the sunlight and the spring wind would blow the greasy ash and brimstone right off her skin.

But looking at her father's face in profile as he turned the key in the ignition (his down-turned mouth, the flesh starting to sag under his chin), this was her question: if you were going to latch on to one story to explain everything, why that particular story?

THE FIRST PERSONAL letter Olive got from Peter was a straightforward proposal of marriage. It arrived in early February 1953. He told her that Jim Elliot had been led by God to ask Elisabeth Howard to give up her ministry to the Colorado Indians and come to El Oriente. Jim had built a fine new house up on the ridge, and he and Betty had recently been married in a small ceremony in Quito. And now Peter was alone in the Tidmarsh house, and was himself considering marriage. "I've always known that, if I were to have a wife, it would be you," he wrote. "It was just a question of whether God wanted me to marry at all. And now I see that He does. We may never entirely understand His reasons for subjecting us to this painful separation, but I know we are the stronger for it."

The word *sorry* did not appear, or the word *love*. It was as if he were hiring her for a job. He'd worked out all the logistics. His first three-month furlough was a year away; they could wait and talk this over then. But if she agreed to an engagement now, they could be married when he came home and she could return to Ecuador with him. And doors would open for her, she could use the intervening year to get ready. For example, she could take a Missionary Medicine course (he recommended one in Los Angeles) that would be tremendously helpful in their ministry, and was open only to individuals who had already been assigned to a mission field. He prayed that God would advise her.

And then this last paragraph:

Olive, just knowing that you exist in this world, a girl so fine and so true—on the darkest days it's the only hope I have. I am so tormented, my thoughts poison everything around me. But then you come to me, and you are whole. I need you desperately. I share every moment of every day with you. I can't bear to be apart from you any longer.

And it was signed, *Sillence*.

THE AUCA SCALE

8

THE DUSTY LITTLE CAR PARKED beside the garage used to be Sharon's. A blue Ford Fiesta with a Jesus fish on the bumper—Abby's dad gave it to her when she turned eighteen. She swipes the ginkgo tree crap off the hood and windshield and drives to the gas station on Robson Road. There she fills the tank and washes the windshield and checks the oil the way her dad taught her. The oil is fine and so is she.

Out on the road by nine thirty, she's already in a movie. The sort of film that starts with collecting up all the players from across two continents, a minute or two of backstory for each. Abby's in her dad's house in Portland, alone, paralyzed, her path blocked no matter which way she turns—and the phone rings. And then she's on the I-5 heading south, driving a car that belonged to the mother she lost so tragically in her youth, and this is a crane shot, or maybe the crew is up on the ridge. No, they'll have a helicopter tracking her as she barrels along. The soundtrack . . . Abby reaches into the console and pops a CD blindly into the tray. The music is playful and spunky—it's her mood, it pulls her forward, snatching up details from the landscape, plucking at the trees she spins between.

She passes Salem and for a while she's in a tunnel of flickering brilliance, where trees shoot their shadows over the highway. Then she's at Gold Hill and she doesn't remember Grants Pass. Maybe the strobe did something to her brain. They used to drive a lot, she and her dad, in his old Pontiac. They drove and drove and drove, especially the summer after Sharon died. They didn't talk much in the car. David was constantly sleepy and Abby was tall for her age, so sometimes he let her take the wheel. Not on this highway, though. On this highway he always made her bury her face in her arms, because strobe light can cause seizures in young people.

She turns the music off. All night, when she surfaced from sleep, she was thinking about the part she might be asked to play. What if the director gave her a monologue, and she offered to read it in different voices? Nobody else they audition will know the characters well enough to do that. Well, she didn't actually know Marilou very well, or Barb Youderian. Even Olive is a mystery. And her two real grandmothers, Marj and Betty—it was hard to know what they actually thought. When Sharon was sick, her granny Marj used to visit and spend all day cooking up soup and chili and ladling it into containers for the freezer, while Abby sat at the kitchen island writing up labels. Once in a while Operation Auca would come up and her granny would say, "Well, it was hard, but at least we were all a hundred percent in agreement." Could that possibly be true?

She sees a first billboard for Sacramento, and stops for a taco. By early afternoon she's across the California state line. The notion of a movie, the phone call from Walter Varga, feels less and less real. It's dangerous, it's reckless, taking off to California without telling her father. She tries to call up the voice of this serial killer who did such immaculate research to lure her to LA. He sounded all business, a little uninterested even, like he was doing his job but didn't care all that much whether she turned up or not.

The bigger issue is how her father will react if she gets a part in this film. She feels a little sick at the thought. All the criticisms that have prickled in her mind for years, things she's never talked about with a living person—they'll be given words and splashed on a big screen. The outside view. Walter Varga talked about the cultural context, and about an anthropologist. What will that mean for *them*? Will she be asked to portray her character as stupid, or deluded? It's one thing to drift away, it's another to publicly trash the women who raised her. Her beautiful mother, who truly believed in heaven but fought for her life, fought to stay with Abby. Her kind granny Marj, and her grandma Betty, who may not have been warm but was sure about things, and clever, and brave, all of which you need to be. *Olive.*

And then she thinks, Olive herself opened the door just a tiny crack, last time Abby was in Seattle.

They were looking at the *Life* magazine article about the killings. Olive had cut the pages apart and slid each one into the plastic sleeve of a photo album. She'd added a cover page with a verse hand-printed on it: *Faith is the substance of things hoped for, the evidence of things not seen.* The pictures were very familiar. A body face down in water, being towed by a canoe. Who was it? Abby was glad not to know.

Sitting side by side on the couch, they studied the portraits of the wives.

"When I was little, I'd look at these pictures and think of you all as ancient. But look how young you were."

"I was the youngest. I was twenty-four."

The other wives are holding children in their portraits, but Olive stands alone, her big eyes on the photographer as if to say, *Now what?*

"Did you all believe in this mission? Did nobody have any doubts?" Abby's voice was rough with fear, asking that.

Olive lifted those same eyes, made even bigger by reading glasses, and said, "You couldn't afford to understand it any other way. Think how hideous that would be."

Maybe that was what prompted Abby to start looking in the library, where she found the anthropology book that's in her backpack. She knew without reading it that it would be dangerous. Standing in the stacks, she let her eyes skim over the preface. Elisabeth Elliot, Rachel Saint—they were named. She couldn't bear to read on, and she couldn't abandon it. She's already renewed it once.

Will Rachel be in the film? She remembers her great-aunt Rachel mainly from when she brought the two Amazonian men to Seattle. "New Christians from a Stone Age tribe in the jungle, bearing witness to God's victory over savagery," was how Rachel described the men. They didn't react to being called savages, but of course they didn't understand English. For that whole hour in the church in Seattle, they sat alert, expressionless, their hands on their knees. If they were surprised at the fascination they inspired in a huge crowd of white Americans, they gave no sign. Sitting, they seemed bigger; Abby was struck by how broad their shoulders were, straining their cheap grey suits. There was a Q & A at the end, which went on a long time because Rachel had to translate the audience's questions into Waorani for the men, and then translate the men's answers into English for the audience. Mainly Enkidi, the old man, spoke. He had a deep and confident voice, and his language seemed to be full of consonants. No matter what was asked, his response (as Rachel translated it) was always a variation on, "When I was a child, we lived very, very badly and our souls were dark and black." Rachel talked swiftly and casually to the men. It was clear that she wanted to impress everyone with how close she was to the Auca, that she was like family.

"Can you tell us about your culture?" someone asked. "What was your art like, and your music?"

Enkidi's answer, delivered in Rachel's blunt way after a little back-and-forth, was, "We were like wild animals before the missionaries brought Christ to us."

"Let me just add," Rachel said. She mentioned criticism she'd faced, mainly from journalists who accused her of destroying the Auca culture. She laughed at this. The Auca would not even exist as a people if she had not intervened! They were killing themselves off at a tremendous rate. And in fact (and this was hard for people to grasp) *they didn't have a culture.* Take music: The Auca found the missionaries' singing hilarious. They were incapable of melody themselves. All they knew was the drone that accompanied their demonic rituals. Many of their chants had no meaning whatsoever; others described and celebrated spearing. The missionaries had of course forbidden chanting—but how can you worship the Lord without singing? So hymns had to be written to the Auca scale, in faith that God would use these primitive songs to teach the beauty of true melody.

She asked whether the congregation would like to hear the Auca version of "Jesus Loves Me."

"You might not recognize it—the Auca scale has only three notes, and this song takes on more of the flavour of the jungle every time they sing it—but it will give you some sense of what we're up against."

She spoke to the two men and Abby saw a silent signal pass between them. They lowered their eyes and sank into it, producing the song as one voice—a nasal sound, like the Jew's harp Abby had once heard a busker play in Pettygrove Park. They chanted the same line over and over, but every few lines the pitch went up a tiny bit, and one word changed. It took her deeper, each repetition, stirred her in an unfamiliar way. It was something you'd have to have different ears to really hear.

"When you go, sweetheart . . ." her mother said. And now she will go.

It's RAINING AS she approaches Arbuckle. She spies a Roadway Inn the exact shape of a Monopoly hotel and decides to stop. She has nine hundred and fifteen dollars in her savings account. She's never stayed in a motel on her own, and she feels like a kid walking into the office. She slaps the little bell on the counter, trying to project confidence. A hand splits a bead curtain and a man inserts himself between its strands. His big face gleams as if he's just risen from a tanning bed. He looks full of self-pity and resentful at being interrupted.

She asks if he has a room available and he names a price. He wants a credit card, but he finally lets her pay with her bank card and gives her Unit 6. It's on the ground floor with a door that opens onto the parking lot. There's a faint smell of cigarette smoke. She pulls her jacket out of her bag and dashes across the street and buys a sandwich at a gas stop. Chicken and avocado, what a find. Back in her room, she brews tea in the coffee machine. Coffee-flavoured tea, always a treat. It's getting dark. She stands at the window for a minute looking out across the parking lot and then she pulls the blind down and turns on a light. If she's successful in this audition, she'll soon experience the Amazon sunset, darkness that falls like a black curtain at the same time every night.

She sits back at the desk and finishes her sandwich, drinks down her tea. She tries the TV, but the remote seems to be dead. It's early, but she barely slept last night. Once in bed, all she can hear is the faraway whine of the traffic. She commands herself to relax, alone in this impersonal room. She does relax, the bed is her friend. Her cheek against the pillow, she drifts towards sleep.

And then, on the edge of it, a drone starts up in her brain, a monotonous, hypnotic drone, and she pulls herself upright and sits in the dark listening.

It's the Auca singing.

In the night a man, a hunter with two wives and six children, will stir awake and start chanting in a minor key, laying a bass line to the chorus of tree frogs and night birds. The chant will spread through the open-walled longhouse, from his hearth fire to the next, and then along the ridge to the next longhouse, until the whole dark forest is droning. Monkeys curled up in woolly sleep hear it the way they hear the rain.

Her mother knew it as a child. Abby only heard it that once, on a night so full of pain and surprise that she's carried it for years without understanding it. A strange bit of theatre, that night in Seattle, in which Amazonian men in grey suits from Walmart played well-rehearsed roles and yet seemed the only authentic presence.

Rachel had warned everyone, "You will find they don't look at you as they sing. They're not being rude. It's just their way." But in fact, in casting his eyes down from the platform, Enkidi, the older man, was looking straight at Abby. All the time he was chanting, his eyes were fixed on her with an expression of utmost sweetness.

WHO IS RACHEL SAINT?

9

THOUGHTS POP INTO YOUR HEAD every minute of every day, and it's not easy to tell which are your own human (possibly silly or wicked) impulses and which are orders from the Almighty. In Rachel's experience, God's directives, however quietly they come down the pipe, tend to be harder and shinier than the average thought, as though they've been dipped in enamel. But even then, it can be hard to tell for sure.

Her third year in Peru, she avoided Lima and went to Quito, Ecuador, for her annual furlough. She was racked with toothache and people said that Ecuador's dentists were a higher order of butcher than Peru's—and besides, Quito was closer to her mission station. In Quito, she stayed at Hotel Andaluz, a decent hotel a block or so off Plaza Grande. She was well aware of her brother Nate just a hundred and fifty miles to the southeast, in an Ecuadorean town at the edge of the rainforest. He'd had an aviation accident some time ago. And wasn't there a new baby in the house? So at the start she thought, If my teeth are fixed in time, I will go to Shell Mera and try to help out.

She'd headed to a dentist near Alameda Park, expecting to spend precious weeks lying in agony in a chair with her mouth pried open. Dr. Sanchez-Smith met her with a wide smile, his own mouth a display case of what he could offer by way of gold inlays. Rachel said no to the gold but yes to novocaine, which cost less than a hamburger in America. And praise God, Dr. Sanchez-Smith had deft hands and an open schedule, and in a week she was toothache free! So then the next morning she sat on her balcony at Hotel Andaluz as the sun rose over Mount Pichincha, drinking hot chocolate and eating crusty bread with butter and marmalade, stretching her bare legs out to the sun and noting how nicely the jungle ringworm on her left calf was healing. And my brother Nate? she prayed. Below in the street, a donkey brayed into the cold, thin air, and she seemed to see God smile. Take this, Rachel. Take three more weeks at Hotel Andaluz. Well done, thou good and faithful servant.

It was at the end of those three weeks that a maid tapped on Rachel's door with a note from someone named Carlos Sevilla.

She had never heard the name. The letter was in Spanish, and she whispered a translation as she read.

> My dear Señorita Saint, I am the owner of a modest hacienda in El Oriente, and I count Señor Nathaniel Saint as a friend. He is a man of many surprises. Can it be that his sister is presently in Quito? If so, why have I not made her acquaintance? My wife and I are currently at our residence on Calle Ambato. Would you join us for dinner tonight so that we can remedy this sad state of affairs?

She knew from his quaint effort to charm that the man was a Spaniard. The thought of leaving Quito had begun to add a melancholy edge to every small pleasure, and she was grateful for the diversion, and felt suddenly buoyant. She ordered a bath for five o'clock and sent her dress to be pressed, an ivory dress with a lace collar. After the bath, she sat by the window in her wrapper and spread out the damp ends of her hair (still thick as a girl's, still snatching sequins of pale gold out of the sun) and listened to the voices of the street merchants floating up from the square. Always the same nasal call, whether they were selling combs or avocados or little bunches of coca leaves. Her combs and hairpins were in a felt bag, and she began to arrange her hair, working by habit, without a mirror. She'd never socialized with white South Americans—*El High*, her partner in Peru liked to call them—and she had no idea what to expect. Maybe she should pin it looser, so waves formed around her face. Or should she be thinking of a hat? On the bureau sat her Christmas cake tin with its painted lid, three fat robins squatting on a pine branch. The feathers Chief Tariri had given her lay coiled inside, grey (owl), yellow (toucan), tan (eagle), green (parrot), neatly stitched onto a basketry circle, just the size of a lady's ring hat in America. She went to the mirror and settled the ring on her hair. No, wear it lower, closer to the brow. Wear it the way the Shapras of Peru wear their feathers— like a crown.

The lobby was empty. No one at reception to witness her descent of the wide marble stairway, no one lifting his head in surprise from the back of the leather sofa. Only the derelict matador they called a *portero*, hurrying over to assist and cajole. That pencil moustache all catawampus, and front teeth missing. "Do not walk alone, señora," he said. "You will not be so lucky another time."

"It isn't luck I count on," Rachel said. She shook her shawl open and he reached out to help her with a mirthless laugh. There were more thieves than honest men in Quito, it was a fact. Rachel's first night at Hotel Andaluz, she had set out for a stroll up Garcia Moreno and a man had scurried past her and grabbed her camera right out of her hands. She was still breathless from the altitude, but she chased him down and cornered him in the entrance of a hat shop and, trembling, he handed it back. The second day a gang of bootblacks swarmed her in Plaza Grande and snatched at her handbag. But the strap was solidly over her arm and she pinned the closest boy against a stone bench, breathing in the grease of his hair, till he cried for mercy. That was all in the first week. They knew her now.

"*Buenas noches*," she said to the *portero*, stepping into the noise of the street. She set off up Calle Garcia Moreno, crossing the Plaza, oh, *walking*. At the station in Peru, the only place to walk was the trail to the yucca field, a hundred yards of snake-infested mud. The streets of the old town were still busy, well-dressed Quito families taking the air, the little girls with their shiny black plaits, the smell of brilliantine. Mountain Quichua draped in wool, the women with their bowler hats and babies tied to their backs—all stared at the tall, fair, robust American woman striding so confidently over the cobblestones. God had made her fair for reasons known only to Him, and He had made her big for wrestling her brothers into obedience. For serving at the Colony of Mercy in New Jersey, where the winos would get into potato-peel moonshine and stagger out into the yard and she'd have to drag them back to their cots. For walking through the jungle settlement where Shapra warriors sat in doorways polishing their rifles and watching her with spiteful eyes. God made her big because He could! A melody formed like a burr in the back of her throat, the words unspooling somewhere deeper. *Immortal, invisible, God only wise, in light inaccessible hid from our eyes.*

She crossed Plaza Grande, running her tongue over her molars, enjoying the silvery feel of her new fillings. All month she had played the tourist, which of course meant visiting the churches, though she was Quaker-born and Presbyterian-raised, and the incense turned her stomach, the penitents crawling on bleeding knees up the aisles and planting desperate kisses on their idols. But she was something of an expert in stained glass, and never tired of watching the way figures came alive in the light, even if she detested the Papist fetishism, the sallow, languid-eyed saints with iron halos like stovetop lids clamped to their heads, and the popes or whatever they were with the towering, pointed head-dresses they wore to make themselves look like gods. Lima had its excesses, but nothing that compared to the obscenity of Quito's

Iglesia de la Compañía de Jesús, where seven tons of gold were smeared onto the walls of a chapel that looked like the inside of a jewel box. She went into it and into every other church within walking distance, and she took a bus up to the Monastery of San Diego with its huge Last Supper painting, in which Jesus is served a roast guinea pig lying on its back like a dog wanting its stomach scratched. *Cuy*—the artist used it as an obvious ploy to pander to the Indians. *Cuy* was on the menu at the hotel; the chef served it whole with a hot pepper in its little mouth. American tourists liked to order it and take one tiny bite and carry on noisily, coughing into their napkins, crying out the names of their childhood pets, while Rachel sat alone at a table in the beautiful courtyard and dined on trout and barbecued pork, thanks to the tithes of the faithful at the Presbyterian Church of the Covenant in Milford, Pennsylvania, and to the power of American dollars in a tinpot economy. At home she'd be living on Boston beans, here she was rich. Dreams are tawdry compared with what God offers His loved ones.

She came to Calle Ambato and turned up it and began to climb, breathing hard. A hill like a loaf of bread plunked into the middle of Quito. Casa Sevilla must be on it. She climbed farther and the streets dropped open to view like canyons. The glory of the scene—later she would understand it as her first intimation of the mighty plan God was putting in motion that night with a simple invitation to dinner—the sun sliding effortlessly behind the mountains, spilling its last light on the houses of *El High*, turning them pink, and Quito spread like a plain of broken pottery below, a window catching the light as if someone was signalling her with a mirror. She stopped to catch her breath and marvel. *If they could see me now* was in her mind, a habitual thought, although in the three years she'd spent in South America, *they* had rather paled as a cadre of watchers. She'd floated up, up and away; the bands between her and them had stretched thin and finally snapped. It was just this: her on the cobblestones with her white shawl over her white arms, and the swifts wheeling in their nightly roost, the glamour of the evening silvering everything.

WHEN THE MAID ushered her up the stairs, ten or fifteen guests were already out on the rooftop with glasses in their hands, sucking on cigarettes, not émigrés like the Sevillas (or so she judged) but the business class of Quito, older Ecuadorean stock, their features betraying a touch of Indigenous blood. Don Carlos Sevilla was exactly what he must be, a handsome, wiry, white-haired man with a huge moustache. He greeted her warmly, offered her the typical limp handshake, congratulated her on her choice of hotel, and told her that he was from Andalucia himself. *"¿De dónde es usted, Señora Saint?"* he asked. And where are you from? So, for the first time ever, she had the opportunity to offer up her testimony in Spanish. Her mother, the lovely young heiress. Her father, the impoverished artist. The party seemed entranced, feeding her the Spanish words that eluded her. How do you say *life drawing*? *"La mujer desnuda,"* she hazarded—and Don Carlos said, *"El dibujo natural."* The torches guttered in the wind, and the stars hummed a few feet above them. But after a bit her listeners began to joke and interrupt, and two men drifted over to the rooftop wall and laughed about something in the street below. Rachel was trying to tell them about raising her brothers, a young girl shouldering an extraordinary burden, and her anger spiked. "Believe you me," she cried, beginning to improvise, "a willow switch was never far from my hand. I did not spare the rod, and the truth of the proverb was born out, because all five of those boys are walking with the Lord today."

"All dead?" A woman pressed a hand to her throat in consternation. It was Señora Sevilla, your typical fretful Spanish matron, her dyed black hair pulled into a bun.

"No, no." Rachel dropped her voice, shocked as always by how little Catholics know of the Scriptures. "Spare the rod and spoil the child—it's a Biblical proverb. Those boys were not spared, and they have grown up unspoiled."

And then they were in the dining room, and—

"Señora Saint," Don Carlos said, gesturing to the seat to his left. He had written to her as *Señorita*, but now he'd seen her. In this light his moustache was stained yellow with tobacco. The room itself was narrow and painted the yellow of overripe corn, a colour eschewed by most of the world but dear to the Latin heart, and the guests lounged in their heavy chairs, chattering in quick, intimate tones, laughing and toasting each other with extravagant gestures. It was a terrible faux pas to have launched into her story like that, but every part of her life was so tightly stitched to the next that if you pulled at one live thread, the whole thing unspooled. Now she sat close-mouthed among them, big-haunched and blond, plain, chaste, solitary, her white hands empty of wineglass or cigarette, a ring of jungle feathers on her head, silent but sensing her voice still undulating freely through the smoky air, falling in who-knows-what form on mocking ears. She sat smarting at their indifference, thinking, I opened my heart to them and plucked out its particular treasures and freely handed them around to be ridiculed.

"Coping all right with the altitude?" said a male voice on her left. In English, imagine! She turned eagerly towards him.

He was an American, a fellow from the Midwest, but so dark-complexioned that he had not drawn her notice. "Don McGrath," he said, sticking out his hand. One of those black Irish, she thought. A petroleum engineer for Shell Oil. An American working to bring modernity and prosperity to Ecuador! Rachel made an observation to this effect, and he said, "Well, no, not exactly." After a huge investment and years of exploration, Shell was pulling out of Ecuador. The field tests hadn't lived up to promises, and the Arabs were taking over the market. He'd been left behind to sell off company assets in Shell Mera, Coca, and Arajuno.

Across from them sat an Ecuadorean man with the bulging eyes of a Boston terrier, listening with interest. "*No ha terminado*," he said emphatically. It's not over. He went on to say in Spanish, "Don't dismantle too much. We're going to get the oil companies back." He had a distinct air of authority, as if he spoke on behalf of the government. In fact, as it came out, he was principal secretary to Velasco Ibarra, Ecuador's previous president. He claimed Ibarra was certain to be re-elected next month, and nobody at the table seemed inclined to dispute this.

A lovely Indian girl served them fried fish, chunks of beef, yellow rice with bits of grass in it, fried plantain, and hominy corn. Setting into his dinner, Don McGrath insisted in his crude Spanish that Shell was gone for good. It wasn't just the poor field tests, it was the violent resistance of the Indians in the region. American shareholders could not stomach news bulletins that their engineers had been found in the jungle stuck full of lances like porcupines.

The man with the bulging eyes just shrugged. "Chevron will invest if we promise military support. We're already talking."

"Well, with all due respect, I wonder where you were through Ibarra's last term. You left us at the mercy of savages. You could have gone in at the first sign of trouble and strafed their huts."

Don Carlos was listening to this conversation with keen enjoyment, as if it was the sort of entertainment he'd hoped to provide. But instead of jumping in, he turned suddenly to Rachel, peering at her through the sprigs of his eyebrows. "So your father was an artist. Do *you* paint, Señora Saint?"

"No."

"A pity." He lifted his wine goblet. "I could sit for you. I might even persuade you to do a *dibujo natural*—you'd be amazed to see my scars."

They held each other's gaze for a minute, and then he smiled (*I mean no harm*) and began to enumerate his scars for the benefit of the whole party. Lance wounds to his thigh and his shoulder, from an

Indian attack on a jungle trail when his carrier had been killed and he had trekked out of the forest alone. Eight days he walked before he reached help, maggots gnawing at his wounds. Then he told them about a canoe expedition into El Oriente, about trying to navigate a bend in the river and being driven close to shore by the current, and the lances suddenly raining down on them. In that attack he gave better than he got; he managed to shoot into the forest, where afterwards they found two bodies. On and on he talked, one adventure leading to the next. His interest in Rachel, his conversation about painting—it was all just a ploy to get to this.

The beef was absurdly undercooked. With a sideways glance at Don McGrath, Rachel dropped hers deftly onto his plate and he snapped it up. It was hard to get a foothold in this conversation. When it came to Indians and their barbarism, she of course had the Shapras of Peru, who decapitated their enemies and by some devilish process shrank the heads down to tiny doll faces with witchy hair, which they flaunted as badges of their prowess, hanging them in their doorways. It was a story to dine out on, but the woollen tapestries seemed to have blotted up the oxygen, and the stifling air was fouled by smoke from huge brackets of candles and from the infernal cigarettes everybody smoked even as they ate. Don Carlos was talking now about going into a deserted Indian hut, gun loaded and cocked, and finding a life-sized human form carved from balsa. He understood it to be a dummy used for training purposes. The torso was scarred by lance thrusts. A heart had been painted on it in *achiote*, a red dye.

"And a white moustache?" Rachel managed to say, and everyone laughed, and the sea of their regard lifted and swept her warmly up. Then she was restored enough to ask the question she'd been wanting to ask all along. "Are these savages the Lowland Quichua?"

No, no, it's the Auca, everyone said. You don't know about our Auca? They live to kill. Don Carlos's first plantation was in the heart of Auca territory. He worked it for four years, until the day he came home from a trip to Shell Mera and saw pillars of flies where the bodies of his workers lay face down on the fields. His entire workforce (twelve Quichua and two whites at the time) had been slaughtered. Thank God his family was safe in Quito. This was decades ago, but nothing had changed.

Don Carlos put his fork and knife down and gazed at her with eyes that were at the same time warm and impersonal. "I have been looking at your feather headpiece all night," he said. "Who gave you this crown, Señora Saint?"

"A Shapra chief. On the Marañón River, just across the border in Peru."

He got up and went to the sideboard and pulled something out of a drawer and carried it to the table. A ring of jungle feathers. "May I?" he asked. He reached for her feathers and lifted them off and placed the two crowns side by side.

They were almost identical. The same pattern of alternating colours, although the bands of green in Rachel's were slightly wider.

"Where did you get yours?" she asked him.

"I picked it up by the Curaray, the time our canoe was attacked. Took it off one of the Auca men I shot. I've never seen another like it."

Rachel examined the basketry inside, the way the feathers were tacked onto it. The two crowns could have been made by the same hand.

"You've been working with the Shapras," said Don Carlos. "Do you speak their tongue?"

"Passably."

"I've heard that the different Indian tribes don't even understand each other. Can this be true?" The word he used for Indian was *infieles*.

"The Shapra language is related to the Candoshi. But many of these tribes have no words at all in common with any other. Their languages are what we call isolates."

He seemed very struck by this. He took a drink of wine and daubed at the patch of mouth visible between the swags of his moustache. "Well," he said eventually. "A strange business."

The servant they called Joaquina was passing out little dishes of crème caramel. She came to Don Carlos just then and he put a hand on her wrist. "This girl has stories to tell. She's Quichua, but when she was a child, the Aucas stole her from her home on the Arajuno River. Those devils killed both her parents, but they took her alive. She lived with them in the jungle for a year, until she spied a party of Quichua fishing on the river and was able to escape."

"Did the Auca not attack the Quichua fishers?"

"No. They allow the Quichua to enter their territory to fish. But white men are always attacked. Always."

"What about white women?"

He laughed. "That hasn't been tried."

Every single thing that happens is from the Lord. The Sevillas were profane, irreverent people, and their hearts were closed up tight and padlocked with the seal of Rome. Yet God used them. They decided to throw a party and He planted a thought: Let's find an American woman so Don McGrath is not all on his own. Or, Let's invite that *evangélica* for dinner, they're always good for a laugh. And she came, and wore her Shapra feathers, and there on the tablecloth in front of her lay another beautiful, almost identical crown from the forest.

She had her voice back now and began to question Don Carlos. These people go about naked? They don't trade in rubber? The priests have never tried to convert them? What about my brother Nate—has he been trying to reach them?

"How do you convert an infidel if you don't speak in his tongue?" Don Carlos asked.

"Does this girl speak the Auca language?" Rachel gestured towards Joaquina, who stood with her hands clasped and her face turned shyly away from them.

"No, señora, she's forgotten. She was a tiny girl when she lived among them. But at Hacienda Ila we have an Auca woman who escaped the jungle in 1947. She is fluent in Quichua now, but she has not forgotten her mother tongue. The next time you visit Señor Nate in Shell Mera, you must come to the hacienda. If you know enough Quichua to converse with her, Dayuma will teach you all about the Auca."

10

HER STORY WOULD HAVE MADE a splendid children's book, as people often said at the fundraising events she held along the Eastern Seaboard one long winter before she went to the mission field. They compared it to *The Five Little Peppers and How They Grew*, a book she herself had adored in childhood, and the similarities only grew with the telling. Poverty and piety are an irresistible combination.

I was born in Pennsylvania, the third child in a family of eight. Sam. Phil. Dan. Dave. Steve. Nate. Ben. Seven boys and me the only girl. My mother was from a Quaker family named Proctor. This is a name that, as you know, means great wealth in America, and my mother was educated at Wellesley. She was a famous beauty whose many suitors included the poet Ezra Pound and the novelist Ralph Connor. But to her family's dismay, she fell in love with an artist. He was pious, but he was penniless and her parents disowned her. That red-bearded artist was my father, Laurence Saint. He was awarded a scholarship to study art in Paris—a wonderful honour that he declined because the studio would have required him to paint and sculpt nude models. So it was his moral fibre that barred him from a conventional career as an artist.

Instead, he was inspired to turn to stained glass, the art that most speaks of the glory of God. Early on, he vowed to use the classical methods in his glass work. This required a great deal of research, for many of the ancient formulae had been lost, and every penny my father earned was spent on study trips to Europe. My mother accompanied him, as she was needed to translate documents from the French and the Italian—and so we saw God's purpose in educating her as he had.

An immense sacrifice was required of the whole family. My two older brothers were taken out of school and sent to work, and I was the one who raised the five little boys. I was only a girl myself, and while my father and mother toured the grand cathedrals of Europe, I became mother and father both to that mischievous gang. We lived on peanuts, I always tell people, and they think I'm joking, but in fact many times our pantry was bare but for the sacks of nuts my brothers took in trade for performing odd jobs. The role I was asked to assume would have quelled many young ladies, but God gave me strength, and today all those boys are following the paths of righteousness. Two besides myself are missionaries in South America: Phillip, who serves God in Venezuela, and Nate, a missionary pilot who works out of Shell Mera, Ecuador.

As for my father, his obedience to the will of God was one day rewarded. Back in America, his research completed, he was riding on a train when a stranger was drawn to him by the beauty of his face. "You resemble portraits of Jesus," the stranger said. "In fact, the Lord Jesus Christ is my Master," my father said, and went on to tell the man about his sacred vocation. As it happened, that stranger was a wealthy businessman in charge of the construction of the Washington Cathedral. From that providential encounter, my father was commissioned to create the cathedral windows, and I had the honour of posing as a model for one of them. One day a wealthy widow named Mrs. Parmalee happened to see my window, and was so affected by it that she sought me out and invited me to be her companion for a grand tour of Europe. Her husband had made a vast fortune in the horse-drawn carriage trade in Boston. This was 1932, and by the intervention of providence their money had not been lost, neither when the automobile took over the trade nor in the Great Crash.

It is a trip I shall never forget. We had first-class passage on the RMS *Aquitania*. A suite in the Savoy Hotel in London. We visited all the greatest monuments and museums, often guided by distinguished scholars, because Mrs. Parmalee was known in society. We had hoped to tour the Continent, but Mrs. Parmalee fell ill and we were obliged to sail for home earlier than expected. On the last night out, Mrs. Parmalee called me to her stateroom and said, "Miss Saint, I make no secret of the fact that I like the cut of your jib. Will you consent to live with me in Boston?" She promised that if I would sign on as her companion, she would have legal papers drawn up the minute we landed in New York, naming me her only heir.

As you can imagine, this invitation knocked me for a loop, and I spent a wakeful night seeking the will of the Lord. In the early hours I was moved to go up to the deck. I stood in the prow of the ship, wrapped in a warm cloak and with my hair loose on my shoulders, the opulence of wealth behind me and in front of me only moving darkness. There I watched for dawn—but it was in the *west* that I saw a pale light grow. Not the eastern flank of my own country, as you might imagine, not the Statue of Liberty. It was the light of the jungle. There, against the black sea, I saw a tangle of vines and palm trees, and under it a group of brown people, naked, with long black hair. And they turned imploring faces towards me, and raised their hands to signal me. "Come and help us," they called.

An hour later, I sat across from Mrs. Parmalee at the breakfast table and said, "Ma'am, I appreciate the great honour you have offered me, but I have had a higher calling."

So, EVENTUALLY, PERU, and a Shapra settlement on the mucky bank of the Marañón River. Which perfectly fit the bill, as to vines and palm trees and needy brown-skinned people.

She left Quito in early morning after the Sevilla party and made the onerous return to Peru. By the time she'd struggled up the riverbank to the Shapra settlement, her legs were cramping from three hours in a small plane and eight hours in a dugout canoe. The whole village streamed out to meet her, the children grabbing at her skirt, eager to see what she'd brought back from Ecuador. But her partners Loretta and Doris were nowhere to be seen. "They're in the house with José María," one of the children said. José María was their language informant, not the brightest candle in the box but the only youth they'd found willing to sit at their folding table for the equivalent of twenty-five cents a day and watch while they made marks on paper. He was their sole convert to date, unless you counted the chief, Tariri, the one who gave Rachel the feather crown, and by then she didn't.

She climbed up to the house, the porters trailing after her, and there sat José María with his head hanging down. Wearing his shoes (which, as they were strictly ornamental, signalled this as an occasion) and clutching a fistful of dirty bills. Loretta with her fiercest face and Doris all droopy and dispirited. "It's a year since his mother died. He tried to buy a Mass, but the priest said he didn't have enough money. So he came to us. He's begging for a discount rate to get her out of purgatory."

José María—his name alone illustrated how bedevilled these

people had been by the priests. Rachel walked the settlement as the sun dropped beneath the canopy. It was a single trail that wound between palm huts and the racks for drying tapir skins. She passed by Chief Tariri's hut, as squalid as the rest, although larger. He would be inside, glowering from his hammock. Such an unpleasant little man. How long will he be your chief? she'd more than once asked the people. There was some nonsense about a boa that had put its lips to Tariri's and passed him something on its forked tongue—a shiny pebble, which he swallowed, and still carried. The *arotama*, they called it. He would be their chief forever.

The Shapras of Peru had lived with rubber traders and oilmen for three generations, but they clung to their superstitions. More to the point, they had lived with priests. She passed by the shrine, a plaster god in human form writhing on a wooden cross, blood oozing from the heart painted on its chest, its face lewd, its eyes rolled upwards. She passed by fires where people sat, finishing up the evening meal. Some ignored her, others greeted her elaborately, bowing and scraping—another form of begging, she had long ago decided. A few actually crossed themselves at the sight of her. And she thought of her vision on the deck of the *Aquitania*, the brown-skinned people calling, *Come and help us*. Once, when she told her story, someone said, "They spoke English?" "They spoke the language of the spirit," Rachel had replied. "It's a universal language."

She had got it wrong, she thought as she came to the end of the path and turned to go back. The Shapras of the Marañón River did not speak the language of the spirit, at least not to her. They weren't even naked. They wore torn T-shirts and filthy jeans. Shapeless cotton skirts and sometimes Maidenform bras in lieu of blouses.

There was the chief's hut again. His new wife, a pregnant child, came out just then, and stooped to fill a gourd from a pot by the entrance. Rachel nodded to her. Some of the village men would be sitting with him. Although she'd been away for a month, although she had once spent two weeks in this house lending support after the chief's wife died, and Tariri, at the end of it, had ceremoniously presented her with a feather crown, no one would look up if she went in. She would stand and wait, cut to a different scale, painted from a different palette, and they would go right on talking, enumerating their ancestors and their feats in killing jaguars, boas, and Indians from other clans. This rudeness, intended to remind her of Chief Tariri's stature, would continue for twenty minutes before they greeted her. *Give not that which is holy unto the dogs,* she thought, feeling her rage ignite. *Neither cast ye your pearls before swine.* The Shapras had a word for pigs, and she knew it, but *pearls?*

She turned away and followed the lower path to the river.

The porters who had ferried her in from Nauta were down at the bank, drinking *masato* with the local men. "I'm going to bring down a letter for you to carry out in the morning," she said to the only one who would meet her eye. She climbed back up to their little house. Her partners were eager to talk, but she said, "Tomorrow," and went to her room, ignoring Doris's doleful face. Doris, who one night had shaken Rachel awake, sobbing, because she'd found a white-headed pimple in her cleavage and thought it might be the protruding head of a guinea worm, who (if we're going to call a spade a spade) did not have the mettle to serve in the tropics. Loretta, who was strong enough, spunky and resourceful, but brittle somehow, preoccupied with private griefs and rages. Had they ever really been a team, the three of them?

She lit a lantern and sat at her desk and began a letter to Cameron Townsend, her mission director. "I am writing to request a change of assignment. My work on the Marañón River is done. The Lord is calling me to Ecuador." And in the process of writing those words, she felt an airy space open up in her chest and she discerned that it was absolutely and splendidly true.

God wants me to serve the Auca Indians, a savage people who (as you no doubt know) have never heard the name of Christ. They have eluded contact for centuries, they have not fallen into the clutches of the priests, they remain a ripe and fertile ground for evangelism. I have reason to believe that they are culturally and linguistically related to the Shapras, in whose language I now have mastery. I praise God that, in His omniscience, He prepared me to work with the Auca by leading me first to Peru.

11

OVER A YEAR SINCE THE accident, but Nate is still in an upper-body cast. He moves like a cockroach, stiff but quick.

"So how did it happen?" Rachel asks, settling into a chair on a screened veranda that has a wonderful view of Mount Sangay with its snowy fields.

"I ran out of fuel, flying into Shandia."

"You don't have an auxiliary tank?"

"I do, but mud wasps got into the fuel line and plugged it up. It was a sick feeling, let me tell you. I went into a glide and tried for the Napo, thought I might come down on a playa. But I didn't have enough air under me, the left wing caught a tree."

While Nate is grounded, a pilot named Johnny Keenan is doing most of his circuit with a float plane. The church at home is raising the cash for another plane, a brand-new Piper Super Cub, and Nate hopes to be back to flying in the new year. In the meantime, he's supervising the building of a hospital in the town, and they're still running the missionary guesthouse. Shell Mera itself is nothing, three rows of shacks assembled by the wind. But the guesthouse, which overlooks the airstrip, has every modern convenience, and they're at a third the altitude of Quito. The beauty of the rainforest, the refreshing air of the foothills, and all the comforts of home.

He paces from one end of the porch to the other as he talks, swinging his arms. The itching under his cast is driving him crazy. Finally he charges into the kitchen and comes back with a pitcher of water and a tin funnel. "Honey?" he says to Marj, and she hoists herself up and goes to him. He stands with his head bent while she pours water into the crack between his spine and the cast. "Ahhhh," he moans extravagantly. "Ahhhh." Water seeps from his cast and turns his khakis black.

"That's exactly the worst thing to do," Rachel says. "You should be trying to keep it dry. You're going to develop a deadly fungus."

He grins his easy shortstop's grin. She can see him outside with his brothers, sliding down a snowy slope or swinging on a rope over the river, his face tanned bronze and his hair bleached silver, yelling, "Rachel, Rachel, look, look," every blessed minute of every day.

They sit down to eat in the kitchen. The cupboards are painted the blue of a bird's egg, probably the latest thing in Idaho. Marj has a Quichua girl to help. As they eat, she washes up the pots with big, careless motions, banging them together as if they are car parts. The children whine and Marj picks up their spoons and cajoles them with mouthfuls. Rice, plantain, fish. Peas out of a can. Marj is from the Midwest, a nurse by training. A plain girl, not pretty enough to have been chosen by Nate, that's the main thing about Marj. There's no baby, Rachel got that wrong, although there will be in a few months. The third. Their girl is about five and the boy Rachel judges to be nine months and a day younger. She studies them and they stare back, unsmiling. They have a Marj-like squatness to their faces, but they got their hair and their eyes from the Saints. Yellow. Blue.

Sam, Phil, Dan, Dave, Steve, Nate, and Ben. Two short of a baseball team, everyone said. Sam and Phil slept in one room, and Dan, Dave, Steve, Nate, and Ben in another, all in one big bed, three at the head and two at the feet, the quilt stretched tight as a drum by ten grubby hands pulling at it. Nate she remembers best, for what a lovely-looking little fellow he was. Her parents were in Europe when he was tiny, and mornings she'd get up to find him sleeping on the floor across her doorway. She'd trip over him and he'd scramble up and trot behind her to the kitchen and clutch her leg while she stirred the porridge.

"So what brings you to Shell Mera, Rachel?" he says. "Wasn't your furlough last month?"

They've been dying to know since they saw her piles of luggage, and she's ignored their hints. "Well, as it happens," she says, "I have some very big news. Cameron Townsend has asked me to spearhead a new mission into Ecuador. Wycliffe Bible Translators is establishing a base here, and that base is me!"

They stop eating at that, even the children, who sense drama. Marj is the first to respond. "Here? In Shell?"

"For the time being."

They are frozen with astonishment. It's Marj who speaks again.

"All the language work you did with the Shapras—and now you're launching into a ministry in Ecuador? You can't be serious! You . . . you have the Lord's leading on this?"

"Of course."

"And you have a visa?"

"I do. In fact, Cameron Townsend and I met last week with President Velasco Ibarra in the palace. He was extremely interested in my work in Peru. I'm coming in at his particular request."

She's longing to tell them the whole story. She's been waiting for days, imagining how excited they'll be, the questions they'll bombard her with. But silence falls over the table like a ton of bricks. It's not just that they aren't curious—they seem actually hostile to hearing about it.

"Will you be working alone?" Marj finally asks. "Do you have housing?" She's put her hand on Debbie's cheek, trying to shush her, and she's looking at Rachel with worry and dismay. No matter, it's Nate's reaction Rachel cares about, and she wishes now she had talked to him alone.

It's five or six years since she's seen him. A man in his prime now, but the boy's winsomeness still in his face. She looks appealingly at him, but he says not a word. His face is blank, even the surprise scrubbed off it. He tips the last of the fish onto his plate and goes back to eating. Some instinct warned her against mentioning the Auca, and in the light of this reaction, she's glad. She'll be months studying Quichua, in any case. It's the lingua franca of El Oriente, she can't do anything without it. And what was it Don Carlos said? There is an Auca girl at the hacienda, and if you learn to speak Quichua, you can ask her about her people.

Nate sits shovelling rice and fish into his mouth as if it's his first meal in a week. He's still wearing that baseball cap, shoved back. She feels familiar ground under her feet.

"Nate. You've left your cap on."

"You're right, I have," he says. He looks her straight in the face and gives her another jaunty grin.

THEY PUT HER in an upstairs room with a large window, and she pays them the weekly rate posted in the radio room. "I know we're family, but I insist," she says, pressing the money into Marj's hand. But when Marj is gone, Rachel discovers the invoice the cold-hearted shrew has already set on the dresser.

It's been a thrilling few weeks, but she sits on the edge of the bed tasting disappointment. Maybe they're jealous. They may have got to Ecuador first, but she's the one with tribal experience. It must bother them that she's a real missionary, while they just offer material support. And when you think of it, it must gall them that she arrived in Ecuador and right off the bat had an audience with their newly re-elected president. Oh, she longs to tell Nate about the beautifully carved mahogany chairs they sat on while they talked. And what a scrawny chap Ibarra was, an aging egghead with thick, circular, black-rimmed spectacles, who told them all about his vision of a transformed Ecuador, ushered into the twentieth century with the help of foreign investors. Roads, industry, schools. Secular schools—he'd had it with the Catholics, who bred subservience into the people. His face glowed, a beautiful man. He promised as many visas as they wanted to go into El Oriente and establish schools. They'd have full rights to radio and air, providing they built airstrips for general use. Their mandate was to speed the transition to an oil future, where the Achuar, the Shuar, the Cofán, and the Secoya would provide much-needed labour for road building and the like.

Cameron Townsend had coached Rachel over supper the night before they met with the president. "We go in as language specialists and teachers and pilots. We don't preach. We don't set up churches. Remember, we are not the Wycliffe Bible Translators. We are the Institute of Linguistics. You will be talking to the president of Ecuador himself, but this is not the place to witness for the Lord. Ecuador has never given a visa to a Protestant missionary."

"I wouldn't feel comfortable lying," Rachel said.

"Listen," Cameron Townsend said. "People used to come up to Jesus all the time and say, Who are you? He never told them. Who do men say that I am? That was his answer."

She didn't actually have to utter a lie during the meeting, thank God. At one point, Velasco Ibarra's attention was caught by her Shapra feathers, transformed now into a ring hat with a bit of black netting tacked to the front, an enhancement suggested by Doris and executed by Loretta before she left Peru. The feathers reminded him of flying over El Oriente during his last term, and he told them how the natives—*los infieles*, he called them, the way Don Carlos had—had thrown lances at his plane. "But the lowlands really are our orient. Ecuador has no future without oil. Are we going to abandon our richest territories to our most primitive people?"

Rachel spreads a towel on the bed to protect it from her shoes and lies down. Nate needs to put his pride aside. There's no competition in God's army. Maybe they'll even lure Phillip here from Venezuela. Think of the years God spent building the Saint team, unconventional, intrepid, exceptional in any enterprise they turn their minds to. "San Felipe, San Natanael, Santa Raquel," someone mused at the Sevilla party. It takes her breath away, to think of the separate ways the Lord brought them to this point.

In the meantime, this room is a palace. A little island of America, with a light bulb dangling from the ceiling and a big window overlooking the airstrip. It even has a gecko, showing its green tail to her from the top louvre.

12

NATE AND MARJ ARE ABLE to provide Quichua word lists, and Rachel spends her days at the desk by the big window memorizing them. Her third week there, a young American gets off the bus from Quito and walks across to the guesthouse with a duffle bag on his back. He's pale and thin and has a tremor in his hands. Marj greets him with sympathetic cries. "They discharged you far too soon," she says. "Look at the colour of you. Oh, poor Peter."

Peter Fleming is new to the field and deep in language learning himself. He's from the west coast, sponsored by one of those primitive congregations, Anabaptist or apostolic or whatever they call themselves, where the working poor sit on folding chairs in a wood-frame hall and sing without books or an organ. But he seems very nice. When he hears Rachel is studying Quichua, he tells her he has a package of materials his predecessor Dr. Tidmarsh made up, a grammar she might find useful. "I'll make you a copy," he says, and in spite of his fatigue, he spends the next two days in the radio room typing up the pages for Rachel. He gives it to her without a fuss. "I enjoyed doing it," he says. "It was a good way for me to learn."

They talk on the veranda while Marj puts the children to bed on the other side of the window. He tells her about the flood that destroyed all their efforts of the first six months. He tells her about his work with the Quichua in Shandia, the medical clinic and the boys' school, how difficult that ministry is. Indians walk by on the road as they talk, and they watch them together, and it's clear to Rachel that it's too late to rewind history and save the Quichua. They're like the Shapras, they've had just a big-enough dose of Christianity to inoculate them against it for life. But what's to be gained by discouraging this young missionary?

He's had three medical evacuations in the last year. "That is par for the course," Rachel says consolingly. Her own malaria came and went her entire first year on the Marañón River. It took her a long time to recognize what it was. "It felt like a miracle at first," she says. "Being cool, for the first time in months. I dreamed I was sledding. Nate was there, sliding on a tea tray, and the snowflakes parted like a mosquito net. But in the morning, shivers began to chase over my arms, waves of gooseflesh, and I started trembling. I walked through the settlement with my arms folded, trying to hide the fact that I was shaking like an old man with palsy. Stop it! I kept scolding myself—you're doing that on purpose! But I couldn't stop."

"I went through that stage too."

"And were you a little crazy?" she asks. "When it really set in, I thought the child who hauled our water was *Jesus*. I tried to go down to the river myself because I didn't want our Lord fetching and carrying for us. The can I took was half-full of kerosene, and I filled it to the top with water. Then I slipped in the mud and sprained my shoulder, just to add to the general misery. My partners were beside themselves!"

"I didn't hallucinate," Peter says. "But I had—I guess you'd call it poor control of my impulses."

Rachel senses a juicy story. "What did you do?"

"Oh, I wrote a letter I should never have written. Fortunately, no one mailed it and I had the chance to burn it when I was lucid again."

This boy is articulate and educated, not what Rachel assumed at all. He wrote a university thesis on Herman Melville. "Melville," she cries, thrilled. "Herman Melville courted the grandmother of a dear friend of mine." It was Mrs. Parmalee's grandmother, in fact. So then she tells him about her own mother's academic career and various suitors.

"Ezra Pound!" he exclaims in his turn. He's sprawled on a bamboo chair, so thin he seems to be part of it, and he turns his eyes towards the town and recites, "'Empty are the ways, empty are the ways of this land, and the flowers bend over with heavy heads.'"

She beams at him. Even Nate has no idea who either Herman Melville or Ezra Pound are. All that interests Nate and Marj, really, are the children, and the properties and efficient functioning of generators and kerosene refrigerators, and whether they are being swindled by their grocery supplier.

A day or two later, Pete's partner Jim Elliot arrives, having walked the jungle trail from Shandia. His hair is drenched with sweat and his shirt is plastered to him, but he bounds up the steps of the veranda, noisy, exuberant, the cock of the walk. "Nate's got a sister?" he says when he shakes Rachel's hand. "I thought the Pennsylvania Saints was a full team of heavy sluggers."

"We are," she says, staring him down.

An American couple, Ed and Marilou McCully, are joining the work—that's why Jim trekked out from Shandia, to welcome them. Late that afternoon they roll in on the bus, carrying their eight-month-old son. Ed and Marilou flew Chicago–Houston–Quito, no stinking ocean freighter for them. So just yesterday they had cornflakes for breakfast, just yesterday they were driven up the turnpike to O'Hare Airport. They look hot and exhausted, but still unmistakably *new*. As they mill around the veranda, shaking hands, embracing, the clouds part to reveal the perfect cone of Mount Sangay, forty miles away. Nate has combed his hair and put on a white shirt, buttoning it up over his grimy cast. Standing beside him, Rachel can feel his excitement. It's been cloudy for a week, but, a proud host, he laid Mount Sangay on especially for them, the snowfields pink with the failing light.

Jim Elliot leads them in prayer, thanking God for Ed and Marilou's safe arrival. "You are bringing your team together, Lord," he prays. "We can only watch in humility and awe as your plans are made manifest. We ask that you counsel and guide us as we prepare for the glorious harvest that lies ahead."

Marj has been saving a case of Pepsi for the occasion and she hauls it out. They drink their Pepsis, they talk and laugh. Marilou McCully is a good-looking woman in a mint-green suit and navy pumps. It turns out she's expecting a second baby, she's not just buxom as Rachel assumed at first, and she and Marj are soon sitting with their heads close together, murmuring in low voices, their hands straying now and then to their bellies. The children are crazy for pop, they guzzle it down and beg for seconds. When their whining turns to shrieks, Marj announces that it's time for bed. Marilou stands up too. She swivels towards Rachel, telegraphing a polite invitation. Oh, I don't think so, Rachel says to herself, pressing her bum firmly back in her bamboo chair.

The men talk aviation. High-octane fuel, directional gyroscopes. Their voices are low and casual, in a different register now. The sky gathers up colour and the cone of the mountain darkens against it. On the other side of the wall a child cries, and one of the women murmurs in comfort. They talk about Shell Oil, about a whole town abandoned in the jungle, and all the spoils to be bought up. "Don McGrath!" Rachel cries. "An American I met in Quito. He's in charge of selling off the assets. You could look him up—he's staying at the Cordillera Hotel. He—"

"That rathole," says Nate. "I was almost knifed on the street outside the Cordillera."

They're in a row against the house, with Jim on the railing facing them. They drift to the subject of the Catholic Church. Nate knows all the priests in the region. The Americans and the Spaniards tend to be Communists, but the Italians are even worse, mean-spirited, ignorant, and superstitious. They teach the Indians that Protestant missionaries are *supai pagris*, devil priests. "The priest at Macuma, where Roger and Barbara Youderian serve, is a real piece of work," he says. "Roger gave out mosquito nets to the new Christians, and the priest went around warning the people that the nets would trap demons inside during the night. Can you believe it? And when Roger started administering penicillin by injection, Father Bruno—"

"Nate," Rachel says. "Don't call him Father. You have an earthly father and a heavenly Father, and those men are neither." His mouth turns down in irritation and he doesn't look at her. "Not that I disagree," she adds, "about the priests. The stories I could tell you from Peru." No one responds. "Even President Ibarra is disgusted by them. He told me they used to be carried from village to village on a litter, demanding tribute."

More silence. *You met President Ibarra, Rachel?* she waits for someone to ask. *However did that happen?*

Jim launches into a story about the day he and Pete arrived in Shandia. "First day there, we've just trekked eight hours through the jungle, and we open up the Tidmarsh house and of course it's crawling with roaches and rats, and then we hear a voice and there the guy is at the door. He's put on his robes and his long crucifix, and he's come over to the house to order us to leave. It's *his* village, he says. That was our welcome party! I'm trying not to laugh, but then I look over at Pete here and I kind of lose it."

Peter shrugs. "He didn't exactly order us to leave. He's worked in Shandia for fifteen years, and he said that within a month the Indians would be playing us off against each other. You can't deny that he was right—that's exactly what's happening. There are a lot of settlements in El Oriente with no Christian presence, and he thought maybe we could agree on certain territories."

"Well, I said to him, with all due respect for your fifteen-year ministry, Father Alfredo, I have not exactly noticed a Christian presence in Shandia." The bedroom light comes on and falls yellow over Jim's face. He looks at Rachel. "Sorry. You're right, Miss Saint. We shouldn't say 'Father.'" He hitches himself sideways, swinging one leg up onto the railing, and says to Ed, "The guy's from Albuquerque."

"He's Chicano?"

"What I want to know is where he's getting his booze these days," Nate says. "A few months ago he had a full case of whiskey shipped here from Quito, but Johnny takes one look at it and says, 'No way I'm flying that in.'" He hunches his shoulders as if his cast is bugging him, twisting his head from side to side.

Beside him, Rachel sits still in her chair. I am Miss Saint, she thinks. I am neither fish nor fowl.

Suddenly Nate's on his feet, he's thumping on the window frame. "Marj! Marj! Get out here. Bring the kids. We're going to have a show. And turn off that bloomin' light."

Only then do the rest of them notice grey puffs rising from the cone of the mountain. The yellow light goes off and Marj and Marilou hurry out to the veranda, each carrying a sleepy child. The screen door slams and the volcano erupts, comets of orange light shooting in all directions. They're all on their feet, they cry out in amazement. It's an excess of beauty, it's from another world. Lava like molten gold races down the slopes of the cone. Rachel closes her eyes and the sight is stamped on her eyelids. I am God, and this is my work. All the hurt falls away, all the petty resentment and competition: you are frail and flawed, but here you are and here I Am. "Immortal, invisible, God only wise," she finds herself singing, and a beautiful male voice picks the song up—Jim Elliot's, it's Jim's voice—and then they're all singing, they move into four-part harmony, and she feels, rather than hears, the deep thrum of the bass voices. "We blossom and flourish as leaves on the tree, and wither and perish, but naught changeth thee."

It's a song from Rachel's childhood, but never in childhood did she hear it with so much wonder.

LOOKING FOR A quiet place to work the next morning, Rachel opens the door of the radio room to see Jim Elliot studying the map on the wall. The eastern Amazon basin, with little flags on pins marking the fifteen mission stations Nate serves when he is able to fly.

"Come in, come in," he says. "Don't let me stop you. I'll be out of here in a flash." He pulls out the desk chair for her. She sets the Tidmarsh grammar down, and he gestures to it. "That's a terrific help, isn't it. Quichua is a nightmare of a language!"

"You're not just kidding," Rachel says. "You know, don't you, the Quichua used to tie knots into coloured strings as a form of writing?"

"There's a metaphor if you ever need one." Jim laughs.

They are just the same height. They look at each other directly and she feels his clear gaze taking her in, not dismissing her. She sits on the office chair and he perches on the edge of the desk. "Every evening I turn to God, and I say, Lord, you reached down at Babel and touched the tongues of the folks there, and next morning they woke up speaking different languages. Couldn't you just reverse that miracle for us? Because I promise you, if we had a unified language today, we wouldn't be wasting it on building any old tower. We would use it to spread the good news of Christ to all the nations. But so far the Lord hasn't taken my advice."

He gets up and goes back to the map. "And Quichua won't be any help where I'm hoping to go. This is all Auca country. You've heard of the Auca? Entirely unreached. Nate doesn't even fly over their territory. If he had another forced landing, he'd end up in a stewpot."

Hope or fear, she's not sure which, surges through her. "How far does Auca territory extend?"

He shows her. It's a wide belt, bounded by the Napo in the north and the Curaray in the south, and by the border with Peru in the east—although that border is a fluid thing, isn't it, and would be meaningless to forest dwellers.

She tries to keep her voice casual. "And you said you're intending to try to reach them?"

"Well, I don't know how to answer that question. When God called me two years ago, I thought it was to the Auca. But I haven't figured out a way to make that happen yet. We don't know where they are, and the other Indians are not about to guide us. So for now I'm working with the Quichua. It's kind of hard to know if you've misunderstood your calling. Sometimes I wish God would speak up so I could be sure I've got it right."

"You know why He whispers, don't you? It's to keep you close to Him."

He smiles politely and she regrets preaching to him like that. To get the friendly mood back, she tells him about all the obstacles she faced when she first tried to enlist as a missionary. She came home from her grand tour with Mrs. Parmalee, her heart full of her wonderful vision, and enrolled at the Philadelphia College of the Bible, where she worked like a Turk for three years. And when she graduated, the mission board turned her down! A weak back, they said. Nothing about her was weak. They (those men, they were all men) saw her strength and it scared them silly. *Silly* was the only word for it, and it set her back by ten years. How do you make sense of it when God's very own servants set out to block you? "It was only after the war," she tells him, "when so many men had been killed and they were desperate for recruits, that they finally accepted me."

"Miss Saint," he says, "there is a flat and sterile spirit in the church in America. Frankly, I was happy to leave. I long to fight for Christ in a real battle with evil, where you can smell the stench of demonic forces. You must have sensed that in Peru."

That she can attest to. She tells him several stories about the Shapras, their history of head-shrinking, and the chief's shenanigans, which leads naturally into the story of the night Chief Tariri sought her out in so much distress, wanting to pray.

"I can't imagine the joy you must have felt," Jim says, "ushering a heathen soul into glory. I haven't had a single convert here. I walk around feeling like such a failure. Satan can really use it to drag you down. I look at the Quichua, and honestly, I question whether they are my real ministry. They're like children. They'll say anything to get on the right side of you. Basically, all they want from us is trade goods." He pulls a chair out from the wall and sits facing her. "Do you work alone?" he asks.

"Cameron Townsend promised to send me a partner, but so far no word on that."

"Well, there is a wonderful liberty in singleness. The first missionary, the Apostle Paul, preached celibacy, but very few Christians take him seriously. The Catholics, whatever we might think of them, got that part right. It's a huge sacrifice, and I have been struggling with it for years. For a while Ed McCully shared my vision, and he and I were planning to come to the field together, and then Marilou strolled into his life, and that was that."

"Well, yes," she says. "I often think of the freedom Nate would have had if . . . well . . ."

They sit looking comfortably at each other, their knees almost touching. He's rolled up his shirt sleeves. The veins lie along his arms like cables, outside the muscle, just under the skin.

"You said something about a stewpot," she says. "But the Auca aren't cannibals, are they?"

"I don't think anybody knows for sure. Tidmarsh heard somewhere that they bury their children alive, and their sick, and the elderly. Anybody they don't want around anymore. When you think of it, a hundred generations have gone by since our Lord came to earth. All those centuries under Satanic influence—it must have a terrible impact on a people." He reaches a hand towards her. "Would you join me in laying that ministry at the throne of God?"

His hand is damp with sweat, but it's firm and strong, and God help her if she doesn't thrill to the touch as they bow their heads in prayer.

THE SHANDIA CREW stays in Shell Mera for almost a week. Johnny Keenan's not flying; his float plane is down and the parts he needs have been back-ordered. Hiking in to Shandia takes eight hours, and Ed and Marilou need to acclimatize first. Plus, they need to hire porters and sort out all the gear that just arrived in steel barrels from the port at Guayaquil, some of which (the record player and Marilou's sewing machine, for example) will not be carried in.

It's an absolute tonic to have them there. Jim alone has the energy of ten, he makes a festival of every meal. They spend the days in prayer and fun and singing and conversation. It's a foretaste of heaven, that week, God's children enjoying themselves together in God's presence. It was never like this in the station on the Marañón River. The spirit is very different in a house full of men.

The only dark thread is Nate, who never speaks to Rachel

unless he has to. Now that the gang is there, he's started to mock her openly. One day when they're singing together on the veranda, he gestures grandly at the end of the song and says, "With thanks to Miss Rachel Saint on the bagpipes." And more than once, when a question comes up, he says, "Maybe Rachel can ask her friend Velasco about that." She brings out meanness in him, and she has no idea why. You'd think he'd be grateful to her—it was her vision on the *Aquitania*, and he grabbed it up. And the missions were happy enough to sign him on the instant he was old enough. Nate and Phil, they're both in South America thanks to her, and neither of them has ever acknowledged this.

It's always in her mind to ask him about the Auca, whether he's seen any sign of their settlements as he makes his rounds by air, but any ambition she shows for outreach into the field seems to invite his ridicule. He knows she met Don Carlos in Quito; he refers to him as Daniel Boone. One day Rachel asks him to show her on the map where the hacienda is. It's on the Ila river, with no settlement nearby.

"Have you ever flown in?"

"How would I land?"

"What do you mean?"

"Hard to land without an airstrip."

The red flag closest to the hacienda is the Shandia mission station.

"Could you fly in to Shandia and walk from there?"

"You could."

"How long a walk would it be?"

"Three, four hours."

"Is that how the Sevillas get in and out when they go to Quito?"

"No. They go up the river, they use a barge." He peers at her. "What's up? You got a thing for Daniel Boone?"

That's what it's like with Nate.

Jim, though! Jim, she can tell, holds her in respect, and even seeks her out. Something burns so bright in Jim, a bright flame of faith. Rachel knows cant, she's encountered it far too often in Christian circles, and she generally prefers a more modest manner. But Jim seems entirely honest, both in his spiritual victories and in his doubts. This should be the norm in the body of believers, but sadly it is not.

They talk in low voices, up at the end of the veranda, mostly about the singleness issue. It pains him to see Ed and Marilou together; it's hard to understand what God is up to when he believed for so long that Ed would be his partner in the work, and when he himself surrendered his dream of a lifetime of love and companionship with a soulmate, and ended up having to recruit Peter. "When did *you* first realize that God was calling you to be single?" he asks Rachel.

"Well, in fact, I feel more like a widow," she says. And she tells him. The man she loved was named Raymond. He signed up for the war and was sent to Italy. Rachel's brother Sam was a telegram messenger at the time, and he came home one day and told her he'd carried a black-edged telegram to a house on Spiggot Street. He'd forgotten the soldier's name—that big guy with the Alsatian, he said. Rachel didn't even know Raymond had a dog, but she knew right away that it was him.

"Oh, I'm very sorry," Jim says kindly. "Were you engaged to be married?"

"No," she says simply, and it seems this only deepens the tragedy.

She's never told a single soul before, because she took the whole thing as a lesson in the follies of the heart. Raymond Molgat filled her dreams in the years after she was turned down by the mission, when she was drying out drunks at the Colony of Mercy, a dark, dark time, all those long days and longer nights in a mouse-smelling house crammed with wretched men who under other circumstances might have been husbands for her, but all of them ruined by the last war, ruined by going or by not going—and then there he was with his long legs and black beard, a new usher at the Church of the Covenant, a mountain man, her brothers called him, and it seemed the two of them were a perfectly matched set. For a long time she watched and waited, thrilling to the realization that God had planned this from the outset, that the missionary business had been *a test*, the Lord checking to see how willing she was, like God asking Abraham to butcher his own son Isaac. And then one Sunday morning the banns were read out in church, and she sat in the pew among her brothers and actually reached up to bat at her ears because she thought they were playing tricks on her. *Raymond Molgat and Margaret Mallender.* Margaret Mallender! A stick insect of a girl who would have to clamber up on a chair to kiss him properly. The day Raymond got engaged to Margaret Mallender was the day she learned that her own heart (which had offered her so much sterling proof in the way of smiles and conscious glances) was a treacherous counterfeiter.

And so what to think now, when the same currents begin to course through that same beating heart?

She's not a pathetic fool. Jim is a decade younger than she is, and full of the sort of easy charm that draws everyone to him. Nevertheless, there is such a thing as sensing exactly where an individual is in the house at any moment, there is a spontaneous sort of laughter that bubbles up in your chest when you're around a fellow who has as many jokes and silly songs as he has, there's the softness that comes over you at the sight of muddy brown shoes at the door, their backs broken down from the wearer's haste in thrusting his big feet into them because children in the yard are calling for someone to throw a ball or a porter on the road is struggling alone to straighten the load on his donkey. There is all that. Oh, her heart is deceitful above all things, and desperately wicked. But it is the only heart she has.

And then there is, in the early morning, a sense of waking up to herself, lying on her side in her beautiful room with the wide window. Opening her eyes and fumbling for the hem of the mosquito net and reaching for her clock. Ten after five. Her drying underpants a row of silvery flags in the morning light. She drops the net and rolls over and lies listening to the birds. Rachel Saint. She is Rachel Saint, tall and big-boned, her stomach a mound under the sheet, a woman spurned by men, reviled and persecuted by the world, but created and beloved by Almighty God. She lies in bed and feels His love silver her very core. God is planning something great for the Auca. It will be an extraordinary work, like David Livingstone's in Africa or the Apostle Paul's, wherever he went. God has called her and given her certainty. He's brought her to this house, and He's called that gifted man sleeping down the hall. Celibacy, Jim said, holding out the word like a chalice. Holding it out to her, to Rachel Saint.

13

"So what exactly is *chicha*?" Ed McCully asks, helping himself to a third big scoop of macaroni.

Nate and Marj groan, they gag.

"I know it's a drink, but I don't really know what it is."

"It's made from yucca," Marj explains. "You know, manioc, the tapioca root. The women chew it up and spit it into a kettle, and then they let it sit for a few days before they drink it."

"*Masato!*" Rachel cries, dropping her fork. "In Peru they call it *masato*, the Indians live on the stuff. They use exactly the same method. Not long ago the chief's wife died and—"

Marilou has a hand over her mouth. "They drink each other's spit? That's just revolting. Why doesn't somebody introduce them to a mortar and pestle?"

"I think their saliva starts the fermentation," says Marj. "That's what I've always assumed."

Peter has been reading about it. "The bitter varieties of yucca contain cyanide. Not enough to poison you, but over time it can cause goitres. The enzymes in saliva neutralize it. That's why the Indians prepare it the way they do."

"But how would they possibly know that?" Ed asks.

"It's hideous to drink, kind of like raw egg white with lumps in it. But it's quite nutritious, apparently. I'll get Perfecta to bring some in." Marj smiles mischievously at Marilou. "It's just the thing for morning sickness."

"Does it make you drunk?"

"I don't think so. For fiestas they let it ferment longer."

Rachel finally manages to jump in. "I have a very funny story about *masato*, what you call *chicha*." She raises her voice. "*Masato*, also known as *chicha*, almost caused a civil war on the Marañón River."

Finally she gets everyone's attention.

"About a year ago, the chief's wife died. She was just a young woman, and she collapsed and died overnight, nobody knew why. The whole settlement was in a terrible tizzy, because the chief was threatening to murder one of the other men and steal his wife. So I went over to his house and insisted he see me. What's this I hear? I said. He didn't deny it. I have no *masato*, he said. The kettle was right there and I could see he was running low."

"This was the guy you told me about?" Jim interrupts. "The head-shrinking chief you led to the Lord?"

"Yes, it was Tariri. He had a huge pile of yucca in the corner but nobody to cook and chew it, because they consider it strictly women's work. 'There will be no killing of husbands and stealing of wives on Rachel Saint's watch,' I said to him. 'I'll get someone to make your *masato*.' But you know—I couldn't! I couldn't find a single girl who wasn't spoken for. And so the next morning, I took my partner Loretta by the arm and I said, Come on, girl, we're on duty at the chief's house. And we did it—we went every morning to that filthy little hut and boiled up his yucca and then sat on the floor and masticated it and spit it into the kettle."

Their laughter explodes.

"It is not easy work, let me tell you," Rachel shouts over the hilarity. "I already had terrible toothache, I was just waiting for my leave so I could get to Quito to the dentist, and I was in true agony." She's laughing so hard herself, she's in danger of peeing. "I was in agony, but I went faithfully every morning for two weeks, chewed and spat, chewed and spat. Finally one of the clans came back from a trip upriver, and they had a daughter they were willing to give him, so we were off the hook."

Nate almost falls off his chair. "What's their wedding ritual, Rachel? Maybe it's chewing and spitting! *With this mush I thee wed!* Hahahahaha. Maybe you're married and you don't realize it! You better get on a plane back to Peru!"

Her laughter dies. She fixes on him a face she perfected on the *Aquitania*, where they sat at the captain's table, and everyone drank like fish, and she witnessed all sorts of godless imbecility and endured shocking ridicule. She fixes this face on her brother, and he shuts up fast, and then she hears Jim.

"He was in the market for a wife! Oh, Miss Saint, Miss Rachel Saint, it could have been your lucky day."

SUCH IS HER pain that she spends the next hour kneeling at the throne of God. She waits with a folded towel under her knees, pressing her face into the pillow. She can hear the others moving quietly below, but no one comes up the stairs to inquire as to her sudden exit.

You gave me *victory* over this, she says to the Lord. Just the other morning. So what the tarnation is going on?

It takes God a while to answer. I'm not fond of lies, He finally says. There's the little matter of the conversion of Chief Tariri.

Chief Tariri of the Shapras, who had so raised her hopes six months ago when he knelt with her in his hut on the banks of the Marañón River and prayed in a paroxysm of emotion, clear evidence of guilt and the conviction of sin. And then, two days later, a terrible massacre took place upriver. When Chief Tariri returned to the settlement, she went straight in and confronted him. "*Did* you invite Jesus into your heart?"

He looked directly at her and said, "Yes. But He didn't come."

Anger rises like bilge water in her chest. For God to rebuke her with this! And in any case, what is a lie? Sometimes the moment you imagine and long for, the event that should by rights have transpired, that's where you're going to find the real truth.

She sends this up to the Lord, but it's too subtle for Him and a long silence follows. And then she digs in. Consider my grievance against you, she cries. *Marj.* You seem to adore Marj. You've made her plump and happy, given her everything. You want truth? The plain truth is that my sister-in-law has created a full-time job for herself as a broodmare. And now this Marilou person! How can they even use the term *missionary*? So tell me why they are respected when I am not. Is this fair?

Fair, God says. It's not a word I recognize.

Well, maybe you should enlighten me, Rachel rages (silently, silently, her face pressed into the pillow), as to why do you call single girls out to these stinking jungles only to be sneered at by their own people? The danger and the loneliness, don't you consider that enough? Having nobody to trade glances with at the supper table? Never a loving hand on the nape of your neck? Is the workwoman not worthy of her hire?

Nothing comes back. She waits, but nothing comes back.

Her feet have fallen asleep, they're dead from the ankles down. She hauls herself up and undresses and gets into bed. Doors open and close in the hallway. A man's voice next door, and then a woman's—Ed and Marilou, talking just too low for her to make out the words. She listens in vain for Jim. Her thoughts fall away, she starts to drift. Pictures crowd into her mind and transmogrify, the way they will. Dolls in sparkling dresses in the alcoves of the cathedrals, angels or brides or the glory of the Lord. It was a virgin who bore our Lord, wasn't it? She's lying on her side and her shoulder is cramping. She rolls over, washed back up to wakefulness, and there's the answer, as vivid as if it were backlit: the Auca in their green world, faces turned imploringly towards her. A stained glass window with its pure and simple lines, a private shrine to hope.

THEY ALL LEAVE and the house falls quiet. It's better, Rachel can give herself to her work without distraction. The new hospital opens and a doctor flies in from Quito for a two-day clinic. Nate comes home without his cast, red as a lobster. Then Marj goes over for what Rachel presumes is a checkup and that afternoon the children, Debbie and Ben, spy someone on the road and shriek to high heaven—it's Mommy carrying a baby (also red as a lobster) in the crook of one arm. Marj, all on her own, walking back to the house—well, my goodness! David, they're calling him. It seems Nate is naming his sons after his brothers.

But *Debbie*? He only had the one sister, Rachel thinks with a little rub of hurt.

A week or two later, Nate boards the bus to Quito, and that same evening, just before sunset, they're sitting on the veranda and a shiny new Piper Cub comes into sight over the trees. Yellow. They all run out to the airstrip and clap and cheer when it touches down. Nate clambers out, arms raised. "Back in business, praise God!"

After that, he comes home every night with news from the stations, what goods he carried in, what gossip he heard, who was sick and who was injured, the Indians and missionaries he flew out to the hospital. The work crews he flies into the jungle, because it seems the men have bought an abandoned Shell Oil town. And Marj is back to her old job in the radio room, with the radio squawking all morning, *Shell Mera, stand by, Shell Mera, stand by*. She still has the muscular Perfecta working in the kitchen, and she hires a thin girl named Sofia to help with the children. And then, of course, what is bound to happen (what is carved into Rachel's destiny, stamped like a label on her forehead) begins to happen: Marj in the doorway, holding a child by each hand. "If you could just give me a couple of hours? I am swamped down there. Sofia didn't show up again and Perfecta has gone out to buy chickens. The baby is sleeping, but these two are driving me crazy. Ben has his truck, he'll play with that. Won't you, Benjy? And Debbie has her new colouring book."

The pleading face, the little backside jogging down the stairs even though Rachel has not uttered a word.

The girl thrusts a page into Rachel's face. "Auntie Rachel, I'm doing this one next." Heroes of the Old Testament, a robed boy at an old man's knee.

"Very nice," Rachel says. She was just finding shelf space in her mind for seven personal pronouns of three syllables each.

The girl settles herself on her tummy and picks out a crayon. "This is for her hair."

"That is not a girl. That is the prophet Samuel, who lived in God's house and listened to God's voice. And that crayon is blue. Don't make his hair blue. You will ruin your book." The girl lowers her forehead to the floor, overcome at any thwarting of her will. "Samuel's hair was brown. Look at the lovely waves. Find a brown crayon, now."

She turns back to her notes. Seven pronouns in the Quichua dialect, two words for "we." *Nuqayku, nuqanchik*. Who worked out this orthography, *q* with no *u*?

The boy is banging his truck on the floor, making revving noises. He drives it over Rachel's foot. She sends him to the other side of the bed. Then he's back, driving the truck right up her leg. Rachel moves out of his reach. "You're a lot like your father when he was little," she says. "Although he listened better."

"I listen," the boy says sulkily.

Nuqayku, nuqanchik. How can they both mean "we"? *Nuqayku* means "we not including you" (we're going but you're not), *nuqanchik* means "all of us." A useful distinction, when you think about it.

The boy smacks the truck hard against her toes, butting at her ingrown toenail. "Oops," he says, peering up at her for a reaction. "That was a truck accident, Auntie Rachel. The truck smashed into a cliff."

"What does your mother spank you with, Ben? Does she use a strap?"

"She doesn't spank us."

"I know that can't be true." Rachel gets up and gathers her underpants off her clothesline and unhooks the cord from the window. "Stand up," she says. "And stand still." He obeys, watching curiously while she knots one end tight around his waist. She leads him around the bed and fastens the other end to the bedpost. "Pretend you're a doggie," she says. "Aunt Rachel has work to do."

He barks for a bit and then begins to holler and finally to blubber.

"He's crying, Auntie Rachel," the girl calls from the floor. "He's crying, Auntie Rachel. Auntie Raaa-chel, Benjy is cryyyy-ing."

Rachel senses Marj in the doorway, but she keeps her head bent over her work as Marj, stiff and silent, unties the boy and leads the children out. "You know," Rachel calls to her back, "I did not do jungle training in Mexico, I did not translate the gospel for headhunters in Peru, to come to Ecuador and look after other people's children."

And then, no surprise, her concentration is shot. She lies on the bed and she and her gecko watch each other for the rest of the afternoon. She knows what she is doing where children are concerned! For months stretching into years, while her mother and father swanned around Europe, she raised five rambunctious boys. She was fourteen when her parents left, and she remembers them hustling to the train station almost at a gallop, so great was their relief to be escaping. "There should be a law against that sort of thing," Mrs. Parmalee said when she heard this story. "You were only a child." "I was never a child," Rachel said. Of course, Phil and Sam got jobs at a warehouse and they paid the rent, but how often did she see them? And when her grandparents came to take her to the grocery store, when they drove up in their beige-and-maroon town car and saw the boys like a gang of hoodlums and paupers tossing a rag football in the Saint yard, she could not bear the superior look on their faces. "We're fine for now," she said, although the oatmeal and potatoes had run out and she was feeding the boys boiled cabbage, all that was left in the garden.

In the mirror, in the stateroom on the *Aquitania*, she was as beautiful as a Dutch doll. Yet the English did not warm to her. She stared, she spoke her mind, she knew the rutabaga as a turnip. Her social deficiencies were endless conversational fodder to Mrs. Parmalee. "This is all new to Rachel," she would say, gesturing to the linen napkins and the crystal and heavy silver. "They're poor as church mice. Dear child—I'm not sure how she grew to such a size. They use their coffee grounds three times over. They wear shirts and bloomers made from the mother's gowns."

Then the next day, Mrs. Parmalee would introduce Rachel as the heir to the Proctor fortune. "Her mother is a famous beauty in Pennsylvania," she would tell people. "She was the belle of Wellesley. Ezra Pound was her lover, but she threw him over." People thought Mrs. Parmalee was crazy, but still they sought her company. Money will buy you any amount of friendship. Well, it did not buy Rachel's.

When she came home empty-handed, without so much as a parting gift, her mother was furious. "You have no idea what was at stake. All you had to do was get along with her."

"You mean the money."

"Yes, of course the money."

It was noon and her mother was still in bed, in worn sheets cut in half and sewn back up sides-to-middle. She was not having a baby this time, it was something else. Her hair was unwashed and tangled, the colour of dirty linen.

"But you didn't want money. You gave it all up."

"Oh, Rachel," she said. "I had no idea."

The gecko gazes at her, its throat going in and out in contemplation. I thought Mrs. Parmalee offered to make you her heir, it says. Sometimes I think she did, Rachel says. It's hard to remember what actually happened. Sometimes she pictures the stateroom on the *Aquitania*, and there are piles of yucca in the corners.

There's an atmosphere at supper, and *frosty* is the only word for it. A missionary family called the Youderians are at the table, an ex-soldier and his horse-faced wife, two fretful children. They're en route to Macuma, a Jivaro settlement a few hours south. The bus from Quito broke down, so they hired a private driver and rolled in hours earlier than expected. Supper will be slim pickings; apparently Perfecta couldn't find fresh chickens. "Family hold back," Nate says in a low voice when Rachel passes him in the hall.

"Youderian," Rachel says after the grace. "That's a different sort of name. Where are you folks from?"

"Montana," the man says, looking right past her. A morose and unfriendly chap. Does he hate Ecuador in general or just other missionaries?

The platter comes to her. It's meat loaf and Rachel does not hold back. If they will not honour me, then I must honour myself, she thinks. At such moments she feels it clearly, the shiny *arotama* she swallowed at birth.

THE NEXT MORNING, Marj appears in her doorway and tells her that Jim Elliot will be staying in Shell Mera for a few days. He went to Quito on his own, and he's on his way home.

Rachel feels the skin on her arms prickle at the news. She turns towards the window to hide her gladness.

But there is more. "I want to ask you if you would mind moving downstairs. With the Youderians here too, we are going to need your room."

"The Youderians are leaving tomorrow," Rachel says. "As you well know. There's plenty of room."

"Even with the Youderians gone," Marj says, "we have a problem. We're not comfortable billeting you alone upstairs when single men come in. It doesn't look good."

"I've stayed upstairs with Jim and Peter before. Each of us in our own rooms. I don't believe the police had to be called. I don't believe the world came to an end."

She turns to look at Marj, who is still standing in the doorway, patting the little simian sleeping limply on her shoulder. She might be pretty if her eyes were not so fatally close together (for peering through keyholes, Rachel's mother said privately to Rachel, the first time Nate brought his girlfriend home).

"Well, as it happens," Marj says, "several families have booked the second floor in the coming weeks, so I'm afraid we'll have to consider this move permanent."

Rachel goes over to the hangar. Nate is there, in overalls. He lifts his shoulders when she tells him. "Nothing I can do about it," he says. "Marjie is the boss."

"Really? You are called by Christ to be the head of your home.

If Marj does not submit to you as to the Lord, well, then you have a real problem."

He turns his back and starts digging through a bin of nuts and bolts.

She walks towards the door and on impulse goes back. "You know, when you were little, you used to call me Mommy."

He looks over his shoulder at this and his mouth turns down unpleasantly. "I never called you Mommy. That was Ben."

She steps back out into the cruel light of the airstrip. She can still see him, the lovely-looking little fellow he was. How much he resembled her. She can see their dad in a shop, in warm conversation with a lady in a red hat. "Nate was painted by Botticelli," he said, "and so was Rachel." How attached that little boy was to her! Even after his hair and his voice darkened and he developed the goaty smell they all took on at a certain age, even when he stopped talking to her, she would sense his yearning floating across the room. Now he won't look at her.

It's a narrow cell they dump her into, at the opposite end of the house from Nate and Marj's spacious bedroom. *For whosoever has, to him shall be given. But whosoever has not, from her shall be taken away even that which she has.* She is in Coventry, whatever that means, down past the radio room, the storage room, Nate's darkroom. She is a mile from the toilet. She has a tiny window, but there's no real airflow, no space for a desk. She'll be forced to work at the kitchen table, or on her bed. She does have a bed, be thankful for small mercies, and after she's dragged all her things downstairs, she falls to her knees beside it and presses her face into the coverlet. A picture comes to her, Nate under a turned-over chair, she's feeding him peanuts. Is this a game or a punishment? She can't tell. All dead, your brothers? laughs Señora Sevilla. She sees one of them lying face down on the daybed in the kitchen, his shoulders heaving. A big boy, a man really, crying like a baby. Was it Nate? She drifts off, kneeling at the bed, and then the pain in her knees brings her back to herself, and she gets to her feet and undresses and crawls under the cover.

THE YOUDERIANS LEAVE, the plane from Quito lands. Jim Elliot has a surprise in tow, a wife. A tall, thin woman, and he beams as he leads her up the steps of the veranda and introduces her as his *honey*, gazing at her as if she's Helen of Troy.

They were married in Quito two weeks before. A glorious surprise, even for them, and it all happened because, after Jim had wrestled with the question of marriage for years, God simply spoke to him and said, Enough.

"What were you doing at the time?" This is Marj, her face all aglow at the joyful prospect of another missionary bride.

"I was sitting on the stoop in Shandia checking my scalp for ticks. The Indians groom each other every night, and there I was, working at it all alone, feeling sorry for myself, and God said, Go on, then, propose to Betty. I'm tired of listening to you moan about it."

Betty doesn't hit him, she just watches with cool eyes and a little smile. She's bony and plain-faced.

"How did you propose?"

"I wrote her a letter. Get yourself over here pronto, I said, and then Johnny Keenan let me hitch a ride to Quito and I sat myself down in the guesthouse and waited, and after what seemed like years, my angel rode up to the door in a taxi, dressed to the nines in a blue frock and red coat."

"You're making me sound absolutely desperate." His angel smiles, showing a gap between her front teeth you could drive a truck through.

"Well, you've been giving me the runaround for years. But we won't tell folks that part."

Now they're moving into the big house he built on the ridge. "Just the two of you?"

"For the moment." He winks at Elisabeth.

"And how is Peter going to manage on his own?"

"Oh, he's got plans too. He's working on a little gal named Olive, writing letters into the wee hours. He'll wear her down in no time."

It's the sort of brutality God specializes in, putting His finger on the bright thread of your desire and saying, I'll take that, if you please. Cracking you open to the marrow of your bones, digging out the rosy pith, and stuffing mogey cotton in instead.

Rachel hears her own voice. "Do you mind if I ask you a question? How exactly did you get visas? As Plymouth Brethren missionaries?"

"Somebody advised us to apply as linguists, and it worked."

"And you're all trained as linguists?"

Jim shrugs. "I took a summer course."

"I see. Because President Ibarra mentioned to me that they are going to start checking the formal qualifications of foreign workers."

She retires early to her narrow cell. She's been reading through Isaiah in her evening devotions, but God's on His own with that tonight. In the lounge, the others chat for hours. Their raucous laughter gusts down the hall. On the floor, the cockroaches whisper. Does Marj not sprinkle lime powder? Rachel sleeps, and in the distance someone tortures an infant, and she rolls over and sleeps again.

In the dark, in the quiet, she finds herself standing outside the net, intent on an errand elsewhere in the house. Scorpions, God says, breaking His silence. Put your shoes on. She squats to buckle them and makes her way down the hall, passing the kitchen and the radio room. Crossing a patch of moonlight from the windows in the lounge, seeing in the silver light her alabaster limbs, the strong, bare legs of a mountain woman. She comes to the stairway and tramps methodically up and turns down the corridor. Past the upstairs toilet. Past the bed where the lovers float together in a single dream. She walks the length of the house and tramps back downstairs. A sinister noise has started up, she moves towards it with the resolve of a watchman. Squawk, squawk, squawk, squawk. It's Nate's room, and she's at the doorway, and she understands. They're at it, Nate and his bride, Nate and the curly-haired Cyclops, they're riding the bedsprings, panting with one voice, panting, grunting, moaning (hard work, the making of a saint!), huh, huh, huh, huh, huh. She stands still, skewered by the noise. If she had a willie, she'd lift it and piss on the floor. Just here, against their closed door. The boys did that sometimes outside her bedroom. One winter the whole house stank of piss.

They yelp like foxes and fall silent. A quick business when you think about it. She waits a beat. "I hope to God it was worth it," she calls into the crack of the door.

A startled gasp, an angry shout, and she turns and strides down the hall and into the bathroom, where she hooks the little hook and lowers herself, breathless, onto the toilet. She's beginning to feel cold. Her feet hurt, and the sacks of flesh on her chest. She lifts them with her hands to ease the weight. Jugs. Useless jugs of fat she's toted now for almost thirty years.

Footsteps in the corridor, a line of light under the door. "Rachel?" Nate says in a low voice. She can feel his fury through the thin wood. She sits still until he leaves and she hears his bedroom door close.

Back in her room, the mosquito net hangs bride-like over her bed. Her heart is beating funny. She presses her hand to her chest on the left side, below her breast. The skin underneath is bubbled in some places and scaly in others. What fresh hell is this? She pulls off her nightgown and finds her flashlight and peers into her hand mirror, holding her breast up. A big patch of broken skin the colour of beets. The same rash under her right breast. She drops the mirror on the side table, and the beam of her flashlight catches the white splash of her nightgown on the floor. And there's her bible, which she declined to open for evening devotions.

Well, you're up now, the Lord says.

Let me put my nightgown back on first, she says. She shakes the scorpions out of it and struggles into it and crawls into bed, arranging the mosquito net, stuffing her pillow behind her. Then she's propped up in her little tent, trying to catch her breath.

The Old Testament, God says. We're at Isaiah 54.

She tucks her flashlight under her chin. The light on the snowy pages dazzles her. She finds the chapter and puts her eyes to the words, but she can't read. Whatever language this is, she says to God, I don't speak it.

Listen, God says. You think I'm cruel. But you don't see the whole picture. Just read when I ask you to read.

Isaiah 54

Sing, barren woman, you who never bore a child;
Burst into song, shout for joy, you who were never in labour;
Because more are the children of the desolate woman than of her
who has a husband.
Do not be afraid; you will not be put to shame.
Do not fear disgrace; you will not be humiliated.
You will forget the shame of your youth and remember no more the
reproach of your widowhood.
For your Maker is your husband—the Lord Almighty is his name—
the God of all the earth.

It's eight by the time she wakes up. Outside her window, fat drops of water plop into a barrel. Has it rained? No, it's an oropendola in the ficus tree. The night heaves its way to the surface of her mind, a hot, hallucinatory night, like a malaria dream. She listens for a hum in her blood, but all is quiet there. She slept, she's refreshed.

She gets out of bed and dresses with a sense of occasion, tucking in the hem of her favourite pale-blue blouse. Sunlight lies on the floorboards of the kitchen. The children are eating their breakfast and Marj has the coffee made. "Good morning," they all say.

Rachel cuts two slices of bread and butters them, and the bagpipes in her chest start to drone and fill her with a silent vibration. *Rolled away, rolled away, rolled away, every burden of my heart rolled away.*

Nate carries in a wooden crate, the top pried off. "The Quito flight is in," he says. Condensed milk, tinned ham, marmalade! "Carlos Sevilla was on the flight. He's got a ton of cargo. He's hired a barge for the hacienda. They're just loading it."

Rachel closes her eyes for a minute, not speaking to God, just letting Him speak to her. Yes, he says, I meant what I said. She gets up, she leaves her bread and butter on a saucer on the yellow oil-cloth and walks out the door. A crowd is milling around the cargo shed at the far end of the airstrip and they part at the sight of her.

Don Carlos stands outside the shed in a panama hat, smoking. "*Bien, bien, bien,*" he says, tipping his head. "*La patrona del Perú.*" The patron saint of Peru, our lady of the languages.

SINGING IN TONGUES

14

HE RESPECTS HIS DAUGHTER'S NEED for distance, he really does—just one quick call after breakfast to make sure she's safely settled with Olive. Turns out she's not there and Olive hasn't heard from her. David tries her cell and she doesn't pick up. He's scrolling through his contacts, trying to decide which of her friends to call first, his hands starting to tremble, when the land line rings. Sean Youderian. "Pastor Dave! Sorry about the telephone tag. It was just—all hell broke loose here yesterday."

"Before you launch in," David says, "you don't happen to know where Abby is, do you?"

A silence. "I might. She didn't tell you?"

"Tell me what?"

"She's headed to LA. She's got an audition later this week."

"What?"

"Yeah."

"You set this up?"

"Well, sort of. I passed her photo and contact info on to Walter Varga. He's the director. I thought we might have a better chance if somebody else approached her."

"This is for one of your films?"

"I'm a producer."

"I just saw your parents at Wheaton. They didn't say a word."

"Yeah, well, I asked them to keep it on the down-low. We were in some really heavy negotiations with funders. But it's full steam ahead now."

"So Abby—you said LA?"

"Yuh."

"She was driving down on her own?"

"I guess."

"Where's she going to stay?"

A little silence. "You know, Dave, if I could give you a word of advice. Maybe just lighten up on Abby. She's not a kid. She knows what she's doing."

David almost hangs up. I'll track her down, he thinks. There was a world of hurt between the two of us after that talk. She's getting her revenge.

But here's why Sean called—to brief David, which he does, at length. After years of beating the bushes, they've put solid funding in place for a feature film on Operation Auca. They? Sean rhymes off a string of names and titles. There's always been money out there for this story, but his team has a particular vision. First, the story's not going to be watered down. The Lord's hand is going to be visible in everything. Second, the film is going to be pitched to a secular audience, to non-Christians, to the world at large. No more preaching to the choir. A lot of people think those two mandates are incompatible, but picture a Venn diagram. Where the circles overlap, you've got a viewership that's spiritually hungry and a message that'll rock their world. And now they've found a super-wealthy businessman who is grateful to God for his prosperity and wants to give back. He's not a young man, he's dealing with heart disease, and he'd like to live to see the film. The shoot is scheduled for September, and in fact Sean is flying to Ecuador on Thursday with a few other guys. "So here's the thing. You up for joining us in a day or two?"

"What?"

"We could use you to consult on locations."

"You can't be serious."

"'Course I'm serious."

"You realize it's years since I was in Ecuador."

"I do realize. That's why you're perfect. You're going to walk into a scene and say, That was not here, that was not here, nix the cell tower in this shot, whatever. Find a few donkeys."

"I was just away, for Betty's funeral. I can't take off again."

"Don't you have a youth pastor? That Ryan guy? He's dying to step up."

He'd be able to abandon his sermon on the Islamic caliphate, he thinks, and then, to counter the unworthiness of that thought, he suggests September. "Wouldn't it make more sense if I went when you were shooting? Like, in terms of consulting on details?"

But Sean gets an idea in his mind and reason only irritates him. David finally says he'll think about it.

"What's to think about? Dave. *Dave.* You get an all-expense-paid trip to Ecuador. You get a consultancy fee—we should be able to stretch to a couple K. You get a screen credit—wouldn't that be cool? You're helping us take our story to a new generation. What's the downside?"

"Well, Sean, I'll tell you what it is. I'm not sure I'm keen on working with you. I'm pretty disappointed in something Abby told me—"

"She got things wrong," Sean interrupts.

"So there was nothing to it?"

"Let me just say—it was not what she thought. And I've got to believe our Lord forgives."

On this mixed note, the call ends.

David sits stunned in front of his cereal bowl. Oh, God, you have surely broken this day wide open. He goes out the back door into a fine June morning, his cellphone in hand. He sits at the picnic table and texts Karen at the church. *Working at home for a bit.*

The timing is astonishing. Betty dies, Abby is in crisis, and then this. How amazing it would be for Abby. Potentially life-changing. She's made the mistake of trusting in her emotions. A little dryness of the spirit and she thinks God has abandoned her. But then He reaches down and He says, *This.*

Ecuador—David's green world. It gleams in his mind, the leafy longhouses guarded by a harpy eagle, the courage and sacrifice. It's a beauty of a proposition. He's never been back. At first because of Sharon, who was so sick for so long, and then, well, it's hard to say. It was a relief to have a bit of distance from some of the problems there. Things in Tiwaeno were bad enough when he and Sharon were in Ecuador, but worse in the last years of Rachel's life. All sorts of rumours about dementia, heavy metal poisoning, something to do with the diet.

Everybody else went, all his Operation Auca cousins and their kids. It seemed they needed to take a pilgrimage to see where the men had lived and died, and of course he didn't need that. One of the McCully granddaughters, Cheryl, went maybe a year ago and e-mailed to tell David about a tour she took in Cuyabeno. She called it the Toxic Tour and went on at length about the pits of abandoned crude, how fouled the rivers were, and the health problems the local people faced. A lot of people have this romance with the rainforest, and they want Indigenous lands to be left untouched. It's a form of nostalgia. They don't expect us to ride around in horse-drawn buggies in America, but they get all worked up when native people move into the modern era. Anyway, *los afectados* she talked about—they were Secoya and Cofán, not Waorani.

Of course Ecuador will have changed, but he could play a role in taking people powerfully back to the story. And they'll shoot at the guesthouse in Shell Mera, he thinks with a spurt of excitement. Frame houses don't last long in the tropics, and it was abandoned and boarded up in the 1960s. No one had the heart to tear it down, and now it's been rebuilt. Churches in the US raised the money, and crews of volunteers flew down to do the work. David wasn't involved in that project, but if he says yes to Sean, he'll see the house. He pictures Abby in a cotton housedress, standing in front of his mother's blue kitchen cupboards, buttering bread for sandwiches—but then he thinks, *Betty*. Betty's part is sure to be bigger and more dramatic.

He picks up his phone and crafts a text:

Just had a call from Sean and it looks as though I'm going to be a consultant on his movie. Feeling pretty hurt that you didn't tell me what was up—but holding you in my prayers. Abby, sweetheart, I need to know where you are and how you're doing. Love Dad.

He sets the phone down and almost right away it pings. Not Abby. It's an e-mail from Sean.

just in case you're having doubts about God's leading it thrills me to forward you a song we hope to use on the soundtrack. it's by singersongwriter leo duric a brilliant artist and a real man of God and if you google him youll see hes on the cusp of a massive breakout. ran into him and told him about the project and a week later he sent me this song. says he's never had music given to him like this before.

David touches the link. Digital instrumentation and a voice that's pure California schmaltz, all vibrato and emotion. He can't make out the lyrics. They're not in English or Spanish, nor do they sound like any Indigenous language he's ever heard. It must be like a Cirque du Soleil song, written in a made-up language so nobody in the world is privileged above anybody else.

He sits in the spring morning with his head bowed, listening. To a yearning song intended to baffle everybody on earth equally.

MARJ'S MISSION

15

THEY ARGUE IN THE MIDDLE of the night with a sodden baby sleeping between them and they don't make up in the morning. Nate grabs some breakfast and runs out to the hangar to load up for his northern circuit, and then Marj sees him hurrying back to the house and she thinks, Okay, he's coming in to apologize and to kiss me. But all he says as he dashes through the kitchen is, "Toilet." While he's in there, Marj senses someone on the veranda. She opens the door and Sofia's daughter is pressed against the wall, waiting to be noticed. "My mother can't come today," she says in Quichua. "She's dying." Marj is used to this sort of melodrama from her Indian house workers. "Tell her I'll see her tomorrow," she says, or tries to say. The girl seems to understand, she nods and takes off, and Marj goes back into the kitchen. It's exactly seven and the radio is already squawking. David is writhing in the carriage, frantically searching for his food source. Debbie is playing with her doll on the floor. Benjy is somewhere else, ominously quiet. Then there's a tap on the door and the priest from Shandia walks in, looking for Nate. Nobody thinks of this house as Marj and Nate's home. The priest is dressed like any ordinary working guy, in chinos and a worn blue shirt.

"He's just leaving to do his northern circuit," Marj says. "He won't have time to talk to you, I'm afraid." She bends to pick up the baby. Nate's a stickler for his schedule and normally he'd be taxiing down the runway by now. She hears the bathroom door open and he steps into the kitchen behind her. No pleasantries are exchanged in any direction. The priest tells them he hiked in to Shell Mera to see the doctor. He asks Nate if he'll fly him back to Shandia in a day or two.

"Listen, I could tell you I'm fully booked all week, but I don't want to lie. We won't be carrying you fellows in or out anymore. It's a new policy." Nate's voice is even, but Marj knows its registers, she knows this colourless tone.

"Us fellows?"

"You know what I mean."

"And why is that?"

"We just want what's best for the people. We don't fly liquor in either."

Father Alfredo's eyebrows notch down. He and Nate stare at each other like two species of primate meeting in the forest. "You'd fly in empty and leave a man to a dangerous eight-hour slog through the forest just because he's a Catholic."

Nate gives him one of his grins. "I seem to remember you were against us even building an airstrip in Shandia." He's wearing his huge new wristwatch, and just then the alarm in it rings. "I have to go," he says, and does.

Guests will be arriving in a few hours on the bus from Quito, Peter Fleming and his wife. Cramps are crabbing at Marj's belly, the first time since the baby, and Sofia is a no-show again, and now an irritated priest is standing in her kitchen while David grovels at her, trying to get his head into the opening of her blouse. She swings him up and down to distract him. "That watch!" she says. "It's annoying, but it's the only way Nate can manage his circuit. Every station he stops at, the missionaries are starved for somebody to talk to."

The priest just keeps standing there. It would be the Christian thing to offer him a cup of coffee, but then he would sit down, and how do you give your breast to a baby in front of a priest? He's about forty, with thinning hair, and he looks like a nice man, someone who doesn't enjoy the taste of anger. His skin is fair and unevenly tanned, as though one freckle is trying to take over his face. It makes his pale-green eyes look eerie. She asks him where he's staying.

"In the hotel, if you can call it that."

"And I hope nothing's seriously wrong?" She's a nurse, she can ask, and people are usually glad for someone to tell.

"Nah. A bad case of piles. Makes trekking pretty unpleasant." Debbie hits at him with her doll, wanting to show him its open-and-shut eyes, and he leans over and examines it. "Did your father just insult me?" he asks her.

"Yes," she says eagerly.

"I realize alcohol is a big problem in Shandia," Marj says. "Jim says the traders are giving the Indians palm spirits for their tapir skins. He told me one of the men from the village passed out on the trail and in the morning the kids found him half-buried by scavenger beetles."

"So I heard."

"I just mean, it must be hard for priests to preach to the Indians about alcohol if they use it themselves."

She's going to offend him even more, she can't seem to help herself, but he actually appears amused. "Just for the record, I'm not a priest."

"You're not?"

"I'm a friar. We take the vows of poverty, chastity, and obedience, but we don't perform the sacraments. I'm a Capuchin. Do you know the word?"

"I know the monkey. By friar, do you mean a monk?"

"No." He launches into an explanation involving cloisters and vineyards and the copying of manuscripts, but it's hard to listen with David gumming the side of her neck. She's afraid he'll give her a hickey. She pries him loose and sticks a finger in his mouth, and all she really catches is the last word.

"Mendicant," she says thoughtfully, as though she's been listening.

"It means we subsist on the charity of others."

"You do? So do we. Well, we have a base of donors in the US." Marj notices then that he's carrying a letter. Letter writing seems to be his hobby; every week he posts six or seven. Pen Pal Boy, Nate calls him. "I'm sorry, really, about the flight. But give me your mail. I'd be happy to take that."

Then his face turns dark under his mottling. "You'd be happy to take it? You're the authorized agent—you don't have any choice in the matter." He puts it on the table and she picks it up with her free hand and drops it into the mail sack for Quito.

"Don't make us out to be petty. It's not that."

"It's not? You know, I understand your visas are based on a reciprocal arrangement with the government. Regarding providing transportation in the region."

"I really don't know the details. But if Nate says he can't carry you, there's nothing I can do about it."

He watches her for another minute and then reaches into his back pocket and pulls out another letter. "Why don't I give you this one too," he says, and leaves without saying goodbye. He walks like someone whose bum is hurting.

She waits a minute after the door closes and then lifts the second letter and studies the envelope. It's addressed to a government office in Quito, the Ministerio del Interior. It's stamped, but it's not sealed—maybe he was having second thoughts about what he wrote. Holding David squirming against her with one arm, she slides the letter out of the envelope and shakes it open. It's in Spanish. But even an Idaho farm girl who (newly married and swiftly pregnant) puked her way through language school can make out phrases like *son misioneros protestantes* and *iglesia evangélica* and *la conversión de los indios*. And the words *avión* and *servicio de aire*, over and over. He's a little rat! He's ratting on them! But does he have any pull at the ministry? Seemingly not—the letter is addressed to *Señor Ministro*. She seals it up for him and righteously drops it into the mailbag.

Perfecta is banging above with her broom, stretching out the cleaning because it's more peaceful upstairs. Marj needs to think about supper. Peter and Olive will arrive around four, they're coming in on the bus from Quito. Maybe Perfecta can get fish at the dock. The children will usually eat fish without a fuss. *Benjy.* Marj dashes down the hall and finds him in their bedroom, running a dead cockroach along the baseboard like a toy truck. She makes him throw it in the toilet and drags him to the radio room to play with Debbie. Still cradling David, she takes a call from Roger Youderian, the missionary at Macuma who can turn a request for a five-pound can of lime powder into a ten-minute life-and-death saga. "I'll put it on your list for tomorrow," she says firmly. *Over and out.* Finally she settles on the rocker in the kitchen, where she can watch the kids through the glass while she feeds David, who pauses now and then to use her nipple as a teething ring. She has never heard of a healthy child resisting solid food this long. They've had wild battles, but in the end she needs him to nurse too, and when she gives in, he lies looking victoriously at her out of the corner of his eye as he sucks. Not long ago, her mother wrote, "Tell me about an average day." She wrote back, "Mother, you have no idea what you're asking." Then her mother wrote to say, "You are Martha in the Bible, burdened with care. Find time to sit at the Lord's feet." She didn't know whether to laugh or cry. Not Martha, she's Jesus Christ himself, walking on water. Benjy has his face up to the window. He doesn't respond to her smile, just presses his nose against the glass. She should have scrubbed his hands after the cockroach. Oh, well. She was up three times in the night, once before the fight and twice after. *Who can find a virtuous woman, for her price is far above rubies.* Even Nate has no idea. She and Nate are on a teeter-totter. She's squatted awkwardly on the ground, pots and pans and the shortwave radio and all the account books on her lap and her three children clinging to her head and shoulders, while Nate, dashing and handsome, is perched silhouetted against the sky, chatting with God and the angels, immune to the very notion of gravity. If she tried to tell him how she feels, he'd get her a watch with a timer. *Ring ring*, and she'd pry David off her nipple and say, That's it for now, kiddo. Poor David—he wasn't even allowed to be born on his own terms. Marj wasn't due for another week, but Dr. Johnston had flown in for a clinic. Her back was killing her and when he said, "Would you like me to break your waters while I'm here?" she couldn't resist. So then there was David, dazed and bleary like a bear cub dragged out of a cave in the middle of winter. Maybe that's why he's hanging on to her now. We all have our ways. Mrs. Dr. Tidmarsh used to order a particular candy from Quito, some melting caramel thing, and allow herself one a day. She told Marj she thought about that candy from the minute she got up in the morning until she finally ate it in the evening. Until she finally *et* it, she said. You have to have some little thing for yourself, she said. Mrs. Dr. Tidmarsh—now, of course, she's back in England, paralyzed from the fifth vertebra down, and when they talk about Nate's accident and how terrible it was that he was in a body cast for a year and how wonderful that God fully restored his health, no one ever mentions her. That sadness lies in Marj's chest like sludge, like the silt left in a building after a flood. Her abdomen tightens just then like a mini labour pain, and she breathes until it eases. The cramp leaves a new sadness behind, for the priest, who will be forced to trek a day through the jungle when Nate could have him home in half an hour. Marj had hemorrhoids when she was pregnant with Benjy. It was shocking how much it hurt. She and Nate came to Ecuador to do good, to make things better for people, and the priest looked at her warmly and then switched to looking at her like she was the enemy, and in a way she is.

David has stopped sucking, he's drifting off. She lays him carefully on his side in the carriage and seats the older two at the table and gives them a snack of milk and some little crackers that are too stale for the adults to eat. The mailbag is sagging open on the kitchen table, and there's the priest's letter, the first one he handed her, a fat letter bound for the US, to somebody in North Carolina named J. Sampson. Just *J. Sampson*. No *Mr.* or *Mrs.* or *Miss.* It feels like he's taunting her. Flaunting something, his privacy, or the way rules don't apply to him. She picks up the letter and tests the seal. Glue is always gummy in this humidity. You can tease a flap open without having to rip it at all, and envelopes reseal themselves with just a little pressure. "Dear Podge," the letter begins. Podge?

Dear Podge,

It's siesta. I was going to write this letter after breakfast and just as I sat down a man from the settlement upriver was at the window saying, "My wife is dying." This is not always as dire as it sounds. There are only two states of being in the Quichua tongue, living or dying. You're on the upswing or you're on the down. Nevertheless I packed up my kit and went back with him by canoe. I found a woman of about forty with a low fever. Likely pneumonia. I started her on an oral course of penicillin. Her husband was not pleased. He wanted what he called "sticking medicine." This is the fault of my new neighbours, the jolly gospellers. They give penicillin by injection because they have a refrigerator to store it, and the Quichua are convinced it's a more powerful magic.

F tells me you're back in the States and receiving mail at this address. I think it must be 18 months or 2 years since we wrote each other (fall 1953?). I seem to remember regaling you with stories of my then-nemeses, the Tidmarshes (Marmite-eating Brits, straight out of Somerset Maugham, although much-loved by the people). Their tenure in Shandia ended with a plane crash, and I had a year on my own (as it were), with the occasional company of the priest who comes from Coca to say mass, a Spanish Franciscan who is a progressive thinker regarding the Indigenous peoples. I was contemplating asking the Ministry to impose some sort of territories on Pastaza Province so we and the evangélicos are not constantly undermining whatever progress each is making. But just as I was working myself up to write that letter, two American men stepped out of the trailhead from Shell Mera, followed by five or six porters laden with all their paraphernalia. And that was that. As with termites, once you see the evangélicos in the flesh, it's always too late to do anything about it.

Marj finds that her hands are trembling. The first personal envelope she's ever illicitly opened and it is turning out to be gold. Well, okay, the third or fourth, but the others were not worth counting. She shoos Debbie and Benjy out onto the veranda and sinks into the rocker. The letter is one-sided on onion skin, and (judging from a little smudge) written in real ink. She counts the pages. In what sort of reality would you have the leisure to write a six-page letter?

My new neighbours are from the Pacific Northwest and are totally green. They spurn my counsel so, absolved of all responsibility, I lie in my hammock on the ridge above the Rio Talac and watch events unfurl. They spent their first few months here extending the airstrip and building a school, a clinic, and a house right on the banks of the Jatun Yaku. They were almost finished when the river rose overnight and washed it all away. They moved up the bank and started again. It rained for five days and nights and the river rose higher. Elliot, the boss of the operation, stops by my house and postulates that the end times are upon us, when weather systems will go crazy and usher in the apocalypse. It floods like this every second year, I say (a slight exaggeration, as this flood was spectacular). But the Indians build their houses right on the riverbank, he says. Well, yes, they do. Palm huts. They build them in a day. I deliver this information and settle back into my hammock. Donkeys live a long time.

But they've succeeded with rebuilding their airstrip, which now runs from the Jatun Yaku to the Talac. An airstrip in the rainforest is no small enterprise. Just the building of it changes a settlement, because all the able-bodied men are on wages. And then of course it's built and the gringos start bringing stuff in. Bags of concrete. Chainsaws. Generators. Cans of diesel lashed to the plane. The pilot who serves these missionaries has fabricated some sort of rig to carry in sheets of tin for roofing. He's an American, eponymously named Saint, an enterprising fellow. He has about him the glamour of those who slip the surly bonds of earth—the young men in the settlement all imitate his way of wearing his cap (while I, formerly the object of their admiration, can hardly walk due to an infirmity I won't bore you with). Anyway, in a few short months this settlement has been transformed—for those who can afford it. Me, I'm sticking with thatch. It's cooler than tin and quieter in a rainstorm. And it's entertaining. I get both snakes and rats living in my roof, and every week or so they put on a show.

As for my own ministry, not a lot has changed since our correspondence lapsed. Please take for granted my avid interest in all you are up to and write me at length. M told me about your reading club and I laughed out loud. We don't need Sigmund Freud to tell us what a snake means. My own stash of reading is low. Send Graham Greene if you can. Start collecting records for me. The gospellers are corrupting me. Now I want a generator, not for the lights, but for music. I want Robert Schumann, Carnaval. I discovered it the year I was in Atlanta and enjoyed it, but I didn't know then (I just learned from an old New Yorker M sent me) that Schumann composed each of those 21 pieces as a portrait of one of his friends. Send me the album, and I will tell you which piece is Podge.

The handwriting is pleasing and clear, and something between the lines makes emotion swell in Marj's throat. It's not the priest's words that move her—it's being inside his mind, like stepping into an otherworldly garden full of delicate plants she's never even imagined. He thinks of himself as doing good and them (Nate, Jim, Pete) as doing bad: this hits her again with a force that dazes her.

She'd like to keep the letter, she longs to keep it. But it's Thursday, she has to bundle up the Quito mail, so she presses the envelope under a can of evaporated milk until it's resealed and drops it into the bag. Perfecta is back in the kitchen and looks at Marj with reproach, as if she knows what's going on. But reproach is Perfecta's usual expression. The radio squawks. It's Helen Swift, she runs the mission guesthouse in Quito. She's calling because Peter Fleming asked her to let Marj know that he and Olive have decided to take a commercial flight to Shell Mera. The driver just took them to the airport. That means they'll be at Shell in an hour. She doesn't say why they're not taking the bus, and all Marj says is, "All right, then, thanks for letting me know, over and out."

Don't confuse a two-way radio with a telephone—that's a lesson Marj learned the hard way her first year in Shell Mera.

OLIVE AND PETER are finally moving to Shandia after months of language study. They're slated to stay with Marj and Nate for three or four days while they sort out their gear. But yesterday Olive ended up in the hospital in Quito. They talked about postponing the move, but when she was discharged, they couldn't go back to the guesthouse because Helen had given their room away. Helen was the one who suggested they come to Shell Mera anyway, that they fly instead of taking the bus. She thought it would be a good place for Olive to recuperate, with Marj being a nurse.

Olive sits on the veranda all afternoon, pale but resolute. Marj, who only met her once before, sees that she is not the sort of girl to make a fuss about things, she is not a girl who will use her troubles to get sympathy. She plays Parcheesi with Debbie and braids her hair. They spy a narrow strip of lawn moving like a green river and call Marj out to see. A phalanx of ants, stretching from the road to a cave opening at the foot of the kapok tree. Hundreds of thousands of them, each with its little flag of green.

"Leafcutter ants," Marj says. They must have a practical reason for stashing all those leaves underground, but they always look brave and obedient and somehow deluded to Marj.

"I wonder if Shandia has ants like this?"

"No question. If you're short of protein, you can eat them. The Indians do."

Emotions flicker on Olive's face, as if her feelings are all dialed up. She's not beautiful in a conventional way, but she's lovely all the same, with her dark eyes and eyebrows and her fair hair. Marj's mother was firmly against beauty, the way it made girls vain and then faded, leaving them with nothing. But surely, Marj thinks as she goes back to the kitchen, a mother could rejoice in some middle ground.

Nate is home now, he and Pete are out by the hangar. Perfecta appears on the path from the dock. She's managed to buy a lovely three-pound trout and Marj chops up four or five tamarillos to spread over it while it bakes. She never knows what to do with tamarillos. She'll call this *trucha con salsa*. She puts rice to cook and makes a salad with avocado. Olive comes in and offers to set the table. She moves slowly, lining the cutlery up precisely. Marj feels slow herself, weighed down by the fight she had with Nate. Soon it will be bedtime and they'll talk.

But after supper, after she's gotten the kids to sleep, Peter comes down the stairs and says, "I wonder, would you mind sitting with Olive for a while? She's quite upset."

Olive is lying on the bed crying like there's no tomorrow, trying to muffle the noise with a pillow. It's stifling in their room, as though her sorrow has clogged the air. Marj goes to the window and opens it wide. She sits on the edge of the bed and puts her arm around Olive.

"I miss my mother," Olive says when she can finally talk. This is her second miscarriage; she lost a baby at Christmas.

"Oh, my poor girl," Marj says. "I'm sure you do. Did you manage to phone her?"

"No, I didn't call. I never told them we were expecting. It would only have worried them. I'm their only kid, I am all they think about." Olive lifts herself up on one elbow and digs in the pocket of her skirt for her hanky. "I feel bad about causing so much trouble. Peter and Jim wanted to be single missionaries. They should have stuck with their plan."

"You didn't force Peter to marry you."

"Oh, maybe I did by some kind of telepathy. I just wouldn't let it go." Her voice is a little hoarse from all the crying.

"Let me tell you, I know what Pete was like before you got here. I can't believe he ever thought he could get along without you."

Olive gazes at her gratefully and then her shoulders start to shake and she presses her face back into the pillow. "You know what?" she says when she comes up for air. "I'm sort of glad this happened. I've been to Shandia and I'm scared to death of living there. How would I have managed in that hut with a tiny baby? And so, if you want the truth, I'm glad!" She is overtaken with sobs again. "Oh, oh, oh, oh," she cries.

Marj leans over Olive and strokes her hair. "Olive. Are you having pain?"

"No. No, it just hurts so much. Here." She touches her heart. "I wish I hadn't said that. I didn't even know I was thinking it until I said it out loud."

"Olive, darling. It's totally natural. And having to go through this twice, well, it's heartbreaking."

"The first time wasn't this hard. I didn't realize I was pregnant until it happened. My body felt different, but I didn't know what it was. I thought it was just, you know, all that loving."

She manages a smile, and just then the generator goes off and the light goes out. The tumult of the forest fills the sudden quiet. "Daddy turned the jungle on," Marj and the kids always say. Olive slides over on the bed and Marj stretches out beside her. Her own cramps are gone, but she feels as if her limbs are made of cement and it's a huge relief to lie down.

"Pete confided in us when he proposed to you," she says. "And we were all so excited when you wrote back to say yes."

Olive emits a little breath of pleasure. She lifts her left hand and looks at her rings in the dark.

"It must have been strange for you to be apart for your engagement."

"It was. It was really strange. Pete's dad came to the door one day and asked me to go for a drive. He said, 'I am under strict instructions from my son,' and he took me to a jewellery store. Pete had money from when his mother died, and he told his dad I was to have whichever ring I wanted." She doesn't strike Marj as a talkative girl, but her words come out in a rush. "I had no idea how much money there was and I was too shy to ask, so I picked out the ring I liked best from the tray with the smaller diamonds. The big ones didn't appeal to me anyway. And then afterwards, we were sitting in the car and Mr. Fleming swivelled around, and I had this awful feeling he was going to put the ring on my finger and even try to kiss me—like, give me the kiss Peter had sent for me. So I reached over and took the box and put the ring on myself! It was kind of a funny moment."

Marj feels pressed into the mattress by the weight of her breasts. The left one has a hot, hard patch above the nipple and she reaches up and starts to massage it gently, because she can't deal with another bout of mastitis. "You were, what, twenty?"

"Twenty-two."

"I was twenty-three when we got married and twenty-five when we came to Ecuador. But I still felt like a kid. And then . . . well, you have to grow up fast on the mission field."

"Pete leaving the way he did—I kind of grew up then. I don't see life the same way now. I used to think he was perfect, for one thing. It's probably a good thing I got over that." Her voice is not childish exactly, but it's soft and light, and she speaks with the west coast accent that always sounds citified to Marj. "He had no idea what to do when this happened last Christmas. He's been better this time."

The moon is almost full and the light from the night sky has seeped into the room, showing everything up in tones of silver and grey. Olive and Peter's clothes are arranged on hangers (hangers!) along the row of hooks and their suitcases are stacked on the bench, both of their sun hats on top. They're a tidy pair. Marj's thoughts drift down to the mess in the kitchen, to the children. The baby will be halfway through his first heavy sleep, he'll be starting to dream about her.

"It is very hard to lose a baby, let alone two," she says. "But you're right, having children on the mission field is not easy either. Schooling is a big problem. We're facing that in a few weeks with Debbie. Am I going to send my six-year-old on her own to boarding school in Quito? Nate and I are on different sides of that question. And honestly, as hard as it is to face a miscarriage, I think you should treasure this time on your own with your husband. You have the privilege of working closely together. You have a very special calling. My work is interesting, meeting missionaries from all over. But you will be winning souls for Christ."

"Souls," Olive says in her soft voice. "Exactly what are they? That's what I wonder. Did the baby I lost on Tuesday have one?"

Marj is shocked into silence. They're on their backs staring up at the mosquito net tied into a huge knot above them, and

Olive is very still beside her. Finally Marj says, "That's the sort of question only a theologian can answer. Why don't you talk it over with Jim?"

Olive lets out a little snort. "When Jim talks, I see his mouth move, but I don't understand a word he's saying."

Marj has to suppress a laugh. It's always bugged her, the way Jim Elliot goes on, although she has never before encountered anyone who didn't revere him. "Well, Pete, then," she says. "You and Pete will be a huge comfort to each other."

She has no idea if that is true. At supper Peter was pretty much silent. No doubt he's finding this hard, though Marj sensed that the quiet at the table was mainly out of respect for Olive and her misery. How much of the family burden do men ever carry? They couldn't carry it and do what they do. She's pretty sure that, in spite of their decorum at supper, Pete and Nate will by now have given in to temptation: they'll be sitting in the dark, drinking Pepsi and trading stories about the Auca Indians.

IN THE NIGHT, Nate turns on the bedside lamp and drags her up out of a deep well of sleep. David is wailing against his shoulder.

"Holy cow," Marj moans, shielding her eyes. "This has got to end. I'm going to start putting Tabasco on my boobies." She shrugs herself up against the pillow. "This is newborn behaviour. He will take a few swallows and then he'll fall right back to sleep."

Nate hands the baby to her and lies down himself, facing in the other direction. He's never liked to watch her nurse. He'll be back snoring again in two minutes if she doesn't talk fast.

"Listen, Nate," she says as she pulls down her nightgown and gets David settled. "I'm sorry we didn't get time together before bed. I had to go and sit with Olive. She's really taking it hard, poor kid. And then I had to set the bread for tomorrow, we were down to one loaf. But I wanted to talk—I thought all day about what you said. I know this is a big thing to you. But you have to listen to me. Nate. Nate."

Sometimes she misses his plaster cast; she could rap on it with her knuckles to get his attention. Finally he rolls over.

"Nate, I am in quicksand up to my knees and sinking fast. If I keep very calm and focused, we will maybe survive until these kids are all out of diapers. But we can't take on a whole new ministry."

It was Tuesday he spied the huts. He's been looking for years, just out of curiosity, criss-crossing the territory south of the Napo any time he had spare fuel on his flight home. He's seen abandoned houses several times, because the Auca apparently move around a lot. But the day before yesterday he located an inhabited settlement for the first time. Beside a little stream an hour's walk north of the Curaray, hidden away in dense forest. First he spied a yucca plantation, a *chagra*, big and well tended. Just past the *chagra* he saw four palm-leaf longhouses, spaced out among the trees. And he saw people on the paths between the houses. He took a good look and noted the coordinates and then turned around and flew back to Shandia to tell Jim and Betty. Marj is hurt about that part of it, although she's not going to say so. She can feel Nate's excitement, still as strong as yesterday. It's like having a stranger in their bed, preventing them from talking frankly.

Nate folds his pillow so he can lie on his side and watch her face. "There's nothing for you to take on," he says. "This won't make a single difference to your work. We'll just start a campaign of gift drops, get them interested, let them know we're friendly. That's all it is."

"That's all for now, but eventually you will want to go in."

He shakes this off.

"Nate. Of course you will. Otherwise, what's the point? Remember what it was like for us when you crashed? When you sent out that distress signal and then went dead? You give me one more shock like that and it will finish me altogether. Nate." She waits until his eyes focus on her again. "Honey, I am really tired."

He reaches over and cups her forehead gently. "Eagle wings," he says. That's his shorthand for: *Those who hope in the Lord will renew their strength. They will soar on wings like eagles; they will run and not grow weary, they will walk and not be faint.*

"That verse has a lot more to do with you than it does with me," Marj says.

David is already asleep, as she predicted. Nate notices, and gets out of bed, reaching down for him. When he straightens up, she sees the length of the baby's body against his, and it shocks her. That is *all her.* Every molecule of that child's body came from hers. "Thank you, honey," she says when Nate comes back. It's kind of him to get up with David, he almost never does it, but he hasn't changed his diaper, and the clammy mess between David's legs will wake him up extra-early and quite possibly leave him with diaper rash. So really, how much help is it?

He turns off the lamp and crawls into bed. As her eyes adjust to the dark, she makes out the thrilling angle of his shoulder. Prudently, she shifts over on the bed, leaving a safe zone between them. Oh! The tireder she gets, the more she wants him—it's nuts. She's turning into nothing but a body, the rest of her is shutting down. That's what having babies and nursing babies year after year does to you. Her hunger for Nate and its astonishing satisfactions—it's the sort of thing she would have thought belonged to the worldly and the unsaved, who live to be intoxicated. Or at least to women who are sexier-looking than she is, women who would be a natural match for Nate. But it turns out it doesn't matter. Rhythm, speed, steadiness, guts—that's what Nate cares about. He throws something her way, throws it hard and fast, and deftly she catches it.

"Nate, I hate to let you down," she says.

He doesn't respond.

"I hate to let you down, but I really don't get it. All we do, your huge circuit, and the way you maintain the plane and the generators, and the things you invent, and keeping all those missionaries safe, and building the clinic and hospital—it's more than enough."

He rolls onto his back and lies staring upwards. "The priest, when he was here today—did he talk about Rachel? Did he say what she's up to?"

"Rachel? How would he know anything about Rachel?"

"He's been going in to the hacienda. Jim told me. He hikes in every month to work with Don Carlos's campesinos. To pull teeth and say Mass or whatever he does. He might know if she's making any progress."

In the dim light, Marj stares at Nate with sudden understanding. "This is about Rachel."

He makes a dismissive noise in the back of his throat and lays an arm over his eyes.

But it is! It's about Rachel, who walked around the house for months crowing about the glory of her mission, constantly singing, "Will there be any stars, any stars in my crown, when at evening the sun goeth down?" Before Rachel came, the Auca were just a galvanizing rumour. Then she took off for the hacienda, and someone happened to mention that Don Carlos had an Auca woman living there, and Nate asked Don Carlos what Rachel was doing, and he said she was learning the Auca language from the woman, and then Jim said Rachel had more or less confided in him that she felt called to reach the Auca, and they would joke about her walking into the forest and ending up in a stewpot. Through the months, Nate has more than once mused about Rachel's progress, wondering how fluent she'll be by now, and whether she'll have a plan for making contact. And now he's spied the houses, and he sees a chance to scoop her.

Marj raises herself up on one elbow and studies Nate. The day Rachel with no advance notice climbed off the Quito bus (this was months ago, before David was born), Marj instinctively put her in an upstairs room as far away from them as possible. And a good thing, because when they went to bed, Nate couldn't contain himself. "Why is she here? Why is she here?" He kept putting this to Marj as a serious question, as if she should know. "First she follows me to South America, and then she follows me here. I don't want her in the house."

"Whatever did she do to make you feel that way?"

Then he told her things she had never heard before about his childhood, the years when their parents were so often away, when she ran the house like a tyrant.

"She was mean to you."

"Yeah, she was mean. Of course she was mean. Dad had one of those leather straps teachers use, and she strapped us with that. Morning, noon, and night. But it wasn't even that. Probably we deserved the lickings. It was more . . . Well, I don't know, Marj. I see the way you are with the kids, and she was not like that."

"But she wasn't your mother. She was only a kid herself, left with all that responsibility. It's your mother you should be mad at."

"I hardly know my mother. Rachel *was* our mother. She was more than our mother, she was like our king. We had to obey her every command. And we were so poor. We couldn't heat the house properly, we were never warm. I had terrible chilblains, I had pneumonia half the time. We were hungry! She was getting money from our grandparents and not buying food with it."

"She was spending it on herself?"

"No, not even that. One day Ben found dollar bills half-burned in the stove. It was like our real problems weren't big enough, she wanted this drama where we were suffering and starving, like children in a fairy tale. So she could have more power over us. Or so she would look like some sort of martyr to everybody in the town."

It was hard to believe. Rachel didn't strike Marj as having much flair for drama, or caring a lot what people thought of her. And this story was crazy. Rachel's eyes were as pale and strange as a husky dog's, but she didn't seem insane, just lonely, overbearing, and with very little talent for getting people to like her. But who knows? Marj was always baffled when she peered down into the weird old stage set of Nate's childhood, at a family both high-falutin and impoverished, like banished heirs to a throne, full of culture and full of its opposite, strange to a degree she was only gradually discovering.

"Nate," she says now, leaning over him to get his attention in the dark. "Forget Rachel. You're not ending up in the jungle with a lance through your heart."

This does get his attention. He rouses himself and sits up in the bed, pulling up his knees.

"You know, Marj, I haven't told you everything. I didn't tell you exactly how it happened."

"Okay. So tell me."

"Well, remember there was a really low ceiling on Tuesday? The clouds were rock-solid all day, they never broke. But when I was flying home, just as I was crossing the Napo, a hole opened to the southwest. It was shaped exactly like a keyhole, and it was low, close to the horizon, so the sun was streaming through at an angle—it was like one of those pictures you see of the Rapture. Everything was in 3-D. The big old kapok trees were throwing shade on the canopy, and I could see the shadow of the Piper skimming over the jungle ahead of me, almost as if it was leading me on. That was how I spied that dimple in the forest. The *chagra*. I would never normally have seen it. It was like I literally saw God's hand. I saw God reach down and open the clouds with a finger. He was saying, Look, Nate. Look. There you go." His eyes are fixed on her through this whole story. "If God's calling me, Marjie, he's calling you. You made a vow."

He drops back on his pillow, and after a minute she lies down too.

He has never, ever pulled this before. Not *once* since the day she stood with a bunch of woody-stemmed lilacs in her hand

and promised to obey him. The minister explained what the vow meant: Nate obeyed the Lord, and Marj obeyed Nate with the same respect. It struck Marj then as an efficient arrangement—and she knew she had more hope of dealing with Nate than she ever did with God.

She lies on her back and listens to the song of the crickets and frogs and cicadas, and to Nate's breathing, which, now that he's said his piece, quickly turns to a gentle snore. Possibly she sleeps, because the next time she opens her eyes, the room is bright and her thoughts are clear and Nate is lying on his side looking at her.

Who can find a virtuous woman, her children rise up and call her blessed.

"Listen," she says, rolling over to face him full on. "I'll stop fighting you on this. But Debbie is not going to boarding school in Quito. I'm not sending my little girl to an *orphanage* a hundred miles away."

In the morning light, she sees a blink of assent so quick only a wife would catch it.

16

AT HOME IN IDAHO IT's fall, the cottonwoods will be turning yellow. Here in the big guesthouse on the Rio Pastaza, the lounge becomes a first-grade classroom. Their daughter is thrilled, gravely taking on her letters and numbers. School is what this fall will always be about for Debbie: for her whole life, she'll remember sitting on a stump stool in a neon-green yard, watching leafcutter ants and reading *Dick and Jane*.

Davey. That fall he finally develops a taste for solid food, and Marj orders canned applesauce by the case. But still he lies in bliss as he nurses, patting the top of her breast as if to console her. All this drops into a crevasse in his pristine little brain, so deep he'll never dig it out. He'll always love applesauce, and one day he'll love nestling with a woman, but he won't know why.

Ben. That fall Benjy turns four. When Nate takes off in the mornings, Ben climbs into Marj's lap in the radio room to watch, it's their new morning ritual. He watches until the plane vanishes and then he gets down and goes outside and rides his new tricycle up and down the veranda, scooping up impressions with his bright-blue eyes. The clouds, the geckos, a yellow dog he sees and later dreams about, Oresto with his scythe cutting the grass, the puffing white mountain. He's at the in-between age, still floating in the ocean of sensation but starting to feel *yesterday* like solid ground beneath his feet.

For Marj, this fall will always be about Operation Auca, and the deal she made with her husband and the dangerous place it took them. The silences between them, which used to feel companionable and now feel cold. He's standing on the veranda watching a condor over the river, and she leans on the railing beside him. For a second she sees him the way a stranger might, this beautiful, remote man in his prime, his coiled energy, his quick impulses (so private, like a car engine whose inner workings she can't imagine). And then he's her husband again, and her senses open to him, his musculature and the easy grace of his posture, his beautiful hand on the veranda railing.

Without a word she goes back to the storeroom and begins to unpack the grocery order. She pries open a crate of macaroni, stacking the boxes neatly on a shelf, feeling a bit sick to her stomach. She has no divine illumination to counter Nate's, just an instinct about the whole chain-of-command thing. You obey your husband, who believes he's obeying the Lord, but what if your husband got it wrong?

She was never called to be a missionary. When she was a girl, when missionaries came to speak in her church, she always felt a secret cringing, like they were announcing themselves as water dowsers, or spirit mediums, some job that required a special gift nobody normal would want. She knew exactly what she did want. She wanted to go to Boise and train as a nurse, she wanted the protocols and the expertise and the navy cape, and she wanted to share an apartment with her high school friend Susan, a suite in a particular building she had often admired as they drove by. And that's what she did, all of it, including the apartment in the block with the stained glass transom over the door. Then she agreed to a blind date with a mechanic in the air force, a lonely guy from the East stationed in Boise, and that was that. South America was just part of the Nate Saint package from the beginning. Ecuador, where she would run a house and raise kids, just like her mother did, except there are more vermin here than on the farm and supplies are harder to get.

She did kind of regret putting her nursing aside. But one day, when they were new to Shell Mera, Johnny Keenan radioed and said he was bringing in a Quichua man who had been attacked by the Auca. He hadn't been able to rouse anybody at the clinic and he asked her to meet the float plane at the dock. The man was dead by the time Johnny landed. He had been speared six or seven times, and they had yanked the lances out to get him into the plane and that had done even more damage. Marj had dealt with her share of terrible car accidents, working in emergency in Boise, but this was like nothing she had ever seen.

Nate is wrong, there's no other way to understand it. He asked her to barter his life and safety for their little daughter's welfare. A deal like that is never meant to hold. If he knew for sure he had God's leading, he would never have made a deal. He would just have said, No, Marjie. You have to listen to God. Now it's her job to bring Nate to his senses, and she knows she can. She feels something like exhilaration at the thought.

She makes macaroni and sausage meat for supper, a special treat. "You said *we*. About the gift drops to the Auca. Who did you mean?"

"Ed McCully. The settlement I saw from the air is pretty close to Arajuno, and we can use the airstrip there. And Jim. Jim's been keen for a long time."

"Well, we'll need to get everyone in for a meeting."

"What?"

"The fellows. Marilou. Betty."

He stares, she can see his mind working. She looks mildly back, giving him nothing, and reaches for his plate to start the cleanup.

Marilou and Betty are both missionaries in their own right, which gives them an authority Marj might not have. And, she thinks as she dumps soap into the dishpan and stirs up a few bubbles, they are both extraordinary. Marilou lives in the most isolated and dangerous station, she has two tiny boys, and she takes everything beautifully in stride. She had a fancy job in the US, she was the music director of a huge city church, the first lady music director they had ever had, and when Marj saw her walk up from the airstrip with her navy high heels and her fuchsia lipstick and clip-on earrings, she said to herself, This girl will not last a year in the jungle. But Marilou has thrived. She claims to like working with the Quichua more than with the musicians at Chicago First Baptist, who she says wasted all their energy on gossip and infighting. She says the Indians are *more civilized*, much kinder to each other and to her. So for her grit and her happy nature and her lack of airs, Marilou is respected by everyone.

And Betty—she's almost like one of the men. Before she married Jim, she worked on the other side of the mountains, with the Colorados, Indians who spread mud and red dye on their hair to make stiff lids of it, and paint horizontal black stripes on their faces and bodies. Alone—she worked there alone. And she is terrific in meetings. She speaks with absolute confidence about spiritual things, as though Jesus has just been sitting in the flesh at her breakfast table talking to her. Even pregnancy didn't put her fully in the women's camp. Right up until the ninth month, her belly looked like a tightly packed knapsack, and Marj always pictured her unclipping it at night and setting it on a chair before she stretched out in bed, her usual lithe self.

She dries the milk glasses and lines them up on the shelf. She can't drop in to visit Marilou and Betty, and she can't talk freely on the radio. She can only count on their good sense and their love for their husbands. She can only make sure Nate ends up in a room with both of them.

And Peter and Olive, she decides. Cautious types.

"Why don't you include Peter and Olive?" she says to Nate, who is still at the table nursing his tea. "You can't involve one Shandia couple and not the other."

He frowns.

She drops the dishtowel and goes to him. "You really need a haircut," she says, reaching over and touching her fingers to the back of his neck. "If you can find the clippers, I'll do it after the kids are in bed."

He seems willing enough when they pick a date. She sets about getting the rooms ready and plans out meals for fourteen. On that morning, Nate flies them all in. Olive and Peter arrive first. They seem relaxed and happy, they've got their honeymoon glow back. Then Jim and Betty and their baby, Sharon, six months old now, a little blondie who looks just like her dad. Then Ed and Marilou and their two sturdy little guys. Where did Marilou find that skirt? An Inca design that is so much nicer than anything you see in the market at Baños. Nobody mentions the purpose of the meeting. Marj can sense anticipation in the air, but nobody says a thing. Perfecta has made canned-ham sandwiches and they eat lunch on the veranda. It's always a joy to be together and to see each other's kids. A hoatzin screams from the big tree, and Marilou's older boy screams back and makes them all laugh. Marilou's eyes hold Marj's for a minute, thoughtfully. We'll be all right, Marj thinks. They finish eating and the women go upstairs and settle the little ones for their naps, and Marj asks Sofia to keep all the kids up there while the adults gather in the kitchen.

Nate is the one who opens the meeting, standing tall against the turquoise cupboards, wearing jeans and the white shirt that is such a beast to iron (she was up until eleven), her golden-haired husband flushed with excitement and glowing with that special light the priest noticed. He's not nervous, he doesn't know what it is to be nervous, but he is sober with this new role. She's never known him to try to sway people with words. Facts, yes, words, no; normally he uses words like a technician, like a man accustomed to the shortwave radio. But to her surprise, he starts his story early in the morning, taking them into his day, recounting all the judgment calls he has to make, what it is to be constantly monitoring cargo weight, fuel, time, the radio, the wind, the clouds. He takes them into a landing, coming in low over the trees, avoiding the chickens and the children that wander onto the airstrip, dodging potholes, responding to the Indians who crowd around the plane, ministering to the missionaries, who haven't seen another white guy in weeks.

And then flying home with a bit of extra fuel in his tank, and making the discovery. He paints the picture with incredible vividness, as he did for Marj in the night: the keyhole in the clouds, the light streaming through like in the Rapture. And people on the paths between the houses, hearing the plane, lifting their heads in the sudden light-and-shadow. Men, women, children. How did he know they weren't Quichua? They were naked as jaybirds, he says, and the hush in the room is broken by excited laughter.

He speaks over them with evident emotion. "Lots of days I feel close to the Lord when I fly, but that day, I literally saw His hand. I saw God reach down and open the clouds with a finger. Look, Our Lord was saying. These are lost souls, whom I love and gave my Son to save."

Nothing is as moving as the heartfelt eloquence of a man not given to words. They're all silent then, and in the silence Marj senses something like awe. Surely the presence of the Lord is in this place.

Nate gives that silence its due and then he speaks again. He's been doing daily reconnaissance over the Curaray River. He's found a long playa not far from the Auca settlement. He's not keen to land on sand, but he's done it before in a pinch. They'll prefab a platform in Arajuno and fly it in and hoist it up into the trees by ropes. That's where they'll sleep, so they have a vantage point and can't be ambushed. He'll fly supplies in every morning. And then they'll wait and pray.

He keeps talking, and Marj understands.

This is not a meeting to discuss the risks and vote yes or no; this is a meeting to brief the girls. The plan is glorious and complete, it's an extravagant bird in full flight. A tree house features prominently in it, and code. The men have been hatching it for weeks, standing in the shade of the airplane on jungle airstrips, heads together. Working out the details of a *ground mission*, not just gift drops the way Nate promised. He keeps talking, and she looks around the room at the women she counted on to speak up and sees carefully guarded expressions. He keeps talking, and she understands that he's far ahead of her, that she's a baby in treachery compared with him. While her days were taken up with scheming, he was cementing his plans. Look at me, Nate, she breathes, and he does, his eyes straight on hers, a high red flush around them, and she reads in them what only she can read.

It's not what she thought. It's not, *This will teach you that you can't undermine me.*

It's this: *Please, Marjie. Please give me this.*

He finishes and leans back against the counter, and Jim takes the floor. Marj sits with her hands clasped to control their shaking, letting her panic out in little breaths. Oh, dear God. Jim, his job is to address the concerns of the wives, who will naturally worry. They'll have the hardest role, sitting at home waiting for word.

Nothing to do but pray—but they need to remember that that is the most important job of all! He wants them to know that the men will spend several months doing gift drops before they ever embark on a ground mission. And they have put a meticulous safety plan in place for when they do go in. They'll go in at full moon, nobody's going to sneak up on them. They'll take in the portable two-way radio and extra batteries. They'll build their tree house first thing, and one man will be posted up there to cover them with a gun as long as they're on the beach. He himself will be in charge of weapons and ammunition. He owns an Enfield bolt-action and a carbine and he's ordered two more. Not that they would ever shoot an Auca, and send an unsaved soul to eternal perdition. But the Auca only have lances, so firing into the air will scare off anybody who arrives looking for trouble. Jim grew up in Oregon, where kids are born with shotguns or rifles on their shoulders, and he'll be conducting target practice with the men. He learned the hard way not to go turkey hunting with greenhorns. With a grin, he ducks his head and parts his hair to show them a four-inch furrow across his scalp. He got that scar when he was fourteen. His buddy didn't know the proper way to hold a rifle when he climbed through a barbed-wire fence.

It's a long meeting and at a certain point Sofia can't contain the children—they giggle and shriek from the stairs, they invade the kitchen in a horde. Marj clamps a hand over Benjy's mouth while Jim closes the meeting with a prayer, and the men escape outside, and the wives open their arms to that clinging, prodding, whining, wailing gang in their stinking diapers. Marj takes Davey from Sofia and undoes the top two buttons of her blouse. Three nursing mothers—no, only Marj is breastfeeding, Marilou and Betty (modern women) are heating up bottles of diluted condensed cow's milk on the stove. Four Christian wives, no doubt they all made the same vow Marj did. Well, possibly not Betty, she was married in a civil ceremony in Quito; who knows what she promised. Marj strokes Davey's head and breathes in the smell of him, and thinks fiercely, *Jim*. He didn't want to dwell on the threat of violence, he said. It was not the guns that would keep them safe, it was the Lord. *Safe*. Where, when you thought about it, would they be safer than in the Lord's arms for all eternity? He was poised as he spoke like a pole vaulter about to start his sprint. "If God asks the ultimate sacrifice of us," he cried in his ringing voice, "what greater glory could there be? Than to be ushered through the gates of splendour in our prime, obeying our Commander's voice, giving our all?" The kitchen is still full of the distress of that moment. But how can you talk about it with Betty sitting right there? They chose their husbands, but they didn't choose each other, they hardly know each other. They said almost nothing in the meeting and they're still not talking, just murmuring softly to their children, who are hungry and thirsty. In an hour the men will invade, ravenous, and Marj needs to start supper. She has a pile of flank steaks waiting, tough as leather.

"Hold Davey, will you?" she says to Olive, pulling him off her breast, reaching for her buttons. She runs out to find Perfecta, and drags her in and puts her to work at the counter pounding the meat with the mallet, the sort of job Perfecta is good at. Then she gets out the pitcher of orange Kool-Aid she made earlier, and lines up a row of tumblers and starts filling them, though her hands are shaking. She lifts her face to Marilou, their eyes meet.

"How are you feeling about all this?"

"Well, it seems we're putting the cart before the horse, just a little." Marilou pulls the bottle away from her baby and holds it up to check the level. "Why are we talking about going in? We need to find some way to learn the language first."

"Not necessarily," Betty says from the other side of the table. "The Auca will teach us. The men have all taken courses in the monolingual method."

"But it takes time to coax language out of new subjects. And if those subjects . . ." Marilou stops mid-sentence and turns her attention back to her baby.

"Isn't your sister-in-law learning the language?" Olive asks over Davey's head. "I thought she had an Auca informant at the hacienda. Why don't they work with her?"

"Nate doesn't think that's a good idea," Marj says.

All three of them look at her with stony faces, and with a lurch Marj realizes that the fraught atmosphere in the room is not just about Jim. Nate upset them too.

Right at the end of the meeting, Betty spoke up to suggest sending a newsletter to all their supporters back home and getting prayer support. Her voice was strong and confident as always and Marj could tell she was getting under Nate's skin. He cut her off. No, he said. It's essential that the mission be kept a secret. He went over the code they were to use for radio communication. Marj stands by the counter, her blouse sticking to her all the way from her armpits to her waist, and looks into her friends' faces and decides that they deserve to know what this is about.

"Nate doesn't want to involve Rachel. In fact, he doesn't want Rachel to know. When he says we have to keep Operation Auca quiet, it's mainly because he doesn't want word getting back to her."

This only makes things worse. "He doesn't intend to include Rachel?" Betty is astonished. "I just assumed she'd be a big part of it."

"Didn't she come to Ecuador especially to reach the Auca?" Marilou says. "That's what Jim told me. He figures she's working hard on the language."

"How will she feel when she finds out?" That's Olive's soft voice. "I mean, I don't really know her, but I can only imagine she'll be terribly hurt."

The room fills with their confusion and disapproval. The rhythmic *thwap* of Perfecta's mallet on the meat could be the blows of Nate and Marj's cruelty. Frustration slides down over Marj's eyes like a red screen. Her mind flips through all the things she could say about Rachel, not just Nate's stories but the weird things she did when she stayed with them. "Rachel . . ." she says hesitantly, and then Rachel herself surfaces vividly in Marj's mind, her eyes dull and wounded.

Who can find a virtuous woman? She opens her mouth with wisdom, and in her tongue is the law of kindness.

"Rachel . . . I think she *will* be hurt," Marj says at last, "and that makes me feel bad. But we know her a lot better than you do. And Nate feels the mission would be in jeopardy if Rachel got involved. He is very clear in this decision. Nate was the one who God led to the settlement. Not Rachel. So I think we have to trust him on this."

"Well, we knew it wouldn't be easy when we signed up," Marilou says vaguely. She sets the bottle on the table and gives her baby a cursory pat on the back, and then she stands up. "I'll be back in a sec to help with supper," she says, her voice wobbling a little. "But I need to go upstairs for a bit."

MARJ GIVES MARILOU twenty minutes and then, Davey on her hip, goes looking for her. Her daughter is in the upstairs corridor, swinging on Marilou's door, chatting. Debbie loves Marilou.

"You need to run downstairs now and let Mommy and Auntie Marilou talk for a bit," Marj says. She manages to pry Debbie off the doorknob with her free hand. When Debbie tries to grab the doorknob back, Marj slaps her backside hard and says, "Go downstairs this minute. Don't you dare disobey me." Her voice is so witchy that Debbie careens down the corridor wailing.

Marilou's baby is in the crib and Marilou herself is lying on the bed. She has a balled-up hanky in her fist and when she lifts her tear-swollen eyes to Marj, she is an ordinary frightened girl, her face splotchy and unbeautiful.

"Oh, Marilou," Marj says, closing the door and going to her.

Marilou sits up against the pillow. She gives her face a quick wipe. "I'm okay now," she says. "I just had to have a little cry." She smiles ruefully at Marj. "I'm not sure why it hit me like that. I thought I was fine. Of course, the day I heard about it I was really upset—"

"So you knew?"

"Ed told me a while ago." Marilou swings her legs over the edge of the bed and sits up. "It's just . . . it feels so dangerous, and so close. They speared the engineer who lived in our house. He was an American, and they speared him."

"Really? Did the Shell people tell you that?"

"No. I just know." Her voice breaks. "I've seen him. It's like he's in the house. I see him with . . . with all his . . . *injuries.*"

"Oh, Marilou," Marj says, reaching for her. "Marilou, you're dreaming. You're afraid, and it's natural, because you love Ed so much. But it won't happen to us. The boys have God's leading."

"No, I know it won't. Ed says God has given him an absolute promise that the men will all be safe. I believe God. I do." She hunches up a shoulder to wipe her cheek. "It's just—I'm pregnant again."

"Oh! Oh, honey. Are you sure?"

"Yeah, I'm sure. I'm almost three months along. Due at the end of January."

That baby in the crib is six months old and his brother just turned three.

Still with Davey on her knee, Marj moves over to the bed and puts her arm around Marilou. They sit in silence for a long time. Not (as in months past) because the glamorous Marilou doesn't need advice from the likes of Marj. They sit in silence because there is nothing anyone can say.

From there, Marj goes up the hall to Jim and Betty's room. Not someone to waste a minute, Betty is sitting at the desk with what looks like language notes spread out in front of her. Marj stands in the doorway. "Listen, I wanted the chance to ask you on your own. Are you convinced Operation Auca is a good idea?"

"Not entirely," Betty says, and Marj's heart leaps. Betty straightens her thin back. "It seems needlessly complicated," she says. "This long buildup with airdrops. Why not just go in? Since God showed us where the settlement is, that's what we've been thinking. We've been talking about going in by canoe, Jim and I and the baby. Who's going to attack a man with his wife and baby? But we really value the fellowship of this team, so if everyone is sure they have the Lord's leading on this, then we're prepared to go along with it."

"You were thinking of taking your baby in?" They both look to the centre of the bed, where Sharon lies on her tummy in a golden heap.

Betty turns back to Marj. "Well, either we trust God's promises or we don't," she says evenly.

Her tawny eyes never, ever blink. Her thinness seems like a spiritual victory, as if she's had every molecule of doubt burned out of her.

AFTER EVERYONE HAS been flown home to their stations and it's just Marj and Nate and the kids in the house, Marj walks down the hall to Nate's favourite hideout, the darkroom. The door is closed. Nate might have a film in one of the baths, but she doesn't care, she flings the door open without knocking. His head snaps up. He's sitting reading an old *Time* magazine, obviously hiding. She says, "You promised me you would only do airdrops."

He doesn't look the least bit ashamed. "Are you going to stand against the Lord in this?" he says.

It is the worst moment of their marriage. She walks back to the kitchen and sets about making the bread. She sprinkles yeast onto a dish of warm sugar water, and then pulls out the flour canister and begins to sift the flour to get the bugs out. Is there an instance in the Bible where God spoke to a woman and contradicted what her husband said? She can't think of one, but she doesn't know the Bible as well as she should. It occurs to her that she hasn't prayed in months, possibly years, except maybe to her mother. What's to be gained by nagging God? No doubt He's as besieged moment by moment as she is.

She checks the yeast. It's only produced a few feeble bubbles along the edge.

Then he's at the doorway. "Marj. Did Dunlap radio in from Quito?"

"No."

"He was supposed to send out a torque plate for the brakes last Friday."

Something like hot metal fills her chest, a feeling she would call hatred in other circumstances. For Dunlap, whoever he is, for Nate, for men. For torque plates, and lances, and Enfield bolt-action rifles. Chainsaws, sledgehammers, stinky football pads, khaki-painted tanks with guns sticking erect out of them. Men in uniforms, swarming the decks of ships, cheering like imbeciles. All through the war, when they sat in church and prayed for the troops going into France and Italy and the Philippines, she thought, This is *men*. This is all men, God included. Men in their gangs. Men doing what they want to do. Jim, Ed, Nate—remember the day they roofed the house? Goading each other on, vying to be the biggest fool on the ridge-pole. Operation Auca. It is all about *men*.

Well, discounting Betty.

IN THE GAUZY morning light filtering through the mosquito net, Marj says, "The girls were asking about Rachel. Wondering why she's not involved."

"Did you tell them what happened when Jim and Betty turned up after their wedding? How Rachel threatened to tell the government they're not trained as linguists? If Rachel gets involved, this mission is doomed." His voice is low, his hand is splayed on her thigh. "You know, Marj, Rachel almost ruined my chance to be a pilot. It's because of her I never got to fly with the air force."

So he's back to that. It's an old story—how thrilled he was when the Japanese attacked Pearl Harbor, and how he waited in line the day the recruiting office opened, and then, the night before his medical, fell sick with a fever—the return of his osteomyelitis. It was from a skiing accident he'd had when he was twelve, when he hit a rock and his ski broke. Six years later, splinters of wood were still working their way out of his shin. So of course the air force turned him down.

Normally at this point Marj says, How in the world is that Rachel's fault? and Nate says, I didn't have proper skis. None of us did. We would race down steep, rocky hills with barrel staves wired to our boots and tree branches for poles. Can you imagine? Rachel was in charge of us and she completely ignored the danger, she was just glad to get us out of the house. Then I had that ugly gash in my leg, and she pooh-poohed it. Until the infection got so bad she had no choice but to take me to the doctor. I'm just lucky they had penicillin by then. I'm just lucky my leg didn't have to be amputated.

To which Marj always replies, You got training as a mechanic. You weren't asked to drop bombs and kill thousands of people. And eventually you got to be a civilian pilot. I think that's a wonderful example of the way God works.

But this time she just lies in silence. On the other side of the wall, thudding starts up, wood on wood. It's David bouncing in his crib, politely signalling time for breakfast. He'll be rehearsing his dazzling morning smile, it's always in place when she puts her head in the doorway.

"Nate. In the meeting, Jim said he was going to hold target practice. Why do you need target practice? If you're only going to be firing warning shots in the air?"

"He just misspoke. He meant gun safety training."

David lets out an experimental holler and then goes quiet. The thumping has stopped.

"Don't think about it," Nate says. "We won't be using the weapons. We're just carrying them so you girls won't worry. We fire even a single warning shot and we can forget about making friendly contact with the Auca in our lifetime."

After a minute he says, "I was thinking about using the spiral bucket." This is one of Nate's inventions—a canvas bucket he lowers on a long rope from the plane, circling above until the bucket hangs steady close to ground level. He first dreamed it up for mission stations that didn't have an airstrip, so he could deliver essentials like penicillin. He doesn't have all the kinks worked out and he hasn't tried it with the new plane. "I thought, if I get good at it, we could lower the gifts to the Auca in the bucket. It feels more respectful than just dropping stuff from the open door of the plane. Here, neighbour, you'd be saying, here's a small token of our concern for you."

"Neighbour?" she says, raising herself up on an elbow.

"Well, we have to call them something. On the radio, I mean." Nate lifts his hand and caresses her cheek with the backs of his knuckles. "I took it from the Lord's greatest commandment: *Thou shalt love thy neighbour as thyself.* We do actually love the Auca— they just don't know it yet."

She gazes down at him. His handsome face is illuminated, not from the window but from within, from his heart, which she has always known to be good. She drops back to the mattress.

Debbie's light voice starts up. She'll be peering down from her bunk bed, her hair a shiny waterfall, chatting to her brother in the bunk below.

Morning. Nate hoists himself out of the nest, swivels his shoulders. Gathers himself to flap off to his secret haunts in the jungle.

17

THEY PUT THE GIFTS TOGETHER with the greatest of care. An aluminum kettle. A bag of salt. A little bag of coloured buttons and some ribbons. Nate will do a gift drop on the same day every week, so the Auca will start expecting it. This will build trust.

The first drop is October 6. Nate and Ed find the clearing empty, but they drop the gifts anyway. The second is October 13, and Nate says six or seven people rushed over in excitement when the gifts landed between the longhouses. After that, the sound of the Piper coming over the trees draws a crowd every week.

In the morning they watch Nate take off, Benjy in Marj's lap. Marj runs her palm over the bristles on the top of his head, enjoying their bluntness. She's just given him his first crewcut. "Who's that in the airplane?" she asks him.

"Daddy," he says flatly, bored by the question.

The fourth week, Nate jacks up the gift lode: he starts to drop machetes. Because it's such great sport to watch the excitement on the ground when the people look up and see what's falling towards them.

"Nate," Marj says. "Didn't Shell Oil try airdrops before they went into Auca territory?"

"Yeah, they did."

"Didn't they drop tools like machetes?"

"Could be."

"And weren't some of the Shell employees later killed by machetes?"

He's sitting on the stool, staring at her wordlessly. "Okay," he finally says. "I won't drop machetes."

He flies the men in so they can practise with the spiral bucket, and Olive comes to Shell Mera with Peter. The men spend the afternoon at the airstrip. The trick, as Marj understands it, is to pit centrifugal force against centripetal force, and somehow factor in drag. Marj watches Nate's first pass over the airstrip, discovers that the weight swinging from the end of the rope is her new kerosene iron, and takes the kids to the lounge.

An hour or two later, she hears the men in the backyard with the football. They sound excited. It must have worked.

Olive comes to the kitchen to help with supper. "I can make boiled yucca taste just like mashed potatoes," she says. "It's my only jungle skill."

So Marj surrenders the yucca to her and turns her attention to browning the pork chops.

Olive stands close to her at the stove. "I need to tell you something."

Marj poured too much oil into the frying pan and the pork chops are spitting like crazy, drilling minuscule fiery darts into her hand. "You're pregnant?"

"No. Not that. It's just—Peter is thinking seriously about pulling out of the operation."

"He is?"

"Yes."

Marj dials the flame down and turns towards Olive. "What's that about?"

"Well, he's been praying and praying about the mission, and he can't seem to get any peace about it."

Shouts float in through the window and they both glance over and watch Jim throw a long pass. Ed lifts into the air and hooks the football down with exceptional grace.

"Peter is a really intelligent person," Olive says. "I don't know if the others recognize that—he always feels like a junior partner in this group, especially with Jim. And you know how it is, he wants to be one of the gang. But back when he was recruited, he kind of fell under Jim's thrall, and he doesn't want that to happen again. So he's stuck. He's stuck between wanting to belong and wanting to be his own person. That might not be how he would explain it, but it's the way I see it."

Shouts draw their eyes back to the window. Ed and Jim have added a tackle element to the game. But Pete—as if in deliberate illustration of his wife's point—Pete is standing with his back to the house, batting the heels of his hands against his thighs in a parody of eagerness. *Please throw to me. Oh, please don't.*

In bed that night, Marj says, "So I hear Pete is thinking about pulling out of Operation Auca."

Nate's shoulder moves under her cheek. "Yeah, sounds like it."

"Apparently, he doesn't have assurance that this is God's will."

"Yeah, that's what I hear."

"Well, that worries me, Nate. Don't you think God might be trying to tell you all something?"

"He's telling us something I already suspected. That Peter is not cut out for this operation."

"You would go in with just three?"

"We'll still be four. I've been talking to Roger Youderian."

Roger Youderian! One of the missionaries on Nate's southern circuit. He works with Frank Drown at Macuma, a thirty-minute flight away.

"Do the other men even know him?"

"No. But they're prepared to trust me with this."

Marj knows Roger, though, and she is absolutely dismayed. "The guy is *miserable*," she says, thinking of his dour presence at her kitchen table. "You can see it at a glance. You could have asked Frank."

"Roger's a decorated war hero," Nate says. "He was a paratrooper. He fought in the Battle of the Bulge."

"What does that have to do with anything?"

"He understands what it means to obey orders no matter what you feel."

IT IS ALWAYS possible she's wrong. That God has something splendid in mind, that He's picked out their husbands to do something nobody has been able to do for centuries. If that's the case, then *she* might be increasing the jeopardy. By not being wholehearted, by secretly hoping they'll come to their senses. Isn't there a story in the Bible about a battle that was lost because the soldiers had unbelievers in their midst? She longs for counsel from someone from outside their circle. She thinks of the friar at Shandia, Fray Alfredo, the things he knows and the unexpected opinions he holds, ideas that crash like a wrecking ball into the walls of her mind, opening up startling new vistas. Nate comes in with a fistful of letters from Pen Pal Boy himself, and she feels that eager pulse you might call a leading of the Lord.

I'm just back from a hacienda on the Rio Ila, where I minister to the campesinos in exchange for three days of the sort of living made possible when a workforce of a hundred is wholly devoted to the comforts of ten. What does the good brother do for the campesinos? you ask. You'll be surprised to learn that my rudimentary medical skills now include dentistry. A friar retiring from Puyo left me his clamps and when I was next petitioned by a man racked with toothache and infection, I felt obliged to use them. Young, handsome Indians are without doubt defaced for life by my crude practice, but they might be dead of sepsis without it.

One of the patients I saw at the hacienda was the forest woman Dayuma. I believe I've mentioned her to you. It's sad to see her with tooth decay, as when she arrived at the hacienda six or seven years ago she was in splendid health. But last week the glands in her throat were the size of chicken eggs, and I had no choice but to pull her left canine and incisor. I gave her a good shot of rum, offered her a rosary to hold, and I was in position (with my knee on her chest and my knuckles in her mouth, as it were) when a large white figure galloped across the yard and pounced shrieking upon me. It was an American missionary lady staying at the hacienda. She protested that she planned to take Dayuma to her own dentist in Quito. Sadly, indenture at Hacienda Ila does not provide for discretionary jaunts to the capital, and at Don Carlos's insistence, I went ahead with the extractions, started Dayuma on penicillin, and sent her sobbing back to her quarters.

This woman, by name of Rachel Saint, is very fond of Dayuma and did not soon forgive me, but the chance to talk English is irresistible. Turns out she's the sister of the pilot at Shell Mera, although she's a good deal older. I gather she was drawn to the hacienda by the romance of the Auca, a passion she shares with Don Carlos. Miss Saint dreams of accompanying Dayuma into the forest to preach to her people. I did my best to press upon her the folly of this. But her conviction of a divine call to the Auca is unshakable. Dayuma was years ago baptized into the Catholic Church, christened Catalina, and has been taking the sacraments every time a priest goes into Ila. This means nothing to Miss Saint. Dayuma will be her first convert, she says proudly.

Miss Saint is apparently a linguist and she was eager to show me her notes. So we found the overseer and he opened the school-house for us, where she works with Dayuma. I can't speak to Miss Saint's linguistic competence, but her enthusiasm and industry are undeniable. She's created a comprehensive phrase book, and paging through its sections gives you a vivid sense of forest life: Actions. Animals. Beliefs. Family and Kinship. Food and Drink. The House. Hunting. Governance and Warfare.

I was impressed with her passion for the work, but I told her about the Záparo people who, like the Auca, resisted all contact with the outside world for three centuries. And then the rubber *trees along the Napo were tapped out and the traders started going up the tributaries, and the temptation to trade for firearms and machetes was too much. Fifty years ago, the Záparo in El Oriente numbered 200,000 and now they are virtually gone. She did not believe me. She asked me how they could all disappear in one generation, and I said, "They succumbed to the sort of thing you are dead set on taking to the Auca."*

But it was futile. The two are together every hour Don Carlos allows, this mountainous American woman and her small Indigenous friend. Dayuma is a gentle girl, quite extraordinary in her quiet warmth, and no doubt very lonely. She is homesick for her own people; every time I speak to her she tells me of her worry for her mother and sister and brother. But she fled the forest because of reprisal killings, and is afraid to go back. A lonely representative of a society we know nothing about.

Goodness is a lot more complicated than Marj ever imagined. When she was ten or eleven, an evangelist set up his tent at the fairgrounds in Boise, and her parents drove the family in to a meeting, just the one. The preacher was almost sobbing by the time he got to the altar call, haranguing them to come forward and lay their sins at the feet of Jesus. Escape the lake of fire, be welcomed to heaven for all eternity. Marj looked up and caught her mother's eye. Her mother gave a quick, private shake of her head. *No need,* Marj saw in that look. You are a good girl. And she was. Behaving properly just seemed logical. Wouldn't God's will be much the same as your own good sense? But now they're on a runaway train into the fantastical, and God is not doing much to stop it.

Nate starts to use the bucket. Not only do the Auca get its purpose—they start to send things back! On Nate and Ed's sixth visit, they cut the bucket off the rope and tie the rope around their own gift. It's a feather headband. Nate brings it back to Shell Mera. He tells Marj how wonderful that moment was for Ed—feeling the tug on the bucket line while the people below were tying the knot (a perfect hitch knot). The sense that, just for a moment, his hands held Auca hands through the proxy of the rope.

Nate pulls the crown out of a sack to show Marj. She takes it in her hand and feels her own tears rise. The Auca are *real*. They live in this material world. They were driven naked out of the Garden of Eden to a place very much like it, and have made their home there for centuries. They are mothers with children, camping as her family camped when she was a girl. They don't have matches, propane stoves, or axes. What do they have? How do they understand the world? What does this crown mean, this artful arrangement of feathers in alternating colours? Are they wondering about her, as she is wondering about them?

Then, a week or so later, Nate's sister, Rachel, delirious, is carried in through the door in a white nightgown. She's in a very bad way, grey as a mushroom, and with no idea how she got there.

"God performed a miracle," she says the next morning, lifting her fever-scrubbed face from the pillow. "He sent a plane to pick me up—and you know, they don't even have an airstrip."

"It was a *float* plane," Marj tells her, trying to hoist her up in her bed so she can sip some tea. "One of Don Carlos's men walked out to Shandia to tell the missionaries you were sick, and Jim Elliot radioed us, and Johnny Keenan flew in to the hacienda and landed on the river. You don't remember?"

She has no memory even of falling ill. She remembers being carried down the staircase at the hacienda, only that. The porters had her on a stretcher and they could not make it in one go. They put the stretcher down on the stairs while they caught their breath, and she thought she was tobogganing. Lying there naked with her heart exposed, pulsing in the cold air. She's surprised to find herself in a nightgown. She examines the lace trim on the bodice and denies that it's hers.

"You were wearing it when you arrived," Marj says. "You don't need to worry, you weren't naked. And Doña Sevilla packed up all your things and sent them out. Your bible's here, if you want to read."

Everything Rachel owns in the world was neatly folded into her leather suitcase. Strangely, there were no language notes at all. While Rachel floated in fever dreams, Marj went through it all carefully. No vocabulary lists, no file cards. No notebook with section tabs.

They've put her in the downstairs room she stayed in before. It's narrow and stuffy but more convenient for nursing during the day, when Marj is busy with the radio. Nate would have checked her into the hospital, but Marj didn't think Rachel would survive the Shell Mera hospital.

The doctor is at the clinic and he kindly comes over. He takes Rachel's pulse, her blood pressure, and her temperature. Rachel never opens her eyes. "*P. falciparum*," he says. Marj walks him out to the kitchen and he gives her a supply of malaria medication from his bag.

"*P. falciparum* is the most dangerous strain," Rachel says when Marj comes back.

"It's the most common strain," Marj says. She hands Rachel a pill and a glass of water.

"It can cause kidney failure. I should be monitored for edema." Rachel pushes up the sleeve of her nightgown and presses her fingers hard into her forearm. She starts counting. It takes ten seconds for the dent to vanish. She'll need to be checked again in an hour. If no one will nurse her, she will have to nurse herself. "No creatures on earth are as unsympathetic as nurses," she says. "You think suffering is entirely normal."

"It's true, we do," Marj says.

"As long as it's happening to somebody else, eh," Rachel says.

Her hair is greasy and she reeks of sweat and yeast. She needs a good sponge bath. Marj carries in a pitcher of hot water and a basin and sets to work, scrupulously gentle, feeling guilt and duplicity drip from her fingers. In spite of her illness, Rachel is fatter than she was, especially in the chin area. It's the hacienda living Fray Alfredo wrote about.

"I won't wash your hair today. You don't have the strength. But tomorrow you'll feel better and we'll do it then."

All this exertion wears Rachel out. Her head falls back and her breath deepens.

Marj picks up the pitcher and stands by the bed for a moment. She's struck by Rachel's thick braid on the pillow: previously golden, now streaked with pewter. She's not quite forty, but her illness has opened a window to her future, the broad-faced, doughy old woman she will be. A woman no one loves or wants. It's a terrible thought: how could you persist in drawing a breath in this world if not a single soul loved you? Rachel committed the offence of not being loved and they turned against her for that. Not just Nate, but the wives, when Rachel stayed in Shell Mera all those months. And we were so *good*, Marj thinks. So nice and so good. We never talked about her behind her back, we wives. Not once, which is pretty darn amazing. We just made a silent wall against her.

MARJ HAS SEEN people cycle through the phases of malaria before, the aches and chills and then the raging fever and delirium and terrible restlessness. Two jaguars are fighting inside her, Rachel says, an expression apparently used by the Auca. One night when Marj brings supper in, she is lucid but strangely unlike herself, full of sisterly warmth and confidences. "I've been working with Dayuma," she says. "She's the Auca girl who came to me in a vision many years ago, when I was crossing the Atlantic."

"Have you been able to lead her to the Lord?"

"It's early days for that. We need more language first. In Peru I learned not to force things. Because the people will just say what you want them to say, and then you don't know where you're at."

"And how is the language work going?" Marj manages an unconcerned voice.

"Well, it was discouraging at first," Rachel says, taking a big spoonful of soup. "I went into the hacienda full of hope that the Auca language would be a dialect of the Shapra I had learned in Peru, but it turns out they don't have a single word in common, not that I've discovered. I think the Auca language is a true isolate. But we're making real progress. Dayuma speaks Quichua and some Spanish, so that makes things faster."

"Are you learning a lot about Auca life?"

"I am learning a lot about killing!" she cries, the blue beams of her eyes flashing. "There is a savage they call Moipa rampaging through the jungle, killing people on a daily basis. Dayuma ran away because of him. She relishes stories about spearings, and believe you me, she has a lot of them. She recites them almost like a song. She says the same thing over and over, she moves on and then jumps back. She never looks at me and her eyes are half-closed, like she's going into a trance. It's quite something to witness. But it's helpful when you're trying to learn the language. If I miss a phrase, I know I'll hear it again. And she makes the wildest gestures, and grunts and groans, like a person might as they're dying from a spear through their spleen. I don't think this is all for my benefit, it's just the way she tells stories. So, yes, I would say I'm making great progress. Let me show you my beautiful phrase book."

But of course it's not among her things, and she's terribly upset.

"It's blue," she says. "It's a lovely blue hardcover book with marbled end sheets. I bought it in Lima and saved it for a special purpose. You should see it! My lists are wonderful. Everything is in it."

Marj is desperate to talk to Nate, but he's down at the docks. She finally goes to bed and falls asleep for an hour and then wakes to find that he's not with her and the generator is still running. She puts on her slippers and robe and goes up the hall and sees that the darkroom door is closed. She taps and he says, "Turn the hall light off if you want to come in. I've got something in the bath."

He's sitting on his stool, bathed in the red light from his developing lamp. She can tell right away that he's just as worked up as she is. He stopped by Rachel's room to say good night and Rachel called him Father. But he thinks she was faking delirium, just to yank his chain.

He doesn't get up to offer her the stool. She spies a wooden case under the table and pulls it out to sit on. She feels painfully the separation between them. How petty (she thought at one time, weeks ago) if this is all about Rachel. But it's not petty at all. It's not something you can resist, the iron engine of your childhood, it drives you forward until the day you die. Nate has a wife and three kids, but his new family is ghostly compared with his old.

"How much of the Auca language do you think she has?" he asks Marj. His eyes look demonic in this light, and hers must too.

"Quite a bit, I think. But they didn't send her notes out with her."

"Well, I wish I knew how to get some phrases out of her without making her suspicious. Because I've had a really good idea." He drains his Pepsi, and then he tells her about a new, enhanced use for the spiral bucket.

This is what he could do, if he had the language: he could take a public address system up in the plane and put a *speaker* in the basket, have it dangling by a wire, so the Auca below will hear friendly greetings and gospel messages coming from the basket.

"You would really do that?" Marj says. "Instead of going in on the ground?"

"Oh, I don't know. Probably not. It's just a dream I have, because I like the technology."

Marj leans back, the edge of the counter like a blade in her back. Yes, she thinks. That's how it can be done. Safely done. If they had the language, they could share the gospel through a loudspeaker from the plane.

So then she tells him about the notebook full of language, still at the hacienda, just a three-hour walk up a jungle trail from Jim and Betty. It's blue, she tells him. It's a hardcover blue book. It's her master phrase list. It's likely in the schoolhouse. Jim would need to find the overseer, he has a key. The overseer will let another American in to pick up Rachel's things.

Who can find a virtuous woman? The heart of her husband doth safely trust in her. She will do him good and not evil all the days of her life.

18

THE QUININE FINALLY TAKES HOLD. When Rachel's fever peaks now, it's only 102. She's getting bored. She's alert to every noise in the house, full of questions. Soon she'll be mobile, lurking in the halls, spying on their lovemaking, manhandling the children. Soon she'll be noticing the flights to the northeast, overhearing conversations, finding caches of trade goods destined for the bucket, and she won't rest until she figures it out.

Sure enough, late one afternoon, Marj is in the lounge with Debbie and David when Benjy gallops in screeching, "Mommy! Come right away! Auntie Rachel is in Daddy's room and she won't listen!"

She's in the darkroom, with the door open for light.

"This is Daddy's room," Benjy shrills. "We are not supposed to be in here. None of us. Not even Mommy." Delighted, he slips past Marj and past his auntie and begins to grab at things Nate has laid out on the shelves. Marj swings him around and out of the room and pushes him up the corridor, feeling the wing-buds of his shoulder blades under her hands. Plunking him down in his bedroom and closing the door, she goes back for Rachel.

"My Shapra feathers!" Rachel is literally wringing her hands. She's staring at a row of photographs clipped to the clothesline Nate installed for drying photos. Portraits, eight-by-ten glossies. This is what Nate was developing the other night: the missionary men of Operation Auca with friendly smiles. He wants to drop them from the plane, so when the men walk into the forest, the people will recognize them and think, These are the kind fellows who bring us the gifts. Why would we spear men who wish us nothing but good? And in the photos, Jim and Nate are holding the feather crown the Auca sent, and Ed—for whatever reason, Ed has chosen to wear the crown.

"Those fellows stole my crown!"

"No, Rachel," Marj says. "Your crown is in its tin in the top drawer in your room. Doña Sevilla sent it out. Let's go back and I'll show you."

"I wonder where they got that one? They look like the *Masons*. Have they started some sort of secret fraternity?"

"Who?" Marj asks stupidly.

Rachel allows herself to be led to the hall. "The boys. Nate and Ed and Jim. Have they started a club?"

"Oh, no doubt."

"I knew it! I know boys. Do I *ever* know boys!"

The situation is impossible, Nate agrees. He flies to Shandia and has a private conversation with Jim and Betty. The next day the two of them call in around noon, all neutral and businesslike, and ask to speak to Rachel. Marj helps her down the hall to the radio room.

"Jim needs my fellowship just now," Rachel explains to Marj after the call. "He's going through a bad patch. And Betty is struggling to look after that little girl. I'm sorry to leave you like this, but the need there is greater. They don't have all the comforts of home the way you do."

"I thought you weren't keen on looking after other people's children," Marj can't resist saying.

"Well, I only met Betty the once," Rachel says. "But she didn't look like a natural mother to me."

PERFECTA IS THE laundress, she's the only one who can handle the mangle. *Mangle*—even the word puts you off. But when she has time, Marj pegs up the laundry herself, because it's the only chance she has to get outside into their beautiful yard, the green of childhood dreams, and trimmed every third day year-round by a man with a scythe, Oresto, with his sharp eye for snakes. It's lush and velvet, it's a *dell*. As a child, Marj sang "The Farmer in the Dell" without the vaguest notion what a dell was, but the minute she saw this yard, she knew.

She yanks the laundry line along on its little wheels, dipping into her clothespin apron, humming as she pegs up the sheets. The year he was grounded, Nate hired two workmen, and under his supervision they built Marj this wonderful laundry shed. It's a neat, cement-brick building with its own water pump, and roomy enough for the washing machine and the mangle and rinsing tubs and a work table and twenty-five feet of clothesline. The clothesline is on a pulley and runs into the shed through an opening like the slit in the wall of a medieval castle. This is so you can pull the clothes inside when it starts to rain. Farm wives in Idaho would kill for this shed. But then, farm wives in Idaho are not running a hotel in Ecuador.

Something moves in the corner of her eye and she turns her head to see a brown figure striding across the green. Fray Alfredo, walking with a great deal more ease than at his last visit, and dressed in a long hooded garment like a bathrobe, with a white cord knotted around his waist. Warmth fills her at the sight of him. He's grown a beard since she saw him last, and he's a startling sight, an ancient figure appearing out of a brash new forest.

"*Buenos días, Señora Saint.*"

"*Buenos días.*"

He reaches out his hand, strangely formal, and she wipes her hand on her skirt and shakes it.

"It's very pleasant back here."

"It is. Sometimes I think I'm still on our farm in the Midwest. I hear geese honking and cows mooing. The honking is tree frogs, I know, but I have no idea what the mooing is."

"It's the tiger heron. The *puma garza*."

She feels the joy of their peculiar one-sided intimacy, and she reminds herself to watch her words.

"There's something I'd like to ask you, Señora Saint."

"Of course."

"What do you know about the forest people living around the Curaray?"

"The Auca?" she says. And looking into his face, she understands that this formality is the demeanour of a very angry man.

"Well, as you call them. *Auca* is a word the Quichua use for all the forest peoples—the Jivaro, the Shapras, the Shuar and Anshuar. It's a term of disgust. When we use it, it's as if we are calling the people dirty savages."

"So what is their name?"

"I believe, from a conversation I had with the forest woman at the hacienda, that they call themselves Waorani. Which just means 'the people,' as distinguished from the animals around them."

"How did you figure that out?"

"Well, they have many hunting taboos—the hare, for example. Dayuma tells me that they don't kill hares because the hare has Waorani eyes. It strikes me that a hare's eyes look rather human, and I deduced the name from that. I gathered something else from Dayuma's comment—that the Waorani have a strong taboo against cannibalism."

"Oh," Marj says. "That's so interesting."

"It is. And I wonder if you might share with me what you know. Regarding the size of the population, for one thing."

"I don't think anybody knows that."

"I also wonder if the Waorani have ever been exposed to measles or flu or polio or tuberculosis? Do they have any immunity at all to our diseases?"

"I don't really know. Maybe you want to talk to Nate."

"Why Nate?"

"What do you mean?"

"Why refer me to your husband? Don't you bear any responsibility for what happens out of this mission station?"

Emotion floods through her. His keen eyes are fixed on her. It seems their intimacy is not one-sided after all. He sees her, a plain woman made lovely by work, by faithfulness, and by loyalty. He sees the bargains she's made, he sees she's not equal to this challenge.

"Fray Alfredo, say what you want to say."

"I will, then. The Waorani people have shunned the outside world for centuries. They have thrived on their own. They are masters when it comes to navigating the rivers. They know the forest like the back of their hand. It's only from the sky that they're vulnerable."

"You know about the airdrops."

"Yes. The Indians in Shandia and Arajuno notice everything and they talk to each other. The other day I was out near the airstrip when your husband flew over. Some Quichua men heard the plane coming—they always hear it about two minutes before I do—and do you know what they did? They stripped off their shirts and pants and picked up sticks to use as pretend lances. As the plane flew over, they danced around naked and threw those lances up at it. I asked them what was going on. They were pretending to be Waorani. Maybe he'll drop a few tools for us, they said. They're furious that their enemies are getting all these goods and they are not. Having a machete of his own would transform life for the poorest of those men."

He's even angrier than he was that day in the kitchen, and her heart gives a painful squeeze. She bends to picks up another little nightshirt so he won't see her face.

He takes a step closer. "Have you thought about the chaos you will cause? Not long ago, Shell Oil provoked a civil war among the forest people. They dropped a machete from a plane, a man picked it up, and the others speared him to death for it."

Marj drops the nightshirt. "So you want them to live forever in the Stone Age? Killing each other, never knowing God? I thought you were supposed to be a man of faith yourself."

He lifts his hands in an *I give up* gesture and turns to walk back to the road.

"Let me just point out," Marj calls to his back, "we're not the ones who came in with the conquistadores and slaughtered the Indians by the thousands."

"Well, you're not finished yet, are you," he shouts without turning around.

NATE FLIES ROGER and Barbara Youderian to Shell Mera for a few days to get them up to speed. They bring their two kids, a four-year-old girl and a tiny boy. The orientation meeting has to be moved to the evening because they are so late getting back. Nate doesn't respond to the radio, but finally Marj gets a terse call: on our way. They arrive and Marj directs the Youderians upstairs to their room and then follows Nate to the darkroom for a quick chat.

"Whatever happened?"

"It was Roger. We were ready to leave, and then he wouldn't get on the plane. Finally he said he would come if I let him bring some special equipment. Marj, it was *body armour*. He's made himself a breastplate and a belly plate out of an iron drum. It weighs a ton. He can't even walk properly in it. I tried to let on it would put me overweight, but he forced me to itemize my load and he could see I was lying. Marjie, I ended up bringing his body armour. It's in the hangar under a tarp."

Marj doesn't want to rub it in, so she doesn't say anything at all.

The day is not going well, and in fact began very badly. She woke up with a terrible feeling in her belly, not fear, as you might expect, but sadness, as if something awful had already happened and she hadn't been able to cry. The feeling has dimmed, but it's not entirely gone. While they waited for Nate to come back with the Youderians, she was alone in the kitchen and had a chance to sort the mail. Fray Alfredo had written a letter to his friend M, and she eased it open and furtively read it, squinting her eyes to see through the black cloud of acrimony that rose from its pages. A long rant about his trek back to Shandia. He and his porter took a wrong fork halfway along and wasted two hours on a narrow trail where he was almost bitten by a bushmaster. Of course, he blamed this on Nate. Then there was this, which floored her because, when she went back over their conversation out by the laundry lines, she could not put her finger on a single thing she had said that absolutely betrayed her:

Beyond controlling the airspace, the gatekeepers in the gospel house in Shell Mera handle all the mail to Quito and quite possibly vet my letters. (Hello, my dear, if you're reading this: Yes, we Papists were handmaidens to the conquistadores, we will be making reparations forever—but that was in the sixteenth century. For you, nothing has changed. You say you love the indigeni, but all you really want are their souls. How can you hope to minister to people you despise?)

"We're eleven for supper," Marj says to Nate. "I need to go and get cooking." God help me, she thinks, because suddenly the slightest demand feels overwhelming.

In the ammonia-smelling dark, Nate reaches for her hand and lifts it to his chest. "Marjie, will you come to the meeting tonight?"

"I thought you just wanted the men."

"No," he says. "I need you there."

BARBARA YOUDERIAN IS a calm presence, clear-eyed, uncannily like a girl Marj admired in her nursing class but never got to be friends with. She's subdued today too, a slender girl balancing a huge weight. They do the dishes almost in silence, and Marj is glad: her mind is on the meeting. I will speak, she's been telling herself. I will tell them everything Fray Alfredo said. After the children are in bed, she gets out the precious can of cocoa powder and, as they come in for the meeting, dips everyone a mug of hot chocolate. Pete and Jim and Ed—Nate flew them in that morning. Not Marilou, who is not travelling much these days, and not Betty, who has, well, Rachel. As for Peter, he seems to want to demonstrate his goodwill by coming to all the meetings, although this actually causes a lot more trouble for Nate, and no one is keen to include him in the discussions.

They sit around the table and fill the Youderians in on the day the Auca man appeared in the yard in Arajuno. Nate and Ed share exciting news from this week's flight over Terminal City. The Auca have built a bamboo platform like an observation deck, as if they're trying to get closer to the plane. And on the platform, a model plane is mounted! Ed trained the binoculars on it, and he was amazed at its perfect proportions and fine details.

"Well, that cage is really something too," Nate says.

Cage? Marj thinks.

The Auca sent out a live parrot. It was in an intricately woven cage, and it had a banana as provision for its journey. They send gifts up every visit now, often food wrapped in banana leaves. Fish, yucca, a smoked monkey tail. Nate and Ed don't always manage to spool the line in. They end up dragging the gifts over the canopy to Arajuno, and things don't fare well in the landing. The pottery vessels the Auca sent were all smashed to bits. Two squirrels were both DOA. But the parrot survived. It was lying on its side, stunned, but Ed dumped a mug of cold water on it and it started moving. Now Marilou's kids have a bad-tempered parrot for a pet.

And so they are making gains in building trust. They drink their hot chocolate, and Ed and Jim tip back their chairs and spar as usual, but Marj is struck by how flat their voices are. Everyone seems privately anxious. It may be the effect of the new recruit, who sits at the end of the table taking notes, saying very little but exuding a dark energy, his face so long it seems a mask, and his eyes deeply set, ringed with black and full of what, from her experience in hospitals, Marj can only call suffering. He asks who's been assigned to do the operational plan. They admit they don't know what that is. It specifies each man's task every quarter-hour, he says.

"No one so far," Nate says.

Roger says he'll take it on. He'll also create a list of symbols to be drawn in the sand in case of emergency, so rescuers flying over can see them.

The Quichua say that at any moment you are either living or dying. In their terms, this man is dying, and it gives him a strange authority. Marj finds herself longing for Fray Alfredo. I should have dreamed up a pretext for Nate to fly him in, she thinks wildly. He could have talked to them. She can't bear the thought that she might walk out of this meeting with nothing changed.

Nate is all business. He's got a formula for measuring distance on the ground against the speed of the plane, and on a windless day recently he flew over Palm Beach dumping a big scoop of bright-pink plaster of Paris out the door every seven seconds. From counting these markers, he was able to calculate two hundred yards of runway—long enough, but just barely. The question is *when* they will go in.

"Well, actually," Jim says, "the Lord has answered that for me in unmistakable terms. But before I get to that—does everyone have the Auca phrases?"

Nate and Ed do; in fact Marilou was able to use them when the Auca man appeared in her yard. But Roger and Barb don't, of course. Jim dictates the words phonetically and they write them down. Apparently they mean: *I want to be your friend. I like you. Christ died for you.* Roger, who doesn't seem to know about Rachel, asks Jim how he got the phrases.

Marj holds her breath. If he lies, he will be lying for me, she thinks. But he simply acts as though he didn't hear. "As for the timing," he says, "I think it's imperative that we land at the next full moon, which is right after New Year's. If we leave it too much later, the rains will start and the playa may be washed away. And— you fellows will laugh, but it's actually Satan's shenanigans that have convinced me the time is right."

Marj sits with her hands clasped in her lap and does a trick she has to blur her vision: she doesn't look away but neither does she take in Jim's face. Just his words, just his hoarse, impassioned voice. He describes how restless he's been for the last month, how depressed. He can hardly pray or read Scripture. He feels anguish at his lack of progress with the Quichua, who parrot everything he says to them but never change. Even this new mission was starting to turn to ashes in his mind. Why should they assume the Auca will be any more responsive than the Quichua are? For a few days he stopped eating, food sickened him. It was Betty, his wise help-meet, who first grasped what was going on. *Satan is trying to prevent this new mission.* Satan senses that his domination of El Oriente is coming to an end, and he is throwing his worst at them. So, having realized the cause of his depression, Jim is more eager than ever to get the ball rolling. Last night, something happened that sealed his new resolve: he learned that Operation Auca is no longer a secret.

"The friar at Shandia came over to the house. Somehow he's

figured out we're doing airdrops on the Curaray. He wouldn't say how he knew. He wanted to tell me stuff about the Auca, how they're busy killing each other off in vicious reprisal spearings, for one thing, how unsettled they apparently are right now. He was all worked up, he thought we'd drop our plans right away when we heard this. But really, it clarified everything for me. I went to bed, and during the night a terrible sound woke me. A hideous scream—it took me a minute to figure out what it was. And then I realized: God was allowing me to witness the cry of a dying Auca as he hurtled headlong into Christless damnation without even a chance."

Jim stops for a minute, and Marj focuses her eyes and sees that his face is working, as though he's fighting tears.

"Brothers and sisters," he says in a voice thick with emotion, "we can't afford to wait another month."

Is there a space as comforting as a tidy kitchen? The saved and the unsaved alike have their kitchens, many as pleasant as this one, with its cream-coloured walls and aqua cupboards (a colour scheme Marj dreamed of when she was a girl) and the cream-and-orange canisters lined up in descending order (a wedding present from Marj's auntie) and the wide window through which a cool breeze blows in from the river. It's dark now, the window is a black square filled with the invisible jungle. The dangling light bulb floods the kitchen with harsh, hot light, and against that black square their faces bob, white and ghoulish, unattached to anything, and out of nowhere a memory comes to Marj, a story from her childhood, something that happened to people on a neighbouring farm.

This family had the same sort of cellar Marj's family had, an earthen cave that you accessed by lifting a ring and pulling up a square of the kitchen floor on a hinge. As at Marj's, all their preserves were kept down there in rows of dusty jars on home-built wooden shelves. One day in early spring the mother sent her daughter, a teenager named Margaret, for a jar of canned cherries. After what seemed like forever, the woman said to her son, "Reg, go down and see what's keeping Margaret." A few minutes later the kids still weren't back, and she called and got no answer. Her husband, who'd been snoozing on the daybed in the kitchen, was awakened by her shout. "What are those darn kids up to?" she said to him. He got up with a sigh and went to the hole in the floor and lowered himself down the ladder. The woman was busy getting supper on, she ran out to the garden to pick some greens. When she came back, the kitchen was still empty and the house was silent. Then a terrible dread seized her and she lit a kerosene lantern with trembling fingers and lay down near the cellar door, dangling the lantern into the dark. And saw the first pair of legs, her husband's, sprawled on the earthen floor below.

There is a kind of gas that pools in earthen cellars. You breathe it, this air from the subterranean reaches of your own home, and it smothers you. The woman, whose name was Nora Prescott, had never heard of such a thing before it took her entire family.

She sits very still, aware of Barbara Youderian motionless beside her. Barb's skin is warm against Marj's arm, but instead of moving away, Marj leans a little closer. No one would dream of digging a cellar in the tropics, she thinks. In the tropics, you build on stilts. Flooding is the main concern, and, of course, termites. Everyone said Nate was crazy to build their house in Shell Mera out of wood beams and planks, but they couldn't afford cement blocks at the time. So Nate bought *dishpans* and set the foot of each wooden stilt in one of them. He filled the pans with kerosene, which he faithfully tops up every few months so termites can't get to the house.

Nate. In every corner of this house you see his loving care for his little family. The Christmas tree he made of balsa wood and painted green. "Joy to the World," they sang in the lounge after they put it up. In English, because you have to have some little thing for yourselves. Marj had managed to dig out the Advent calendar her mother sent a few years ago. The candies were long gone, but there was a tiny picture under each flap, the star, the shepherd's crook, the donkey. The children leaned against their dad, lifting one flap after another, studying the pictures. *Behold, I bring you good tidings of great joy, which shall be to all people.* Four fair heads bent close together, working out the story—and recalling that moment now, every fibre of Marj's body thrills to a truth so vast and so rich she can hardly take it in. Debbie, the serious sweetness of her six-year-old face, delighted to have Nate's full attention for the moment. Benjy, with his hand in unthinking affection on his baby brother's shoulder. Nate, glancing up at her: his trust in her, his energy, the quicksilver springs that feed their life together. It is absolutely enough, she thinks. That moment is enough to sustain me forever. And yet there is more. That's the thing about God, that's what He's telling her. If you belong to me, this joy will never end. Other people perish, but you will not.

LOCATIONS

19

OLIVE PHONES, AND IT'S A huge relief to hear her calm and mild voice. She says, "I talked to Abby last night."

"She called you?"

"No, I called her."

"She's not picking up when I call."

"I know. But she asked me to let you know she's fine."

"Olive, how are we supposed to sort things out if she won't talk to me?"

"She said she'd get in touch with you soon."

"Where is she?"

"She's in California. I didn't get the exact place."

"I'm supposed to leave for Ecuador tomorrow. I can't go without knowing where she is."

"I know. I think she'll be at Isabel's." Isabel is one of Olive's old friends.

"Did she say that?"

"Not exactly. But I said, 'If you're going to be in the LA area for a few days, why don't you stay with Isabel?' And she said, 'That's a great idea.' So you have to stop worrying, David. She is fine."

They hang up and David sticks his Cheerios bowl in the dishwasher and glances at the clock on the stove. He's got a million things to do and Sean wants to Skype at ten o'clock. If it weren't for worrying about his daughter, he'd be feeling pretty excited. *De parte de Jehová es esto: Es maravilla en nuestros ojos.* It's fun to be easing himself back into Spanish. This will be a much-needed spiritual reboot. He can't help but think that faith is less complicated in South America. If you ever said that out loud, people would accuse you of calling Ecuadoreans simple. And it's true he's been away for a long time, but from all he hears, Ecuador is still a society of old-fashioned sins. Purse snatching. Teen pregnancy. Public drunkenness. Not the moral atrocities bubbling up in America, not giving hormones to children to block their puberty so doctors can surgically alter their sex, not the *churches*. Sadly, that's what comes to mind as he tramps down the stairs in search of his big suitcase: the drive-in services where desperate people sit weeping alone in their Lexuses, the preachers with their sordid hookups in public toilets, the congregations who've sold their souls to vulgar politicians, the hucksters on TV selling survival products for the apocalypse, cancers you'd have to call them, noxious outgrowths of your very own cells, so that even straightforward utterances of the gospel are so tainted by association that you stand at a microphone in front of a huge congregation and are seized by the feeling that you should just—

Shut up, Pastor Dave.

Under the basement stairs, a trash heap of paint-splattered groundsheets and a broken ladder and extension cords. His stationary bike, a bad idea from the beginning. The basement. Always finds it a little creepy. People die from gas that collects in their basements. His mother actually knew a family. Sharon used to laugh when he pounded back up the stairs to the kitchen. Thank God you made it back.

David hauls his big suitcase out of the heap and bats the dust off it. He'd prefer to travel light, but he'll be dealing with two different climates in Ecuador. Inside it is the film camera in its battered brown leather case. It was a gift from the old photographer. He died not long ago, around the same time as Marj. David's brother Ben saw a notice online and forwarded it. This camera was a gift to Sharon.

David remembers everything about the night Cornell Capa gave it to her. It was before Abby was born, over twenty years ago. Betty was speaking at a missionary conference in New York and David and Sharon were home on furlough. They met up with her afterwards and walked across the park in the dark. This was before Betty and Stan were married. Betty had just given a terrific address to a packed auditorium, and she was in fine form, striding along in a houndstooth jacket. She knew the way to Cornell's apartment, a brownstone on the Upper West Side. Cornell was mostly retired, but his wife, Edith, still worked as an editor. She had dyed brown hair and she wore a wool dress the red of ripe berries. David remembers her serving them date loaf and soft cheese. Their place was crammed with books and magazines and records and photographs and art, all their interests and ideas carried into that apartment and never carried out.

They sat and reminisced about Cornell's visit to the Waorani settlement, his second time in Ecuador. A hellish trek in, Cornell said, and the first thing his eyes lit on at the end of the trail was this little blond girl in a gang of other kids, all of them naked as the day they were born. Of course, you couldn't exactly phone ahead to announce a visit, so it was a wonderful surprise. He arrived bearing rare treats. Camembert in cans. Chocolate bars. Everything a melted mess, but they ate it all anyway. He had dragged in absurd piles of gear (well, his porters had), and he taught Betty to use a camera. They did a book together, a beautiful book that sold hundreds of thousands of copies. The American woman's story of living with her husband's Stone Age killers, and Cornell's photos. The little girl was at the centre of it.

"Do you still speak the language?" Cornell asked.

Sharon shook her head. "Sadly, no. I wish I did. It would be a big help in our work right now."

"But she's got a big streak of Wao in her," Betty said. "You cross her and she puts her hand on her hip and gives you this exasperated look—that's the Wao."

Cornell was gazing at Sharon with great fondness. Of course, her fair hair was a gift, he said, visually speaking. It made the story more moving to their readers, who wanted to see Americans as agents of light to benighted peoples. "I conspired with Elisabeth to tell the story that suited her purposes," he said.

He sat with his feet up on a settee and held forth in his deep, rumbling voice. They were under the spell of that voice, of Cornell's Hungarian accent and the pleasure he took in his words, and the spell of that cozy room, and of Manhattan, its silver pillars of light in the narrow opening of the drapes. He called the Waorani the People in a way that made you hear the capital letter. "I have never lived in a more peaceful community," he said. "Or among more resourceful individuals. The People were technicians par excellence. The blowguns alone. And in such splendid physical condition. I was a joke in the jungle. I was useless—worse than useless, because I ate so much. Rachel made a big deal of the fact that I'm Jewish. She kept saying to the People, 'Cornell is from Jesus's clan.' I could see them looking sideways at my belly and my big flat feet. The People are revolted by body hair, they pluck it all out—and look at me! I set your ministry back by years."

Betty laughed and laughed. He was not a Christian, but he was the man God had sent, and it seemed he could get away with saying anything. For hours that night they sat warming their hands on the embers of his dazzling story.

SEAN AND THE locations manager are sitting by a tiny pool against a backdrop of green foothills. At David's suggestion, they're working out of a hotel close to the airport at Shell Mera. On Skype they look conspicuously alike. The sunglasses, the baseball caps.

"I just read your father's biography," the locations manager says to David. "Oh, man. Man."

"Ah, that's great. And how's everything going with you guys?"

Sean closes his eyes and swivels his head. This looks like a *no*, but it means *No words*. They met their Waorani language interpreter this morning, a woman named Carmela. As soon as they can book a plane, they're planning to fly into Tiwaeno, the settlement where Rachel and Betty lived. Three of the men involved in the massacre are still alive, and live there.

The locations manager says, "I'm trying to decide whether to go too. What would you think of Tiwaeno as a location? Could we use it as the site where the killers lived pre-contact, where Nate did the airdrops?"

"No," David says. "Out of the question. It's nothing like a pre-contact settlement. Why would you make the effort to haul a crew all the way in there?"

Sean says, "I've been hoping we can use the actual beach on the Curaray for the massacre. I'm going to find a pilot to take me in."

"There's no way. There's nothing there. It washed away a few years back."

"It was good when we went down for the baptisms."

"Yeah, well, that was years ago. I've talked to people about it recently. That playa's gone. The ironwood tree where they built the tree house is gone."

"There's other rivers and other beaches," the locations manager says.

"As for the Waorani settlement," David says, "you're going to have to find some old people who know how to build the traditional longhouses. You need a certain kind of palm, but it's everywhere."

"None of the Waorani still live in longhouses?"

"Well, the Tagaeri and the Taromenane likely do, up in Yasuní, but no one knows their exact location."

Sean stirs. "There are still uncontacted Auca?"

David can see this news spark between him and the locations manager.

"There are clans living close to the Peruvian border. *Los Pueblos en Aislamiento Voluntario*. It's against the law to approach them. The people have absolutely no immunity to outside diseases. The government has established what they call an intangible zone. Don't even think about it." He tries to change the subject. "You couldn't send me a copy of the script, could you?"

But a few issues have been identified with the script and it's in rewrites. David would be better off waiting for the new draft. If he wants something to read in the meantime, Sean suggests he pick up a copy of the bible. Not *the* Bible, but a screenwriting book that spells out what a movie has to do scene by scene. It's based on the elements of the hero myth, and the archetypal hero, of course, is Jesus, with His death and resurrection. "It's extremely cool," Sean says. "You use this formula and you're giving people the gospel message, whether they realize it or not."

"Is Rachel going to be in this film?"

"Rachel?"

"My aunt. Rachel Saint."

"Yeah, that's one of the things we're still talking about."

After they sign off, David wanders into the living room. The dog is curled up in the leather recliner and he doesn't have the heart to throw him off. Poor little guy. It's off to the kennel for Gizmo.

His phone pings. It's a text from Abby.

Dad, how do you translate this sentence? *Tus abuelos le dispararon a mi tío.*

Your grandfathers shot my uncle. He sinks onto the couch.

CORNELL IN THE JUNGLE

20

THE TRAVEL GIRL AT *LIFE*, whose name was Gloria, whose first language was Spanish, who had pretty ears with pretty rhinestone earrings in them and a photograph of Bernie Schwartz (a.k.a. Tony Curtis) on her desk, told him he would need a pilot to take him to the little town where the group's headquarters were. "I'll be on the phone tomorrow while you're on your flight to Ecuador," she said. "The minute you land in Quito, give me a call and I'll let you know what I've arranged. Here's a list of my contacts and their numbers. Here's some cash to get you started. Their currency is the sucre, these are hundred-sucre notes, and each one is worth about seven US dollars. Here's your ticket to Quito. You're flying Delta through Houston. The car to La Guardia is going to be outside your building at 6 a.m. sharp." *Don't sleep in, Cornell*, her look added.

"You are an angel," he said, folding the worn bills and sticking them in his back pocket. "Isn't that what *Gloria* means? Angel?"

"No. It means glory."

"Oh, well, same thing, huh."

Time to go home, Cornell.

He was just back from a trip to DC and he'd need different gear for this one. In his apartment he dumped the dirty laundry from his suitcase onto the floor and then repacked into his duffle: extra chinos, two shirts, socks, shorts, his shaving kit. A cap, a rain jacket. He located his old flask in a drawer and filled it with Canadian. How many cigarettes? He conjured up his brother, Endre, an old pro at this sort of thing, saw him standing by the bed drawing on a butt so short he had to pinch it between his thumb and forefinger. Ten packs, Endre said. You never know if you'll see a store and besides, they're great currency. And ten rolls of thirty-five-millimetre. Dig out those waterproof pouches. This is the jungle.

The windows were dark, but it was only seven o'clock. He lay face down on the bed and woke up at ten, hungry as a bear. He went to the bathroom and splashed water at his bleary eyes, fingering the crease where he'd lain on the strap of his duffle bag. There was nothing in the place to eat, so he went out and walked three blocks up Sixty-Third to Pogo's, where they served something called "hot pot" at all hours. It could have been goulash if only the cook understood paprika. He gave his order to the bartender and was making his way to a table when he spied one of Endre's old girlfriends dancing on the square of red linoleum beside the jukebox. Her name was Edith. He had run into her maybe twice since Endre died, the last time with a tall art director he vaguely knew, a misanthrope who affected a plaid waistcoat. But there she was with a couple of tourists, Midwesterners Cornell judged them to be. Bill Haley was playing and they were passing her back and forth, her hair and her skirt flying like a teenager's.

He veered over towards the dance floor and snagged her with one hand. She was startled, but he saw in her eyes that she was glad and she tripped after him, laughing.

"Where is Mr. Fear and Trembling?" he asked when they got to the table he had his eye on.

"He drowned in the East River," she said. She wasn't drunk after all. Over her shoulder he could see the bolo ties making rude gestures in their direction, and she turned halfway and screwed up her face at them.

"What are you drinking?"

"Don't you have a wife yet, Cornell?"

"Not that I recall."

Oh, Edith! The way she put her hand on your arm—there's still love in the world, you think. It was a decade now since she and his brother were together. She was Cornell's age, five years younger than Endre. Cornell adored her back then and he trusted that Endre did too. By then his brother was no longer Endre Friedmann, he had reinvented himself as Robert Capa, and he was in Europe for a long time during the war. So Cornell would arrange to meet Edith at the movies, where he would sit with one arm around her shoulders in brotherly affection, strands of their cigarette smoke drifting up into the projection beam. One day the movie was *Gaslight*, and as they gazed for two hours at Ingrid Bergman's luminous face, he sensed a tightness growing in Edith. It turned out that Endre had photographed Ingrid Bergman when she was in Germany to tour the troops, and Edith knew it. When he got back to New York, he made light of it, said Bergman was a big baby. But then, a month or two later, he was moving to Hollywood. He could be a real asshole when it came to women, but Cornell was not inclined to judge him too harshly for that one. Although, honestly, on the merits, it would be hard to choose. Edith had this lovely warmth that rose like colour in her face, and a way of resting her eyes on you while you talked, and those pleasant breasts. You could picture her living in a house in Yonkers, walking her children to school. But it was strange, she'd devoted her life to bringing a bit of happiness to lost poets and filmmakers on Eighth Street. Though when Ingrid Bergman threw Endre out, Edith wouldn't take him back. He ended up moving in with—who? That girl who tried so hard to be sophisticated (Cornell could picture her perfectly, a sour smile, her short hair dyed red as if she were imitating Gerda Taro from Endre's Paris days). The sour girl and Endre broke up shortly before Endre was killed, and it must have been a nasty breakup, because even Endre's violent death didn't satisfy her; she slammed the phone down when Cornell called and she didn't come to the funeral.

And so. Endre saunters into Cornell's thoughts for ten seconds, and he's worked his way through four lovers.

Cornell caught the waiter's eye and signalled another round for Edith. Feeling tremendous relief to be in her company, to know that the same thing was in both their minds. It wasn't even that he missed his brother, whose involvement in his daily life these last years had been mainly to exasperate him. It was more, when he had a day or two of respite from thinking about him, that he was nagged by the sense that he was neglecting something at his peril. *There is still work to do here.* Maybe Edith felt the same way, because from the minute she raised her eyes on the dance floor, he knew she was eager to talk.

His hot pot arrived and he dug into it, and she went to claim her coat and bag from the table where the bolo ties were sitting.

"They weren't really such bad guys," she said when she got back. "They're calling you Bigfoot."

"I'll Bigfoot them right up the arse." He stood up and reached to take her bag. It was a stout leather briefcase, crammed full. "What have you got there?"

"Manuscripts, Cornell."

He'd forgotten what she did and it clearly pissed her off. "But what, I mean?"

"Oh, a first read of a couple of novels. They're both, I don't know, about adultery, what else? And I'm editing some essays on Ralph Waldo Emerson."

"The guy who lived by the pond?"

"No, you schmuck," she said affectionately.

"Why are you dragging it all around town?"

"I'm working at home tomorrow."

"Well, come to my place. I've got something I want to show you."

It was raining, just a light mist, as they walked back. Midnight by then, and he was regretting it just a bit, knowing she'd never go to bed with him and thinking about his early call in the morning. But then he glanced at her walking hatless through the rain and thought, What a stroke of luck.

She knew the apartment, it had been Endre's at one time. She walked in and switched on the lights and took a turn through the living room without taking her coat off. Nothing on the walls but Robert Capa photographs.

"You've turned the place into a shrine."

"No. What am I going to hang but photographs? I'm not vain enough to put my own up. These . . . these are new. I just wanted the chance to study them."

He gestured to the row of framed contact sheets. He'd moved the furniture out from the wall where they hung and installed new lights.

A few months ago, the sour girl with the short dyed hair, Red, let's call her, had appeared in Cornell's office on Herald Square and handed Cornell a cardboard valise with metal corners. Inside, the valise was fitted with cardboard cross-hatching like an egg carton, and each little cell held a coil of negatives. On the lid of the valise was a legend in Robert's handwriting. Dates and places. All from 1944 and 1945.

"Where are the rest of his things?" Cornell had asked sternly, trying to hide his delight.

"He took everything else. He just forgot this case."

Endre would never have left his negatives. She'd hidden the valise, the cow. She was punishing Endre, or extorting him. Now he was dead and it didn't matter. But she hadn't thrown it in the trash, and she didn't ask Cornell for anything for it.

He printed the contact sheets himself and was amazed. The liberation of Paris. A visit to Picasso's studio. The Battle of the Bulge. A sky filled with paratroopers, Endre among them; that was when they freed the territory east of the Rhine. In many cases Cornell had seen the three or four shots that were published, but he hadn't seen the whole narrative. They were all so fine. Sometimes the focus was off, but every shot was well composed. Endre always knew what he was shooting and his timing was uncanny. It had been like that from the beginning, from the early days in Paris when Cornell was developing Endre's film in the bidet in their hotel lavatory.

He tried to pick a few sheets to mount, but in the end he hung them all. Because his brother was in every shot, just outside the frame.

He poured a drink for Edith and for himself. They toured the gallery with their glasses in hand. This work was from the years when Edith and Endre were theoretically together. She was in awe.

"He saw everything," she said. "Everything."

She was entranced by the scenes in Chartres, where French women who had slept with the enemy were paraded through the streets with their heads shaved, and Robert had had to run backwards at the head of the pack to catch their faces—and really, was there a more dramatic sequence of photographs in the world? The shocking pelts of hair on the cobblestones, mostly dark but a few grey, old women shamed for their daughters' sins. A girl's hand protectively over the scalp of her half-German baby. The crowd, their faces: they've just been freed from the Nazis, it's their own hatred that occupies them now.

The perfect frame—it was near the end, as though it had taken Robert a while to work his way fully into the story. A bald girl strides through the mob, her eyes on her baby. Her father carries her bundle, everything she owns tied hastily into a tablecloth. Quick, quick, desperate and quick, a gang of gleeful girls running to keep pace. It wasn't her humiliation Robert caught, it was her stony-faced refusal of it. Once Cornell had picked that shot out, it seemed to him that the difference between it and the frames around it was incalculable. When you looked at them all together, almost-there was nowhere.

"I use these as a test when I bring a girl home. Can she pick out the money shot? Because if she can't, we're done here."

Edith pointed to it without a moment's hesitation.

"I'm keeping you," Cornell said, dropping a kiss on the top of her head.

She didn't flinch. But he was homely and shambling, his hopes were dim.

"What is it, though?" she asked. "What makes it the best?"

"It's . . . irreducible. You can't take anything away, or add anything."

"I guess that's it. I wonder whether he knew when he got it. Do you? Do you know when you get the shot that it's going to be the one?" She tipped her face up to him.

"Sometimes I have a pretty good hunch. And sometimes I never get it. That's the difference between Robert and me."

They sat at either end of the couch with their stocking feet companionably together and talked until the bottle was empty. Afterwards, Cornell remembered saying at one point, "He wanted it. It was the only next thing for him." His death, he meant. They had washed up on a peaceful shore in the US after the typhoon of their youth, and the big war was over, and Endre had no idea what to do or be.

It was a terrible thought, and Edith didn't buy it. She laid her hand on Cornell's shin and said, "I guess it's easier to think that way. But people are pretty good at reinventing themselves."

Then she talked about the book she was editing. She said that Emerson had had a little daughter who died, and she was interested in what he wrote about losing someone important to you. She wanted to show Cornell a passage in the manuscript in her briefcase. She got up and dug it out and flipped through the pages. She paused, her face grave in the warm light, and read out:

"'This calamity, it does not touch me: something which I fancied was a part of me, which could not be torn away without tearing me, nor enlarged without enriching me, falls off me and leaves no scar. I grieve that grief can teach me nothing, nor carry me one step into real nature.'" She raised her eyes from the page and looked at him steadily. "Ralph Waldo Emerson. And his darling daughter had just died. I'm trying to understand what he meant."

She read the lines again. But it was late, the words washed over Cornell leaving nothing behind. Finally she tore the bottom half off the page and held it out to him.

"Hey."

"This is a copy. I can type the page again."

He took the paper and shoved it into his trousers pocket and poured them both another drink. All he could think to tell her was the bargain he had made with his own grief: that every time the vat of bitter brew was thrust at him, he would drink it down, on condition that it was finite, that he would never have to swallow that particular foul mouthful again. So far the drafts kept coming. But he held out hope that there was an end.

"Really?" she said. "Because if the pain is gone, so is the one you loved. It means you've forgotten."

"Is it over for you?"

She lifted her shoulders. "It's different for me. It's ages ago, Robert and me."

Her eyelashes cast spiky shadows on her cheeks. She *was* ten years older, he could see it now in the way the light fell on her face. And he loved what he saw. She might lie to other people, but she didn't lie to herself.

IT WAS THREE in the afternoon when the Delta flight made the steep descent into Quito. Same time zone, the stewardess told him, same population as Manhattan but five times as big—it was a gargantuan mountaintop village. In the terminal he said, "*Telefono?*" to a uniformed kid leaning against the wall and tipped him a lilac-coloured bill.

Gloria's voice came over the line.

"What's a hundred sucre worth again?" he asked.

"You set him up for life," she said. "Listen. The US rescue service is flying in an R4D at four o'clock. To the town I mentioned, Shell Mera. I talked to a Major Nurnberg. He said they'd take you."

Cornell was near a window overlooking the tarmac. He could see a plane with US navy insignia, but it looked like a DC-3.

"No, that'll be it," Gloria said.

Two uniforms were smoking by the ramp. Cornell stuck out his hand. "I'm from *Life* magazine. I'm doing a story about the missing Americans."

"You going in with us?"

"That's the idea." He set his gear down and pulled out his own cigarettes. "Where'd you fellows fly in from?"

"Panama."

One of them could have been a twelve-year-old, the big goofy teeth. "You won't get a story if we don't find these guys."

"How'd they get lost?"

"They're not lost. They been killed by Indians. Nobody's saying, but I'd lay money."

"They hiked into the jungle?"

"They flew in. They got a pilot with a single-engine."

"How long since they've been heard from?"

The kid looked to his partner, who shrugged. "Sunday?"

Today was Thursday.

"A guy flew over yesterday in a float plane. He seen the Piper on a beach and he says it's stripped. And he's pretty sure he seen a body."

"He didn't land and check it out?"

"Nobody's going in without backup. Jungle injuns are scary fuckers."

It was a half-hour flight to Shell Mera. Cornell ended up on the floor of the R4D and he couldn't see a thing. Ten minutes in, he was swamped by nausea. Endre flashed him a wolfish grin. You asked for it, he said. You could be shooting that feature on Lawrence Welk.

He got queasily off the plane to find that they weren't in the jungle yet. This was a shabby little town on the seam where the rainforest was stitched to the mountains. The airstrip ran along the edge of a wide delta. The Rio Pastaza was somewhere over there, a marine said.

Major Nurnberg stood on the tarmac directing traffic. Cornell stuck out his hand and said his name.

"You're the newspaperman?"

"Photographer. *Life.*"

This didn't seem to register. The kid with the teeth was dragging a crate away from the plane. "Hey, girly-boy," he yelled. "Pick that fucking thing up."

"Why such a big airstrip here?" Cornell asked.

"You're in Shell. *Shell?* The oilmen pulled out and the preachers moved in." His voice was mild, but he had a belligerent bearing and he never looked at Cornell.

Cornell asked about an American-style frame house overlooking the airstrip, a large, two-storey affair with a screened veranda.

"That's their headquarters."

Cornell filled his lungs with the green-smelling air. His nausea was gone. "It's very pleasant," he said. "I was expecting a furnace."

"We've still got some elevation. You get these microclimates along the slopes of the Andes."

Four aircraft sat on the tarmac. Two cargo planes with US insignia and a big amphibian with a flag Cornell took to be Ecuador's. Also a little Bell helicopter with its bubble of a windscreen.

"Brought it in on Tuesday," Nurnberg said.

"But you haven't started the search?"

"Chopper was in pieces. Takes two C-47s to transport it, two days to put it back together. We've got an operation planned for tomorrow."

Cornell was eventually shown a map in a plastic sleeve, the spot the five men had headed into, where they had set up camp, hoping to lure some nearby Indians out of the forest, an uncontacted tribe called the Auca. The pilot flew out every evening, overnighted at a jungle station called Arajuno, and flew back with supplies in the morning. Last Sunday, the men's sixth day in the jungle, they scheduled a radio call to their wives for 16:30. That call never came. A ground party had left from Arajuno two days ago and was expected to arrive at the site midday tomorrow in a flotilla of canoes. About twenty Ecuadorean soldiers and a couple of other American missionaries, including a doctor, in case the men were wounded in the jungle. Nurnberg had promised Dr. Johnston that he'd have aerial surveillance in place over the Curaray by 1200 hours. The fear was that the Auca would be waiting in ambush. The ground party had hired a crew of friendly Indians as porters, and they'd serve as an advance guard. About the Auca, about the purpose of the lost Americans, Nurnberg had no intel. He did promise Cornell a seat in the chopper, as well as a rubber poncho.

They went to the mess tent and a marine served out some reconstituted glop. Just as they tucked into it, an American woman appeared at the entrance, carrying a tray of hot dogs.

"The freezer was a little overstocked," she said when the marines cheered. She was a short woman with curly dark hair, and she had a little blond girl with her. "Debbie's brought you boys the mustard. We want to thank you for all you are doing to find Daddy, don't we, honey."

The little girl leaned against her mother, shy and staring. The woman took the jar from her, and she scooted out of the tent.

Nurnberg got up to talk to the woman. When he sat back down, he said, "That's the pilot's wife. Quite the little gal."

"I wonder if you'd take me over to the house and introduce me."

He didn't respond and Cornell asked again.

"She's been on the radio all day. Two canoes of friendly Indians went into the site from Arajuno. She got a call to say that they found a body in the water, just the one. The girls don't know yet whose husband it was."

21

THAT WAS THURSDAY. IT WAS Saturday noon before he got back from the Curaray. Saturday and Sunday he sat on a folding canvas stool the mess sergeant gave him, his back against the freight shed, his leg throbbing from an injury he'd sustained in the collision of two dugout canoes. Sat smoking and watching the missionary house. It was not clear to him what they knew, whether anyone had briefed them. DeWitt, the helicopter pilot, was out helping the Ecuadorean army search for the killers, and Dr. Johnston and Major Nurnberg were on their way home with the ground party, still dodging lances on the Rio Curaray. The house was quiet.

Cornell had been thirteen when his father died in an upstairs bedroom in their house in Budapest. His mother came home from the market and went upstairs to take off her second-best dress and was greeted by the blackened face of her husband dangling from a noose. That's what Cornell hated his father for most, doing it there, installing a hook especially for the purpose, earlier, a day or two before, and (if he knew his father) taking wounded satisfaction in the fact that no one noticed and guessed why. Endre might have figured it out, but Endre was in Berlin by then, or maybe Paris, he had left Pest a few months before. Cornell's mother had two sisters living nearby, and they were already at the house when Cornell got home from school. He heard the wailing and commotion a street away.

This house stood in a verdant glen with swallows flying over it, blue sky reflecting off its windows, a testament to American opportunism. Sometimes a little boy came out and rode a tricycle up and down the veranda for a while and then went back inside. Indians Cornell had learned to call the Lowland Quichua walked by on the road. Some of them apparently knew; they paused and crossed themselves. A donkey was tethered on the edge of the delta, and a small boy came to move its stake. Several times a float plane landed on the invisible river, and twenty minutes later two or three Americans would emerge from a path and walk soberly up to the house.

Young marines interrupted his vigil to scrounge cigarettes. He handed a pack over and said genially, "Now fuck off, okay?" From time to time the company in the house spilled onto the veranda and even the yard, where they stood talking with their heads close together. Some had babies on their hips. Later, when they were all inside, he heard singing, a chorus of voices lifting in a simple melody.

He had no idea how to frame this story because he didn't grasp what the story was. He sat with eyes half-closed, trying to refuse the images from the Curaray. They had scoured the campsite from the air and found nothing, so the helicopter lifted and moved back to the river and began to follow it downstream. It was dark between the forest walls, like being at the bottom of a canyon. About a hundred yards from the campsite a tree had fallen into the river. Cornell was the one who noticed a white bird on a branch close to the water. No. It was a foot snagged in the foliage, the sole of a bare foot. He shouted and De Witt moved closer. The backwash of the copter opened the water to reveal the smooth, muscled form of a man's back. Cornell couldn't fit those two body parts into a coherent human shape.

He was right out of his depth. Endre never just photographed carnage as such. He might shoot a row of corpses lining a road in Belgium, but his focus was the old woman walking the centre of that road, casting her eyes to the side. Her expression told the story.

What was the story here—or, to be more exact, what was the *Life* story?

Last Wednesday, Cornell's editor had sent him to Washington to shoot what he called a perfect *Life* story. It was a national competition of marching bands. For a full day he trained his lenses on college kids in snowy uniforms mincing across a square, spinning their cymbals skyward. Cornell had never paid much attention to parades, and this one struck him as grotesque. Unruly pubescents buttoned into uniforms and marching in straight lines, dreaming of glory, revelling in conformity, blasting out the tunes other kids had marched to their deaths to. That's what he saw and that's what he shot, and then, ears ringing, he packed up his cameras and went across the street to a bar where a radio murmured from among the amber bottles on a shelf, and learned that five American men were missing in the Amazon. For whatever reason, he was moved to call his editor and to come to Ecuador, where he failed to get a story, and almost died.

They evacuated the site on the Curaray in a panic because a motherfucker of a tropical storm was dropping down on them. They'd found only four bodies and they lined them up face down in a shallow grave. Soldiers were desperately kicking sand into it when the pilot waved Cornell towards the helicopter. But he couldn't leave, he had nothing, so he ended up joining the ground party, wedging himself into the cavity of a massive dug-out tree trunk between an overgrown American missionary and one of the wheels of the Piper, which, along with several unwieldy sheets of corrugated tin, his new friends were determined to salvage from the site. As he planted his ass in the bottom of the canoe, the sky broke entirely apart and all he could see was the bent shoulders of the man in front of him. Water poured onto Cornell's head and shoulders as from a spout, and water rose in the tree trunk. His trousers were plastered to his shins and his shoes were ruined. The canoe shuddered and ran to ground. This is where they attack, the missionary shouted in his ear, at the river bends. They leapt out and dragged the thing through brown water where, the missionary shouted, caimans and water boas lurked. Nurnberg was up ahead, screaming orders. Again and again the canoes ran to ground, and the rain never let up. After several hours of this hell, Nurnberg called a halt. He'd spied an open area he thought they could defend. While armed guards prowled the site, the soldiers threw shelters together, using the sheets of tin. Cornell squatted in one of them, deafened by the hammer of the rain. His duffle bag was in Shell Mera. He went through its contents in his mind, the dry shirts and socks, the flask. He thought about the fifth man they were abandoning. He thought with wonder of himself, just yesterday morning riding a yellow cab through Manhattan as the bagel sellers opened their kiosks.

The rain stopped. The light rose. The air was still water-drenched, but they were able to spread out a little. Cornell lit up a cigarette, guiltily. He could see hunger on the faces of the soldiers around him, but he had brought only the one pack from Shell Mera. The Indians cut massive banana leaves for beds and built a smoky fire. The American who had prayed by the grave stood by the fire and prayed again in Spanish, evidently invoking the Americans who had been lost. *Señor Jaime, Señor Nathaniel, Señor Rodrigo.* This was Art Johnston, the doctor Nurnberg had mentioned. Afterwards, Cornell made his way over and asked, Could I ask you about this mission? He said, Yes, but not tonight. He looked pale and exhausted. No doubt these men had been his friends. An Ecuadorean soldier passed out tin plates of rice and beans with something stringy on the side. Cornell ate and then shot off a roll of film. Night fell, and the racket of the forest replaced the racket of the rain. Guards were organized in two-hour shifts. The missionary who had shouted in Cornell's ear in the canoe offered to share his rubber groundsheet, but before Cornell could lie down, his stomach declined to wrestle any longer with his supper and he lurched to the edge of the forest and chucked it up. Then he and his bedmate lay down side by side in the breathing, croaking, crawling dark, Cornell's cameras and the missionary's flashlight between them.

His name was Frank Drown and he had the bland, handsome features of a TV announcer. He said he was stationed at a jungle settlement to the south of Shell Mera, where he'd worked alongside Roger Youderian, one of the dead men. He was a talker, and the horrors of the day were eating at him. He had a pathological terror of dead bodies, and when they beached, he was overcome by a stench he assumed was rotting flesh, though it turned out to be just a pot of pork and beans the fellows were preparing for their supper the day they died. Then, out in the canoe that recovered Roger's body, his gorge rose again and he couldn't hook the tow rope to Roger's belt loop.

"God does this," he said, his white face close to Cornell's ear. "He knows what our weaknesses are, and in His fatherly love, He challenges us on exactly those points. I failed the test. One of the Indians had to do it. Amazonian Indians don't know fear. When we got the body to shore, and we had to lift it—"

"They don't feel fear? That's why you send them in first?"

Frank was taken aback. "Why, it's only prudent. They know the forest. They can read the signs, how the monkeys and birds are behaving. Whether savages are waiting in ambush."

"I think it stinks. They're not even armed."

"Very well. We'll let you lead the charge tomorrow, shall we?"

Cornell lay back. He'd tied the hood of the poncho tight around his face, and his flesh was slowly cooking in its rubber case. The taste in his mouth was foul.

A crash, very near, and its echo.

"What was that?"

"Just a tree," Frank said after a minute. "Their roots are shallow, and when it rains . . ."

"Listen," Cornell said. "What can you tell me about the Auca?"

"Nothing," Frank said.

By morning, Cornell's stomach had settled down and the sky above the canopy was blue; the storm had been a bit of staging laid on by a director with a taste for melodrama. The forest was prepared now to show them its splendour, a thrilling sight. But his chinos were still wet, they were cutting into him. Crotch-rot, he thought. His left leg hurt like hell; it had been jammed between two of those brutal canoes in one of their mad scrambles. He limped a few steps into the jungle and unzipped and directed his piss into a fabulous terrarium. Carnivorous flies feasted on his neck. He resorted to cursing in Hungarian.

They were back on the river when the beating of heavenly wings filled the sky and the whirlybird dropped down between the forest walls. DeWitt beckoned in the open doorway. Cornell glanced back to see Major Nurnberg giving a thumbs-down.

"No!" Cornell hollered. He was waving both arms like a maniac. "Yes! Yes!"

So. The lily-livered Manhattan photographer was coptered out to Shell Mera and for two days sat on a canvas stool and smoked and watched and waited. His shoes were bloated and shapeless, his leg was turning purple, and rather than subsiding, his insect bites were brewing up new venom. He sat against the freight shed even while the equatorial sun was straight overhead, letting it burn the memory of the rainforest off him, the bloated bodies hanging in brown water, the white foot fixed in a tree, the failings that bled up from his core and blossomed on his skin. From time to time he reached down for his sore leg and lifted it manually to ease the aching. When nothing happened at the house, he studied the faraway Andes, a child's drawing of mountains. Then the two marines were in his face, driven back by boredom, and he pulled out his flask of Canadian Club and passed it around, an instant hero. When it was empty, the three of them walked in the direction the marines called uptown. A small boy ran towards them crying, "*Carne! Carne!*" and led them triumphantly to a tiny kitchen crammed with heavy-bottomed sacks of corn, where a woman with a baby tied to her back sold tin plates of food through a window. Cornell peeled off one lilac-coloured bill for the cook and another for the boy. He had no idea what he was eating, but he liked it. Misery has a short memory.

On the way back to the airstrip he noticed a white form behind the mission house, and said goodbye to the marines and cut across the yard. A tall and very thin girl in a sleeveless dress was standing like a crane beside a tree, studying the bark. He walked across the grass towards her, trying not to limp. She saw him and gestured. "Look. Look at the size of it."

The light was failing by then and he couldn't see anything. She bent and picked up a stick and touched it to the trunk and a patch of bark repositioned itself. Then he could see it: a tarantula with a mottled body as big as a mouse. It moved again, packing itself like a dilapidated umbrella into a knothole in the trunk. Perfectly still now, though the hole was too small to accommodate the entire hairy apparatus of its legs.

Her eyes met his in shared amusement. "It thinks it's hidden because it can't see us," she said. She smiled, showing a gap between her front teeth. She was, he guessed, in her late twenties. She had light-brown hair pulled into a ponytail, and she was barefoot.

"Shouldn't you have shoes on?"

"I should. They keep the yard trimmed so short that I think I'm in New Jersey."

"You don't live here?"

"No. I work at the Shandia station. It's about a day's trek north and east. I'm Betty Elliot. And—you are?"

He told her his name and that he was a photographer doing a piece on the missing men. He kept a bit of distance, conscious of the booze on his breath. "What exactly is your work?"

"I've just started a girls' school. And we've been running a medical clinic out of the house. But my main focus is learning the Quichua language so I can translate the Scriptures into it. Our mission society requires us to write a grammar and have it approved before we can begin to translate. So right now I'm working on that. It's such a challenge."

"Languages are brutal."

She looked at him critically, no doubt hearing his accent. "What languages do you speak?"

"Yiddish. Hungarian. French, sort of. Parisians don't enjoy hearing their language massacred. I guess it was because of language that my brother and I took up photography. You say it all without words."

"Yes, well, you don't know a brutal process till you try to learn an Amazonian language. It's not just that we don't have common roots. It's—well, it's a whole different way of looking at the world." The gap in her front teeth gave her a rakish look, but everything else about her was intent and focused. "Quichua verbs all have endings that indicate *evidentiality*. Whether the speaker saw what happened with his own eyes, or inferred it, or learned it through hearsay, that sort of thing. It's so hard to master. And so—well, you end up casting the Holy Scriptures as a sort of hearsay. Because there's no verb form that allows for divine revelation. I have all these girls in front of me with such spiritual hunger in their eyes, and it's almost like their language doesn't let me share the gospel with them."

"Hearsay," he said. "It sounds like *heresy*. I wonder if one is the root of the other?"

Her eyes sharpened. Darkness was falling fast, the air was cooling, and he could feel his sunburn pumping out heat. This girl was tanned to the point that her face was the same colour as her hair.

"Just think if God had allowed humanity one language," she said. "Our work would be so different."

"Isn't there a fable about that? About a time when everybody spoke the same language?"

"It's not a *fable*," she said, amused at his ignorance. "It's in Genesis. All the nations got together to build a tower. The Tower of Babel."

"Right—I know that story from a rabbi. He called it the Tower of Hubris. Jehovah dropped down into their bedchambers at night and scrambled everybody's brains—right? When they went to bed, they all spoke Hungarian, or maybe it was Yiddish, and in the morning they each spoke something different, and they never figured out how to get past it. They had to schlep their stuff onto their camels and walk off in different directions." He smiled at her, hoping to get another glimpse of the toothy gap. "Hey, maybe it was Esperanto."

She gave her head a little shake. "It was Hebrew," she said, as though this was a matter of historical fact.

He had no idea how to talk to these people.

A yellow square fell onto the grass—they had turned a light on in the house.

"That house must be full tonight."

"It is. Johnny Keenan brought in almost everybody in the area. The fellowship is so rich—but sometimes I can hardly breathe and I have to get away."

"Very sad that their mission ended the way it did."

"Ended?" She seemed genuinely surprised. "As long as the Auca are unreached, this mission hasn't ended."

"Well, you have to concede it's a setback. And a great tragedy for the families."

But she wanted to quarrel with that too. "I don't think the word *tragedy* has any meaning here. We have no idea what God has in mind. His ways are not our ways." She began to move slowly towards the house. She told him that she used to work with the Colorado Indians on the other side of the Andes. She had a gifted language informant, a man named Micadio who was fluent in both Spanish and Colorado. One day he was killed and no one would tell her why. Then later, she was travelling to a meeting in Quito and the suitcase containing all her language notes and files was stolen off the back of the banana truck. "I prayed and prayed," she said. "I was convinced God would return it. But he didn't. A whole year's work down the drain, and no way to go forward. Why? Why would God allow such a thing to happen?" She turned her keen face towards Cornell. When he didn't answer, she said, "It forced me to trust in Him. I had no option. And so I think about that now. This—on the surface, it's devastating. But we don't see what God sees. The very fact that He would call for the sacrifice of five such wonderful men—well, it suggests that His plan for this is . . . *glorious*."

In the yellow light from the window, he could see her shining eyes and the cloud of insects around both their heads. He didn't take against her as he had against missionary Frank. She was a loping greyhound of a girl, a plucky young woman working alone in the tropics and putting her mind to the hardest questions there were.

"You said 'five wonderful men.' You don't think it's possible any of them escaped?"

"No. They're all dead. How could it be otherwise?"

"Well," he said, "from my point of view, it's a terrible tragedy.

Listen, I usually travel with a *Life* journalist, but I'm on my own this time. I really need to speak to the families. I haven't wanted to intrude. But I wonder—"

She interrupted him. "*Life*. You mean *the* magazine? THE *Life* magazine? That's who you're with?"

"Yes."

She looked at him intently with her mouth slightly open, and he saw that he had found himself a go-between. "I'll set something up for you. Not tonight, but tomorrow. Are you staying at the airstrip? I'll come over and get you. For tonight—I need to go in now, but—" She paused, thinking. "Would you like photos of the men?"

She ran up the steps. It was ten minutes before she came back and handed him a big brown envelope. "These pictures—you might think of them as calling cards. Nate tinted the first set so they'd look more realistic, and then the men dropped them from the plane so the Auca could get to know their faces. I've written the names on the back. The fifth man was Peter Fleming. I don't have a photo of him, but I'll get you one."

Cornell took the envelope over to the mess tent, where a generator was running. Four headshots of American men in their late twenties or early thirties. Probably too young to have served in the war. He studied the photos, trying to animate the faces, and also, heavily, to match them to what he'd seen on the Curaray. Good-looking men, all smiling with determined goodwill. Three of them held a ring of feathers such as jungle dwellers might make, held it up beside their faces, and the fourth was wearing the feathers. He turned that picture over. The man wearing the feathers was named McCully. He turned the next one over. The name on the back was Elliot.

He sat back. Betty Elliot.

Nothing in that woman's manner had suggested she was a grieving widow. Nothing. It wasn't just that she was composed—she was animated, and engaged. She'd talked as though she was outside this tragedy, with space in her heart and mind to turn it over and look for its finer meanings.

He slid the photos back into the envelope. A strange fatalism takes you over when the unthinkable happens. Eagerly, so eagerly, you try to leap straight from stunned disbelief to the distant shore of acceptance, avoiding all the shit in between. *Well, it's happened, what can you do? Life goes on.* People call this "shock." In his experience, it protects you for about two days. Three at most. This was a week in.

But of course the news had come out to these women in drips.

DEWITT CAME BACK the next morning. Cornell walked over to the chopper to get the news. They'd located the Auca settlement from the air, DeWitt said. They found the longhouses burned and the yucca ripped up, hastily harvested. The Auca had vanished, moving deeper into the forest, which apparently was what they always did after a massacre.

Cornell asked whether the Ecuadorean army was going to try to track them down.

"Doesn't look like it," DeWitt said. "Colonel Izurieta's been on the shortwave with the missionaries. They want him to leave the Auca alone."

"Why would they have a voice in that?"

"I don't know. Seems like they run the fucking place." He lifted his sunglasses to the top of his head and Cornell saw his eyes for the first time. Lashless, sore-looking. "Want to go see what's uptown?"

But Cornell kept his vigil by the freight shed. It was early afternoon before Betty Elliot came across the tarmac to get him. The sun was bright, eating at her from both sides, but when she got closer, he saw she was carrying a tiny child.

He got up and walked towards her. "Mrs. Elliot," he said. "I'm so sorry. I had no idea when we talked last night that your husband was part of this excursion."

She shook her head, dismissing his chagrin. "I realized you didn't know, and I should have told you, but I guess I was glad for the chance to talk to someone who was not feeling terribly sorry for me. I think the Lord sent you over just as I stepped outside, because it helped me to talk to you."

She looked older this morning, and very tired. Gaunt, he would call her now, rather than slim, and he was conscious of his own knowledge from the Curaray. He was an eyewitness, as the rules of evidentiality went.

She gave her child a hitch on her hip. "Mr. Capa, this is Sharon. She'll be a year old next month."

Cornell put a finger out and touched the kid's hand and she smiled and clung harder to her mother, as cute as a baby monkey.

"She looks just like her daddy," Betty said.

"He must have loved her to pieces."

"He loved everybody. He loved life. Nobody loved life more than Jim."

"I am so sorry."

"Well, Jim always knew he was expendable to God's purposes. We both knew it. Anyway, I came to tell you. We just got a radio call. The ground party's back in Arajuno, and Dr. Johnston is going to be flown here to brief us. Would you like to photograph that briefing? In an hour or so?"

"Yes, of course. Could I come to the house now? I'd love to take a few pictures while we wait."

"We can ask."

He went to grab his camera bag. As they crossed the tarmac, he tried to thank her, saying, as he'd said many times before, "I know it's very hard to face a camera at a time like this."

"I think you'll find that all the wives can testify to God's sustaining grace. In fact, we are grateful to *you*." She paused by the steps to the house. "You know, about ten years ago, a group of missionaries were killed by savages in Bolivia. The world never heard about that sacrifice. It was like they gave their lives for nothing. So when you said you were from *Life* magazine, I understood that God had something different in mind this time."

22

AGAIN THE DOCTOR STARTED WITH prayer, and for the first time Cornell heard his words in English: "Lord, our hearts are heavy with grief today. And so we turn to you, the great physician who heals all wounds, and ask you to be among us in your tender loving-kindness and mercy. It's a dark path you have given us to walk, but we see the footprints where you have gone before, a God who knows grief, a loving father who sacrificed His only son. You ask us to bear nothing you have not borne yourself, you deliver no pain you can't succour. We trust you, Lord, we call down your presence among us today, we ask that you minister personally to each of these your sisters in their hour of need."

They'd closed the door to the hall. Just the five wives in the kitchen now, with the comforting angel of death Dr. Johnston at the head of the table, and Cornell Capa, God's recently recruited documentarian, leaning against the counter with his camera in hand, attempting to wrap himself in a cloak of invisibility. Children in the radio room pressed their faces against the glass, and women came to take them away. Kids were underfoot in every corner of the house, and everywhere the sound of their fretful crying, as if they had shouldered that task for their elders. Everybody Cornell had seen walk across the tarmac in the last two days seemed still to be here. A few Ecuadorean officials, but mostly missionaries from other stations in the area and personnel from the US, white, middle-class Americans of a certain type, earnest, tidy, bland. On their side of the glass, immortality still reigned. Death was close, they'd felt the cold draft as it beat past them, and still they moved and breathed. But inside the kitchen a crossing-over was happening, it was a transformation as profound as death, the shattering of happy families. He was present to it, he was a witness, their eyes all closed, but his open to a scene made sacred by their courage—he watched them and felt his skepticism slip away.

"Lord," Dr. Johnston prayed, "five of your saints had a happy homecoming last week. And though our impulse is to cry out in pain, to weep with sorrow at being left behind, we know that your divine purpose is being realized here on earth, and we praise you and thank you that we can be part of this holy work, and put ourselves in your loving hands, as these five saints did."

It was over. The women lifted their heads, eyes on the doctor. He told them matter-of-factly that the ground party had conducted a thorough search of the site on the Rio Curaray on Friday afternoon. Four bodies had been found and positively identified. Peter, Roger, and Nate had died of lance wounds. Their bodies were in the water, a little way downstream from the playa. Jim had been killed with a machete, and his body was caught in the branches of a fallen tree at the edge of the river.

"Marilou," Dr. Johnston said gently. He turned towards the wife Cornell had just photographed under a tree in the yard, a pregnant woman who had picked up a toddler and held him for her portrait, keeping her eyes on his bright little face. "Marilou, I think you know that six brave Quichua from your station canoed in to the site on Wednesday. They saw the plane and a single body in the river, and they recognized him as their beloved Señor Eduardo. They were too frightened to disembark onto the playa, but they took the time to pull off one of his shoes and toss it up on the sand so he could be positively identified later. I saw that shoe.

I wasn't able to bring it out, but I checked the sole and the size was stamped on it. It was a thirteen and a half."

Her face was a study in grief. "I know, Art," she said.

"I'm so sorry, Marilou."

"Don't be sorry," she said. "Think how kind God is, how He attends to the smallest things. Even now, in the middle of all this. He sent Fermin and Ernesto and the others in to find Ed's body before it washed away, so we could all be certain. I'm so grateful."

A smattering of gooseflesh rose on Cornell's arms. Good old God.

Dr. Johnston told them that a storm had been gathering and he'd had to make a quick decision about what to do with the four bodies. It did not seem feasible to bring them out after days in the tropical heat. He said that the playa was beautiful, an airy palm grove with white sand, that their husbands had been buried in the shade of a huge ironwood tree, and that he had conducted a service for them. "It will always be a sacred place," he said. "Everyone who passes by will sense the presence of God on that playa."

Dr. Johnston picked up a canvas sack of mementoes he'd brought back. He pulled out a pair of wire-rimmed glasses. They were muddy; he apologized for that, but he'd wanted to come straight here. "Peter's," they said, and looked at Olive. A sweet-faced young woman from the Pacific Northwest, a girl new to South America, a girl who had not objected to the word *tragedy* when Cornell had photographed her in the yard.

She had stepped alone to the spot Cornell indicated, no child in her arms. Someone noticed, and ran over and passed her a big black bible, and that was what she held. As Cornell adjusted the angle of her shoulders, he mentioned the fact that her husband hadn't had his photo taken with the rest.

"Peter wasn't really part of Operation Auca," she said. "He didn't feel he had God's leading. But he wanted to support his friends, so when he heard that Nate planned to make a supply run every day, he asked if he could help with that part of it. He decided this just the day before they went in."

"Oh, Christ," Cornell said without thinking.

"I know," she said in a small voice. "Even tragedy is not what you expect. It's . . . sloppy."

She reached out now to take her husband's glasses, not looking at them, just holding them on her lap.

Dr. Johnston handed out wedding rings. The notebooks he'd found up in the tree house. Journals, bibles, half-finished letters. A big stash for Betty Elliot, who was silent, sitting entirely still, only her eyes moving.

Dr. Johnston had a watch. "Nate's," Mrs. Saint said. Its hands had stopped at 3:12.

"What time was it when Pete and Nate flew in on Sunday morning?" Dr. Johnston asked.

"About eight thirty." This was Roger Youderian's wife, who had been staying at Arajuno with Mrs. McCully. "Marilou sent a meal in for the boys, blueberry muffins and a quart of ice cream."

Marilou lifted her shoulders. "Just a little treat."

"And what time was your last call from Nate?" someone asked Mrs. Saint, whose first name Cornell had written in his notebook an hour ago but had now forgotten.

"Around eleven o'clock." Her brown eyes brimmed with life. "He said the men were impatient that morning, Jim especially. He wanted to walk in to the settlement. So Nate agreed to fly over to see what he could see. He radioed me from the air. He had spied a party of men on a trail, walking in the direction of the playa. He said, 'They're on their way. They'll be here for the Sunday service. I'll call you at four thirty and let you know how it went.'"

She spoke calmly. It was heartbreaking. Cornell liked them all. His admiration for them was infinite. And there he was, squeezing off shots.

Then Johnston took a camera out of his canvas bag, a fine little Leica.

"Nate's."

"It was lying in water. It's too bad—those pictures might have shed some light on what happened."

"Oh, maybe they're from Friday," one of the women said fervently.

Cornell spoke for the first time. "You might be able to salvage something. Do you want me to take the film and develop it when I get back to New York?"

"You can do that here," Mrs. Saint said.

The meeting was over, the children could no longer be contained. Mrs. Saint walked quickly down the hall. He followed her to a darkroom, a well-equipped darkroom. A stainless-steel daylight tank and reels. Four large trays, all the chemicals lined up and labelled. No running water, but a barrel with a long hose. A good thermometer. A standard enlarger with an excellent lens. It was even equipped with a drying cupboard, a clever affair with an electric hair dryer fixed into it. The room was windowless and the doorway had a strip of felt top and bottom to seal off the light. Mrs. Saint closed the door to show him, flicking the light off.

"Nate built it especially, when he built the house."

"It's wonderful. It's—professional."

"I know. He—"

Her voice broke and a long wail tore through the dark. Cornell reached for her and tried to guide her to the stool, but she was caught in the vise of grief. She was bent over in the dark, her face on the counter. He stood with a hand on her shoulder while she wept. Her beloved husband so present in this room, or so horribly absent.

Finally she quieted and he sensed that she had straightened up and was trying to clean her face. He pulled out his handkerchief, and she took it with a whispered thanks.

"We promised each other we wouldn't do that."

"Not cry? How could you not cry?"

"We don't want people to think we're questioning God."

"Oh, I don't think that." He reached around her and turned on the light. "Would you like to stay and keep me company while I see what's on this film?"

She seemed glad for the distraction. She perched on the stool and he could see her trying to calm her breathing by an act of will. He began to line up the beakers, getting things ready so he could work in the dark by feel. He was still pressing his memory for her first name.

"Have you been a photographer for a long time?" she asked after a minute.

"Twenty years. My whole adult life."

"And you develop and print your own work?"

"Not anymore. But I always worry when I don't." He gestured towards the drying cupboard. He couldn't resist telling her. "My brother was a war photographer, and he went into the D-Day landing with the troops. That day, under constant fire, while men were dying all around him, he shot off a hundred and six frames. All but eleven of those shots were destroyed by a lab in London. The kid in the lab knew everyone was eager to see what Robert had, so he closed the doors on the drying cupboard to speed things up and the emulsion fried three of the films and half of the fourth."

"Oh, that's terrible. How did your brother react?"

"You know, I never heard him complain about it. But then, those eleven frames made his career."

He put the chemicals in a water bath to standardize their temperature. Room temperature was seventy-four degrees. He'd have to cool this water a bit. "You wouldn't have ice, would you?"

"I'll get you some."

When she came back with a little bowl of ice, she said, "I can't stay. It's chaos out there. I have to give the kids their supper and put them to bed."

"Aren't there others who could do that?"

"Yes. But not tonight. The kids are missing their dad. I'll get them settled and I'll try to come back when you're ready to print. I'm really hoping the pictures are from Friday."

Then she was gone, and he turned off the lights and set to work, winding the film into the daylight tank, counting off the minutes, shaking it methodically. The film in Nate Saint's Leica was twenty-four exposures. It looked as though nine frames had something on them, and then the rest of the film was whitened by the water. When he'd finished fixing the strip, he clipped it into the drying cupboard, set the temperature to low, and went down the corridor and out the door for a smoke. The whole gang seemed to be in the kitchen. He slunk past, avoiding all eyes. He'd begun to hate them in the hours they'd waited for Dr. Johnston to arrive. Not the wives, but the others, who struck him as feasting on the crumbs of tragedy. No doubt Frank Drown will be among them, back from the Curaray.

In the night, lying on that rubber sheet in the jungle, they'd heard a sound like a savage wind keening over steppes.

"Howler monkeys," Frank said. "You can hear them for three miles. They roar like that to guard their territory. The sound is pneumatically amplified by the bones in their necks. It's curious, though ... the loudness of the male's howl is negatively correlated to the size of his testicles. You're familiar with the term *negative correlation*?"

"You know quite a bit more about the monkeys out here than you do about the people."

Frank had stirred, irritated. "As it happens, the Auca are outside human ken."

"I beg your pardon?"

"They know what it is to have devils inside of them."

"I have no idea what that means."

"My point exactly." He'd lifted himself up on one elbow. "Did you take note of the plane? Did you see how viciously it was attacked? They ripped all the fabric from the fuselage. They bent the struts of the landing gear. Steel—they bent steel! Think of the malevolence—they were crazed with malice."

"Maybe they're just tactical. When the US Army went into France, they disabled a lot of German equipment. Lit the gas tanks of the trucks, threw grenades into the fucking panzers."

"Well, that was *war*," Frank said.

"What was this?"

He declined to answer. After a minute he said, "You talk like an American, but you're not, are you."

"I was born in Hungary."

"So you're a Catholic."

"I'm Jewish. I fled the Nazis."

"Ah, a Jew. Like our Lord himself." He mulled this over. "Do you know the Lord?"

"Not personally."

"Very few people grasp that as you do. The need for a personal relationship. I would say it's a good start."

A vague figure on the veranda had Frank Drown's stooped posture. Cornell stepped into hiding around the corner of the house. He smoked two cigarettes and then went back to the darkroom, and a Quichua woman came down the corridor with a plate of food from Señora Saint. Rice and fried luncheon meat and canned peas. He ate it and then he snooped through the darkroom. Nate Saint had a lot of gear besides his photographic equipment: batteries, extension cords, lanterns, an audiotape recorder, a slide projector, boxes of slides and audiotapes, all neatly labelled. On a shelf was a stack of leaflets on cheap paper with the headline "*¿Dónde vas a pasar la eternidad?*" During the night in the jungle, Frank had turned his flashlight on to show Cornell a similar paper he was carrying out. Nate Saint had been found with a lance through his heart, he said, and this paper was wrapped around its shaft, tied on with palm fibre. Cornell had been half-asleep. "The Indians wrote a message on a paper?"

"No, of course not. It's a gospel leaflet. The fellows must have dropped it from the air."

"These people are literate? In Spanish?"

"How could they be literate?" He turned the flashlight off and laughed softly in the dark. "I don't know why Nate would . . . I guess you just try what you can. But my point is, without being able to read, without knowing the language that leaflet was written in, the Auca understood that it threatened their savage ways, and they rejected it in the clearest possible terms. That is an understanding that can only have come from Satan."

And here was a stack of those papers. Maybe the missionaries thought they had magical properties, like Tibetan prayer flags.

The film was dry. He didn't bother printing a contact sheet; he was going to want a good look at every frame. He'd make a double set of prints, with the assumption they'd give him one.

So then he moved to the enlarger.

Camp-out photos, boys having a jungle adventure. The tree house slapped together with the sheets of tin that had proved so useful to the rescue party, and two heads peering out of it. The plane, and three men lounging in the shade beside it, killing time, rubbing themselves with bug oil. A bare-chested American standing in the river exuberantly holding up a huge catfish. That was Jim Elliot. A match for Betty in vitality, Cornell would say, although more conventionally good-looking. From what the doctor said, he knew it was this man's body he'd spotted in the tree in the river.

Frame four was a single human figure. Watching the image appear, Cornell felt the hair on the back of his neck prickle. It wasn't an American. It was a naked, brown-skinned man. Young, and sturdy, not an ounce of excess fat on him, his chest and face hairless. He's wearing nothing but a fibre band around his belly as a jockstrap. His earlobes are stretched around big round plugs. His hair is long, but cut short around his face and over his ears. He looks straight at the camera. His face is expressionless. He has what appears to be a model airplane slung over one shoulder, and behind him a long, slender machete is stuck by its point into a log. The background is a river.

Then Cornell couldn't work fast enough.

An Indian girl walks away from the camera, long hair hanging down her back. You can't see her face. Another shot of her looking over her shoulder at the airplane. Same stretched-out earlobes, her hair cut into the same thick fringe. She's young, attractive, unsmiling, unaware of what the photographer's up to, checking things out. Then a shot of her face-on, leaning back in a pose that looks almost seductive. She's holding an open magazine, holding it strategically, as if someone gave it to her to cover herself.

In the foreground of frame eight, a different woman sits on a log. She's older and stouter, and she has deflated breasts such as Cornell has never seen, flat, triangular flaps. Her head is half-turned to look at the girl, who clutches a drinking glass in one hand and whose other arm is full of stuff, as if she's been given so many gifts she can hardly hold them all.

They had made peaceful contact, at least at first.

And of course the wives knew—they'd been communicating with the men all week. That's why they kept mentioning *Friday*.

Frame nine was the money shot, Cornell decided, and someone other than Nate Saint had taken it. The young man is squatting comfortably on his haunches and Nate is crouched beside him with one knee in the sand. Two good-looking men in their prime. The Indian man's body is compact in relation to Nate's, he's much smaller. The man's mouth is wide open, he's eating what looks to be a hamburger, and a hand reaches in, dribbling something from a small bottle onto his back, bug oil, it must be, as if they can't introduce him to America fast enough.

Nine printable frames. Then, on the film, the encroaching water like spilled blood.

THE NEXT MORNING, Cornell was out on the runway early. The two mechanics from the rescue service were at work on the copter, breaking it down. This mission was over.

He still hadn't seen Nurnberg. Rumour had it that the R4D was going to fly in from Arajuno that morning and then straight out to Quito. Cornell spied a marine moving around and asked him if he knew what time the plane was due.

"Zero eight hundred."

He glanced at his watch. It was ten to eight.

He had exactly two cigarettes left and he wanted both for himself, so he walked up the tarmac a way, his duffle bag on one shoulder and his camera bag on the other. Out of cigarettes and out of film, something he'd been careful to avoid for his entire professional life.

He glanced over at the house, thought of the brave women pulling themselves out of their solitary beds and getting breakfast for their kids. This morning he'd woken up to the pain of this calamity. A shitty, shitty thing. Eight little kids growing up without their dads. Nine: Mrs. McCully was heading home to give birth to another baby alone, her heart full of gratitude to God.

Is it better to have an empty drum of a heart, or to fill it how you can?

He was wearing his city trousers. In the pocket was the half page Edith had ripped out of her manuscript for him. Edith. He opened the folded paper. "I grieve that grief can teach me nothing, nor carry me one step into real nature." The words had force but no meaning. He lifted his cigarette to his lips and then, in the inhalation, he was breathing him in, his brother, more alive to Cornell than the young marine he'd just talked to. His dark, straight eyebrows, his extravagant, hungry features, the lithe way he moved, how fully his spirit occupied his body. His knowing. Oh, Endre. Cornell turned towards the river flats and gave himself over to drinking it down, today's acrid cupful of grief. At a world moving on without Endre—it was unendurable. It crashed at him, wave after wave. Oh, my brother. He spat out a clot or two of it, and the wave subsided a bit, and he reached into his pocket for a handkerchief. Finding nothing, he bent over and pinched the top of his nose and blew hard, the way they dealt with snot playing in the alleys of Pest. When he surfaced, an American woman was standing ten yards away, watching him. A little older than the women in the house, and tall and stout. But she had that same look of wilful plainness about her. He stood for a minute or two to compose himself and then he walked towards her and said, "Cornell Capa," and stuck out his hand. Not surprisingly, she ignored it.

"Rachel Saint," she said. Another wife? He must have telegraphed his confusion. "The sister," she added.

"Oh. My sincere condolences."

She didn't respond.

Maybe she'd flown in from New Jersey or Pennsylvania or somewhere when the crisis broke, to be with her brother's family. But he hadn't seen her in the house. Well, it was a big place, with numerous closed doors along the corridor. She was still staring at him. She had the most intense eyes, pale, otherworldly. She was wearing a white cotton dress and her fair hair was braided into a fat queue, in the style of the Quichua. She made him regret his lack of film.

"You're the photographer," she said suddenly.

"Yes. And I'll be writing a short feature. So any insights you have about what happened, I'd be grateful if you shared them with me."

"Insights." She made a little humph of disgust and looked away.

"Really, I'm very sorry," Cornell said after a minute. "It's a terrible loss for you. I understand your brother was a wonderful man."

No reaction. And she made no effort to leave or to change the subject. She stood like a huge, disconsolate child, her eyes on the orange windsock. She gazed at the mechanics over by the helicopter. Then she turned her head and stared again at Cornell with the same impassivity.

"I have some idea what you're going through," he said helplessly. "I recently lost my brother. He stepped on a land mine in Thái Bìn, in Vietnam. He was a gifted photographer, a bit of a legend in his own lifetime. Robert Capa."

She kept staring, as though she didn't grasp that he was sentient and looking back. Under her gaze he couldn't seem to keep his mouth shut.

"It's very hard to lose someone who seemed to be invincible. My brother was five years older than me and I followed him into photography. Hell, I even took his name. I guess I've tried all my life to be half the man he was."

This unleashed a savage denunciation. "My brother followed my vision to the mission field. He tried all his life to be half the servant of God that I am. Turns out he was nothing but a liar and a cheat."

Ragged trees, and the kid with the rifle, motionless against the freight shed. The snowy cone of a mountain pinned to the sky. Over the delta, white birds lifted and tilted.

Ralph Waldo Emerson was just wrong. Nothing in Cornell's life was ever as real to him as this moment. *Losing my brother made the world real.* That's what he'd like to say to this woman.

"You're flying to Quito?" he asked.

"No."

But she stood waiting implacably with him, as if it made no difference to her or to anybody else where she was or what she did.

WE SORROW NOT

23

THE YEAR BEFORE BETTY CAME as a bride to Shandia, Jim dreamed a house on the ridge and then he built it. So close to the Jatun Yaku that you can hear the murmur of the rapids as you drift off to sleep, so close that the fish are still flipping in the basket when fishermen come peddling their catch to the door. But high, high up, safe from floods: a house that stands in the forest, and is made of the forest, and fraternizes with the forest through its many windows.

Just walking the path to this house is a meditation. You feel you're *rising* rather than climbing. The heat falls away, the squalor of the settlement, the demands and reproach of the people. You come first to a wonderful garden full of native plants Betty can't name, although Jim could. He collected everything, especially orchids, tiny and delicate and spotted, carrying them home in the waist hem of his T-shirt and planting them in a tree. Then you come to the kitchen garden, the avocados, pineapples, corn, papaya, yucca, plantain, tree tomatoes. Then the roses, the gardenia. The orange tree Jim planted the day Betty moved in—it was in instant fragrant blossom. The profligate hand of nature and her husband's husbandry: working together, they re-created Eden on this ridge.

When Betty was flown back to Shandia after the men's bodies were found, the whole settlement streamed out to the airstrip. Olive was on the same flight; she had come to pack up or give away her things, and then she was going home to America. The instant the pilot cut the engine, the Quichua mourning wail began. A collective scream that rose in pitch as each of the women climbed out of the plane, and then descended in three mournful notes. Betty struggled out with Sharon in her arms, and imploring hands reached at her from all directions. The people had *adored* Señor Jaime and Señor Pedro, their hearts were broken. But she could not stop to speak to them. Jim was waiting for her in the house; after two weeks apart, she was desperate to get back to him, and the wail was unendurable. Picture a deep, deep well and wave action starting up in the black water at the bottom of it.

She stepped onto the trail to the ridge, and many of the mourners followed. At the first rise, her servant Gabriel turned and stopped them with a command. The wail hushed and she climbed alone up to the house, her hand on her baby's plump little thigh. She opened the door and stepped inside. Jim, his joyful spirit, was there, as she had known he would be. She walked through the house and sat down on the bed, still carrying her baby, at peace.

SIX WEEKS LATER, bending and pulling out a drawer, she marvels at how God has sustained that peace. She's going through Jim's shirts, picking out a few that are not too worn or stained. She started this job an hour ago, and got lost in thought and wandered away, and now she's back at it because the new pilot will be here soon. His name is Eugene. He was working as a crop-duster in the Midwest when he heard about Nate's death, and within a month he arrived in Ecuador. Not surprisingly, he's poorly equipped for the full range of the climate. Marj radioed to ask if Betty could help, because (practical above all things) she had already given Nate's clothes to the poor of Shell Mera.

A widow's job: all five of them face the wrench of disposing of their beloveds' things. People might picture them weeping over the task. Fray Alfredo, for example, has very definite ideas about mourning. Not long ago, he climbed the trail to the house to offer his condolences. "How are you, really?" he asked, his mild eyes full of sympathy.

"I'm doing well," Betty said.

"There is often a grace period with a bereavement, a numbness, and then the force of the loss hits."

It's true that she was numb for a few hours after the call came, after Marj called to report radio silence from the camp on the Curaray. It was early on the Monday morning and she was turning the handle to keep the shortwave radio going (their radio had a crank, she had to labour to learn the news), and as Marj signed off, Betty looked up and saw Rachel standing stricken in the doorway. Maybe that's why her voice was so strange and so flat—she had to fill Rachel in, and then she had to tamp down Rachel's fury. There was never an instant when they fooled themselves about what that radio silence meant. In the stupor of those hours they had to decide what to do. She was a wooden creature moving, telling Gabriel some version of the news, making arrangements for Johnny Keenan to pick them up with the float plane, packing their things and closing up the house. They walked the Shandia Trail to a stretch of the river where Johnny could land, and then waded into the icy water, Gabriel carrying Sharon, Alberto and María-Elena with the suitcases on their heads. The shock of the water threatened to rip her limb from limb, and God said, *When thou passest through the waters, I will be with thee; and through the rivers, they shall not overflow thee.* She crawled into the back seat, and they handed Sharon to her, and then the plane lifted into the blue and the cabin filled with light, and she was filled with a sort of rapture, just at that lift. In a swoop she was with Jim in his ascension, she could almost see him, striding among the silver-edged clouds piled white on the river.

Numb? She runs her hand over the beautiful mahogany of the bed frame. Everything bears a richer meaning. This bed: it was Jim who built this bed with all its clever storage. Betty knew the mahogany as a tree growing close to the house, and then as a giant crashing to earth, and then eventually as their squeaky four-poster with Jim's shirts folded into a drawer beneath it. In the corner of her eye she sees him on it now, sprawled on his stomach, Sharon sleeping on his back like a baby possum.

We sorrow not, even as others who have no hope. The widow's task is not weeping but *thinking*. Every widow has to grasp the new shape of her life, so that she might embark upon it wholeheartedly. Every widow has to understand how one event led to the next. All along, Betty thought they were seeing what really was, but apparently not, because this new preoccupation absorbs her every waking minute.

Years ago, in the grey city of Brussels, Betty and her brothers were sent into treeless cobblestone streets to hand out gospel tracts in French. Their job was to entice passersby away from the echoing cathedral on the corner and into the bare room behind a shoe shop where their father preached. Then their father was found to have sugar diabetes and they were forced to come home. They moved into a big old house in Moorestown, New Jersey, and Betty's father bought a printing press and set it up in the shed and began to produce Sunday school materials. The house had trees around it and was named Birdsong.

Once, a lady came to stay at Birdsong. She had a smooth, round face and round, black-framed glasses. She wore a blouse the red fabric of which had been made by silkworms, and her hair curved into smiling points at each ear. The lady was to sleep in her bed, so at bedtime Betty's mother got out an old quilt for Betty to use on the daybed in the kitchen. But the lady said, "Oh, no, she must keep me company." They arranged the quilt on the floor beside Betty's bed, and when they were tucked in, the lady talked to her about China, where she served, where millions and millions lived in darkness. "Picture their souls like the stars in the heavens," she said. After Betty was asleep, the lady got out of bed and stepped on her, and Betty let out a shriek that scared the lady, and they laughed and laughed. Then Betty helped her find her way to the downstairs toilet, and afterwards the lady said, "It's cold, come up here." And Betty did, lying still on the rim of the narrow bed while the lady slumbered beside her.

The thing is, the lady's name was *Betty*: Betty Scott. She went back to China and married a fellow missionary named John Stam, and the next year gave birth to a baby girl. In the mail one day a newsletter came. It had a photograph of the Stam family standing by a big gate with a dragon carved on it. At the bottom, four Chinese characters were written in ink, with this note: *For little Betty*. Then, months later, the minister at Moorestown First Presbyterian told the congregation that John and Betty Stam had been murdered by Communists in China for telling people about Jesus. They were at home and they heard a mob coming up the street. While John scrawled a final note, Betty hid her baby in a sleeping bag. Then she and John were dragged out to be killed in the village square.

It was winter in New Jersey. It had rained and then turned cold, and the sidewalks were coated with ice. "What does 'beheaded' mean?" Betty asked as they walked home, and her brother Harvey made a chopping motion to his neck. Their father heard Betty cry out and he wheeled around and smacked Harvey on the side of the head and sent him sprawling.

Later, Betty's father came to her room and sat on the wooden chair. Betty was still kneeling by the bed. "God will be looking for someone to take Betty Stam's place," he said. "Yes, I thought so," she said. Her chest and her throat hurt terribly from crying. She was nine years old. She wore Harvey's outgrown boots with butcher twine for laces. She parted her hair cleanly behind her head and braided it herself into two tight whips. She was nine years old, but she was not a child as she knew other children to be; she had been born knowing everything. After supper, her father brought her an address and she sat at the kitchen table with fingers blue from the cold and wrote a letter to Betty Scott Stam's parents to tell them she would do it when she grew up.

One of the first fruits of martyrdom is the way it inspires others. Like Eugene, who now needs shirts.

This one, Betty thinks, holding up a white shirt in thick, soft cotton—this one I cannot bear to give away. She was with Jim in Quito when he bought it.

Excited voices float through the window. María-Elena has taken Sharon outside. The dog barks. Who knows what he's found in the garden, quite possibly a snake. But Gabriel is with them, their faithful house- and yardman who worked for Jim and Peter when they first came, and for Dr. Tidmarsh before that.

Betty slides the drawer closed and leans back against the bed, turning her face in to the mattress. She lived and breathed China for years, and it turned out to be a dead end. Now she studies herself, a pigtailed little girl writing a letter at a kitchen table, working out how horror can be translated into glory.

IT'S NOT EASY to leave that cool house in the murmur of the rapids, but having tramped her way down to the sun-sapped settlement, calling greetings to the people sitting on their stoops or working at their weaving, having put her hand on the heads of five or six children and helped to chase a chicken off the airstrip, having greeted Eugene calmly (he's terrified, he's homesick, she can see at a glance), and having surrendered Jim's shirts (including, in the end, the white shirt she loves), she finds herself sitting on the bench between the airstrip and the playing field, a pile of mail on her lap, unable to drag herself back up to the house.

The burden of thought has lifted somewhat, that's what it is.

It's a very pleasant village with the blue peaks of the Andes above it to the west. Dr. Tidmarsh was the one who laid it out. He persuaded the Quichua to settle and work at a nearby hacienda, and he had the men clear this huge playing field at its centre. Maybe he had cricket in mind, or maybe the commons of an English village, but it gave Shandia a nice formality, the houses spaced out all around the field. Jim and Ed and Pete always dreamed of a football league, although the Quichua boys didn't really take to team sports; they were more inclined to kick the ball exuberantly into the forest or run wildly over to help out their brothers on the other side.

Betty works a fingernail under a flap of her parents' letter. It's in her mother's handwriting as usual, but with her father's turns of phrase. They're distraught that she hasn't come home. This time her father takes up his straight pen to add a PS in his formal old script. "Do you not feel we have lost enough?" He's referring to her brother Harvey, and his self-pity appalls her. She slides the letter back into the envelope, squelching their voices.

They assume her calling was to Jim, and not to Ecuador—that's what is so irritating. She was called to the mission field long before she met Jim. Unlike Marj or Olive, who make no bones about the fact that they just followed their husbands.

On the other side of the playing field, three girls who used to be in her school are cutting palm fronds and fashioning ornate headdresses. Getting ready for some sort of festival, or are they just playing? Jim would have been over there in a flash, chatting and teasing. He was such a gifted fisher of men. Everyone was drawn to him. The girls have seen her, but they haven't called hello or even waved. She lifts an arm and rests her face in the elbow, savouring the darkness. In it she sees a truth that three years in South America have taught her: she does not have the gift of working with people. She never expects people to like her, they so seldom do, which leaves her freer to speak her mind, which tends to offend people. So it's a vicious circle, isn't it.

One of the greater mysteries, why God took Jim from Shandia and left her.

She opens her eyes to see a brown figure cutting across the playing field towards her. Sackcloth Fred, Jim says in her ear. If Fray Alfredo is wearing his cassock, brace yourself.

"Well, that didn't take long," he calls.

"What?"

"A new pilot. A new plane."

"Oh. Yes. Eugene."

"He's American?"

"He's from Wisconsin. Someone donated the plane—a businessman in Little Rock, Arkansas."

They're the only two in the settlement now who speak English, and you'd think they might be friendly. But they're more awkward with each other than they were before. Why? Because he thinks he's been proved right. Not that he takes joy in it, she doesn't accuse him of that. Just that it's between them.

"I hear you've sold your livestock. Does this mean you're going home?"

"We still have chickens," she says, dodging the question. "Gabriel is wonderful, but he has enough to do with the house and the garden."

"Yapanqui," he says automatically. That's their yardman's name in the village. It means *he who honours his ancestors*. Jim and Betty used to call him Yapanqui. Then Jim read somewhere that the name Gabriel meant *he who honours God*, and they were struck by the parallel, and changed Yapanqui's name in the hope that they could change his heart.

Fray Alfredo's eyes fall on the mail on the bench beside her, a brown tube labelled *Life* magazine. Betty's already seen the article, she had a look at Eugene's last week. "That's the magazine story," she says. "Would you like to see it?"

"Yes, of course."

She slips her hand into the tube and tightens the coil of the pages, as you have to do, and she manages to extract the magazine without ripping it. The cover has a photo of a man in a suit, Henry Ford II. But nine pages inside are devoted to Operation Auca. As she hands the magazine to Fray Alfredo, a paper flutters to the ground. It's from Cornell Capa. Just a note to give her his address, if she should ever need it. How kind.

Fray Alfredo reads the article with great interest while she waits patiently in the sun. Of course, it's mostly pictures. The photos Nate took of the three Auca visitors to the Curaray (the young man with his private parts painted over). Cornell Capa's photos of the rescue operation (one shot of a body, not Jim's). The portraits of the wives. The account is factual enough, but a little unconvincing, as if Mr. Capa dutifully reported things he did not in the least understand. How little sense the operation makes if you ignore the spiritual element.

Fray Alfredo studies Betty's photo and then lifts his eyes to her face. "How are you, really?" he asks, as though it took this sombre photograph to recall her situation to him.

"I'm fine," she says, irritated again at the *really*. "Actually, what I feel most is a sense of urgency. Like something very special is about to happen."

And this is suddenly true, and sharp. When Sharon's head dropped into the birth canal, the culmination of months of dreaming—it's like that. But Fray Alfredo's eyes are full of pity. She knows what he's thinking, that she's expecting this to be over soon, expecting the men to come back. Possibly he's right.

"Your husband and I disagreed about almost everything," he says, "but I miss him every day. He had a remarkable energy. I know this must be tremendously hard for you. Whatever you believe about the wider meaning of this loss, you have a human heart."

"You know," she says, "it's only from the perspective of the world that this is a loss."

"Whereas in your view . . ."

"Well, of course it's God's perspective I'm trying to see. We don't talk a lot about martyrdom in the modern church. But six men now have given their lives for the Aucas' salvation. That's a marvellous indication of God's love and purpose. It seems clear that God has moved a step closer to redeeming the Auca."

He freezes, startled. "Six?"

"If you think of the original sacrifice of Christ."

"Oh. I thought maybe you had information about Waorani casualties."

Something dark flutters across the scene, as if he's scared it up from the edge of her vision. This is the sort of scolding turn things always take with Fray Alfredo. She's far better off with just her Quichua friends. From this day forward she is going to scrupulously avoid this man.

She gets up and bends to pick up her letters. "I have to go. I left my baby with María-Elena and she needs to get home for her supper."

"I'd like to have you and your little girl over for tea," he says. "I have a wind-up gramophone—Don Carlos gave it to me. And I've bought some records through a mail-order catalogue. I'll play Schumann for you. Would you like to come one afternoon?"

"Of course," Betty says. The day that pigs sprout wings and fly.

She sets off up the airstrip. The evening rush hour, Jim called this time of day. People trudging home from their *chagras*, packs held by tumplines over their foreheads. "*Imaynalla*," they all call to each other, but they don't stop to talk. Those baskets of maize and yucca are so heavy Betty would tip right over if she tried to carry one. A new metaphor takes root in her mind, herself struggling under the burden of thought.

A woman with a jug on her head. It's Inkasisa, Gabriel's mother; she's on her way home from the river. A wiry widow of indeterminate age, as brown as a nut, as strong and nimble and busy as an otter. She lives with her huge extended family in a hodgepodge of a house near the Shandia Trail. She has always hated Gabriel working for the missionaries.

"*Imaynalla*," Betty calls.

Barely moving her head under the heavy jug, Inkasisa turns hard eyes on Betty. Betty looks eagerly back. Most of the Quichua in Shandia are friendly, ostentatiously friendly. But Inkasisa—what is it that she sees? Betty longs to understand.

With her eyes locked on Betty's, Inkasisa very deliberately raises a hand to her mouth and lays some words into the palm of it. She purses up her lips and blows the words in Betty's direction.

That's a spirit dart, Jim says in Betty's ear.

And it seems he's right, because Betty feels the dart land. In her side, just below her rib cage, she feels it sting.

Quickly, she walks towards their path, trying to shake the sting off, keeping her eyes on the distant blue mountains. When she gets to the top of the ridge, everyone's still in the garden, her curly-haired baby toddling wide-legged between the banana plants. Sharon is racing to catch Chevrolet, whose golden tail bobs just out of her reach. The walking is very new, her father never saw it.

Gabriel has cut a hand of tiny bananas, and he opens a finger for Sharon. They all cheer when she puts the tip of it to her mouth. María-Elena is there, and her little brother Alberto, who comes most days to help Gabriel. It's almost suppertime, they should not be feeding Sharon.

"Gabriel, what does this mean?" Betty shows him the gesture, mouthing words into her palm and blowing them at him. He shakes his head, he won't say.

"It is a prayer," María-Elena says firmly.

A prayer. Betty looks from one face to the other, trying to decide who to believe.

He WAS A miraculous gift to Betty. Jim Elliot, the heartthrob of Wheaton College, where both Betty and her brother Charlie were freshmen. Betty knew him slightly, they had one class in common, New Testament Greek, at which Betty excelled. Wheaton was considered the Ivy League of Christian colleges, but generally speaking, it had disappointed her. The girls were all in a tizzy to find husbands. Betty was serious and thin, she couldn't carry a tune, she never caught on to jokes. Team sports horrified her. Most girls could twist themselves into any giggling shape they thought would please, but there was never a danger of Betty Howard being anything other than what God had made her. Her nickname as a kid had been Mantie, short for praying mantis. At Wheaton she overheard the dorm supervisor refer to her as a wallflower. Well, people could call her what they wanted—the Lord knew her as the work of His hands.

That first Christmas, when her brother Charlie invited Jim home to Birdsong, they had a pine tree with real candles. Jim was helping them decorate and he crawled behind the curtain in the attic where they had always been forbidden to go and opened a box and found fifteen or twenty candle holders, pressed tin with clamps on them like clothes pegs; they were from when her mother was a girl. It was Jim who went out to buy candles and Jim who talked her mother into it. If it's going to be beautiful, it's got to be dangerous, he said. The candles burned for an hour, each one making a little shrine of the branches around it. They turned off the lights and sat gazing in wonder, breathing in the beeswax and smoke and pine, singing carols and telling stories about other Christmases. She was never shy, ordinarily, but she could hardly look at Jim. Dumbfounded by his face in the flickering light, its beauty and its danger.

That night, when everyone else had drifted off to bed, Jim and Betty and Charlie sat in the kitchen talking. After an hour or so, her brother, a tactful chaperone, fell asleep on the daybed. Her parents could not have disapproved: all Jim wanted was to talk about spiritual things.

She was sitting on the bench against the wall where as a little girl she'd sat between Charlie and Harvey. Charlie, who had now returned from the war, and Harvey, who had not. It would soon be the second anniversary of Iwo Jima.

"You must miss him terribly at Christmas," Jim said.

She shook her head. "He was never home. He was—well, I don't want to say my parents disowned him, but he wasn't welcome here from the time he was about sixteen. He never accepted Christ. When he did come home, it was just to fight." She stopped for a minute, seeing Harvey's defiant eyes. The raised scars on the insides of his arms, rows of them (how they got there, she could not begin to imagine), the cigarettes in his breast pocket. Always the smell of liquor on his breath. "It was like he was trying to bring Satan right into our house. I don't know how else to describe it. Even when he was a little boy. He had a rebellious spirit from the beginning."

Jim leaned on his elbows, listening with his very posture. "What a heartbreak for your parents."

"They blamed themselves. They used to say you have until a child is eight years old to break his spirit. And they thought maybe they hadn't been hard enough on him when he was little. But they were terribly hard on him. Nobody had more whippings than Harvey. I don't know what else they could have done." She did not cry, her voice was steady, but she felt her eyes sting. "And so now . . . well, it hurts to think that he has no more chances. That he's in a worse place even than when he was crawling on his belly in the Philippine jungle. I know it must grieve God too. Because I know God loved Harvey."

Most people in their church said, You have no idea what happened in his final hours. He knew the way of salvation. You have to trust that he repented and Jesus took him home.

Jim did not offer her that consolation. He said, "God is a God of love. He's also a God of justice."

"Yes," she said.

"It's hard, but it's the heart of the gospel. Our heavenly Father hates sin. Could we wish it otherwise?"

Their faith was like a knife. She sat on the hard bench and felt the sharpness of it at her core. The light shone off his hair. Off the kettle with its coiled handle. Outside in the night, snow was falling silently. Yes, she thought. Where Harvey is concerned.

"Charlie tells me you've been called to the mission field."

They talked for a long time about why China so thrilled Betty: how *foreign* it was, the mystery of the language and the script. It was a challenge that corresponded to her gifts. She ran upstairs and dug out the folding fan Betty Scott Stam's parents had sent her and showed it to Jim. She got a notebook and pencil and demonstrated the Chinese characters.

"You know, I envy you," he said, studying the characters. "I wish God would get around to telling me what He has in mind for me. But He's . . ." After a long pause, he said, "Betty, I'd like to tell you something I haven't told many people."

They both glanced at her brother, who was snoring gently. It was a cold night in a drafty old house, but the grate from the coal furnace was right under Betty and her feet and legs in their wool stockings prickled with dry heat. She swung her legs up onto the bench and smoothed her plaid skirt over them. She tipped her head back against the wall to take him fully in.

That was when she learned about the path of glory Jim saw before him, the very special calling. "It's hard to tell people because it sounds so much like ego. But it's not. I know what I am—I'm *nothing*. I'm flawed and weak and prone to sin. But I'm willing. In fact, I'm consumed with it. With the desire that God should take this wretched life and use it for His purposes. And God has told me He has something really big in mind, a glorious work for the ages, and all He needs is an obedient servant. And I've said, Here I am, Lord."

"'May Christ be glorified whether by life or by death,'" Betty said softly. This was the note John Stam scribbled the day the Red Army came for him.

The brighter the flame, the faster it burns. Jim had rolled the sleeves of his red flannel shirt up over his muscled arms and he seemed to exude warmth. Everything was clear to Betty in that moment. The courage it took for him to confess to such a grand conviction. His passion for Christ—he spoke a language she privately knew but had never had a chance to use. And the energy between them, the heat in Jim's gaze, the filaments of attraction that glittered through the air and snagged up her nerves, here, and here, and here—that delight too was part of God's glorious purpose. *As for God, His way is perfect.*

It was like a drug, this radical obedience to the God of the universe. Once you had a taste of it, you had to ask: why would any Christian choose to live any other way?

They went back to college more or less a couple, and the astonishment was palpable. The Lord was teaching a lesson through Wallflower Betty, saying to the others, *Seek ye first the kingdom of God, and all these things shall be added unto you.* Most Christians give lip service to promises like that, but she was chosen to testify to the reality of it. And then, perversely, as the months and years went by, to the discipline of renouncing the passions of the flesh to more fully serve the Lord. They loved each other from that Christmas Eve on, but it was five years before they married. God made them yearn for each other, and then He asked them to deny their yearning. Of course, China was an impediment at first. But then that changed, and Betty and Jim were free to go together wherever God led, and still Jim did not pop the question. He liked to let on that the delay was down to Betty (My gal has thrown me over, he'd say to people ruefully), but it was always him and his anguished conviction that God was calling him to celibacy. A fraught conversation in a corner of the student lounge (they would talk for hours, praying, sometimes weeping, until she had no idea what she was saying) and in the morning she'd wake up and realize they had put things on hold yet again. Why did he court her? He was drawn to her because he thought she was immune to his charms. He was so charming, always, relentlessly charming, that the world was almost manipulated into loving him. He loved her as a corrective to his excesses. He needed something to tether him to the earth. In that, she failed him—she was never immune to his charms.

And so we wasted years and years, she finds herself thinking furiously. *But*, she reminds herself: God gave us Quito. Swift sky and the rumours of mountains, the houses glued to each other instead of planted on the hills. Sparrows with jaunty crests hopping on the cobblestones. Thin mountain air that emptied out her head and fed her senses. The wood-panelled office where they were finally married, the promises they made in a language they imperfectly understood. A civil ceremony, it perplexed everyone. But they didn't need a servant of God to join their hands; God himself had done it. Their hotel room overlooked Plaza San Francisco, where a *grupa* from the mountains played and the sweet thread of panpipes insinuated itself between heavy curtains. Naked, in the afterglow of sex, Jim told her how maple syrup is made. The sap that comes out of the trees is thirty parts water, and you simmer it forever on a low flame to get syrup. That was us, he said. They waited so long that the concentrated sweetness almost killed them.

It was an apprenticeship in surrendering her will, those years of waiting. A preparation for what she's facing now: the loss of the thing she holds dearest. If she wants proof that their choices were in the divine plan, then she herself is that proof, the composure she feels facing the death of a man she loved beyond measure. Every night she crawls into the bed she and Jim shared, every night she lies down in the sheets where they partook of a feast of delights, and she prays, O Lord, bear me up. Every night she props her flashlight on the pillow and takes up her beloved's bible, Jim's well-worn bible with its soft leather cover and the gilt pretty well worn off its pages, and she finds that her bed inside the mosquito net is a secret tent as it was before. She lies in that tent and reads until exhaustion overcomes her, until all she can do is switch off the light and close her eyes. And God does not abandon her. Every night He prepares a feast for her in words of comfort and affirmation, and when she comes back to herself, morning light is filling the tent like mist rising from the river, and her baby is calling from her cot.

Dear Betty,

It was kind of you to write, and I'm sorry it's taken me so long to respond. It's good to hear your voice from time to time on the radio. I miss you as I miss the whole gang and our lively times together. I have been in touch with the other girls, and thought I would share all their news because I know your work does not leave much time for writing letters. Marilou had a healthy baby boy in February, three little boys now. She's staying with Ed's parents for the time being. Olive is with her own parents in Seattle. I think she's going back to school in the fall. Barb Youderian went home for a bit too, but she's here again with her kids, working in Macuma. It's not easy, I'm sure, but Roger was very unhappy in Ecuador, and Barb loves the work.

As for me, well, of course I can't manage the guesthouse on my own (the generator is on the fritz again at the moment), so Eugene is taking it over. He's flying home at Christmas to be married, and when he and his wife get back, they will be the new Nate and Marj. Everyone expects me to go home, but I don't think I could cope with the US right now. Having to tell our story over and over. And supporting my family would be a challenge. I guess I could get a job as a nurse, but who would look after my kids? My father is not well just now and my mother can't do a lot to help me.

It's a daunting thing to be the head of a family of little ones, but we are all in the same boat, and Marilou and I are working together on a plan. The welfare and education of missionary kids is a great concern of mine. Nate was content to send our kids to boarding school, and I was so determined not to let them go, and that impasse caused a great deal of grief between us. The only sure thing my heart tells me is that I am meant to be with my kids. Marilou shares that concern. She has decided to return to Ecuador in the new year, and she and I have come up with the idea of moving to Quito and setting up a school (making it as homelike as possible) where we can raise our families together.

As for Rachel—you will be interested to know that she and I have had a visit. It came about because of something you said. You mentioned in your letter that you had been reading the diary Jim wrote in the months before the killings, and that it helped you a great deal, that you were moved by the men's devotion and their reliance on God and their caution. You wrote, "The fellows did everything right, and this gives me great comfort. If their plan was perfect, then what happened at the end was also perfect and in the divine plan."

I must tell you that this is not an assurance I share. In fact, Operation Auca has left me with a heavy burden of regret, and one of the things that troubles me most is our treatment of Rachel. So I was determined to make things right, at least with her, and I wrote to her at Hacienda Ila, inviting her to come and see me. One day I heard the float plane land, and there she was walking up from the dock with a suitcase in hand. She had an Indian girl with her, barefoot and wearing the smock blouse and straight dark skirt that Quichua women wear for market day. Imagine my surprise when she introduced that girl as Dayuma. She called her "the first Auca Christian."

I hardly know how to tell you everything that happened in the two days they were with us. Dayuma is lovely, with bright black hair that she wears loose on her shoulders. Her smile is marred by missing teeth, but she is pretty nonetheless and has a quiet poise, a way of looking shyly down but still watching you out of the corner of her eye. I remarked that I would not have known her from a Quichua girl, and Rachel took umbrage at that, insisting that Dayuma is far prettier. She wanted to enumerate all the differences, having to do with the way Dayuma's feet have been shaped by climbing trees, and the holes in her ears. Dayuma bore this inspection patiently. She seems to feel affection and trust for Rachel and calls her by an Auca name, Nimu, which means Star. That Don Carlos allowed Dayuma to fly out to Shell Mera speaks of her new status at the hacienda. She was always a fieldworker, but after the killings Don Carlos dressed her in a calico pinafore and promoted her to the dining room. He has many prominent guests, oilmen and government agents, and he wants to display Dayuma and tell the story.

I was of course curious as to how she made the huge transition from the jungle. Modern conveniences do not seem to appeal to her, and she says she does not like the food at the hacienda. Apparently she experienced extreme culture shock at her arrival. The guns frightened her, and she almost had a stroke the first time she saw a horse. But according to what Don Carlos told Rachel, the thing that terrified her most was the oil portrait of his mother. It absolutely horrified her—how alive the face looked, and yet flattened like a pancake into a wooden frame.

On the subject of pictures, I learned that Rachel had never seen the photographs Cornell Capa developed, so I brought them out. Dayuma did not react to the photos as such, just to their subjects. Betty, she knows the forest people our husbands met and photographed on the Curaray! They are from her very clan! She immediately identified the older woman as her aunt, Mintaka. She put her finger on something in the photo I had never noticed—that the woman's stretched earlobe was once torn right open, there's an obvious scar. Tears flooded her cheeks and she lifted the photo and pressed it against her face. So then of course she examined the others with great interest. The man we call George—Dayuma's beloved brother Nampa would be about his age. She stared at length but finally shook her head, certain it is not her brother, and not able to say who it is. Then we showed Delilah to her and immediately she began to weep again, believing she recognized her sister Gimari, who was just a tiny girl when Dayuma left the forest. So it was a very emotional afternoon. How foolish we were to imagine that the Auca do not love each other.

I did manage to have a quiet word with Rachel, but it was not quite the meeting of hearts I had hoped for. I said, "I know how much Nate meant to you when you were children," and in her stony way she said, "No, it was Ben who was my special little boy." I told her simply that I was sorry we had shut her out. I could not give her any reason for having done so, but all the same, we parted on better terms, and her generosity touched me. I showed an interest in the language, and she asked whether I would like to have an audio recording of Dayuma speaking. We set Nate's machine up. Dayuma took it all in stride and willingly talked into the microphone. I suggested she might tell the story of how she came to leave her people and go to Hacienda Ila. I did not know what I was asking—the story is a fraught one for her, as you could tell by the way she spoke, often crying and apparently reliving brutal attacks. I had intended to have Rachel translate the tape, but she was upset by Dayuma's distress, and said that she had learned to keep their study sessions to single words and phrases to avoid this very thing. After they left, I decided to send it to you. No doubt you are better equipped than I am to derive meaning from an unknown tongue with no translation.

The children need their supper, so I'll sign off. I have sometimes marvelled at people who pour out their souls in long missives to their friends, but it seems I have become one of them. Betty, know that I think often of you and your little girl as we go about discovering what our new lives hold for us.

With sisterly love,
Marj

O GOD, SAVE BETTY

24

THE RAINS ARE OVER FOR the season, and they are facing hot, hot days. Chevrolet has vanished and Gabriel won't speculate as to what happened. Alberto wanders the yard with a wretched face. "Puma," he says. Betty tries to get him to put this in a sentence. Does he mean, "I saw a puma take Chevrolet" or "Others told me a puma killed Chevrolet"?

He starts to cry and Gabriel answers for him. The verb form he uses is *inferential*. "A puma must have killed Chevrolet."

All right, then. Chevrolet may well be back.

She plans to restart her girls' school, but the settlement is in the midst of a fiesta. Palm booths line the playing field with monkey carcasses propped up in them, blackened with smoke to preserve them. The people put cigarettes in their mouths and mock them, because they believe monkeys carry the souls of foreigners. Recently a fight broke out and a man was killed. So Betty avoids the settlement. She needs to keep a close eye on Gabriel. Yesterday he asked her to call him Yapanqui, and this morning when she forgot and called, "Gabriel," he pretended not to hear. When Jim was alive, Gabriel once asked for days off, alluding to an illness in his family, but apparently went into the forest to drink hallucinogens the shaman gave him. He was in a strange mood when he came back. What would she do if she lost him?

In the afternoon, while María-Elena plays with Sharon in the garden, Betty sets up the tape recorder. It's moving to hear

Dayuma's low voice. Jim took a photo of Dayuma when he went into the hacienda and Nate developed it. Meet Miss Rosetta Stone, Jim joked when he showed it to Betty. They regarded her as the key to everything. Where is that photo? She can hardly remember now what Dayuma looked like.

The voice on the tape is tentative at first, but soon gathers vigour. The language sounds profoundly different from Quichua and from Colorado. Is it tonal? Marj is right, you can learn a great deal from an untranslated audiotape, but Dayuma's obvious emotion complicates the listening. She begins a sentence and her voice thickens, and it's hard to know what is feeling and what is linguistic inflection, or possibly a glottalized vowel. In fact, it's hard to tell what are sound effects and what are phonemes. Betty identifies only eleven consonants, if you count ñ. She never hears a fricative. She never hears *j*, or *s*, or *r, f, h, l, v*. (No *j*, no *s*. They will have to find a new name for Jesus.) When she's familiar with the whole tape, she transcribes as much as she can into the International Phonetic Alphabet. There's no way to divide phrases into words. Rachel, with her fetish for the single word! Jim was a little like that, he wanted a magical leap into language. But from the time they took New Testament Greek together at Wheaton College, Betty always knew that the mind forms itself around the language (and even, can we say, the world forms itself around the mind?).

She works at it for an hour, sweat worming down her temples and her ribs. And then her resolve crumbles and she does what she has forbidden herself to do: she goes to the mahogany cupboard and gets out Rachel's blue book of language notes. The notebook Jim carried to the camp on the Curaray, the notebook Dr. Johnston found in the tree house and carried back out and handed Betty at the kitchen table in full view of the others, its cover a little grubby from the journey, smeared with mud. Marj Saint is the only other living soul who knows the provenance of this notebook.

In the days at Jim and Betty's just before Jim flew into the Curaray, Rachel was weepy, softened by her fever. She fretted constantly about this phrase book. "You don't think they will have thrown it out, do you?" she asked.

"No, of course not," Betty said. "Don Carlos is eager to learn the language. He'll recognize how valuable it is."

She told Rachel that Jim was hiking into Hacienda Ila by way of the Shandia Trail. "Don Carlos is selling him piglets," she said, which was true, as far as it went. "He's got a passion for bacon. You know Jim, once he gets an idea."

"Did you ask him to look for my phrase book?"

"Yes," she said.

She was working hard to avoid a lie, but her heart ached terribly when she looked at Rachel; she knew what it was to lose a whole year's language work.

When Jim and Gabriel got home the next day, Rachel heard their voices and called out. Betty went to the room. "I'm sorry," she said. "Men—it's just, he had this idea about the pigs, and—"

"Don't try to tell me about men," Rachel said, turning her face to the wall.

The next morning Rachel's fever broke and she dressed herself and appeared at the table, her long hair uncombed and heavy on her shoulders.

"Come outside and see the piglets," Betty said.

Rachel followed her down the path. It was a jolly scene, Jim leaning against a sawhorse by the shed with a squirming piglet on each thigh. They were thin, hairy creatures, grey with black patches, nothing at all like American pigs. Both of them had neat rows of teats, like the tiny buttons on a double-breasted waistcoat, but no one could decipher their genitals, except to note that they were identical. "He *swore* it was a breeding pair." Jim laughed.

Sharon was in Betty's arms. She was more interested in Rachel than in the piglets. She reached over and clutched at Rachel's hair.

"Sorry," Betty said, trying to pry her fist free.

"I need to braid it," Rachel said, arching her back to ease the pull.

"I'll help you wash it first if you want."

Rachel followed her back into the house. "It was the malaria," she said. "People dream things up when they have malaria. I thought all of you were plotting behind my back."

"Oh, Rachel," Betty said, touching her arm.

That's her sharpest memory from the two weeks Rachel stayed with them: touching her arm, saying, Oh, Rachel.

They were fraught days and Betty never actually examined the notebook.

She opens it. On the inside cover, Rachel has victoriously recorded the five Ws, so essential to language acquisition. Dayuma's voice ringing in her mind, Betty studies the entries, flipping back and forth, trying to locate elements she's identified on the tape. It's a lengthy but crudely annotated lexicon. Its obliviousness to the culture is bizarre. Rachel has an Auca word for cheese. She has an Auca word for nightgown. The diacritical marks, so essential to pronunciation, are baffling. Beyond inaccurate, Betty begins to understand—they seem to be entirely arbitrary, macron and circumflex and umlaut stuck in here and there according to some decorative whim. And the *vowels*. Rachel uses only five, and sometimes *y*. Rachel doesn't actually know IPA.

It is, Betty sees with growing heaviness, an imitation of a linguistic phrase book, as created by a non-linguist. It offers no reliable clues as to how words should be pronounced.

They all want to blame Rachel for what happened. They don't say this aloud, but it's what they all feel. She was cruel to Nate when he was a boy. She came uninvited to Shell Mera and she was a selfish and demanding house guest. She discovered Dayuma before they did, and wrangled an invitation from Carlos Sevilla to go and work with her. She showed up again when Operation Auca was in full swing and poked her nose in, prompting them to act in haste. And now, Betty discovers, she pretends to know linguistics when she does not. So when Jim stood on a sandbar and shouted her phrases into the forest through a battery-powered megaphone, no one had a clue what he was saying.

She goes to bed enraged and she faces the morning sleepless and heavy with shame. Their high-handed taking from Rachel, it was not just theft, or lies: it was a failure to love. They pounced on her strangeness, they revelled in it. Can any good come out of such cruelty? But surely the punishment was disproportionate to the crime.

This is new, and bitter, to think of Jim's death as a punishment.

Her distress grows as the day goes on. She's racked by the need to confess. She sees herself walking to Fray Alfredo's little house on the Rio Talac and knocking on his door. *Forgive me, Father, for I have sinned*—isn't that what they say? In her mind she crafts the penitent letter she will write to Rachel, in her mind she wraps up the notebook and takes it down to Eugene. In her mind Rachel receives this package, and opens it, puzzled, and discovers, in her grief, the full extent of their treachery.

She paces the house, she can't work or eat. After her Quichua workers are gone and Sharon is asleep, she takes up the blue phrase book and sits at her desk. Doggedly, she copies out the five Ws, because she understands that she will be learning this language, and the interrogatives are invaluable. Then she carries the book to the firepit and sets it on the embers left from cooking their supper. She fetches kindling from the bin and builds a pyre over it. The heat snatches at her hand (*for that, Betty*) and then with no thought she's pressing her palm down on the living coals (*for that last theft, when you knew full well*). She sinks back against the cupboard, tasting the pain, resisting reaching for the water pitcher.

Next time she looks at the firepit, there's just one smouldering ruff of paper to be nudged onto the coals.

———

How to understand the darkness she falls into then? Jim comes especially to tell her, I have to go into the box. Not a coffin, it's like the entry to a falling-down house, low and cobwebby. He is fully himself, flushed with life, and she tries in anguish to persuade him not to go (*If you're here now, you've escaped*), but he's immune to her pleas, as though death has already captured his will.

The pain begins to come out of her, not just out of her hand (which blisters and then scabs) but out of her belly. Lying in bed in the mornings, she can't hold it in. Not weeping. It's like a tooth being yanked out of a jaw, the way the pain comes out of her.

One morning she surfaces from a bout of it and hears a tap on the door frame.

"Señora Elisabeth."

Gabriel.

"Yes," she says when she can speak. "I'm sorry. I was dreaming about Señor Jaime."

"That's good he comes to you."

"No. It's not." And then she wants to tell him. "I used to see him in the house, and I loved it. But the dreams are terrible."

The vague shape on the other side of the mosquito net, she tries to bring it into focus. Gabriel, what does he look like? She can't conjure up a single feature.

"When you meet him in your dreams, you must tell him that you're orphaned. *Huaccha mani.*"

"I am not an orphan."

"It means you have not yet found an ancient soul to accompany you. But you're walking in the *ucupachama*, that's good. An ancient soul will find you."

He leaves and she manages to sit up. She can feel it in her chest, the wound where those cries were torn out of her. How wise she was to counsel the other wives against indulging their feelings.

Beloved, don't be surprised at the fiery trial that tests you, as though some strange thing is happening to you. But rejoice that you have been chosen to partake in Christ's sufferings.

The fiery trial. That this beautiful man should die, the horror of it clouds her vision.

The next thing she hears (through Eugene, through Marj), Rachel has gone to the US, taking Dayuma with her. Soon Marj will be gone too, she will move to Quito with her kids. Betty herself seems to be vanishing. She has never liked to eat and she begins to have trouble keeping food down. Her body appalls her. Its thinness. Its persistence. She pulls off her cotton nightgown and sees the corrugations of her poor ribs and grasps why Jim put off their marriage for so long. Because he could not give up the dream of sleeping with a beautiful woman.

The dog is gone too, Chevrolet with his golden fur and friendly tongue. Sharon looks fretfully around for him. Betty has nothing to offer her daughter, her baby's very presence fills her with pain. At bedtime Sharon cries and screams for hours, and won't stay in her cot until Betty spanks her. There's no pasteurized milk in the fridge, so Betty makes up a bottle of distilled water and parts the mosquito net to give it to her. Sharon sits up and bats at it. Her eyes are livid. Another human consciousness in the room, it's unbearable. Betty drops the bottle on the cot and tucks in the net and walks away.

She can't face her bed either. She can't pick up Jim's bible, which was brought back from the Curaray and has dried mud along the margins. She turns the lights off to discourage the bugs, and walks to the door and opens it. She rarely goes outside after dark. The cement is cool under her feet. The forest with its vegetable smell throbs and squawks around her. She tilts her face to the cold stars. They're low and hard, terrifying. Sharon's crying is a hoarse bleat by now. If your child asks for bread, will you give her a stone? But she's spoiled, Jim spoiled her. When she cried at night, he used to take her up and walk her. He seemed to want the comfort himself.

How sick Jim was in those last few weeks, how troubled. This is not something she has let herself think about, it's an occult version of events. But it was terrible, what he went through—it was like Christ's forty days in the wilderness, when Satan came to tempt Him. Like Christ, Jim was swamped by fear and doubt. He said, "Look at the oil engineers they killed. Look at all the workers from the hacienda. Why are we so cocky about going in?" She hardly knew him; who was Jim without his confidence? She wanted to shake him or deliver a sharp clip to the back of his head. Instead, she sat on the edge of the bed, stroking his shoulder, playing the encouraging wife. "You have God's promise of protection," she said. "None of them had that." Hers was the voice saying, Leap off this precipice. For isn't it written, *God shall give His angels charge over thee, to keep thee in all thy ways?*

Like Satan, she quoted Scripture. It takes the breath right out of her chest to think about it.

Save me O God, for the waters are come deep into my soul. I sink in mire, where there is no standing.

She sets up the tape recorder again, and listens to Dayuma's voice, plays it over and over. Not having a translation—it is a good thing, it shatters the illusion that translation is possible. She tries to make the sounds, imitating Dayuma, rewinding the tape after every phrase until she gets it right. She's a gifted mimic, she always has been. Dayuma speaks with a strange vehemence. This story has been in her heart for a decade, with no one to tell it to. Betty tries out that tone, and likes it. Soon she's reciting the whole passage. She paces the house, practising until the sounds feel natural, gesticulating as she imagines Dayuma did. This is echolalia, she's speaking in tongues, she's given the words, over and over, the phrases build in power. Oh, this is not words, there are no words for this.

IT COULD NOT go on like that, and it did not. One day a Quichua youth Betty did not recognize came to her door. He was about fourteen years old. He said he was from the forest east of the Shandia Trail.

"The Auca are at our house," he said. "Will you come?"

"The Auca?"

"Two women."

"Where is your settlement?"

"On the Misahualli."

She knew it, a little. She and Jim had once taken a two-hour paddle up the Misahualli. But this boy had walked to Shandia. "How long were you on the trail?"

"Since the sun rose."

It was just after noon. So if he wanted to get home before nightfall, he would need to head back now.

"Why did you come to me?"

"My father said."

It sounded like a divine commandment. As it happened, a friend from the settlement was up at the house that day, Panka, a calm, dependable woman who had served them as a language informant for years. It had to be providential. "Can you keep my little girl for a day or two?" Betty asked. Her salvation was drawing nigh. While María-Elena gave the boy something to eat, Betty filled her *shigras*. She packed a snakebite kit. A bottle of water. A flashlight. A bit of food.

They set out, walking northeast. The Shandia Trail was an old Shell Oil road, overgrown by thorns for long stretches, but often they could walk side by side. Her guide's name was Amaru. He could not tell her his age. He was reluctant to talk and she soon stopped trying. After about an hour, he turned off the trail onto a path she would never have noticed on her own. Here they had to walk single file. He carried a machete and used it almost as an extension of his hand, expertly slashing the path wider for her. Once he used it to dig a thorn out of the leathery sole of his foot. The path was largely indecipherable to her, but he never hesitated.

He would forget how much slower she walked, and she would lose sight of him and have to call out. Three times they forded streams. Did she want her shoes wet or her feet cut? She left her shoes on. The terrain flattened out and the temperature climbed. She tried to ration the water in her bottle. The canopy rose and closed in overhead. It was a mid-afternoon dusk, like a solar eclipse. She was following Jim in his white shirt as he swung nimbly over a fallen tree. Never looking back, trusting her to stay with him. All her life she had talked knowingly about faith. But this was faith. When you felt nothing but darkness, when you understood nothing, and continued to walk resolutely in the direction God had revealed to you in brighter days.

True dusk had erased the forest when they arrived at the Misahualli. She could just make out three houses perched on a low clay bank. They were the traditional oval longhouses. Amaru led her to the middle one. The interior was ghostly, lit only by a white glow coming from two or three inverted pots. It was *atamuyo*, the oily jungle pods that will burn for hours. Fifteen or twenty people from the settlement had crowded into the house. They greeted her and touched her hands. She did not know any of them, but she and her story were famous to the Quichua all through El Oriente; they called her Señora Jaime. You could hardly breathe in that house from the smouldering termite nests they had hung to drive flies away. The crowd parted to lead her forward. It was evident the settlement had been waiting all day for Betty to solve this.

She turned on her flashlight. Two Auca women squatted on the floor at the back of the house. The women in the longhouse had put cotton dresses on them, but they had the exotic haircuts she had seen in Nate's photos and plugs in their earlobes. In fact, she recognized one of the women as the older of the two women in the pictures taken at the camp on the Curaray, and a shock passed through her. They looked terrified. Nobody could communicate to ask them why they had come. She turned off her flashlight because it was contributing to the women's distress. She thought of Jim's phrases, I like you, I want to be your friend, but she had no confidence in either construction. She squatted beside Dayuma's aunt. "Mintaka," she said gently. She pressed her hand to her own breast. "Betty." But this visibly horrified Mintaka. How could this tall, pale creature know her name? So she turned her attention away to ease their terror. She still had a jar of raisins in her pack, and she called the children around her. The women of the house brought supper for her and her guide. A bowl of *chicha*, fish on a banana leaf. It was wonderful, fresh and tasty. She was just finishing it when they heard a shout from outside, and the terrifying sound of women's screams.

A man burst into the house, followed by several others. Betty could not understand what they said. Some of the people in the house ran out, some stayed, talking in anguish. The same man came back and tried to get the Auca women to go outside to see. They resisted him, pressing themselves down on the mud floor. He tried to get Betty to go. "No," she said, thinking of her daughter. She went just as far as the doorway. A body was carried up to the next house, one arm dangling. "Honorio!" they all cried. Honorio, returning home from a day's fishing, had been found dead on the path, riddled with Auca lances. His wife, Maruja, had vanished, evidently stolen by the Auca. The mourning wail started up. Betty turned back into the house. She could not tolerate the dark, she switched on her flashlight.

Men carried in the lances that had been yanked from the body, they wanted to confront the Auca women with them. The lances were ten feet long, and barbed. They were smeared with gore, it gleamed in the light. Betty could not stop herself from counting. Eighteen. Eighteen lances. She touched the shaft end of one, and it was hard as iron. She could see the Auca women stealing glances at the feathers and carvings close to the heads. They murmured a few words to each other. It seemed obvious to Betty that their warriors had tracked the two women, had observed that they had been taken into a house, and were retaliating. She sat on the floor digging her fingernails into her ankles. Mintaka began a low chanting, as if to comfort herself, and the woman who was not Mintaka took it up. A man said, "These women were sent to cast a spell on us. In the night the Auca will attack and kill us all."

Betty had left her child with a stranger and willingly come to this place. Betty Scott Stam, she thought. It was never about China, it was about giving yourself up to this. She began to have pains in her chest. Others said, "The Auca never kill twice in the same place. They have killed Honorio and they will be miles away by now." An old woman took Betty's hand and said, "Please don't leave us, Mother. We will build you a house." It came to Betty that *she* was the one who had led the Auca to this house, that they had spied her and her guide on the trail. She heard herself say, "You are all in danger with these women here. Let us stay until morning. God will protect us during the night. Then I will take the women out." Rain began to patter on the thatched roof. In a moment the downpour started, and that seemed to settle the matter. Someone led Betty to a *caitu*, a bamboo sleeping platform. She was shivering now, because the temperature had plummeted with the rain. The house emptied; everyone except Betty and the Auca women went next door for Honorio's wake.

In the morning, Mintaka and her friend understood that they were to leave with Betty. Amaru was again their guide, along with another young man who carried a shotgun, although Betty gathered he had no ammunition. Both men were pale, their eyes glazed from the wake. Betty felt light-headed and frail herself. It seemed to her that she had lain awake all night to the raucous sounds from the next house—although at some point her water bottle and flashlight had vanished from beside her, so she must have slept.

They started off. An hour out, a viper slid obliquely across the way. The pattern on its skin perfectly mimicked the splashes of sunlight on the path, but Amaru noticed the movement and called out. The woman who was not Mintaka refused to go farther. The guides speculated that the serpent was an omen. They were also afraid, but they were more afraid to linger on the trail. They pleaded with the woman in Quichua and then harangued her. Finally they started off without her, and eventually she followed, walking almost at a jog and even leading the way at times.

They were all strong and accustomed to trekking; they were constantly waiting for Betty. The path was so slick from the rain that in places the men had to make a harness of lianas to haul her up. Her shoes were bricks of mud and she abandoned them—she was better off with her toes for traction. The sun was high and steam rose from the earth. Both women took off their dresses and tied them to their heads. They all began to be hungry. The guides had packed boiled yucca, but they had shared it early on and Betty's food was also gone. The streams were swollen from the rain, and swifter now. The guides took them across the widest river one by one. They waded up to their waists, groping with their feet for a purchase on the rocks. While they rested on the other side, Mintaka wandered into the forest. She came back with a little basket she had improvised of a palm leaf, filled with grubs about as big as Betty's thumb. Betty shook her head, but the others ate them.

They started off again, and she felt a fiery stab to her right leg, just below the knee. It was a conga ant. She had witnessed such stings but never felt one. The pain spread swiftly until its flames licked at the edge of her vision. It was horrifying, a thousand times worse than a wasp sting. She tried to show her fellow travellers, but they were indifferent. The trail had vanished, it could not hold its own against this voracious foliage. Then they came to a place where all was dead, all the trees choked and ghostly and pale, grown over with mould, a swamp where white muck sucked at their feet. Now they were truly lost, or overnight the country had fallen under a curse.

But then they were on the Shandia Trail—and things were worse, not better. There was no shade. She wanted to vomit. She towered over the others, staggering, afraid she would topple. Her hands and feet were distant and possibly detached. There are three ways to form rock, igneous, sedimentary, and metamorphic, but she was always igneous. Other fragments of learning came to her in their beauty, her beloved scribbler with its cover of Chinese red. It occurred to her to seek shade and sit, but she was a beast that could only plod. In any case, she was no longer hot. I'm cold, she said to her new friends, discovering with surprise that the Waorani had a word for this. And they had a word for skates. I'm accustomed to the cold, as a child I skated on the river. You can endure anything if you think the whole world is watching.

FEAR OF FLYING

25

KAREN, THE CHURCH SECRETARY, INSISTS on driving David to the airport. She's more excited than he is. "So they couldn't find a job for Abby?"

"Oh, you know, things are a little rough with Sean," he says vaguely, because Karen will go crazy if she gets wind of a possible acting role. They turn onto Wilkes, where the traffic is bumper to bumper. Karen is a fearless driver and she nimbly overtakes two semis trying to shut her out of the turn lane. All Dave feels is a sense of heaviness about leaving Abby. Your grandfathers killed my uncle. It makes him a little sick to think that this is the path she's following. *Mi tío.* Who in the world is she talking to that would put it to her that way? He sees an airport sign and the wild idea pops into his mind that she's gone to Ecuador. He'll roll into Shell Mera and she'll be there. It's nuts. But then, how fervently he wishes he'd thought to check her top drawer! He knows where she keeps her passport, tucked under a jewellery box.

Karen brakes to a stop outside Departures and pops the trunk and jumps out to say goodbye. "See you in the movies," she says. She's sweet and funny and she's still looking for Mr. Right. David is cautious with his hugs, because there's no point getting her hopes up.

On his own at the check-in terminal, his jitters begin. What is this questionnaire, firearms, surfboards, explosives, knives—some sort of perjury trap? We weren't meant to fly (is the realization that always wallops him the minute he gets a boarding pass in his hand), it's not in the Bible. So if you're going to let yourself be tossed into the upper atmosphere in a steel capsule, it better be for a sacred and important purpose. A lot of the people lined up in security are going to a country music concert in Houston.

He sinks into a chair in the boarding lounge and surveys his fellow passengers. There they sit in rows, gazing stupefied at their phones. Strangers in a secret cohort who'll soon be hurtling together towards the annihilation of their earthly bodies. Some of them going joyfully home, some facing judgment and eternal damnation. Stop already. To distract himself, he pulls out his phone. Another text from Sean. *Why did the search and rescue party only find four bodies?* It's becoming clear that this movie is pretty much in David's hands. He tried the other day to put it to Abby that she would be Betty's natural heir, but really he's been the guardian of the story for a long time.

It was a new story when he was growing up in Quito. There were still things they were putting together. At a certain age he became passionate about it. When he was eleven, his mother married Abe, a widower who ran HCJB in Quito, and they left the mission school and moved to his house in a Quito suburb. Fatherless kids, they'd felt entirely normal at the boarding school, where nobody had parents. In fact they were luckier than most: they had their mother. So the adjustment to Abe's house was hard, dealing with three step-siblings who had a father and who were calling Marj "Mom." Benjy and Debbie would tell stories from Shell Mera, seizing every opportunity to conjure up their real father (a hero and martyr) in the presence of Abraham Van Der Puy with his funny name and his suspenders and his bushy eyebrows and the coiffed waves of his hair. Benjy still had the yellow model airplane their dad had given him that last Christmas, and Debbie remembered their father making her a dollhouse and the two of them painting it together. Whereas David had nothing. You would think some little thing would have pressed itself into his infantile brain. Instead, he became an avid student of Operation Auca, reading his dad's journal and Betty Elliot's memoir as if they were books of the Bible.

As with the Bible, there were many gaps. It was possible for him, in fact, to know more about what had happened than Nate did. The three Auca who visited the missionaries on the beach—no one knew how to understand it at first, but eventually they did, and one night when he asked, his mother told him. He remembers being on a top bunk in the room they now shared with their stepbrothers, and Marj, with her private new happiness, perched on a chair for a bedtime chat.

"They were from the same clan as the men who killed your dad," she said. "The young man we call George, he took the girl into the jungle because he liked her and he wanted to be alone with her. Apparently he'd been spying on the Americans, and he offered to take her over to see."

"Who was the older lady?"

"She was the girl's auntie. Someone told her that the two young people had slipped away to be alone, so she followed, hoping to stop them and bring the girl back. When they got to the Curaray, George stepped out into the open because he thought it would impress Delilah. So then they had this peaceful picnic on the beach with your dad and the others. And I guess it did impress Delilah, because late in the afternoon the pair of them shook off the auntie and slipped on their own into the jungle. The next morning, members of their clan found them, and they were in big trouble."

Benjy had been pretending he wasn't listening, but at that point in the story his man's voice issued from the cave of the lower bunk. "So they had sex in the jungle?"

"They probably did," Marj said with a little frown. "Yes, I guess they did. And so they were ashamed. And they were frightened because Delilah was spoken for, she was supposed to be marrying someone else. So George made up a story that they had been taken captive by some white men. He said that the white men were cannibals, that they had already killed and eaten Delilah's sister—Dayuma, you know?—and that he and Delilah had barely escaped with their lives and were on their way home."

"Cannibals. Why would he say that?"

"I don't know. But he did, and it was enough to set off a war party. The Auca got busy making spears. The old auntie arrived on the scene and tried to tell them she had been treated kindly by the missionaries, but by then their blood was up."

David remembers the horror he felt. It was worse than the actual killing, this sordid suggestion that his father was murdered because of a stupid lie. This story in which the missionaries had only incidental roles, in which, even after enjoying their Christian hospitality, the guy they called George was *only after one thing*.

At times it is better to know less.

His mother must have noticed his distress. "Think about this, Davey," she said. "Your dad and the others made peaceful contact with the Auca before God took them home. They had that satisfaction. Think how generous the Lord was, in giving them that."

It is not an easy thing, being guardian of a story. He later learned (from Betty, who learned it in Tiwaeno) that when the visitors arrived at the camp on the Curaray, the young woman (whose name was actually Gimari) was eager to talk to outsiders, to ask whether they had seen her sister Dayuma. She kept asking the same question over and over: Have you seen Dayuma? Of course, they couldn't understand her. They didn't even pick up the word *Dayuma*. But as it happened, Jim had a photo of Dayuma with him. He had taken it at the hacienda, and he carried it in because he thought, if the people he encountered happened to know her, it might reassure them to find out that she was still alive. At one point he took that snapshot out of his pocket and showed it to them.

This seemed to thrill Betty. That in the vast jungle of eastern Ecuador, it was Dayuma's sister who came to the beach asking about Dayuma, and that Jim—without even understanding what she was saying—pulled out a picture of Dayuma. Betty saw it as powerful evidence of God's working. It had the opposite effect on David. In Quito he had met an anthropologist at a government reception. The guy talked about trophy collecting, about the way some Indigenous peoples shrank down the heads of their conquered enemies and hung them at the doorway of their houses. And then David found himself imagining the scene on the Curaray, Gimari asking about Dayuma, and this strange white man reaching into his pocket and taking out a flat, grey image of Dayuma's head, shrunk down to the size of the tiny photographs they printed in those days.

His flight's been called. People are starting to line up. He tips his head back, closing his eyes. You have an image of the men in your mind, and you have a vision of the mission, and this had the fingerprints of a screw-up all over it.

THE INTANGIBLE ZONE

26

THEIR NEIGHBOUR AT BIRDSONG HAD three big carp lurking in
his backyard pool, and then he had two. They knew what had
happened, but they couldn't put their hands on the culprit. Betty
climbed the stairs and looked out her bedroom window. A wisp
of smoke rose from the secret place in the woodlot where her
brother Harvey sometimes built his fire. She slipped back down
and ran across the garden and up the path. The fish lay on a shin-
gle, its belly torn open and its bones like a silvery comb. Harvey
offered her a bite and she saw in his face what this meant to him:
he had to sin, his life depended on it. She turned and ran back up
the path to the house.

You can purge a child of evil—they forced castor oil into him.
Betty lay on the floor in the upstairs hall with her face pressed to
the grate while Harvey's spasms and moans rose from the lavatory
below. She could see one white foot flexed on the grey floorboards. She was years younger and she had the same hungry heart.
Be perfect, Jesus whispered in Betty's ear. Give them nothing to
judge. *Nothing.* The breastplate of righteousness, she put it on and
it melted right onto her chest.

She could feel it still, the hard ridge you might call her ribs.

She was on her back in a bamboo cage. Everything was striped
in light and dark. There were no windows, but there was a doorway. Now Harvey had killed an armadillo. He got Betty up and
led her to a room where its shell sat empty on the floor. This was
their clan, he said, the armadillo. The room was lit like houses in

the jungle, ghostly. Feather headdresses were stuck into the walls, the white jaws of peccaries, the brown skulls of monkeys. These were the relics of all the animals whose souls had enlarged his.

A corpse lay in the middle of the room, its arms at its sides. The bamboo platform it lay on was like a giant pan flute. People sat in a circle around it and tossed live coals at each other. The corpse sat up and vomited, and lay back down, and a girl with two thick braids splashed water on the mess and switched the floor clean with a leafy branch. Sometime later she sat up again and the girl handed her a gourd and she drank. Her little blond angel was perched beside her, clasping her feet with tiny hands, her fingers and toes finely etched with dirt. Blue eyes lurid in that dirty little face. Betty tried to speak to her, but she was gone.

Then a small woman, naked, stood in the doorway. She was eating something white. She had no eyebrows and no pubic hair. Her belly had a string tied around it. Her breasts lay flat on her chest, long and empty, all used up. Bits of language lay in Betty's mind like chewed bones. She struggled to sit up. *Biti miti punimupa*, she said. The woman was mightily amused. She repeated the words in a mocking voice. She stepped over to where Betty lay and offered her what she was eating. It was boiled plantain, and Betty ate it, and felt herself stronger.

She was back from walking in the *ucupachama*. The *ucupachama*—she loved the word. She and Jim would muse over it and try to get Yapanqui to explain. Was it heaven or hell, was it the present or the afterlife? It was one of those terms their Quichua informants refused to define, but all the same it had drawn her in. Now she was back, in a house with two forest women. Inkasisa, Yapanqui's mother—her impish, wrinkled face began to appear in the doorway. This chicken coop of a house was her house, and she chortled as though she had captured Betty. Possibly it was the spirit dart she'd fired one day by the playing field. Or possibly Betty was here because Inkasisa had taken in the forest women, who lay in a hammock in the same room as her, curled comfortably against each other, showing no sign of moving on.

In the dark hours she would hear the two of them talking. She'd lie listening to their low voices, her daughter slumbering beside her, and they'd drift back to sleep until the roosters started up, and the dogs. Often the forest women would start chanting then, and Betty would step outside in her nightgown and look up to see a toucan gliding alone across the silvery sky. People would be stirring throughout the settlement. She heard falsetto cries, *yui-yui*, and the light thread of a transverse flute drifting on the mist. Woodsmoke filled the air, and the night scent of jasmine. She crouched, lifting her face to the ridge where their house stood empty. Jim was only spirit now and she was only flesh, squatting barefoot on the beaten earth, feeling the hot pee sizzle out of her.

She thought sometimes about going back to her house. But she didn't go. She stayed with Inkasisa because Yapanqui had vanished and she had no one to look after her up on the ridge. She stayed for the sting of Inkasisa's derision. *This is the gringa who thinks she can speak our language!* She stayed because she could no longer be alone, and her two forest companions were such agreeable room-mates. They were warm and patient with Sharon, playing with her by the hour, carrying her on their backs without complaint. They laughed a great deal; they wanted to laugh, they looked eagerly for reasons. Mintaka was quick and chatty, Mankamu serene and beautiful, a few years younger, Betty thought, but clearly the leader of the two. There was a delicacy in the way she approached people, a natural attentiveness.

She stayed with Inkasisa because the thought of being any-where else terrified her. She stayed because only the Indians could see her there, and they expected nothing of her. She stayed because here she was invisible to God, who for whatever reason had set her free from His gaze.

Dear Mother and Dad,

We are not in David Livingstone's Africa and there is no need to send Charlie to look for me. You would do better to believe Eugene and Marj's assurances, and trust in divine providence. I have not written because I was caught up in events, and then I fell ill. I am much better now.

Some time ago, I was summoned to a Quichua settlement where two Auca women had made an unexpected appearance. The Quichua were eager to send them away, afraid of attacks, so I undertook to bring them out to Shandia. It was indeed a stunning development, as one of the women is recognizable from the photos Nate Saint took on the Curaray. On the journey home I fainted and was carried to a nearby Quichua house, where I recovered and am still residing. This Quichua family has made Sharon and me and the Auca women welcome, and it does not seem prudent to take women from the forest up to my home on the ridge. They have enough to adjust to, without factoring in refrigerators and generators.

So we are currently living with eighteen others in a split bamboo house, where you can see through the walls. The home is managed with great vigour by a woman named Inkasisa. Her husband, who was killed by an anaconda several years ago, was apparently a wonderful hunter, and some rooms have animal relics stuck between the bamboo slats. The house is on stilts, and when you sweep crumbs through the cracks between the floor planks, the chickens squawk and fight below. We four are in one room, Sharon and I on a bamboo platform (caitu) and the forest women in a hammock, Jim's hammock, which Alberto and María-Elena brought down from the house. Those two devoted children also carried down the mosquito net, extra clothing, towels, soap, notebooks and pens, Sharon's dolly, my red fireman's lantern, and my bible, so you see that we have everything we need.

Inkasisa tolerates me because she is so thrilled to host the two forest women. In the afternoon she stations herself in the yard, where cobs of drying maize make a golden carpet, and guests stream into the yard to see them. Inkasisa leads the women out, awkward in their cotton dresses, shy under the stares. She sits them on the broken-down canoe that serves as a sofa, and her guests drink chicha and openly discuss their strange haircuts and the plugs in their ears. Sharon always takes up the task of keeping the chickens off the drying maize. A rooster darts in, beak first, and she shrieks, "Riy kaymanta" (the Quichua phrase for "Go away") and flaps her arms. The Auca women laugh as hard as anyone. "They laugh!" the guests cry. That's what surprises people the most, how ordinary they are.

They are named Mintaka and Mankamu and are both, I would say, in their early forties. I know one of them is Dayuma's auntie, and the other may be as well, although from what I can understand, they are not sisters. The four of us are a family-within-a-family. Mintaka and Mankamu help with the making of the chicha, which they make the same way the Quichua do, although they called it tepae. I carry water from the river and collect firewood. Alberto Grefa brings us vegetables from our own kitchen garden. The Catholic friar Fray Alfredo is often here, and I asked him how much I should pay Inkasisa. He said, "Is she not entitled to her acts of charity?" So we simply do what we can, but we keep a little apart because I am entirely taken up with learning the Auca language. I spend my days following the forest women, a notebook and pencil in hand, perversely refusing (as they see it) to understand their meaning, peering into their mouths to determine how sounds are made, trying to trick them into repeating themselves. They have given me a name, Gikari. It means woodpecker. Day after day I peck away.

Of course, it is never far from my mind that Mintaka met Jim, and, with two others, spent a day with him on the Curaray. One day, someone made Sharon a pointed hat out of a sheet of paper, pinning it with a couple of thorns. Mintaka spied the paper cone and picked it up and put it to her mouth like a megaphone. She stood confidently, staring boldly off into the distance—like a man, like an American. "I will give you gifts!" she shouted in her own language. She deepened her voice, mangling the words a bit. I have always been told I am a good mimic, but she is far better. "Come to the river, I will give you gifts." I know from Jim's diary that he called Auca phrases into the forest through a megaphone, so I felt as though a door had opened. But my language skills are not equal to such a sensitive situation, and when Mintaka dropped the cone hat and went back to sitting on the broken canoe, I did not attempt to open that door again.

Why have they come out? When will they go back? Is their clan still close to the camp on the Curaray, where the men's bodies lie? Fray Alfredo has a high-scale map of the area, but the two forest women cannot read it. And so we wait on the Lord, eager to witness the fulfillment of His glorious purpose in this.

Your loving daughter,

Betty

Every insight she gained into Auca life was like the glint in the gravel at the bottom of Inkasisa's pan when she stood in the river panning for gold. A secret world where a harpy eagle was tied under its tiny thatched roof, and screamed a warning if an intruder appeared. A world where couples longed for rain in the afternoon, because it offered privacy, like a curtain falling around the longhouse. Where pregnant women wove a hammock with an open midsection for the baby to drop through. Where in death, the spirit had to cross the body of a huge worm. A *worm*. Could Betty have gotten that right?

She lived in Inkasisa's home for close to a year, though the progression of the months meant little. The year was marked by its thrilling moments. The moment she learned why Mintaka and

Mankamu had come out of the forest: to find Dayuma, and tell her it was safe for her to come home, that a man who had been a great enemy of their clan was dead. The moment Betty was able to say, "My people know Dayuma. She is a beautiful young woman. She is travelling with a friend and will return soon." The moment they finally understood her and were happy, and Mankamu lay in the hammock in the heat of the day, chanting in a low voice, casting a spell of tranquility over the whole house.

The year was marked especially by the afternoon they sat outside and Mankamu called Betty over and began to look through her hair. She found a tick in her scalp and cracked it with her teeth. While she worked, Betty leaned comfortably against her and Mankamu told a story. On the day she became a woman, she drank *tepae* from a special jar her mother had made the day she was born. Then her father took her hunting. He killed a woolly monkey, a *gata*, and taught her how to tie its tail to its arm so as to form a carrying strap. It was a big, heavy beast, a male, but she was the one who proudly carried it home. A few nights later, her mother discovered that the monkey had given Mankamu nits! It was the work of many days to get rid of them.

Betty understood this story perfectly. She said, "You look after each other."

Mintaka spoke up. "In the forest, we live very well. Not like here."

"What is different?"

"Come with us and see." Mankamu was very charming. "You will see it, Gikari, and you will love it. You will be well there."

So Betty said, "All right, then. I will."

When Dayuma came back, they would go in together.

ONE DAY THE pilot brought her a letter from Marj, and tucked into it was a letter from Rachel. It was long and enthusiastic. Rachel and Dayuma were still in America. They had met Billy Graham and shared their testimony with thousands in Madison Square Garden. Rachel's mission director Cameron Townsend arranged for her to be featured on a nationwide television show called *This Is Your Life*, a clever ambush where, one by one, figures from her past were spirited in to be reunited with her: her father, her missionary partner from Peru, Don Carlos Sevilla flown in from Quito, and even the chief from the settlement on the Marañón River where she'd worked—they were all there, it was amazing! She was presented with gifts by the TV studio, a movie camera and projector. She was in her glory in America—she had clearly taken the place her fellow missionaries had denied her, as advance worker and spokeswoman for Operation Auca. Although, sadly, her Auca friend had been a disappointment. Dayuma wasn't the least bit impressed with anything she saw, even the Manhattan skyline. When they were driven across the Brooklyn Bridge, she hung her head and refused to look. The only thing that caught her attention was a window washer up on a scaffold, scaling a skyscraper. She was intrigued by that.

Now they were resting for a bit, staying at a house in Pennsylvania. So Betty had an address—but she found it hard to think of writing to Rachel. That afternoon she walked up the path to the house on the ridge, where Alberto was working in the garden. They got the key out of its hiding place in the shed, and Betty went in. The shutters were closed and she heard the scuttle of roaches on the floor. She felt her way to the cupboard and packed up the tape recorder, along with her stash of batteries and a box for mailing.

The whole household played with the tape recorder for an hour, and then Betty pointed out to Mintaka and Mankamu that they could send a message to Dayuma. They took the job on eagerly, talking in turns and at length. It was a revelation to Betty, the way they talked—far more quickly than when they spoke to her, and with gestures and the sorts of sound effects Dayuma had made on the tape Marj sent. Betty understood very little. But she was thrilled to think of what this would mean to Dayuma, off in Pennsylvania—familiar voices from home speaking her own language. Ten years of news for the wanderer. To learn that it was safe to go back.

The next time Betty heard the plane, she and Mintaka and Mankamu carried the package with the audiotape down to the airstrip and gave it to Eugene.

Some weeks later, Rachel wrote.

We are thrilled to learn that two Auca women have come out of the forest. How the Lord works! We'll return as soon as we are able. Dayuma is ill just now, but the moment she can travel, we'll be back.

Betty, before I return, I want to tell you that the Lord has been working in my heart throughout these months, and I have come to accept what happened to the fellows. My brother would be alive today if you had included me—I know that. Rachel Saint would never have allowed those boys to play the fool the way they did! But it had to happen. Something very big was needed to break Satan's hold over the Auca. So I know it was in God's plan that you shut me out. God willing, we can now go in together to take the Word to these His children.

27

RACHEL WAS ASTONISHED AT HOW much language Betty had learned, and she was generous enough to say so. She brimmed with energy and happiness in the days they prepared for their trek into the forest. All the gear to gather and pack up! Some she ordered from Quito, but much of it came from Jim and Betty's house, where she and Dayuma were staying. Kettles they packed, and pots and lanterns and matches and dishes and notebooks. Soap and towels and waterproof sheets. Medical supplies. Bales of clothing for both sexes—Rachel insisted on it. The Elliot bodega, Betty had come to consider that house.

"You know," Betty said, "since Mintaka and Mankamu have had to wear clothes, they've been dealing with rashes in their armpits and groin. They can't wait to get back to their birthday suits."

Rachel laughed heartily, new fillings flashing in her teeth. "Even Adam and Eve made aprons out of leaves," she said.

Well, they were in this together. Betty might feel as if she were running a three-legged race with another species of animal, a goat tied to a kangaroo, for example, but Rachel was the partner God had given her, and she was warmth itself to Betty these days. "Oh, my dear," she said, when she first saw her, "you look like you've been pulled through a knothole backwards. And your little girl! You have let that child go native. It's a good thing I'm back."

Rachel: with her bulk and her years and her brisk certainties, she was a gravitational field Betty could not resist. The moment Betty saw that round face in the window of Eugene's plane, she felt herself swim back into visibility, thinner than ever, her knees thicker round than her thighs, a safety pin holding up her skirt at the waistband. Rachel climbed out onto the runway in a pale-pink shirtwaist dress and Betty felt the bird of love land lightly on her shoulder.

She went to the bedroom wardrobe and pulled out what was left of Jim's clothes. His shirts had gone to Eugene, but she made a bundle of his trousers and shorts.

When she came back, they were talking about cattle. Don Carlos had had cattle at his former hacienda on the Añangu, he had them taken in by canoe.

"*¿Chiquitos? ¿Niños?*" said Alberto, who would never try to speak Quichua with Rachel.

"*Terneros,*" Rachel said. "It's the best solution."

To what?

"If we can get the Auca into cattle," Rachel said in English, "they won't be able to move around. And we can have a proper church and school. The Youderians and the Drowns used this method with the Jivaro in Macuma. They managed to break their itinerant lifestyle in five years."

"Not all people can digest cow's milk," Betty said, thinking about China.

"Well, in our village the Auca won't be living on fermented yucca mash, that's for darn sure. It's hard on the teeth. Not to mention that it's unsanitary *and* alcoholic."

Betty had been drinking *chicha* for a year. "Not very," she said.

Rachel ignored this. "We hold a ceremony to smash and burn the *tepae* tubs. Make it official, a day they will always remember. I don't kid myself, I know it won't be easy. Dayuma and I were talking at breakfast about the longhouses. I said, They're going to have to put away their extra wives. We won't have that sort of thing on Rachel Saint's watch. And she said, But women who are alone—they need a man to hunt for them. And I said, If you have beef cattle, you soon lose your taste for monkey meat. And anyway, if they live in one place, the game is going to peter out pretty shortly."

Betty tried to counter this in her mind. Was it possible to reach people's souls, and turn them over to Christ, and leave the people otherwise as they were? "The patriarchs in the Old Testament had more than one wife," she said.

"A fellow living with two or three girls, sleeping with one right in front of the other? You would be fine with that?"

Dayuma was transferring clothes pegs from a bucket into a canvas bag. She had not picked up a lot of English in her year in

America. "Dayuma, how do you think your people will change when they hear the gospel?" Betty asked in Quichua.

Dayuma sighed and thought for a minute. "They will sit in a circle when they eat," she said in her soft way. "With a palm leaf as a plate, and a piece of plantain and a piece of meat on each leaf, instead of just passing around parts of the animal's body. They will take the balsa plugs out of their ears. They will stop plucking out their eyebrows, and stop cutting off the front of their hair."

She was back to wearing the Quichua market costume, the white blouse and straight skirt, and Rachel said that every day she looked more like her old self. The day she'd arrived in Shandia, Betty had not been able to believe this was the girl Marj had described. She wore high heels and a navy-blue skirt and jacket. Her hair was pulled up and fastened with a clip. Apparently she'd lost weight in the US and acquired dentures. Her eyes were dull and she rarely smiled. She had not taken well to America. It was as if she'd been flown to Mars or maybe to a galaxy far outside their own, and what she saw there chilled and appalled her.

To compound it all, she had lain in bed in a little house in Pennsylvania for three months, refusing to eat, barely conscious. A doctor came and said it was just a flu, but she could not seem to shake it. "I think maybe it was a spiritual struggle that laid her so low," Rachel confided in Betty, "because when she got out of bed, she declared that she wanted to be baptized. So I arranged for a baptism in my old church. Hundreds of people came to see the first Auca Christian. It was a marvellous day."

But even Rachel acknowledged that a light had gone out in Dayuma, properly baptized or not. Her reunion with Mankamu and Mintaka was far from the happy celebration they had anticipated; it was more like broken-hearted relatives coming together at a funeral. So many terrible things had happened since Dayuma left her clan. One death after another, a decade's worth of loss.

Nampa, Dayuma's beloved brother, had been killed by an anaconda. That was a painful bereavement.

But now they were all going home.

THEY MADE UP a flotilla of five massive dugout canoes, all heaped with cargo, each with a pilot and a porter. Mintaka and Mankamu, relaxed and happy, were in the third canoe, Rachel and Dayuma in the fourth, and Betty in the last with Sharon: the end of the flotilla was deemed to be safest in the event of an attack. Betty's pilot was a terrifying-looking rubber collector with the kindest of hearts. Darwin, he was called; he said it was an English name meaning beloved. Her porter was a thin-chested boy with the regrettable name of Anticristo.

It was Don Carlos who had worked things out. He happened to come through Shandia with three of his men, and of course was keenly interested in Mankamu and Mintaka. With Dayuma to interpret, his rubber harvesters eventually figured out where their clan was, on a ridge between the Añangu and the Curaray, a half day's journey this side of the playa where Jim and the others had camped. It would take five or six days to get there, the first three by canoe. They would sleep in palm-leaf huts made on the spot. The price Don Carlos named was outrageous, but it factored in the outfitting, porters to carry all their gear, and the very real dangers.

When their guides and porters assembled in Shandia, Betty was shocked at the size of the party and the menace it projected. Ten men in rotting trousers and ragged military vests, red bandanas tied around their big rough heads, rifles slung over their shoulders. But Dayuma knew most of them from the hacienda—indeed, some of them remembered finding her trembling in the forest ten years earlier—and she called them amigos.

Betty and Rachel fronted them the money for the canoes and food, and gave Don Carlos the rest of the fee to hold. The next morning they discovered that he had abruptly left for the hacienda, leaving Betty and Rachel to spell out their expectations for the men. They forbade liquor in no uncertain terms, and at first they tried to forbid guns. But the men needed to hunt on the trail, they needed to protect the party from puma, anaconda, and caiman. The best Betty could get from them was a promise that the guns would be out of sight the day they approached the Auca settlement.

Mornings on the river were idyllic but Betty's body was never built for a dugout canoe. So it was always a huge relief when the guides began watching the bank for a suitable campsite. They stopped around four o'clock, thrilled to be out of the canoes, and the guides would get busy setting up camp. Rudimentary palm huts went up in an hour, wet wood was persuaded to burn—it was a marvel to watch. The men had trawled the river all day and they served fish with rice for supper. Betty had a tin of tea and she would brew up a kettle. Mintaka and Mankamu were taking in two little dogs, gifts from Inkasisa's grandson. A bad idea, it seemed to Betty, but what could she do? After the meal they sat around the fire, laughing at the antics of the puppies. In the undergrowth the ferns were edged in light. Every evening the rainforest gave itself to them tenderly. Not so aloof, not so caught up in its own wild growth, part of God's creation after all.

The fourth morning they said goodbye to the river and to one of their guides. Octavio was left alone with a rifle to guard the canoes and some of the cargo, which the porters would double back to collect. They were deep in Auca territory now. It was a ridged forest that cut you down to size. They moved slowly because their guides and porters were carrying staggering weights. Mankamu and Mintaka had their puppies to deal with. At first they struggled to get them to walk at the end of leashes made from lianas, but eventually they found bark cloth and made slings to carry them. Sharon rode on Darwin's back in a carrying brace the men had fabricated back in Shandia; it had once been a wooden chair.

So far they had slept well and had entirely escaped snakebites, scorpion stings, tarantulas, conga ants—it was nothing short of a miracle. But that morning Sharon woke up with red marks behind her ear. "A bat bit me," she said to everyone. She was speaking mostly Quichua, but she called the vampire bat *tõõnae*, an Auca word, because that's what Mankamu called it. Mankamu was the one who noticed the bites. She went into the forest and came back with a fungus shaped like an ear. It split readily into layers. She peeled a layer off and pressed it to the wound.

On the trail the men were sober and alert, but all morning Mintaka talked, and to Betty's surprise they did not hush her. She did bird calls, she imitated the screech of a spider monkey on the indrawn breath. She marvelled at plants that had matured since she had last seen them. She saw a beehive and borrowed a machete to mark the path so she could come back for it. They walked by a *chonta* palm grove managed by her clan. These were the trees the Auca used to make their iron-hard lances and their ceremonial drink. The trunks were covered with terrifying spikes, but each one had a smooth-barked tree planted on purpose beside it for the Auca to climb to do their harvesting.

Then Mankamu and Mintaka spied the hoofprints of *uré*, collared peccaries, and they fell silent. They wanted to see the herd. Occasionally they signalled to each other with a clicking sound, the sound *uré* make while eating. The forest itself was silent in the heat of the day, just now and then the raucous cry of an invisible bird. It was both farther than Betty had imagined and nearer. All morning she had tried to locate them in her mental map of the jungle, a green firmament wider than all her childhood, throbbing with darkness and barbarism. It turned out Auca territory was just like any other stretch of rainforest, and domesticated by Mintaka's familiarity. Known and ancient paths ran all through it.

Dayuma too remembered this neighbourhood. She pointed out the outlines of a yucca *chagra* they had planted when she was young. It was filled in now with balsa trees. But somehow seeing it broke her fears open, and tears began to slide down her cheeks. "They will spear me in this dress," she said to Betty.

"Well, maybe you want to take it off. I don't think Mankamu and Mintaka will wear theirs." ·

"They still have their *comi*."

This was the fibre band they wore around their bellies. Dayuma was right, her aunties wore their *comi* under their dresses. "They would help you make a *comi*."

"I can't wear it. It means we are *dentro*."

"*Dentro?*"

"Inside," she said vaguely.

"Inside?"

"It says, we are not shy. From birth to death, we are like this." She wove her fingers together.

"Like lovers."

"Yes." She began to cry again.

They were holding up the last half of the party. Anticristo with his heavy burden leaned against a tree, his face expressionless. This girl has reached the limits of what she can take in, thought Betty.

"Leave your dress on," she said. "Even with clothes, you're family. Nothing changes that."

But what did she know? She knew nothing. She had paced around her house reciting Dayuma's story, but even now she understood little of it. She began to think about the night on the Misahualli when the fisherman Honorio was found dead. Eighteen lances—she saw them, she counted them. And then her own fear so took her over that she could hardly walk. She turned and looked for Sharon. She was riding high on Darwin's back, grabbing for lianas. Betty let them pass her on the path, reaching out to touch her daughter's perfect little foot. She tried to form her emotions into a prayer. She tried to call up Scripture verses. But God had a new contract with her, the contract of silence.

Rachel in her cotton dress with her tie-up shoes plodded along in front of Betty. She never looked around. She was like Dayuma riding in an automobile through Manhattan. Yet when they stopped for lunch, she told Betty she had been studying the terrain. She was thinking about where the Auca protectorate should be. If the Auca settled, if you could get them to settle, consider what a vast territory would open up for development. She had had several appointments with people in America, her connections in the oil industry, well, mostly Cameron Townsend's connections, all of whom were eager to invest in Ecuador. The CEO of Maxus was an evangelical Christian; it was wonderful to see how God brought such things together. She couldn't help but think how pleased Velasco Ibarra would be. Can you imagine how wide he would open the doors to the missionaries if they solved the Auca problem?

Rachel is frightened too, Betty thought. She is distracting herself with visions of glory. She always claimed to be personally acquainted with the president of Ecuador, it was a bit of a joke in the house in Shell Mera.

They were in the neighbourhood of Don Carlos's old hacienda, and Betty had thought they might overnight there. But the men considered it an ill-fated place. So in the afternoon, with three hours left of daylight, they followed a path that led to a little stream and set up camp on the ridge above it. They were not the first to camp there: Betty could see several clearings, and the charcoal of other fires. They were near the Tiwaeno River, the men said. But the Auca rarely built their settlements on rivers.

After the huts were built, most of the men loaded their guns and set off into the forest. Mintaka was very excited to join in— she had never been part of a hunt with guns. An hour later, they burst gleefully back into the clearing. Emelio had shot a howler monkey, an *iwa*. Mintaka had it, she seemed to be giving it a piggy-back ride. Its eyes were open and its face looked over her shoulder, austere and thoughtful. But when she dropped it to the ground, Betty saw that its chest was blown open. Blood soaked Mintaka's skirt and ran crimson down her legs. Someone had built a fire and they tossed the monkey whole onto it. "Aren't you going to clean and butcher it?" Betty cried. No, no, they wanted to singe its fur off. Mintaka and Mankamu were more animated than she had ever seen them. It was stifling hot, and they both took off their dresses. Mintaka put her hands on Mankamu's shoulders and they began to dance. The stench of the burning fur was sickening. The fire found the poor creature's black face, and its black lips lifted, its yellow teeth grinned below its black eyes. And then, horrifyingly, the creature shrieked, and laughter rose, everyone was laughing—at Betty, who had leapt back. Oh, it was Sharon shrieking, her mouth stretched into a terrified O.

Betty bent to pick her baby up and held her close, pressing Sharon's face into her shoulder. She too was shaking.

"*Ven, ven*," said Darwin, their Dear One. He and two other men led Betty along a path to another clearing where the buttress roots of a huge kapok tree made a natural shelter. He set about building a new fire—she could make her tea there. They fetched the kettle, and water, and her canvas bag. They arranged logs for sitting. Betty cradled Sharon on her lap, and when she was calm enough, she opened a tin of crackers and a can of tuna and fed her like a little bird. It was early days to break into her emergency rations, but Sharon needed comfort and so did she. Anticristo stayed with them to mind the fire. His bare feet were splashed with blood. At the sight of it, dread returned to Betty. Even in the best of cases, even if they found the Auca friendly, how could she deal with it? The light was fading and she began to feel afraid of the forest itself—the massive kapok with its indecent roots, the lianas dangling like nooses, and the crude fungi gleaming, every square inch alive with bugs and bacteria and parasites, everything squirming with growth, plants growing on plants, plants sucking on air. An old terror opened inside her, the trap door she had fallen through on the Misahualli. Tiny sobs like hiccups still shook her baby. Betty bent her head over Sharon, trying to still her. She sat stroking Sharon's silky hair. Jim's adored little girl.

And then it was entirely dark, and she could see the hunters' fire dancing through the trees, and hear the shouts and laughter of the men. Rachel came up the path and helped herself to tea. "Quite a sight," she said. When Betty did not respond, she said, "The men have made *cochla* and rice." Anticristo got up eagerly and the two of them went back to the other fire.

Betty sat on with her daughter in her arms. She needed to understand how she had come to this place. The year just past seemed to have happened to someone else. She was off her head for most of it, that was the only way to put it. And yet, off her head, she'd brought two Auca women out of the forest, and she had lived with an Indian family for a year, and she had learned the language of the people who killed her husband. She acted from something unthinking, deep in her core. A year ago, Jim in his white shirt had led her into the Misahualli, and all this followed. He came to her vividly as she sat watching firelight flicker off the big fins of the kapok roots, and her anguish about him fell away. She'd had the courage to show him who she was, and he had not flinched at the sight. He saw her strength, and he treasured it. He could have had any woman he wanted, and she was the one he wanted. She felt the deep gladness of this, and also its weight. It was of a scale too big to be reckoned up, his martyrdom and God's purposes. Consciously or unconsciously, she had followed Jim into mystery.

Rachel returned with a plate of food, and people began to go back and forth between the two fires. Eventually, Mintaka and Mankamu made their way to Betty. Mankamu nestled in a fork of the kapok roots and Mintaka, with her bloodstained dress, lay with her head in Mankamu's lap. Sharon was asleep now in Betty's arms.

Rachel sat savouring her tea, undaunted by it all. "Tomorrow will be the fulfillment of the dream of a lifetime," she declared. She began to talk about her call to the mission field, a shorter version of the story than Betty had heard previously, and mostly in Spanish. Soon she's crossing the ocean on a steamship and sees a vision of needy people holding out their arms and calling to her. *Quebi emoe*—she's learned an Auca phrase that fits the bill. "It was a long time before I understood that the people in that vision were the Auca. I had to take a few wrong turns first."

They fell into silence, listening to the forest and voices from the other fire. Dayuma wandered into the clearing and sat down by her aunties. For a while it was only the women at their fire, and then Emelio and Darwin joined them. Emelio said something to Dayuma that Betty didn't catch. And then he said, "You were gone a long time."

"In the other world," Dayuma said.

"What is it like?"

"It's very cold. No one can live well there. That's why Nimu and Gikari came to us."

"*Eso es una locura*," Rachel said. That's crazy talk. She was trying to move them to Spanish. "Dayuma, tell everyone what you saw in America."

"*Automóviles, automóviles, automóviles.*" She did a little seated dance to the words, as if it was a jingle she'd heard on the radio. "*Hamburguesa, hamburguesa, hamburguesa.*"

"Stop that now," Rachel said. "Tell them properly."

Dayuma pressed her lips together playfully, and then she said, "We went to a big *iglesia* that had a row of trees in the front. Smooth palms, which chanted with a big voice."

"*¡El órgano!*" Rachel exclaimed. In English she said to Betty, "I took Dayuma to the Washington Cathedral and she heard that grand organ, the cathedral's marvellous pipe organ. *¿Y que mas viste ahi,* Dayuma?" And what else did you see there?

"I saw Nimu's picture."

"She saw my father's windows. The famous stained glass art of Laurence Saint. She saw the window depicting yours truly!"

"What did you think, Dayuma?" Betty asked.

"*Muy hermosa,*" Dayuma said pertly, and Betty couldn't help but be pleased to see her being cheeky with Rachel.

Not long after, Dayuma got up and walked away in the direction of the stream, evidently going to relieve herself. Betty sat feeling restored, enjoying the crackling of the fire against the wall of forest sound. Rachel always talked with such confidence about her calling and the prospects that lay ahead: light and dark colliding, the love of God confronting primal fear and hatred. Whereas my calling, Betty thought—it's more like a worn stone amulet you might wear on a string around your neck.

She finished a second cup of tea, and Dayuma still had not returned. Betty also needed to pee, so she got up and transferred her sleeping child to Rachel's lap. She didn't bother to dig out her flashlight. Thirty feet down the path, she stopped to let her eyes adjust. When you took time to wait, you soon learned that the nighttime jungle was not that dark. Tonight it was lit by a high half moon. And fireflies winking here and there, and the eternal stars. It was lit by a phosphorescence that seemed to rise from the earth itself. This was what the next months would be, for her and Rachel: a time of waiting for their eyes to adjust.

A little way on, the light caught Dayuma's white blouse. She was sitting on a log just off the path, holding her tin cup of tea. Rocking back and forth, and sobbing.

"Oh, Dayuma," Betty said gently. "You're feeling afraid again." She lowered herself onto the log. "You will be all right. You are their daughter."

"No," she said emphatically. "No, I am not."

"What do you mean?"

"They won't know me. I am born again."

Oh, Betty thought. She slipped an arm around Dayuma's shoulders. How could she begin to explain metaphor? Then she caught a whiff of something sharp and medicinal.

She reached for Dayuma's cup, and Dayuma moved it away and began to cry loudly and recklessly. "Oh, oh, oh, Gikari, oh, I am sorry. I know it's wrong, I know it's wicked, but I'm afraid."

Once you realized Dayuma had been drinking, you could see that she was actually very drunk. Betty managed to wrest the cup out of her hand and dump it. They were all drinking! That was why the men had led her to her own fire. The thought of Mintaka and Mankamu passed out under the kapok tree made her so angry she could hardly speak. "Look at Rachel. Look how calm she is. She doesn't need spirits. She knows God will take care of her."

"Yes, yes, everything's fine for Rachel." Dayuma said this in a bitter tone Betty had never heard from her before.

"What do you mean?"

"She'll be safe, they won't be afraid of her. Her brother's killing is all settled."

"What?"

"Everything's equal. A brother for a brother. My brother for her brother."

"Your brother. You mean Nampa?"

Her shoulders shook again with sobs.

"But was he . . . you said he was killed by an anaconda."

She made a derisive sound. "Everybody is killed by anaconda."

Betty's mind refused to take this in. "Nate?" she finally said. "He shot Nampa? During the attack?"

Dayuma's sobs deepened.

"How do you know? Mintaka told you?"

"She told me in America. She told me on the machine."

The audiotape Betty had sent to Pennsylvania. Dayuma in a

cold, alien land, hearing all that terrible news alone. Three months she was sick. Because Betty, off her head or not, had made that tape and arranged to have it sent, congratulating herself on her cleverness.

She sat on the log beside Dayuma and tried to comprehend. *Rachel's brother.* It was Nate who had fired his gun. But Betty could think only of Jim. She saw him on the wrestling mat, his grotesque grimace. She saw him prying open the crate he had brought from Ambato, the joy he took in those guns, stroking their barrels. She saw him and she felt something precious breaking. He was a *pacifist*, she had always been so proud of that. The pain she felt was ugly, it was unendurable.

You think you have surrendered everything, but there is always something more.

"Does Rachel know?"

"No."

WHAT WAS IT Yapanqui had counselled Betty to say when she walked in the *ucupachama*? *Huaccha mani.* I am orphaned.

In the coolest hour of the morning, they trekked past the abandoned Sevilla hacienda, where so many had died. She would not have noticed it was there. They were a sombre party. They were ill, most of them. Mankamu and Mintaka especially were in a wretched state. After breakfast, Betty had asked the three Auca women to take Sharon down to the stream, and had had it out with the men. Shouting was a great relief. She shouted in Spanish and then she shouted in Quichua. There was no more, they swore, they'd drunk it all. Don Carlos, who was holding their payment—what did they think he would do when he heard? Would they ever work for him again?

They stood with their heads down in shame, or at least a pantomime of it, and she seized the advantage. "We had an agreement and you broke it. You can't be trusted. So now I want your guns. All of them." She had brought a canvas to use as a groundsheet, and she yanked it out of the hut where she'd slept with Sharon and made them drop the guns onto it. "Anticristo," she said. "Come here. Tie this up. You are going to take this bundle back to the river, where Octavio is, and wait for us there."

Rachel was mortified that she hadn't caught on, after years of dealing with drunks at the Colony of Mercy. Yet this morning she'd chosen to believe that Dayuma had resisted the temptation of the palm liquor, that Dayuma had come to spill the beans to Betty. "Dayumaland, I think we should call this territory," she said. "Out of respect for that brave girl, the first Auca Christian."

This was the day. The trail was clear now, frequently used. They were expected to reach the settlement before dark. Unless Betty stopped them. I'll raise my voice, she thought as she trudged along the path, and call to Emelio at the head of the line, Stop! We're turning back. Dayuma would be glad. She was frightened, for reasons Betty could not quite grasp. Rachel would be bewildered, she would certainly fight Betty. But then, as Dayuma had said, Rachel will be okay, her brother's killing is all settled. What does it mean for a killing to be settled? And does this mean that Jim's is not? What did the killing of Jim mean for Jim's wife and Jim's child?

Surely, whatever happened, Sharon, her bright-faced little beauty, would be spared. But what would become of her, if the Auca kept her and did not kill her? Betty Scott Stam, in China, hiding her baby when the Communists came—how is this known? Someone from her mission must have come looking. Betty pictures a scene, a search party pushing into the rainforest and encountering a tiny blond girl. And then it's Cornell Capa she sees, tramping up the trail on his big flat feet. Because he said he would come, didn't he, when they said goodbye in Shell Mera. She told him she was going to watch for a chance to reach the

Auca, and he said, Okay, I'll go with you. He'll find a way in, she told herself. It was a dream, she knew it, but it comforted her.

She longed for the privacy of her thoughts, but Rachel was right behind her, insisting on walking close, ruminating on what lay ahead. Even ignorant of the situation, her talk was uncannily to the point. "This afternoon you are going to meet the men who killed your husband," she murmured in the confiding voice Betty loathed. "And I will meet the men who killed my brother. But, Betty, we don't ask about it. We don't even dream of asking. Dayuma has made this very clear to me. If we ask, they might assume we are planning to venge the killings."

I have to tell her, Betty thought. How would it affect her? Something always protected Rachel. She never changed, she just became more of what she was—that was the essence of Rachel. No lines carved her ivory face. She was a large, crafty child. She used the word *venge* as a verb. Betty felt the taste of her own hatred sharply in her mouth. She did not change either. It was a proud heart that beat in her chest, a savage heart.

A mob of squirrel monkeys flowed down a branch, turning their attentive little faces towards Rachel and Betty. The bond between the two of them was undeniable. The bond of being shut out of the drinking party, the bond of speaking English, of being tall, of carrying toothbrushes and notebooks and sanitary napkins and bibles and scissors, of having the skin peel off your white nose, of wearing shoes, of wearing underpants. Of bearing this thing they called faith; she pictured it in that moment like a blindfold.

If Betty goes in broken and ashamed, will that protect her and her little girl?

The path was low now. Leaves tramped into the mud spoke of recent traffic. Betty's blouse was soaked with sweat and sticking to her. A fallen trunk lay across the path, perfectly level like a closed gate. She crawled over it and turned to help Rachel, the partner God had given her. Jim was not leading her now. She had a knowing Jim had never attained. They always talked of how they would change the Indians, what they would bring to the Indians, but they didn't think of what the Indians would bring to them.

The path they were on led them to a little stream, and they began to follow its bank. This stream was the Tiwaeno, Mankamu had said at breakfast. A harpy eagle screamed, very close, and excitement telegraphed along their queue. They didn't falter, they kept on up the path, her friends Mankamu and Mintaka first, each carrying a squirming puppy. Still wearing their dresses, they hadn't taken them off. Then Dayuma in her cotton blouse and skirt. Rachel, unaware, her head down. Betty, then Darwin with her tiny girl in the carrying brace, sleeping the way only a child can sleep, her head hanging down.

Betty stepped back and put her hand on Darwin's arm to stop him, and then she saw what she had not seen before: under the chair where her daughter slept, he had a rifle fixed.

They were on the same side of the stream as the settlement. The peak of a palm roof with dry thatch. It was up on a mud bank, so they had come in slightly below it. Three Auca men stood on the bank, motionless, watching intently, their faces expressionless. Children had been sliding, brown mud was greying on their legs and backsides. They froze with surprise as Mankamu and Mintaka stepped into the clearing, the puppies in their arms. A baby at the breast sensed its mother's shock and lifted its eyes, not disengaging from her nipple. Smoke drifted in the windless forest and the harpy eagle glared from under its thatched roof.

No one spoke. The people looked past their kinswomen. Their eyes found Rachel and then they found Betty, and the tousled head of her little girl.

It was that peaceful hour of late afternoon, when the work of the day is done and soft light teases the forest open. It had the look of a scene in nature you might walk by. Nothing, not a thing in that clearing, that was not of the forest. In every molecule a silent life moved, a life independent of Betty and indifferent to her. In the hunchbacked eagle with its preposterous crest, in the dark well within her. And these two things, the stillness of the eagle on its perch and the long, unspooling eternity of her soul—for a split second her mind held both of them.

DAVID SAINT,
THIS IS YOUR LIFE

28

THE DRIVER SEAN SENDS TO David's airport hotel is a good-looking Indigenous guy, probably in his forties, maybe early fifties. His hair is blunt cut, his face bony. Not Quichua—he's stockier than Quichua men tend to be. He's wearing a woven bracelet. Probably Shuar, but his name is Spanish, Fidel. He drives a five-year-old red Hyundai. He hands David his business card, and David tucks it into his wallet.

He's tasting mountain air, feeling a little weightless. Quito is to the north—he can vaguely see it, spread like ancient ruins on the mountain slopes—and he feels its pull. But they're heading south. This road is the new Pan-American, a wonderful four-lane highway. You can take it as far as Tierra del Fuego. In fact, you can follow this route north through the US and Canada, all the way to the Arctic Ocean. This is the new Ecuador. This is what oil money did.

Fidel has the reserve and the warmth of expression David associates with Amazonian peoples. He manoeuvres the inter-changes like someone who's done it a time or two before. He comments on David's being a *cineasta*, and David says no, no, *soy pastor*. David tells him that he grew up in Ecuador, and mentions that his wife was also born here, and that she passed away a few years back, and that they have one daughter. It's a pleasure to be speaking Spanish.

"We chose her name from the Old Testament," he tells Fidel. "In the Book of Samuel, Abigail is described as a woman of beautiful countenance and good understanding." He can't resist calling up a photo on his phone and flashing it in Fidel's direction.

"*Muy hermosa*," Fidel says, sounding sincere.

Not, *Oh, I picked that girl up at the airport yesterday*. But it was worth a try.

Silence yawns between them. David turns his eyes to the window. Green fields, larger than he remembers, and eucalyptus fringing the road. Isn't eucalyptus an invasive species? When he and Sharon lived in Quito, they used to drive this direction to hike the trails in Cotopaxi park. The Avenue of the Volcanoes, the old highway was called. It wasn't even paved when his parents lived in Shell Mera. Before Nate had a plane, they made this trip on a local bus crammed with live chickens and sacks of yucca, and it took eight or ten hours. Betty claimed to have done it clinging to the tailgate of a banana truck. Now the volcanic peaks have withdrawn and it's not such an adventure. They'll be in Shell by noon.

David is wiped, actually. It was midnight when he landed and 2 a.m. before he was in bed. He didn't take time for devotions, either last night or this morning. He's working his way through Ephesians, memorizing a few verses in each chapter. *Unto me, who am less than the least of all saints, is this grace given, that I should preach among the Gentiles the unsearchable riches of Christ.* He glances over at the Gentile at the steering wheel. Lord, he prays, you give me the opening and I'll take it. He cracks the window down an inch, hoping to pick up Ecuador on the wind, charcoal smoke and lime and fish and roasting corn. He gets comfortable.

What miracle of a child actor are they going to find to play Sharon? David sees her vividly at six, in the school compound in Quito, standing beside the big red fire extinguisher in the entry of the two-storey dormitory he considered home, barefoot on the cold linoleum, her hair a rough and tangled mess. She and her mother had just arrived unexpectedly from Tiwaeno, where they had lived among the Waorani for almost three years. They were on their way home to the US; Betty had finally reached the breaking point with Rachel. She was up in the private quarters, what they called the lounge, with Marj and Marilou, the sounds of her outrage drifting down the stairs, and this strange little girl had been left stranded in the entrance. Eager missionary kids crowded around, bombarding her with questions. She appeared not to understand English. David was the one who took her upstairs to the mothers. He was only seven himself, but a sympathetic connection started up between them that day. The wisps on the nape of her neck when she pulled her hair up. The narrow cage of her ribs. Those things come to him and sleep is never far behind. Then he's back on the plane as it arcs over the curve of the planet. Green, green, green below, a nubby green carpet, invisible villages hidden in its folds. Did not our hearts burn within us?

By the time he wakes up, they're turning east off the Pan-American, they're near Ambato. Highland Quichua on the streets. Lots of traffic, the smell of diesel. He sits up and closes the window.

"So, David Saint. A relative of Rachel Saint?"

"Nephew," David says in surprise. Was there the slightest hint earlier that Fidel spoke English?

"Nate Saint was your dad?"

"Yes."

"Your hair was white back then. It's almost white again now."

"You've seen pictures of our family?"

"Of course."

"You're Waorani?"

He takes Fidel's silence as assent.

"Where're you from?"

"I grew up in the Protectorate. My parents were converted by Rachel. They were Baihuari—back-river Waorani."

"Your English is perfect. You hardly have an accent."

"I've spent a lot of time in the US. I went to Bible college in

Miami for four years in my twenties. I was sponsored by a church in Iowa. The missionaries arranged it."

"That's wonderful."

"Which part of it?"

"Well, the fact that your family found salvation, and that you had the privilege of an American education."

Fidel emits a derisive bark.

He's obviously spent too long in the US. David sits there doing a full mental one-eighty. "You don't have a Waorani name."

"Rachel named me, actually. I was about thirteen before it occurred to her that I shared a name with the revolutionary leader of Cuba. You know how she hated Communists. So then she tried to force me to change it, but I dug my heels in. Now I carry my Spanish name with pride."

So.

After a minute, Fidel says, "I don't think I ever saw you in the Protectorate when I was a kid."

"No, I worked in Quito. At HCJB. I visited Tiwaeno once, oh, it must have been in the nineties." For a long time when he was young there was no airstrip, and even when there was, his mother wouldn't take them in because of the outbreaks of polio. He finally flew in when he and Sharon were working at the radio station. What he remembers best is the voice of a gringo preaching in heavily accented Spanish as they climbed out of the plane. A huge radio receiver had been fixed to a pole in the middle of Tiwaeno, with a cage around it to prevent its being vandalized. That was David's father preaching. Rachel played HCJB World Radio for hours every day, and as David well knew, HCJB had acquired a stack of audiotapes of Nate Saint practising his Spanish.

"Do you remember what happened when the back-river people were forced out of their territorial lands, or lured out, whichever you prefer, and arrived in the Protectorate?"

David decides not to whitewash it. "A lot of people got sick, and some died."

"Yes. A time of terrible loss. And of starvation. A man was shown the map where Rachel had recorded all the roads being built, the progress of the oil companies. She was very proud of it. That man knew the whole area like the back of his hand, and he stared at the map, tracing the rivers until he understood, and then he fell unconscious to the ground. Fearing for my children, I got faint-hearted, was how he told it after. This incident is recounted in several books. I suspect you've read it."

"I have."

"That man was my father."

So they both had their famous fathers.

David turns his eyes to the side window and tries unsuccessfully to recall Fidel's father's name from his reading. Nincambo, he finds himself thinking. No, that was a man in Dayuma's clan. When Betty and Rachel trekked into the forest, Sharon thought they were going in to meet her daddy. And in her own mind she found him in Nincambo, a wonderful man who was adoptive dad to a lot of children in the settlement, children whose dads had also died by the spear. Sharon fit right in in Tiwaeno. She loved those years.

The Tiwaeno they saw the day they flew in was a dispiriting place. Rachel had been serving alone there for many years. The Waorani were trekkers no longer. The wild game around the settlement was hunted out and Rachel was having sacks of rice and crates of canned tuna flown in. No more palm-leaf longhouses: individual families lived in tiny plank huts with corrugated tin roofs in a row along the *pista*, and the children were clothed and ragged, their teeth black with rot from all the Yupi they drank. They crowded around the plane, pressing David and Sharon for handouts. But Rachel managed the supply shed and she had firm ideas about who got what. You had to look beyond the material, he told himself. You had to think about the eternal benefits to the Auca. But still David struggled to reconcile what he saw with the isolated settlement that lived so vividly in his imagination. It was not his aunt he found himself blaming. He blamed Betty. She had a lot of ideas about accommodating the gospel to native ways, modern ideas, and she and Rachel clashed terribly. Rachel was a bully. No doubt there were reasons for that; possibly she had been bullied herself. But she was who she was, she was never going to change. And it seemed to him that, having brought Rachel in, Betty should have stayed and protected the people from her. Sharon didn't want to criticize. "The people are alive," was all she would say. They might not have been, if Betty and Rachel had not gone in and persuaded them to stop their civil wars.

"How long you going to be in Ecuador?" Fidel asks.

"Eight days."

"Are you flying into any of the settlements?"

"I don't think so. I think I'll be in Shell and Puyo most of the week."

"If you have time, I'll take you on a drive up what they call the Vía Auca. It's the road the oil companies built, south from Coca right through Waorani territory. The government gave parcels of land to homesteaders, so it's mainly been taken over by Quichua. But it's still home to most of Ecuador's Waorani. Some of the men work for the oil companies, road building and laying pipe. But a lot of my people . . . well, the old ways are gone and nothing good's replaced them."

"I take it you blame the missionaries for that."

"Thirteen days of oil for America ruined Waorani lands."

"Yeah," David says, "I've heard that slogan before." He wonders where Sean found this driver. Are they going to have to face an inquisition every time they get into a car?

There is a story here, and it's unlikely that Fidel knows it. One afternoon when David was about twelve, his aunt Rachel and

Dayuma appeared in the courtyard of the boarding school, their arms full of goodies. They had flown into Quito that morning, and a car had picked them up at the airport and taken them straight to the presidential palace. There, they had signed the official documents that gave the Auca their own land. The Protectorate, people called it, but at Rachel's insistence the map read *Dayumaland*. Rachel, of course, could not sign on behalf of the Waorani. They did not have a chief—for some reason they were against the whole idea of leadership, and certainly they were against negotiating with white men in Quito to give up their lands—so Rachel presented Dayuma as the Waorani's leader, and no one in the government objected. After the signing, they walked through Plaza San Francisco and bought treats for a celebration, figs in cellophane, *humitas*, bottles of Pepsi. All the teachers were invited to the party, all the missionary kids, and David remembers them singing, "To God be the glory, great things He hath done."

It was only gradually, as he grew up, that he got the picture of what had happened that day. The Protectorate comprised 8 percent of Waorani lands. (Isn't it actually just an Indian reservation? Abby had asked.) Rachel got a promise that roads would not be built through it and that homestead rights would not be granted to non-Waorani people. In exchange, she agreed that the Waorani would surrender mineral rights and promised they would not interfere with (i.e., kill) oil workers coming in to extract the oil. What happened next was a vicious trick, Rachel said later. She was asked to step outside, leaving Dayuma alone with the government officials—this was to ensure that a foreigner did not exert undue influence—and while she was out of the room, the officials stroked out all the clauses that limited development in the Protectorate. Dayuma was not fluent in Spanish and could not in any case read, but Rachel had taught her to write her name, and when they asked her to, she wrote it.

"You know," David says to Fidel, "Ecuador was going to develop its oil in any case. The army was prepared to support the industry. There would have been a bloodbath. The missionaries just did their best to make sure that transition was peaceful."

Fidel responds with silence. David turns his eyes to the fields on the far side, where labourers in a straggling row are digging up what looks like potatoes. It strikes him that his family's story always sounds better in the US. You tell it there and people are moved to tears.

Near Baños they drive into rain. Terraced fields, and then they're in the clutches of the Andes, dramatic cliffs plunging down to roiling water. This is where the old road was especially treacherous, switching back and forth, barely clinging to the slopes. The new road has guardrails and it also has tunnels, long, long tunnels that strike David as dangerous in their own way, with dim lights intermittently installed, with fallen rocks in both lanes, and water running glistening down the walls.

Mid-tunnel, Fidel starts talking again in a low voice. "You know, I try to understand and to forgive. I think about Rachel Saint, who had no empathy, who had no understanding of my people, who had no respect for them, who referred to them as heathen scum—did you know she said that?—and I remind myself that she was suffering from lead poisoning."

"Who told you that?"

"It was well known. She ate a can of tuna every day for thirty years."

"Wasn't it more likely *mercury* poisoning?"

In the yellow light, David sees Fidel grin. In David's family they rarely talked about Rachel, because you always ended up in this sort of conversation.

They come out to sunlight and they're in the Rio Pastaza flats. Fruit stands line the highway, oranges hanging in long plastic sleeves. They pass a cyclist, a girl with a big orange X on her back.

An American, no doubt. Not Abby, but she makes Abby possible. They drive through Shell, where military jeeps and oil trucks cram the street. They drive past the air base. And there is the house, looming beside the road in its lush glen. Fidel pulls up. It's beautiful. They used a warm cedar to rebuild it. There must be a new chemical for treating wood. They installed new windows and new screens on the veranda. The house looks smarter, no doubt, than the day David's dad finished it.

The rain has let up. "*¿Vienes?*" David asks.

"*Voy a recoger a Sean,*" Fidel says. Smiling politely, reverting to the Fidel who picked David up in Quito.

AN EXCITED FEMALE voice calling in English—it's an American woman running across the green yard. "Dave Saint! Pastor Dave Saint! Oh, I would know you anywhere! It's amazing!"

The house now fronts a whole compound of new buildings, and she's coming from one of them. She's up the steps, in her hand a length of bamboo with the key wired to it. "I am so sorry I kept you waiting. I went across the yard for my lunch, and then I looked out the window when I was putting the kettle on and there you were all on your own."

She gives him her free hand and it seems a hug is in the offing. He's still trying to get a good look at the bronze plaque by the door. NATE SAINT HOUSE. Very classy. "Sean Youderian told me *tomorrow*! And now I have a great big tour coming in. They're from a Baptist church in Georgia, they made this pilgrimage especially to see your dad's house." Kelly, she says her name is. She has a Wisconsin accent. She's lived in this compound for ten years, right through the reconstruction, hosting all the crews. She's forty, maybe, at that poignant tipping point into middle age. "How did you get here?"

"I had a driver." He looks back to the parking lot, but Fidel is gone. My suitcase, he thinks. It's in his trunk.

"Fidel?"

"Yes."

"And how was that?"

"Seems like a good-enough driver."

"But he wanted to vent his grievances?"

"Yeah, he kind of did."

"Poor Fidel. He's full of bitterness. He's involved with—I don't know, some sort of socialist organization. His niece Carmela has learned the language, and she's Sean's interpreter, and I guess that's why they hired him." A huge tourist bus has come up the road and is navigating the turn into the parking lot. Kelly says in a rush, her eyes on the bus, "He's a super-talented guy and everybody had such high hopes for him. But in the end, Rachel had to throw him out of the Protectorate. He was such a bad influence on the young people. It's been quite a disappointment." She makes a rueful emoticon of a face. Her hand is on his arm. "Listen to me! It is such a blessing to meet you. I can't wait until we have a chance to sit down and talk. David, I'm going to head this gang off. I'll give them my spiel in the yard first so you can be on your own in the house for a bit. Maybe you'd be willing to chat with them later? They will be *so* thrilled to meet you."

She's got the door open. She shoos him in and closes it behind him.

The interior of the house looks old and it smells old. He stands for a minute breathing it in, trying to shake off the last few hours. Here it is, just as in the pictures, the radio room with a glass between it and the kitchen, the blue cupboards his mother so loved. Debbie was here last year for the grand opening and she said she spent the whole day in tears. He takes a few steps in. Something moves in his chest at the sight of the stool by the two-way radio, where his mother sat through so many painful hours. A residue of what she must have felt, a brave young woman facing life alone with three tiny kids. She had a great view of the runway from her stool. David looks out the window and pictures the hangar door opening and Nate coming out and starting up the path. He's wearing a white T-shirt and baggy chinos and his sandy hair's in a crewcut. He moves with a lot more energy than David feels these days.

The radio room is lined with shelves displaying all sorts of artifacts. Miniature lances and blowguns. Feather crowns and woven bracelets. Notebooks. A battered bit of the Piper's fuselage. The *Life* magazine article in plastic sleeves. A propped-up frame of Jim Elliot's famous *He is no fool who gives what he cannot keep to gain what he cannot lose*—the motto that hangs over David's desk in the church office.

A collection of children's books in Wao-Tededo, the Waorani language, is fanned out on a counter. He looks at them with interest. When he and Sharon worked at HCJB World Radio, they tried for a while to do a half-hour weekly broadcast in Wao-Tededo. They went to Limoncocha, where the Wycliffe Bible Translators had a centre, and worked with three Waorani informants in translating and adapting Bible stories: Daniel in the lion's den, Jonah and the whale, Noah's ark. Rachel would verify the translations, and then they recorded them for broadcast. In a stroke of inspiration, they asked the Waorani to suggest names for the Biblical characters, and they used Amazonian fauna for the animals in the stories.

The books on this counter are almost certainly based on those audio translations. From the illustrations he extrapolates into English: *Endiki in the puma's den. Kimo and the river dolphin.* It was controversial at the time, using Waorani names, but it's likely standard practice now, as a way to incorporate Indigenous culture.

The three Waorani informants they worked with in Limoncocha had been educated in the mission school, and they all spoke Spanish. The only one he can picture clearly is a woman named Omi. She was the least friendly; there was something about the work that bugged her. One day they were walking back to the guesthouse and she surprised him by asking him whether he'd ever heard the Waorani origin story. About the squirrel that chewed through a cord holding a big tree to the sky. "No," he said eagerly. "There's a *tree* in your origin story?" "*Sí*," she said, with one of her rare smiles. And she stood still and told him the story. A dramatic performance, her voice was passionate. But she was speaking Wao-Tededo. When she finished, he gently pointed out that he didn't understand her language. "*Sí*," she said, starting to walk again. "I realize that."

He steps uncertainly into the hall. The radio room and the kitchen have been restored to 1956, but it looks as though the rest of the house has been modernized. A chain across the stairs has a PRIVATE sign on it. Surely that doesn't apply to him? Before he can make a move, the outside door opens and a girl comes in. She's dressed in spandex and her short black hair is damp and imprinted with the shape of a helmet. It's the cyclist they passed on the highway.

"Hey," she says. She closes the door, but immediately there's pounding on the steps and excited American voices, and the Georgia gang troops in, Kelly at the rear, making apologetic gestures in his direction.

A man in a red baseball cap takes in David and the cyclist. "So you folks made it to the sacred shrine on your own. Where you-all from?"

The girl pointedly ignores him, but David offers, "I'm from Portland, Oregon."

And then a woman with a knowing smile says, "You wouldn't be David Saint, would you?" and everyone wants to shake his hand and get him talking. They bring artifacts over to ask about them. A piece of wood from the old kitchen, honeycombed with tunnels.

"My dad thought he could outfox the termites by setting the foundation piles in enamel dishpans of kerosene," David explains.

"Nobody ever told him there was such a thing as a flying termite!"

They marvel over the lances, hard as iron and their points sharpened to a knife-edge without the use of modern tools. The blowguns so beautifully crafted and balanced, they're a work of art. Did the Auca have a god? someone asks. This question has always perplexed David, and he gives them the best answer he can: the jungle was their god. "They were pagan," a woman offers.

Through the glass, David spies a massive book open on the kitchen counter. It has to be the Wao-Tededo Bible. It was only recently published, the fulfillment of a dream cherished by three generations of Operation Auca families, and a very valuable archive.

It takes forever to work his way through the crowd to the kitchen, and by the time he gets there, the cyclist has beat him to it. She's leaning on the counter studying the large print with great interest, Kelly at her elbow.

"There are only eighteen phonemes in the Waorani language. So words have to have a lot of syllables, to differentiate one from the other. And the Waorani didn't have vocabulary for so many things in the Scriptures—cross, sacrifice, redemption, sin."

The girl raises her head. "Donkeys, sheep, purses, lanterns, robes. Buy, sell, coin, wine."

"Right!" Kelly says. "So instead of using a simple noun, you basically have to write an explanation. I mean, this is just the New Testament, and it's five inches thick. It was very creative and demanding work for the translators."

"So, the Waorani still speak their language?"

"Well, not so much," Kelly says. "The elders do."

"And the elders can read?"

"Well, no, not too many of them."

The girl has a smug little smile. She is clearly trolling Kelly. She waits a beat, and then she says, "The Bible is currently being translated into Klingon. Also into Na'vi. At least, that's what I read online."

"What is Na'vi?"

"The language from *Avatar.*" Kelly's expression is blank and the girl adds with a shrug, "It's a movie."

It's a playful sort of disrespect, the worst kind.

He steps out to the veranda. Lord, he prays. First Fidel and then this girl—couldn't you have ministered to me in some small way? Couldn't you have met me here, after I came all this way with a thirsting heart? No answer. God's out helping some Christian kid in Florida find a parking spot at the mall, Abby says. She smiles at him, pert. *God finds all the prayers of mankind in his Spam folder.* That was a cartoon. She thought it was hilarious.

Everything, every blessed, sacred thing, has to be challenged. *Everything.* Pain heaves in his chest, a solid block of it breaking into pieces. He misses her so desperately. That a child so longed for, finally conceived when they had almost given up hope, so cherished, so gifted, that such a child could willfully turn against truth—a sense of his own failure rises, so sharp his eyes burn.

He stumbles down the stairs and out into the yard. He was always too open; he thought freedom of thought was a safe exercise, given the compelling power of the gospel message. He thought they were special, their family, he saw himself as above the fears that built caution into other Christian parents. He raised a curious and articulate and spirited young woman. Like God, who for whatever reason planted the Tree of the Knowledge of Good and Evil in the Garden, and then had to watch as Eve reached for the fruit that damned all humanity.

Because you take others down with you, don't you. You recklessly knock a crack into the vessel of faith, and the murky gas of doubt seeps in. Abby said she'd stopped talking to God to see if He would keep talking to her. So David has to ask—Lord, why didn't you? Why didn't you try at least as hard as her earthly father, who messages her over and over whether she responds or not?

He walks slowly across the lawn. Some of the Georgians beat

him outside. They're videotaping each other enthusing about the house. Mount Sangay is behind the clouds piled on the river. They probably don't realize it's there, but he could let them know. You have to take it on faith. The gravel parking lot is empty except for the tour bus. Fidel's red Hyundai drives up from the Puyo direction and pulls in. Sean gets out of the front passenger seat, wearing sunglasses, carrying his laptop, and raises a victory fist to David. Then he staggers back against the car, his head lolling. This also means *no words*: it's the ultimate iteration of Youderian wonder. I should get my suitcase out of Fidel's car, Dave thinks. But he's distracted by the American cyclist. She comes down the steps and crosses the grass and unlocks her bike, which was chained to a tree. She wheels it down to the road and soon she's out of sight, heading back towards Baños. Abby is not here and she's not coming. He's known that all along, of course, and he discovers that he's glad.

He hears his name. Kelly, the missionary docent of Nate Saint House, is calling from the veranda. So David Saint, less than the least of all saints, heads back to the house to talk to the crowd waiting for him there.

29

La Virgen de Quito is a patchwork statue, made of thousands of pieces of aluminum welded together. She's relatively new, in David's personal history. He came back to Ecuador after six years of college and seminary, and there she was overlooking the old city, a robed woman embellished with wings, standing on a dragon, which is crouched on a globe. Now it's hard to imagine the city without her.

The driver stops at the top of El Panecillo. Dave pays him and gets out. His plane leaves at midnight and he's dragging his suitcase. He walks once around the monument, studying the statue. She's supposed to be the Woman of the Apocalypse from the book of Revelation. Her face is pretty but vacant. Those wings—oh, why not? And the dragon under her feet has a snout horn, like a rhino. The dragon is not dead, of course, it's just enchained, and the Virgin holds the chain loosely in one hand, waving with the other.

When he was a boy, Marj would sneak them off-campus for a family outing, just Benjy and Debbie and him, and they'd hike up here. You climb and climb and climb, and you get to the top only to discover how low you are, what a little pimple of a hill this is in the sprawling city-plain slung between the mountain ranges. The smell of eucalyptus, the trails for running, the cries of the food vendors—it was his favourite place. While they played, Marj would sit on a bench looking out over the city. If a woman came by with a cart of *espumillas*—the cones that look like ice cream but never melt—they would race back to their mother and she'd smile indulgently and reach into the neck of her blouse (where, to foil thieves, she had tied her change purse to a long loop of shoelace) and pull out a coin warmed by her breasts.

It's quiet tonight, just a few courting couples. Sometimes you can see Cotopaxi, but tonight a scarf of cloud is draped along the horizon. David walks the path a second time, admiring the city spread out in every direction. Then he spies the path he's looking for, and steps through a hedge and down some steps. His favourite restaurant—still here, perched on the slope.

The room is almost empty. A waiter takes the suitcase and lets him pick his table by the long, high window. It's just five thirty, he's organized his day perfectly. "*¿Cómo te llamas?*" he asks the waiter, and the man says, "Marco." David orders a drink and in the time it takes him to down it, the blue sky turns opalescent and then its silvery light drains from it and starts to come on yellow in the buildings. A beautiful and moving transformation. It's always a relief to survey Quito from this height, its individual human dramas lost in haze, just the pleasing adobe shapes, and the sky and the distant peaks. You feel (he realizes) less guilty.

Even as a kid, he carried this weight around. The shoeshine boys jostling him in the square, hungry, ragged—they were his personal responsibility. God had brought him to South America for them. But in those days, he didn't speak Spanish. He had no money for a shoeshine. And he wore canvas runners! He could never enter their mystery, never picture where boys like them laid their heads at night, what they would be as men. They would join the unreached, anguished millions who thronged the streets, but to what end? And so, even then, it was a relief to be up here, where Ecuador became what it was, essentially unknowable.

He signals for another CC. It was the first alcohol he ever tasted—the night they visited the old photographer in that beautiful, warm apartment in Manhattan. Edith poured squat, heavy glasses of the amber drink, and to David's astonishment, Betty accepted one. So David said yes, okay, thank you. Sharon asked for tea and Edith went to put the kettle on, and the light sconces in the hall brushed her hair with amber as she passed. Cornell had the beginnings of Parkinson's and when he raised his trembling hand to drink, the amber liquid heaved in his glass. Already the liquor was moving warmly and swiftly through David's chest, and then more gingerly up the back of his neck to his brain. Sharon, in her orange mohair sweater, he remembers her smiling and asking, "Cornell, is your faith still important to you?"

"I would call myself a secular Jew," Cornell said. He went on to say that this was the sweet spot in American culture, as far as he was concerned. "You're somebody, something more than your money and your ego. Your race was seasoned by great suffering. You have a turn of phrase that makes you sound profound. You can light candles and tell stories, you've got the ancient melodies, you lift your arms and dance—right, Edith? But you're not hostage to all the hocus-pocus."

A trumpet was playing, filaments of music silver in the amber air. Miles Davis, they said. A big orange cat leapt to Sharon's lap and she sat stroking it. Edith refilled their glasses and the secret glow infused the whole apartment. David was—his heart was open that night. The five of them loved each other. His mother-in-law, so much worldlier than he'd known. The old photographer, so homely and so beautiful. His precious wife.

So now, on the rare occasions he treats himself to a drink, it's Canadian Club. Neat.

Marco brings his second drink and hands him a menu in a black leather folder. Then he goes back to the bar where his colleagues linger, talking to each other but alert to their customers. Dark-haired men in black jackets, dutiful members of a modest fraternity. The restaurant is half-full now, couples with heads together talking. David's chronic loneliness rises in his chest. He will never not be alone. You need to get married again, everyone says. But how can you be close to someone, how can you share a heart as troubled as his?

Well, the trip is over. He spent much of the week in a rental Nissan with the locations manager, who, beyond looking like Sean Youderian's identical twin, is *named* Sean. They called him Segundo at first and then Gundo. David still hadn't read the script, but Gundo had a list of locations. He and David drove to Shandia, a beautiful Quichua settlement in the foothills, and found a house that could stand in for Jim and Betty's, their actual house having fallen to ruins in the forest. At Puyo they borrowed a canoe and paddled down the river and chose a long and stable playa that could serve as the beachhead on the Curaray. A single-engine plane was going to have to land there. As David recalled it, Nate needed five hundred feet. He paced the length of the sand and it was good. The topography was wrong, of course, not the high rainforest where the men died, but Gundo valued airport, road, and hotel access above all else. "If Walter's desperate for a canopy," he said, "there's always CGI." They needed traditional Quichua longhouses to stage the scene where Betty meets the two Auca women, and they needed Waorani longhouses in the settlement Betty and Rachel trek into. Gundo couldn't see why the same structures couldn't serve for both if you shot from different angles. David tried to explain the differences as he understood them, and Gundo crossed his eyes. It was all about buy-in. Once you had buy-in, you were good.

Una fantasía, Fidel called the film. David himself could see that it had nothing to do with the Waorani they saw from time to time on the streets of Puyo and Shell, destitute individuals or families who had been flown out to the clinic on an emergency basis and didn't have the money to get home. That's what Fidel said. Fidel spent the week driving Sean Youderian around, and David seldom got to talk to him. He felt a surprising bond with the guy, and started to hope they might drive up the Vía Auca as Fidel had suggested. But any time Fidel had a few spare hours, he barrelled across Puyo to a cement building that was the Waorani Association headquarters, ignoring David's hints to be invited along. Not just a *taxista*, he was (in his niece Carmela's words) an *activista*.

Sean was still obsessing about Tiwaeno, about going in for background, but the Ecuadoreans on the team suggested Quehueire Ono. This was a traditional settlement on the Rio Shiripuno that had been started by people who broke with the missionaries and moved back into the forest. Turned out Fidel had been involved in establishing an eco-lodge near there, where (as one guy from the Ecuadorean service crew put it) rich foreigners could fly in to watch the Waorani practise their lifestyle. That eco-lodge had recently had to close because of oil drilling in Yasuní Park, but Quehueire Ono was still a community, and the idea grew that they might allow the crew to come in and film. They called Fidel into a meeting to ask him about it. "No," he said.

So then Sean was back to talking about Tiwaeno. The plane he booked was a four-seater and one of the seats had David's name on it. By that point David had started to loathe the sound of Sean's voice and the very way he put his words together. "No," he said.

So of course Sean was going to come back from Tiwaeno with a sensational story—you could bank on it. Sure enough, that afternoon when David arrived at Nate Saint House, Sean had just walked over from the Shell airstrip and he was perched on a counter, flushed and excited, waiting for them all to assemble so he could astonish them.

The flight over the rainforest had been stunning. They bounced three times landing, but the Lord had them in the palm of His hand. They were warmly welcomed and taken by canoe to see Rachel Saint's house at nearby Toñampare, although they couldn't go inside as it was shuttered and barred. But they saw her grave. They met numerous individuals who remembered the killings, including three old men who had taken part. All morning they sat chatting over bowls of *tepae*, the yucca beverage. With Carmela translating, first into Spanish and then Wao-Tededo, Sean told the people about the film. He had his laptop with him, and some impulse made him take it out and play the Leo Duric song they intended to use on the soundtrack.

Sean's laptop was on the kitchen counter and at this point in the story he opened it and touched a finger to a key. "I just want to take you to that moment," he said. "That gorgeous melody the Lord gave Leo, and Carmela and I sitting deep in the jungle with these old men God rescued from their savage past, and Leo's amazing voice comes on. The music floats up over the trees—and all the elders fall silent. They listen, and this look comes over their faces, a look of pure wonder, and then (and Carmela here is translating) they say, We know that music. We've heard that song before. Right after the killings, while the missionaries' bodies were still bleeding, we saw a tribe of people in the sky, up over the trees. They were wearing white robes. There was bright light all around. That's the song they were singing."

The synthesizer, and that rapturous voice, and in the blue kitchen they turned stunned faces towards each other. Sean's eyes were rimmed with tears. David sat motionless on a wooden chair. Everybody in that little circle of film people looked terribly young to him. They were young. God chooses his servants. You don't get to choose who you serve with.

First chance he saw, he slipped out. The mountain was painted white on the darkening sky to the south. Always a gift, Sangay showing itself to you at the end of the day. And then another gift, Fidel on his own, leaning against his car in the parking lot. David walked across the gravel towards him.

"It's my last night," he said.

"So I hear. How you getting to Quito?"

"I'm running the Nissan back." David added that he'd be staying overnight in Quito. Just one night because he was eager to get home and see his daughter.

He stood on the gravel, his back to the mountain. This road— the old hospital where he was born was just around the next turn. He'd like to tell Fidel that story, the way his mother surprised the family by walking home from the hospital with him in her arms. He wanted to lean on the car beside Fidel, but he felt reticent. He was six inches taller, but he felt insubstantial beside him. People who knew the truth and rejected it had a strange power. There was nothing you could say to them.

"I wish you and I'd had more time to talk this week," he said.

Fidel didn't respond.

"I don't know if you realize, but my wife was Sharon Elliot, you know, the little girl who was taken into Tiwaeno by Betty and Rachel. I know there have been struggles and difficulties there. I wish . . ."

Fidel listened with his usual self-contained expression. He didn't help David out.

"I've been wanting to say to you, I see the essence of the gospel in what those women did. Their courage in going in, and their grace in forgiving the men who had murdered their loved ones. And to their credit, your people responded to the gospel of peace."

Fidel shrugged. "We took them in," he said. "My people have always been kind to female refugees."

The glory of God and the darkness of the world—it seemed there was no navigable passage between them. David had never been equal to the mission, that's what it boiled down to.

The trucks rolling up the road had switched their headlights on. Behind the house his father built, night birds were starting to call.

"Everybody back home is going to want to know about the movie," Fidel said.

"I guess they will."

"You going to tell them about the angels?"

His tone suggested it was all a big joke.

"You assume the age of miracles is over," David said.

Fidel laughed.

But what David was hoping for (he realizes now) was a miracle of a different kind—that God would fill him with the faith he'd need to stand at his pulpit and look out over his people and say, Something truly amazing happened in Ecuador. We never knew this before, we just found out. There were angels in the sky the day my father died. God sent angels to carry my father home.

He turns his eyes back to the restaurant window. Quito stretches below El Panecillo and above it, its lights are muddled and fading. He finishes his drink and feels a subtle shift, like an automatic transmission changing gears; he feels himself move to a new and more distant relationship with the scene. He should order dinner, but he can't summon up the will to open the menu. He lifts an index finger and the waiter sees him and starts up the aisle. The waiter's name—he's lost it already.

"I need to eat something," David says, and then realizes he's speaking English. "*Tráigame algo para comer, por favor.*"

Whatever you like. I don't really care. Bring me whatever you think is best.

IMMORTAL, INVISIBLE

30

The morning Abby picked up her phone and learned that Sean Youderian was making a movie about Operation Auca and that her dad was going to help with it, she flopped down on the bed in the motel room and cried. With disappointment, but mostly at her endless talent for gaslighting herself. Anybody else would have known Sean was behind this film the instant Walter Varga called. Anybody else would at least have checked it out.

After a while she wiped her face on the pillowcase and got up. She went to the door and opened it. It had rained again in the night and the cars in the parking lot glistened with silver drops. The motel was right on the edge of a little valley, and the air was filled with lemony light. So. She was on her own. She wasn't going to Ecuador, and she wasn't going to have Walter Varga and a cast of Waorani actors to help her figure things out. She stood gazing at a row of cypress trees on the other side of the valley, and then she walked across to the motel office and booked herself in for another night.

It's possible to take up permanent residence in a hotel or motel. There are people who do—rich old women in New York, who treat the bellboys like nephews and leave fortunes to them in their wills. Or that guy whose father wrote a Christmas jingle that paid out royalties every time it was played, so the guy never had to work in his life. This was in a movie, or it's actually true, or maybe both.

She finds that it's not such a bad lifestyle, except for the way her bank balance dwindles. Her room seemed impersonal when she checked in, but it quickly starts to feel like home. The water stain in the ceiling over the bathtub is a turtle with a cow's tail, like the Mock Turtle in *Alice in Wonderland*. There's a new chrome shower head, big and flat, with a transparent sticker on it saying, *Experience the rainforest.* So in the morning, while doors slam on either side and diesel trucks start up, Abby does just that, singing to herself as warm water patters gently onto her shoulders. She gets fresh towels whenever she needs them, and she has a working remote, courtesy of a cleaner named Natalia. Not that she watches much TV. She walks a lot, and when she's not walking, she reads.

The book with the cover photo of children climbing a palm tree in the Amazon: it's not about her family—they're just mentioned in the preface, as one of the external forces that worked to efface Waorani culture. She gets past that and into the discussion of Waorani life. In parts she feels moved with recognition, and in other passages she thinks, My brain is not wired to understand this. She learns about the individual hearths in the communal longhouses. The sturdy little kids who hunt alone with their own miniature blowguns. The hunting taboos that protect certain animals. The songs celebrating the bounty of the forest. The way individuals from clans far away are recognized by their footprints in river clay. The warfare rituals, the sharing rituals.

She spends an hour in the Amazon rainforest and then lifts her eyes to discover an American motel room strewn with clothes and makeup and her curling iron and books and electronics. A Waorani could walk in here and figure out a lot about her by her artifacts. How different it was for a US fieldworker to step into an old Waorani settlement. Most of what the people treasured was intangible. The elaborate lineages, the history written in every tree. The skills and knowledge, the protocols, the songs, the stories. None of that was visible. You could look at the Waorani and think they had nothing.

THE THIRD DAY, she's restless and she leaves the motel and starts driving. She turns when an intersection appeals to her, tending north and west, and then gets the idea of heading for the coast. Billboards say MENDOCINO, and she opens a window and smells salt water. She finds a parking spot along the road and gets out. She stands for a long time looking at the Pacific, a thrilling sight, the white, white surf topping teal-blue waves. Everything in motion, the ocean tossing itself around and clouds sliding loose and gulls fighting the wind as they try to circle the cliffs.

There is no easy way down to the shore. She walks up the road and spies an embankment where a stream enters the ocean through a culvert. There she climbs over the guardrail and inches and gouges her way down. She fights through some prickly shrubs and lands on the beach. A narrow beach, dangerously narrow; if the tide is coming in, Abby is screwed.

She finds a sheltered spot up against the cliff and sits cross-legged on her jacket. The sand is dark grey and damp. She clasps her ankles and settles back to watch the ocean. Everything in the scene is designed to hypnotize. The gulls tilting their out-stretched wings, so you can almost see the planes of air they're riding. The waves chasing in at her and drawing back, over and over. She stares and stares, trying to see a pattern in the shifting bands of colour, the luminous scarves stitched carelessly together, constantly the same and constantly different, the waves small and then huge, flinging themselves open or racing into shore. The longer she stares, the less sense it makes. It's like she's never seen it before. She can't even understand its surface, never mind the secrets hidden in its depths.

It's starting to freak her out, this heaving, disorganized, watery beast that prowls from here to Japan, and she gets up and pulls her jacket on and walks, picking her way through the detritus the beast has coughed up. Kelp. Plastic cups. The wind bites at her. She finds a huge rock with a little alcove in it. It's not in the sun, but it's strangely warm. She leans against it and pulls out her phone: 17 percent. She forgot to charge it last night. She presses Olive's number. Olive picks up on the second ring. They talk for a while about Olive's cat, who is behaving badly, but Abby doesn't want to waste her call talking about the cat. "I've been reading," she says. "I read a book about the Waorani. A field study, by an anthropologist."

"Oh," Olive says, clearly surprised.

"I'll tell you the coolest thing I learned. Apparently they believe that, over time, a human being can literally become a different person. You change in little ways, one tiny thing after another, and at a certain point a critical mass is reached. It's not just a personality change. They believe that you are literally someone else."

"Well, we believe in being born again," Olive says.

"Hmm," Abby says, thinking. Finally she says, "They have this deep respect for the individual. They think it's very bad to impose your will on another person, even on a child. They never had chiefs. They really value autonomy, but at the same time they are very close. They live so intimately together that they almost see themselves as one flesh. If someone is sick and can't eat, the whole longhouse fasts."

"Oh my," Olive says. "I can't see the practical good of that."

"There are lots of intriguing contradictions in the culture. Like how peacefully the Waorani live together, and yet how frequently they killed. It would take me a long time to understand it. Well, I guess I never really would. Anyway, this book was written by a

European anthropologist, and what I would really like to read is *their* story. What it was like for the people when the missionaries came. Well, everything. Dayuma's story—wouldn't it be amazing to hear that?"

"It would," Olive says. "But I believe she's passed away, and I don't think she ever wrote. You could go to Ecuador. Do you think you'd like that? To work with the people yourself?"

"Why would they want me?" Abby lifts her eyes to the restless water. "Olive, I actually called to ask you a question. Do you remember, just before my mom died, when Rachel brought two Waorani men to the US on a tour?"

"I remember that tour, but I was in Hawaii with Ruby at the time."

"Well, one of the men was pretty old—he and Mom actually knew each other when they were children. After the meeting, I had a chance to talk to him. My Spanish wasn't very good back then, but I had planned out some questions. I said, 'Do you remember the attack on the missionaries?' He did remember. He said, '*Por supuesto. Tus abuelos le dispararon a mi tío.*'"

Olive makes a little sound of distress.

"But I didn't really get it," Abby says. "I knew that *por supuesto* meant 'of course.' I knew that *tus abuelos* meant 'your grandparents' and *mi tío* meant 'my uncle.' But I didn't know the verb *disparar* and I never looked it up. Isn't that crazy? Instead, I decided that it meant 'disappeared.' So, I thought, well, Enkidi's uncle disappeared, he fled deeper into the forest after the Americans showed up. All the time I was studying Spanish, I would sit in class reading passages in which the word *disparar* clearly meant 'to shoot,' and I would just think, Oh, *disparar* has more than one meaning."

"Did you not realize the men had guns?"

"Yes, of course. But everybody talks about how they had sworn not to use them. How they would die themselves before they would kill anybody who wasn't ready to meet God. But that's not what happened, apparently. So, does everybody know this but me? Did you know?"

"I've heard a bit about it," Olive says in a thin voice.

"Do you know which of the men fired the gun?"

"I think it might have been Nate. You realize, of course, that it didn't come out for a long time. Because the people didn't feel comfortable talking to Betty and Rachel about the killings. But eventually someone said that Dayuma's brother was shot, and he didn't die right away, and it might actually have been an anaconda that killed him. And someone said that, during the attack, Nate picked up his gun to shoot into the air, and one of the Waorani came and grabbed his arm, so the shot went where he never intended it to go."

"Yeah, right, of course," Abby says. There's a crackling sound, and she thinks the call has dropped out. But she says anyway, "Wouldn't it be better if they admitted what really happened?"

Olive is still there. "You know, Abby, it was a very long time ago, and people thought differently then."

"Olive, they think just the same way now!"

Then the call really is gone. She drops her phone into her pocket and leans back against the rock. I said *they*, she thinks. Not *we*.

A sailboat crosses her line of vision, moving parallel to the shore. It strikes her as a rough day for setting off in a sailboat, but from this distance it looks as though the sailor is gliding along a smooth silvery band and doing fine.

She starts to walk again. The tide is going out, it's finally obvious. She won't need to be rescued from the rocks after all.

THERE'S A TATTOO parlour in the strip mall across from her motel and it's open late into the evening. After she's bought her supper, Abby stands on the sidewalk and watches through the window.

Only one artist is working. The shop is full of motorcycle gang regalia, but he looks like a gentle guy. He's putting the finishing touches on a huge, beautiful moth on a woman's back. The moth has eye-spots on its wings, and when the woman sits up clutching her shirt over her breasts and turns her back to the window, the eyes seem to be watching—and so the moth is both gorgeous and threatening.

The next morning, Abby wakes up feeling strangely clear-headed, as if she's had a fever and it broke. This may not last, so in its light she needs to make some decisions. She dresses and eats a muffin from her stash. The neon OPEN sign at the tattoo parlour comes on just as she walks up. The artist who did the moth is leaning on the counter. Abby has nothing so spectacular in mind, but he listens with interest, suggests various illustrations, and sketches them for her. No, she says. Just the words. She goes through a book and picks out Leelawadee. It's described as a Thai font, but it's totally readable to Americans. He tells her rib cage tattoos are the most painful, and she says, Gotcha.

She lies on her side, undoes her bra, and pulls up her shirt, flinching at the cold of the antiseptic he rubs along her ribs. The pen sounds like a mosquito. Its sting seems to elevate her, like she's floating above the table. She's never even had her ears pierced. You can put a lot of energy into not getting marked in any way. But she is no fool who gives what she cannot keep to gain what she cannot lose.

The artist notices tears dripping onto the paper sheet. "Go ahead and cry," he says. She presses her face into her folded arm. She's thinking of Enkidi, a young boy from the rainforest watching it all, watching his uncle get shot by strangers. An old man now, a long-eared old man, who saw the longhouses broken up, the ancient language forgotten by the young, the stories that died from never being told, the stories displaced by something else.

Culture is a delicate porcelain, she thinks, you can smash it just like that. Or, she thinks, feeling a new wave of emotion, your culture is written so deep in your bones you can never hope to resist it. They thought they owned the Waorani, she weeps. They thought they owned me.

HER DAD'S CAR is in the garage, but the house is dark. Can he possibly have left for Ecuador already? She rings the doorbell and inside a dog goes berserk—not Gizmo, it's the Doberman on the security tape announcing that the owner of this bungalow is out of town. She's been nervous all afternoon for nothing. She fingers her key. The red light of the security alarm box winks at her. He's changed the code, her instincts tell her. It's what he does, just to give her grief. If she opens the door, all hell will break lose.

She walks around to the backyard. It's still warm out and the air smells green. This is a neighbourhood of ragged old cedars and newish houses. Their house is at the dark end of a dead-end street, tucked in under the freeway ramp. Her dad likes that; it reminds him of the rainforest, where you never saw the sun and didn't miss it.

It's getting dark. She should find a friend to take her in. She wanders over to the picnic table and sits on the bench, scrolling through her contacts, calling up faces in her mind. Bethany. Ashley. Joel.

Will. She steadies her breathing, readying herself. Possibly his name provides insight into his character. You always have expectations when you run into a woman named Faith, or Hope, or Joy (or Constance, isn't that a name?). But Will—it's a little more subtle.

She presses his number. He picks up. "Hey," she says. "It's Abby."

"Hey," he says. "I've been wondering where you got to."

"I went on a driving trip and stared at the ocean."

"Cool. What brought you back?"

"I have a library book that's almost due." A dark shadow moves across the grass towards her. The neighbour's cat, a known birder. It presses itself against her ankles, and she reaches a hand down to scratch its back. "What are you up to?"

"Making dinner."

"What're you having?"

"Pasta alla puttanesca."

"Wow. Don't let me interrupt."

"No, I'd like to talk. I haven't seen you in ages."

"So put me on speaker."

He does, and she can tell he's set the phone on the counter.

"This sounds like a really fancy meal," she says.

"It is," he says from a distance. "I make three dishes, and this is my fanciest."

She hears him running water for the pasta, she hears the pot clunk onto the stove. "Tell me all three."

"Well, I do a mean stir-fry. I make what I call frittata, which is eggs whisked up and stuff fried into them. But my specialty is the pasta alla puttanesca."

"And what's in it?"

"Garlic. Anchovies. Capers. Canned tomatoes."

"Capers, wow. You're vegetarian, right?"

"Pretty much."

"And why is that?"

"I don't really have a doctrine. I'm . . . I guess you'd call me a crypto-vegetarian."

She pictures him in his plaid shirt. He'll have the light on over the stove, he'll be working in its yellow glow, his head bent. She hears a sound that might be a knife on a cutting board.

"Will, does this menu include salad?"

"Yes. But I won't lie to you, it's from a bag."

"I thought I heard you chopping something."

"I'm augmenting it with tomatoes."

"You have fresh tomatoes?"

"Vine-ripened."

"Why didn't you use them in the pasta sauce?"

"Fresh tomatoes are contrary to the spirit of the dish."

She hears cellophane rattling, the bagged greens or the pasta. You can't be forgiven, she thinks, if you don't own up to what you did. In her mind she's perched on a stool by the stove drinking wine and watching him. I am literally a different person, she says to him. Or at least, I am learning.

"Okay, my fettuccine is back to a boil," he says right in her ear. He's taken his phone off speaker. "What are you having for dinner?"

"I haven't thought about it. Listen, I'd really like to talk to you. Are you going to be at the library tomorrow? Hey, I can show you my tattoo."

"You got a tattoo?"

"Yup. While I was on the road."

"It's your first?"

"It is."

She'd like to slip her hand up and run her fingers along it, as she's been doing for the last few days—it's like reading Braille. But tonight she's wearing the dress she packed for the audition, having run out of anything else clean. **Everyone guards in their heart a royal chamber. I have sealed mine.** It's something she came across scavenging in the library. Flaubert, apparently. She didn't write the quotation down at the time, so her tattoo is a paraphrase of what must already have been a translation. She likes what it says about having boundaries: my heart and my mind belong to me. At first it seemed a perfect affirmation, profound, clear. But while she was driving today, a different way to read it occurred to her—she may have inked onto her rib cage a vow to barricade her heart against love. That is *so* not what she intended.

"You know, the thing is, just today I realized—I'm not sure the saying works for me anymore."

"Oh, well. You want to evolve."

He says this casually, but the insight relieves and delights her. "You're *right*," she says. "Every year on the same date I'll get a tattoo that expresses what I'm living at the time, and when I die, my grandchildren will be invited to the mortuary to read the story of my life on my wrinkled old back."

"I like it."

"I do too. How's your pasta, by the way?"

"I should check it."

"Then I guess this is goodbye."

It's an abrupt and dramatic hang-up, but she's afraid she's going to start crying. It's been a long time since she talked to a friend.

The predatory cat has vanished. Abby gets up from the picnic table and wanders across the yard. No doubt the trampoline is full of rotting leaves. She shines her phone on it. It's clean and dry. A divine miracle, or else the kids from next door have been using it. She kicks off her shoes. Her dress is tight, but she uses her elbows and manages to mermaid herself up.

She picked a dress with a narrow skirt for the audition because it was Betty she really aspired to. All day she's been thinking about her grandma Betty. The deepest thinker of them all, the questioner. Betty must have lived her life constantly negotiating between what she saw as God's dark necessities and what her heart might have told her. She lived for a year in an Indian home in Shandia with two Waorani women, and she never once asked them about the killing of her husband. "You never asked?" Abby said. "No. I thought—well, if I was going to have a ministry with them, we had to turn the page."

It's hard to imagine. But maybe, Abby thinks (and this thought is more painful), maybe Betty lived her life not listening to her heart at all, what with all the other stuff laid on her.

Abby squirms her way to the middle of the taut canvas belly. In high school, she'd lie up here and daringly peel off her swimsuit, desperate to take full advantage of the one hour of sunlight they got in this yard. And right away a plane would lumber across the sun, showing its riveted underside, and freak her out. But the sky is unoccupied at the moment, no traffic and no stars, just a glow behind the ginkgo tree where the moon may be rising. No, it's not the moon, it's a street light turning the ginkgo into a yellow-leafed goddess. The cold seeps under her dress when she moves, so she lies still. Her high school gym teacher called this the corpse pose. The goal is to be relaxed but alert, to take in everything around you and also everything within. You use your breath as a guide.

She closes her eyes and sinks into it. Unobserved, stripped of superhuman powers, she lies listening to the hum of the cars on the overpass, attending to the in-out of her breath. Trying to tune in to her heart, doing its thing unbidden in her chest.

AUTHOR'S NOTE

THIS NOVEL IS BASED ON events that took place in Ecuador in the mid-1950s, involving five American missionary families. Thanks to features in *Life* magazine, Operation Auca was known across America, and when I was growing up on the Canadian prairies, my parents owned two of Elisabeth Elliot's books. The first of these, *Through Gates of Splendor*, has sold half a million copies and still sells well.

It's impossible to overstate the importance of this mission in evangelical churches. Hundreds (possibly thousands) of young people were recruited "to take the place of the five martyrs." Operation Auca was one of those moving stories that, as far as I travelled from the ideology of my childhood, still lay intact in the back reaches of my memory. Then, in 2012, I read a feature in the *New Yorker* about the politics of oil in the Ecuadorean rainforest ("Reversal of Fortune" by Patrick Radden Keefe) and began to research the wider story of the impact North American evangelicals have had in Ecuador.

It's a delicate thing to write fiction about real individuals, and I briefly considered changing names and identifying details. But for me, the power of this story lay in the fact that it had really happened. I wanted to enter these events and try to understand them. I wanted to look at their legacy, at how stories, like the story based on this incident, persist and shape our thinking in the Western world. And at the same time, I was reluctant to write about people still living.

So here is how this novel works: In the contemporary chapters, the characters are entirely fictional. The nine American kids left fatherless by Operation Auca do not appear in this novel, and neither do their children. David, Sharon, Abby, Sean, and Will are invented. So are the contemporary Waorani characters, Enkidi, Fidel, and Carmela. Several films about Operation Auca exist, but the film being made in *Five Wives* is not based on any actual production.

The principal players in the chapters about Operation Auca in the 1950s, however, are all based on real people, though I treat them fictionally. These include Rachel Saint, Dayuma, Nate Saint, Jim Elliot, Ed McCully, Roger Youderian, Peter Fleming, Marj Saint, Elisabeth Elliot, Marilou McCully, Barb Youderian, Olive Fleming, Mintaka, Mankamu, Don Carlos Sevilla, Yapanqui, and Cornell Capa. Of these, only Olive is still living. Secondary characters in the 1950s chapters are invented (Carol Howard, Inkasisa, Harvey Howard, and Fray Alfredo, for example), with the exception of Alberto Grefa, who still lives in Shandia.

As for "treating real people fictionally"—what I mean is that I use actual names and biographical details, but that the interior lives of the characters and the dynamics of their relationships are entirely of my creation. I read the available biographies and journals of the Operation Auca eleven, and then set those books aside and let the characters walk into my novel with the personalities they had assumed in my imagination. In the missionaries' memoirs, "God's leading" explains almost every impulse. I set out to peer behind that, to explore in human terms actions that astonished me.

I use established facts and timelines, both from missionary accounts and from a handful of secular sources, and I alter chronology in just a couple of instances. Rachel Saint did tour around America with Waorani (Huaorani) converts on numerous fundraising junkets, but she died in 1994, so I tinker with time in having Abby attend one of those meetings. Also for storytelling purposes, I simplify movements in the months in 1958 when

Elisabeth Elliot worked with Mintaka and Mankamu. In reality, the women made several forays back and forth before Elisabeth and Rachel trekked into the forest.

But as for the building blocks of the plot—the stealing of Rachel's language materials, the cultural misunderstanding regarding Dayuma's photo, the shooting of Nampa, Dayuma learning about her brother's death through an audiotape, the missionaries' role in helping oil companies seize Waorani land, the belated Waorani report of singing angels—all these elements are written about elsewhere, although most are not acknowledged in the missionaries' accounts.

The many published accounts of Operation Auca may be called "non-fiction," but like novels, they are attempts to shape a narrative and they have their silences and gaps. Many of the diaries, memoirs, and biographies I read subscribe to flagrant racial stereotypes and idealize, almost deify, the missionaries. Elisabeth Elliot's memoir *The Savage, My Kinsman* (reprinted as a *Reader's Digest* condensed book in 1962) was a thoughtful book for its time, but it is just one of five titles on my research shelf that refer to the Waorani as savages. Thanks to the mythmaking of these books, the Waorani people became known worldwide as "the worst people on earth."

The novel I wrote also has its silences. An intentional silence is at its core: I do not presume to give voices to Waorani people. Some Waorani stories have recently been published in English. *Gentle Savage Still Seeking the End of the Spear* by Menkaye Aenkaedi and Kemo and Dyowe (as told to Tim Paulson, Xulon Press, 2013) is a collection of oral histories by Waorani elders. Stories like these are a vital thread in the project of decolonization. My subject is the actions and motives of the North American intruders.

I'm very grateful to the team at HarperCollins for making this book happen. I'm especially indebted to my editor, Jennifer Lambert, who grasped immediately what I wanted *Five Wives* to be and provided such expert guidance, and to Natalie Meditsky for her clarity. A huge thank-you to Martha Magor Webb at

CookeMcDermid for her enthusiasm and good instincts, and thanks also to Dean Cooke. Grants from the Manitoba Arts Council and the Canada Council for the Arts were essential and much-appreciated support during the years I worked on this novel. Thanks to terrific guides in Ecuador, Rodrigo Jipa and Enrique Cerda, and to Alberto Grefa, who took me to see the ruins of the Elliot house and generously shared his memories. My warmest love and appreciation to friends and family whose help has been absolutely invaluable: Erica Ens (my wonderful interpreter), Sam Baardman, Heidi Harms, Jon Montes, Caitlin Thomas-Dunn, Bill Dunn.

I relied on many print and online resources but would like to acknowledge especially the work of four anthropologists: Laura Rival, James A. Yost, Norman E. Whitten, and Wade Davis. "Other cultures are not failed attempts at being you," Davis reminds his readers. Self-evident, one would think, in the twenty-first century, but these words were on my mind every day as I wrote *Five Wives*.